Maureen Child writes for the Mills   and can't imagine a better job. A seven-time finalist for a prestigious Romance Writers of America RITA® Award, Maureen is the author of more than one hundred romance novels. Her books regularly appear on bestseller lists and have won several awards, including a Prism Award, a National Readers' Choice Award, a Colorado Romance Writers Award of Excellence and a Golden Quill Award. She is a native Californian but has recently moved to the mountains of Utah.

Joss Wood loves books and traveling—especially to the wild places of Southern Africa and, well, anywhere. She's a wife, a mum to two teenagers and slave to two cats. After a career in local economic development, she now writes full-time. Joss is a member of Romance Writers of America and Romance Writers of South Africa.

Discover more at millsandboon.co.uk

TEMPT ME IN VEGAS

MAUREEN CHILD

HOT CHRISTMAS KISSES

JOSS WOOD

MILLS & BOON

First Published in Great Britain 2018
by Mills & Boon, an imprint of HarperCollinsPublishers,
1 London Bridge Street, London, SE1 9GF

Tempt Me in Vegas © 2018 Maureen Child
Hot Christmas Kisses © 2018 Joss Wood

ISBN: 978-0-263-93622-3

1018

TEMPT ME IN VEGAS

MAUREEN CHILD

To my cousin,
Terri Hineline—a strong woman,
a good friend and someone who always knows
how to smile through the bad stuff.
I love you.

One

"This isn't a damn soap opera. It's real life." Cooper Hayes jammed both hands into his slacks pockets and shot a glare at the man opposite him. "How the hell did this happen? Secret heirs don't just appear at the reading of a damn will."

"The only thing that *appeared* was her name," Dave Carey reminded him.

True, but hardly consolation. Cooper stared at the other man for a few long beats. Dave had been his best friend and confidant since college. He was always reasonable, logical and so damn cool-headed that it was irritating at times. Like now, for instance.

"That's enough, though, isn't it? *She* exists. She has a name. And now," Cooper added darkly, "apparently, *half* of my company. To top it all off, we know nothing about her."

Here in his office on the twentieth floor of the StarFire Hotel, Cooper could let his frustration show. In front of the board and the company's fleet of lawyers, he'd had to hide his surprise and his anger at the reading of Jacob Evans's will.

Usually, being in this room with its wide windows, plush carpeting and luxurious furnishings helped to center Cooper. To remind him how far the company had come under his direction. As did looking at the paintings of the famed Hayes hotels that decorated the walls. His father and Jacob had started the company, but it was Cooper who had built it into the huge success it was today.

But at the moment it was hard to take comfort in his business…his world, when the very foundations had been shaken.

Cooper still couldn't quite wrap his head around any of this. Hell, he'd had everything planned out most of his life. Hayes Corporation had been his birthright. He'd trained for years to take the helm of the company and he'd damn near single-handedly made his hotels synonymous with *luxury*.

Though there were five star Hayes hotels all around the world, their main headquarters was here, in what was considered the flagship hotel, the StarFire, in Las Vegas. The building had undergone massive renovations over the years, but it still claimed a huge swath of the famed Vegas Strip, and at night it glowed as fiercely as the stars it had been named after.

When Trevor died, Cooper had stepped into his father's place and worked with Jacob. Since the man had no family, it was understood that when Jacob died, the company would fall completely to Cooper, who had been raised to be king.

Except it hadn't worked out that way.

Cooper looked at Dave again. Now his executive assistant, he and Dave had both worked summers for the corporation, interned in different departments to learn as much as they could and, when Cooper took over from his father, Dave had come along with Cooper. He couldn't really imagine doing this job without Dave. Having someone you could trust was priceless.

Dave sat in one of the maroon leather guest chairs opposite Cooper's massive mahogany desk. He wore a black suit with a red power tie. His brown hair was cut short and his dark brown eyes were thoughtful. "We don't know much *now*. We will, though, in a couple of hours. I've got our best men working on it."

"Fine," Cooper muttered darkly as impatience clawed at his insides. "Jacob had a daughter. A daughter no one knew about. Still sounds like a bad plot in a B movie." Unbelievable. Apparently, Jacob *did* have family after all. A daughter he'd never seen. One he and the child's mother had given up for adoption nearly thirty years ago. And he had waited until he was *dead* to make the damn announcement.

Pushing one hand through his black hair, Cooper shook his head. "You'd think Jacob could have given me a heads-up about this."

"Maybe he planned to," Dave offered, then shut up fast when Cooper glared at him.

"I've known him my whole damn life," he reminded his friend. "Jacob couldn't find five minutes in the last thirty-five years to say, 'Oh, did I tell you I have a daughter?'"

"If you're waiting for me to explain this away," Dave said, lifting both hands in an elegant shrug, "you've got a long wait. I can't tell you why he never told you. I can say that Jacob probably wasn't expecting to die in a damn golf-cart accident."

True. If that cart hadn't rolled, Jacob wouldn't have broken his damn neck and—*it wouldn't have changed any-*

thing. Jacob had been eighty years old. This would all have happened, eventually.

"He gave her up for adoption, ignored her existence for years, then leaves her his half of the company?" Cooper took a deep breath, hoping for calm that didn't come. "Who does that?"

Dave didn't answer because there was no answer. At this point all Cooper had were questions. Who was this woman? What would she say when she found out she was a damn heiress? Would she expect to have a say in how Cooper's business was run? That stopped him cold. No way was she going to interfere in the company; he didn't care who the hell she was.

"Okay," he said, nodding to himself as his thoughts coalesced. "I want to know everything there is to know about—" he broke off and looked down at the copy of Jacob's will laying on his desk "—Terri Ferguson, by the end of today. Where she went to school, what she does, who she knows. Hell, I want to know what she eats for breakfast.

"If I'm going to have to deal with her, I want to have as much ammunition going into this fight as I possibly can."

"Got it." Dave stood up and turned for the door. "Maybe we'll get lucky. Maybe she won't want any of this."

Cooper would have laughed, but he was too furious. "Sure, that'll happen. People turn down billions of dollars every day."

Nodding, Dave said, "Right."

"No, she won't turn it down," Cooper was saying, more to himself than to his friend. "But she's not going to show up out of nowhere and be a part of the company. I don't care who she is. Maybe what we have to do here is find a way to convince her to take the money and then disappear."

"Worth a shot," Dave said. "I'll push our guys to research faster."

"Good."

Once his friend was gone, Cooper turned toward the wall of windows at his back. He stared down at Las Vegas Boulevard, better known as the bustling Vegas Strip, nearly thirty floors below, and let his thoughts wander. He'd grown up in this hotel and still lived in one of the owner's suites on the twenty-fifth floor. He knew every nook and cranny of this city and loved every mercenary inch of it. .

On the street, tourists wandered with hope in their hearts and cash in their wallets. They played the machines, the gaming tables and in the bingo parlors. Every last one of them had thoughts of going home rich.

Why would Jacob's long-lost daughter be any different?

His gaze swept the hotels that surrounded his own and he noticed, not for the first time, that in daylight Vegas held little of the magic that shone on it at night. The city slept during the day but with darkness, it burst into exuberant life.

Cooper's family had been part of Vegas history for decades, he reminded himself as he turned back to his desk. He'd taken his father's legacy and made it a worldwide brand. Cooper had made his mark through hard work, single-minded diligence and a vision of exactly what he wanted.

Damned if he'd let some interloper crash the party.

"I'm sorry." Terri Ferguson shook her head and almost pinched herself, just to make sure she wasn't dreaming. But one look around the employee break room at the bank where she worked convinced her that this was all too real. Just fifteen minutes ago she'd been downstairs on the teller line, helping Mrs. Francis make a deposit. Now she was here, sitting across from a very fussy-looking lawyer listening to what seemed like a fairy tale. Apparently, starring *her*.

"Would you mind saying all of that one more time?"

The lawyer, Maxwell Seaton, sighed. "Ms. Ferguson, I've already explained this twice. How many more times will be required?"

Terri heard the snotty attitude in the older man's tone and maybe there was a part of her that couldn't blame him for it. But come on. Wouldn't anyone in her current position be a little off balance? Because none of this made sense.

It had been an ordinary day in Ogden, Utah. She'd gone to work, laughed with her friends, then taken her spot on the teller line at the Wasatch Bank in downtown Ogden. Familiar customers had streamed in and out of the bank until this man had approached her and, in a few words, turned her whole world upside down.

Now the older man removed his glasses, gave another sigh, then plucked a handkerchief from his suit pocket and unnecessarily cleaned the lenses. "As I've made clear to you, Ms. Ferguson, I represent your biological father's estate."

"My father," she whispered, the very word feeling a little foreign. Terri had grown up knowing she was adopted. Her parents had always told her the truth, that she had been *chosen* by them because they fell in love with her the moment they saw her. They'd encouraged her to search for her birth parents once she was eighteen, but Terri hadn't been curious. Why would she be? she'd reasoned. Where she'd come from didn't really matter as much as where she was, right?

Besides, she hadn't wanted to hurt her mother or father. Then her dad died, her mother moved to southern Utah to live with her sister, and Terri had been too busy with college and life to worry about a biological connection to people she didn't know.

Now that connection had just jumped up to bite her on the butt.

"Yes, your father. Jacob Evans." The lawyer slipped his glasses back into place. "He recently passed away and in accordance with his will, I'm here to inform you that you are his sole beneficiary."

And that summed up the weird. Why would he have left her anything? They had no connection beyond biology. And if he'd known who she was, why hadn't Jacob Evans ever reached out to her? Well, those were questions she would never get an answer to.

"Right. Okay. And I inherited a hotel?" She took a breath and held up one hand before he could speak again. "I'm really sorry. Normally, I'm not this slow on the uptake. Honestly. But this is…just so bizarre."

For the first time since entering the bank and asking to speak to her privately, the lawyer gave her a small smile. "I do understand how unexpected this must seem to you."

"'Unexpected' is a good word," she agreed and reached for the water bottle in front of her. She took a sip and added, "Weird is better."

"I suppose." Another smile. "Ms. Ferguson, your father was a full partner in the Hayes Corporation."

"Okay…" That meant exactly nothing to her.

He sighed. "The Hayes Corporation owns more than two thousand hotels, all over the world."

"Two *thousand*?" She heard her own voice squeak and winced at the sound. But seriously? Two thousand hotels? That couldn't be right, could it? Her stomach did a quick pitch and roll and Terri took a deep breath trying to calm it.

The smell of burning coffee from the pot on the coun-

ter flavored the air, and the bank's furnace made a soft
hum of background noise. Downstairs people were working, talking, laughing, living normal lives, and up here?
Terri was trying to *think*. Tried to remember who she
was, where she was. But her brain had apparently decided it had accepted enough information for one day
and shut down.

Resting one hand on a sheaf of papers he had stacked
on the table, Mr. Seaton looked at her steadily. At least
the gleam of impatience was gone from his eyes. Maybe
he was finally understanding what a shock all of this was
to her.

"Once you sign these papers, it's official," he told her.
"You'll have your father's share in a very successful company."

She tipped her head to one side and quietly asked, "*How*
successful?"

One corner of his mouth twitched slightly. "*Very.* You,
Ms. Ferguson, are now an extremely wealthy woman."

Wealthy. Rich. Also weird. But good. Because her cable
bill had just gone up and she had just been forced to put
new brakes on her car and with winter coming, she really
wanted to get new insulation on her windows and—

She reached for the papers instinctively, then pulled her
hand back. "I'd like my own lawyer to look these over before I sign." Well, her late father's lawyer, but that didn't
really matter, did it?

"Commendable," he said with a brief nod. Standing,
he closed his black leather briefcase with a snap. Looking down at her, he said, "Your new partner, Mr. Cooper
Hayes, is at the company headquarters in Las Vegas. He'd
like to see you there as soon as possible."

"Cooper Hayes." She should probably write that down.

"Yes. His contact information is included in the packet

of papers." He gave her a small smile. "Hayes Corporation is headquartered at the StarFire Hotel and Casino."

StarFire. She'd heard of it, of course. Seen pictures in magazines and now that she thought of it, Terri had seen pictures of Cooper Hayes, too. Her mind drew up one of the images of him posing with some celebrity or other—naturally, he was tall and gorgeous with eyes so blue he had to be wearing colored contacts.

And now he was her *partner.* The idea of going to the StarFire, meeting Cooper Hayes on his home turf, was a little intimidating, but she didn't see a way around it. After all, she was now half owner of the place. A shocked burst of laughter bubbled up in her chest, but she squashed it. Yesterday she wouldn't have been able to afford to *stay* at the StarFire. Now she owned half of it.

Weird just kept getting weirder.

"Okay, thank you." She glanced at the papers, but didn't touch them.

"Ms. Ferguson," the man said quietly, and waited until her gaze met his to continue. "I know this is all new and somewhat overwhelming—"

"Somewhat?" she laughed but the sound she made sounded a little hysterical so she stopped. Fast.

"But," he continued calmly, "I believe once the surprise of the situation eases, you'll do very well in your new life."

"You think so?"

"I do." He grabbed the doorknob and said, "I've left my card with the papers, as well. If you have any questions or concerns, please feel free to call me."

"Thank you."

He opened the door and Jan Belling almost fell into the room. She recovered quickly, stumbling to catch her balance, then flashing the lawyer a brilliant smile. "Hi, sorry."

"No need," he said, lips twitching. Giving Terri one last nod, he left.

Jan slipped into the room, closed the door and hurried over to take a seat opposite Terri. Her short, spiky black hair complemented bottle-green eyes, making her look like a pixie. "Well," she said, "that was embarrassing."

"I can't believe you were listening at the door."

"I can't believe you're surprised. Besides, I didn't hear much. The door's too thick. Stupid historical buildings with real wood doors." Jan took a breath. "So what happened? Who was he and why did he want you?"

Terri laughed as the tension she'd been feeling for the past fifteen minutes dissipated. Jan was her best friend, and the one person who could help her make sense of all of this. "Speaking of a 'can't believe' situation…"

"Try me."

Terri shook her head at the strangeness of it all. "I want to tell you all of it, but I should get back to work."

Jan shook her head. "No worries. The boss says you can take as long as you like. We're not busy, anyway, so start talking."

Turning her bottle of water back and forth between her hands, Terri did. As she told her friend everything, it all began to settle in her own mind. It was beyond strange. Crazy. Impossible, even. Okay, maybe her mind wasn't as settled as she'd thought.

"This is like a fairy tale or something," Jan finally said once Terri had wound down.

"That's exactly what I was thinking," Terri admitted wryly. "So when the clock strikes midnight do I turn back into a pumpkin?"

"Cinderella wasn't a pumpkin. Her carriage was." Jan laughed a little. "And this is reality no matter how strange it all seems. This is amazing, Terri. You're rich. I mean *wildly* rich."

"Oh, God." Terri dropped one hand to her stomach in a futile attempt to calm it. She'd never had a lot of money. Growing up, her adoptive parents had been schoolteachers, so though they'd had a nice life, they'd also driven ten-year-old cars and saved up to take vacations.

Of course, she drove to Idaho occasionally to buy lottery tickets, because who didn't dream of suddenly becoming a gazillionaire? But to have it actually *happen* was almost terrifying.

Jan reached across the table to take her hand. "Why aren't you celebrating? Oh. Wait. Sorry. God, I'm an idiot sometimes. You're reacting to hearing that your biological father died, aren't you?"

"Seems ridiculous to be sad about someone you've never met, but yeah, I guess I am." In the midst of the windfall, there was that sad fact. Terri silently wondered what her father had been like. If he had known who and where she was, why had he never contacted her before? Why had he left her everything? She'd probably always wonder.

Jan took Terri's water, had a sip, then handed it back. "You really had no idea at all about who your biological father was?"

"Not a clue," she said softly. "And now I've got all these questions and no way to get answers and… I don't know. It's all so far out there, it's hard to believe it's really happening."

"Yeah, I get that. But," Jan said, "at least you know he thought about you. Remembered you. And in the end, wanted to give you everything he had."

A smile tugged at the corner of Terri's mouth. "Good

point. Okay, then. No feeling sorry for myself. But I can be a little panicked, right?"

"Absolutely. The StarFire?" Jan grinned. "That's supposed to be an amazing hotel."

"I know." Terri took a deep breath, but she had a feeling the wild tremors inside weren't going to be soothed away. Her entire world had just been rocked.

Terri's mind raced with possibilities. She had a good job, if not an exciting one, but now she had been given the chance for more. Sure, she'd have a lot to learn, but stepping into this new life could be amazing.

"And you *own* it!"

"Well I own half of it, apparently." Abruptly, Terri stood up and said, "How do I go from being a bank teller to being a hotel executive?"

"Seriously?" Jan looked at her. "You're going to make me mad if you start doubting yourself. Okay, fine, there's the whole surprise factor to take into account," Jan said. "But you're smart and you're good with people and you can do any damn thing you want to."

Smiling, Terri said, "Thanks for that."

"You're welcome."

"I don't even know where to start, Jan."

"With a lawyer." Jan stood, too, and her expression read sympathy and aggravation. "Terri, this is your big chance. A chance to get out of the bank, to find a job that really interests you. Take it and run."

All true. Terri had taken this job at the bank because she needed to work. But it wasn't where she'd wanted to build a career. She really hadn't known what she wanted. And the longer she stayed at the bank, the more comfortable it became and the less likely it was that she would leave to find something that fit her better.

She'd always done the expected thing. School. Work.

Maybe this was the Universe giving her the opportunity to burst out of her rut and find out just what she was capable of.

Jan was right. She had to take this chance. Had to try for… more.

"Your new partner expects to see you in Vegas and you've got to figure all of this out before you meet him."

Terri blew out a breath. She wasn't a coward. Never had been. Sure, she'd never been faced with anything like this in her life before, but she could do it.

Couldn't she?

She'd always been the good girl. The good daughter. The responsible one. She'd had dreams of traveling but had accepted that for the things she'd wanted to do and see, she would have to spend years saving money. Now suddenly, the world was laid out in front of her. She'd be crazy to ignore it.

"You're right," she said, nodding. "I'll talk to Mike, tell him I need to take some time off."

Jan shook her head and smiled. "While you're talking to the bank manager, you might tell him that you're going to be taking off *forever*."

Terri laughed. "Things are changing, yes. But I'm not ready to throw my whole life out just yet."

"I think," Jan said as they left the break room together, "someone already did that for you."

"I hate it when you're right."

Jan laid a hand on her arm. "Terri, you're making yourself nuts and you don't have to. Cooper Hayes doesn't need you to run the company. But you're his new partner, like it or not, so you do at least get a say in things."

True, she thought and her mind started racing again. This was the opportunity of a lifetime and she'd be crazy to ignore it or to fear it. Sure, she didn't know how to run a hotel. But she'd stayed in enough of them to know what she liked and didn't. That had to count for something. And her Dad had owned a popular restaurant for decades. Terri had worked there herself as a teenager and learned from her father that the key to success in the service industry was making people happy. Sounded easy, but way too many people didn't understand that.

"Just go, Terri. Grab this shiny brass ring with both hands. And if you need the cavalry, I'm only a plane ride away."

Terri grinned. "Vegas, here I come."

Four days later Terri was in Las Vegas, standing in the massive, opulent lobby of the StarFire Hotel. The floors were covered with wide, navy blue tiles that sparkled as if stars were trapped inside them. The ceiling was high and featured a night sky dazzled by twinkling stars and streaks of light from falling stars leaving trails of gold dust in their wakes. The effect was so real that if not for the crowds and the noise and the fact that it was the middle of the day, Terri would have thought she was outside staring up.

Paintings in gold inlaid frames dotted the walls, and a waiter served complimentary champagne to guests waiting in line to register. The noise level was tremendous, since the casino spilled right off the lobby. Slot machines beeped, pinged and sang out encouragement to the hundreds of people wandering the casino floor.

She turned in a slow circle, saw a gift shop, signs for restaurants and bars and still more people. From what Terri could see, the hotel seemed to stretch on forever. The outside had been impressive, but the inside was like walking into a different world.

One that was hers now.

That thought had her smiling and biting her lip at the same time. She hadn't contacted her new partner, but she had made a reservation, so she dutifully joined the tail end of the line and accepted a flute of champagne from the waiter.

She hadn't told Cooper Hayes she was coming. Terri had wanted a little time on her own, to check out her inheritance. To get a feel for what could be her new life. Or to at least explore the possibilities.

She owed that much to herself and to her parents. They'd raised her to be strong and confident. They'd sent her to college, encouraged her to find her passion. How could she walk away from this without even trying to make it work?

And in a way, didn't she owe it to her biological father, too? She hadn't known him, but he'd clearly kept track of her. He'd left her everything he had, so she was really his legacy, wasn't she?

The line moved quickly and in minutes Terri was at the desk, handing over her ID to the clerk. He was young, with a practiced smile and a name tag that read *Brent*.

"Is this your first time at the StarFire?" he asked.

Terri grinned. "How could you tell?"

He winked at her. "You keep looking up at the ceiling."

"Guilty." She took a sip of the champagne. "It's beautiful."

"It really is." He glanced at her driver's license, tapped a few keys on his keyboard then stopped, turned and stared at her as if she had three heads. "Terri Ferguson?"

"That's right." She frowned a little and tried to get a glimpse of the computer screen. "You've got my reservation, don't you?"

"Yes, ma'am," he said with the crispness of an audible salute. Gone was the easy, flirtatious smile. Brent was suddenly all business. "We've been expecting you, ma'am."

When did she become *ma'am*? "Expecting me?" She'd hoped to fly in under the radar but apparently that wasn't going to happen.

"Your suite is prepared and ready for you, Ms. Ferguson."

"I didn't reserve a suite," she said.

He grinned, printed off two key cards and slid them into a folder with the word *StarFire* emblazoned across it. He returned her ID, handed her the keys, then looked up and waved to someone behind her. "Like I said, Mr. Hayes—and we—have been expecting you."

"He has?" *Well, of course he has, Terri.* Hadn't the lawyer told her as much?

"Your name was tagged in the system so we'd recognize your arrival right away." Brent smiled again. "Your suite's been ready for days. Bill here will take your bags—"

A bellman in his twenties appeared out of nowhere beside her.

"Oh, I've only got the one bag, and it has wheels. I can—"

"It's my job, Ms. Ferguson," Bill said. "I'll show you to your suite."

Of course they'd reserved a suite. Terri had never stayed in a hotel like this one—let alone in a suite. This was so far out of her everyday ballpark, she couldn't even see the stadium from here. But she was part owner now of this amazing hotel, so she'd better get used to it. Right, and that didn't feel weird at all.

"Okay." She swallowed the last of her champagne and slid the glass across the counter to Brent. "Could you take care of this please?"

"My pleasure, Ms. Ferguson. And welcome to StarFire."

Welcome. She followed Bill across the polished lake of a floor toward a bank of elevators. Terri didn't feel welcome.

She felt…on edge. She was about to meet her new partner. About to start a life that she had zero experience with. In a place she didn't know with people who were strangers. Sure. Great. Nerves? No, who would have nerves?

Everything had changed so quickly, she'd hardly had time to take a breath, and now she was in Las Vegas taking the first step into a world she didn't belong in.

Now the question was, could she make a place for herself here? Would Cooper Hayes try to stand in her way? And if he did, was she willing to fight for a new life? Instantly, she thought of all the things she could do with the inheritance her father had left her. She could buy a house, send her mom and aunt on a trip around the world if they wanted it.

The possibilities were endless. All she had to do was prove she could fit in. Be a part of this world. This business.

In her head, she heard her friend Jan saying, "Go for it, Terri. Enjoy it. Life just got way interesting."

Besides, Terri told herself, it was too late to back out now.

That last thought had barely raced through her mind when she saw *him*.

It was as if the crowds melted away. The ambient noise was nothing more than a buzz in her ears. Her heart pounded, her mouth went dry and her gaze locked on what was probably the most gorgeous man she'd ever seen in her life.

Every cell inside her stood up and started cheering. Honestly, even from a distance, he had the kind of magnetism that could turn a woman's knees to jelly. He stood alone, tall and invincible as people hurried past him, instinctively giving him a wide berth. He wore a black suit with a shirt so white it was nearly blinding against the dark red tie. His black hair was expertly shaggy and his eyes were a pale, clear blue so startling, she couldn't look away.

He was watching her, too, but she couldn't tell what he was thinking by the expression on his face. Not surprising, she supposed. A billionaire businessman—especially one who owned casinos—like Cooper Hayes—was probably born with a poker face.

Cooper Hayes. Her new partner.

And a man who could feed her fantasies forever.

TWO

Dave Carey watched the security footage from his office. He'd gotten a text alert the moment Terri Ferguson's name had been entered into the hotel computers. She was here and now he had to find a way to get her gone.

He watched her now on the screen, a cold fist in the pit of his stomach. From his computer he could tap into any camera in the hotel. As executive assistant to Cooper Hayes, Dave pretty much had the run of the place. And it paid to always be on top of whatever was happening in the casino.

"She's hotter than I expected," he muttered, studying the footage of Terri Ferguson as she spoke to Cooper. "That's not good."

Cooper might think of himself as having a great poker face, but Dave had known the man since college. He could tell in a blink that Cooper was intrigued by his new partner. And that wasn't good for Dave.

Hell, none of this was.

He tossed a pen onto his desk, leaned back in his black leather chair and kept his gaze locked on the tall blonde who had ruined his plans. Why couldn't she have been short and ugly with an overbite and a dragging limp or something? No, she had to look like a damn goddess. Who would have guessed that women in a wilderness like *Utah* could look that good? He watched her smile at Cooper and more important, watched Cooper give her that *hungry-lion-looking-at-a-gazelle* expression.

"Damn it." After years of putting in the time, helping Cooper build the Hayes Corporation into a global power, Dave had been on the cusp of finally getting what he deserved. Cooper had promised Dave that soon his loyalty would finally be rewarded.

And now some country-bumpkin blonde with great legs and a spectacular rack put it all in jeopardy.

Standing, Dave walked away from the image of Cooper staring at Terri Ferguson as if he were trying to keep from taking a bite of her. Moving across his office, Dave didn't notice the high-end furniture, the thick carpets strewn across hardwood floors. He didn't even see the wide windows giving him an awesome view of Vegas and the desert and mountains beyond. Instead, his mind was dredging up a meeting with Cooper nearly two years ago.

"Jacob's not getting any younger, you know. And when he dies, the company comes to me. Once I'm fully in charge," Cooper had said, lifting a glass of scotch in a toast, "I'll see to it that you get a major chunk of Hayes Corp."

Pleased, Dave had instantly wanted to know exactly how much they were talking about. But he came at the question subtly. "I appreciate it, Coop," he said, "but what are you really saying?"

"I'm saying that you've had nearly as big a hand as I

have, turning the company into what it is today," Cooper said and Dave silently agreed. He was the one, after all, who ran around setting up meetings, taking care of minor issues before they became big ones and in general doing whatever Cooper didn't have the time to handle.

"I couldn't have accomplished so much so quickly if I hadn't been able to count on you." Cooper took a sip of his Scotch, then set it down again.

"That's good to hear," Dave said, nodding. Lifting his own glass, he took a sip and gave a quick glance around Cooper's private suite. It was palatial and, as always, Dave felt a swift, hard stab of envy that he was just barely able to disguise. He was paid very well and still he couldn't come close to living as Cooper did.

And damn it, he wanted to.

Dave's parents had worked hard all their lives and never got anywhere. They hadn't been able to help him with college. He'd put himself through and getting Cooper Hayes as a roommate had just been a damn bonus. Dave had gotten close to Cooper and slowly cut ties with his blue-collar family as he began to move in higher, glossier circles. By the time he graduated and went to work at Hayes along with Cooper, Dave had turned his back on his own past completely, in favor of his future.

Hell, he hadn't seen his family in more than ten years and if anyone asked about them, Dave kept it simple and told people they were all dead. Easier that way.

"I'm going to want to make some changes once I have unilateral power. Jacob doesn't see things the way I do. He thinks one hotel in London is sufficient. But why have one when you can have two or three?"

Musing aloud, Cooper said again, "Once I'm in charge, everything will change."

"Well, that turned out to be true, anyway," Dave muttered, slapping one hand to the window glass, warm from the October sun. This woman's arrival had ruined everything. Now Cooper had a partner again. He wasn't completely in charge and wouldn't be unless they could get rid of Terri Ferguson. And until that happened, Dave wouldn't get what he'd been working toward for more than ten years.

Oh, he knew that Cooper's plan was to get little Miss Utah out of Vegas as quickly as possible. But Dave wasn't fooling himself about this. He'd seen the interest on Cooper's face as he looked at Terri Ferguson. And if Cooper was that attracted, the urgency to chase the woman off would fade. Pretty soon she'd be settled in, making plans, and Dave's plans would be completely obliterated.

Pushing away from the window, he stalked back to his desk and sat down to stare at the image of the blonde who had, just by being here, become his enemy. As Cooper and Terri disappeared into the elevator, Dave shut down the surveillance feed. There were no cameras in the private elevator or the owner's floor so there was no point in trying to track them.

Alone with his thoughts again, Dave's mind raced with plans, possibilities. He had to find a way to get rid of Terri Ferguson and make it look like leaving was her own idea. He had to convince the gorgeous blonde that she was out of her depth. It wouldn't be easy, of course. But Dave had handled tough assignments for years.

He could handle this, too.

But first, he told himself, it was time to call out the Big Guns, and he reached for the phone.

She wasn't what Cooper had expected.

His own fault, really. He could have done research on her. He'd handed that off to Dave and then never followed up. Mainly because he hadn't wanted to even *think* about having to deal with a new partner, for God's sake. If he had done due diligence, he might have been prepared for his first sight of her.

The world he traveled in was populated by celebrities, wealthy business people and other so-called "elites." When he'd heard that his new partner, Terri Ferguson, was a bank teller from Utah, somehow he'd expected…less. He wasn't even sure what, really. Only that Terri was more—much more—than he'd imagined.

She filled his vision to the point of shutting out everything else. She was tall, which he appreciated. He'd always hated bending nearly in half to look a woman in the eye or to kiss her senseless. This woman probably stood five feet eight inches without the three-inch black heels she wore. Her dress was a deep, rich blue that hugged curves designed to drive a man crazy. The swirling hem of her dress stopped well above her knees, displaying long, shapely legs that were toned and tanned. The bodice was cut low enough to be tempting and she wore a black shrug sweater against the October chill.

Her long blond hair tumbled across her shoulders and down her back in thick, heavy waves and her summer-blue eyes were pinned on him. Just for a second, he indulged himself with another look at the full, rich curve of her breasts and his body stirred in response. Damn it. She was beautiful.

And a distraction he didn't want or need, he reminded himself.

The only reason she was there, in his hotel, was to throw a monkey wrench into the middle of Cooper's business plans. So it didn't matter what she looked like, or that his body was tight and uncomfortable just looking at her. All that mattered was that he get her to sign over her half of the business in exchange for the huge buyout he was willing to offer her.

The bellman skidded to a stop when he spotted Cooper. "Mr. Hayes. I was just showing Ms. Ferguson to her suite, sir."

"So I see." Cooper took two long steps forward and stopped right in front of her. He was close enough to see the flash of something…interesting in her eyes. To hear the quick intake of breath and to notice how she squared her shoulders as if preparing for battle. Which, whether she knew it or not, he told himself, was the right reaction to this situation.

"You're Cooper Hayes," she said and he deliberately refused to notice the low pitch of her voice. Decided to not wonder how that voice would sound as a whisper in the darkness.

"I am," he said. "I've been expecting you."

Bill stood there, swiveling his head back and forth, watching the two of them as if he was at a tennis match.

"Sorry I'm late?" She smiled with the question and her eyes lit up. Completely irrelevant.

"You're not late. I just thought you would arrive sooner than you did."

Cooper noticed the bellman now getting even more interested in the conversation and he had no interest in supplying his employees with entertainment. Fixing his gaze on the younger man, he said, "I'll take it from here, thanks."

"Yes, sir." Bill shot Terri what Cooper thought of as a sympathetic glance, then Bill turned and hurried back to the main lobby.

"Wow, he moved fast." Terri sent a quick look over her shoulder. "Do you inspire fear in all your employees?"

"Not fear," he corrected. "Respect."

"Oh, of course. Wide eyes and a dead run are sure signs of respect."

He took a breath. Apparently, she'd be harder to intimidate than the people who worked for him. "Are we going to talk about the bellman, or would you like to see your suite?"

Terri grinned. "I can do both."

"Why am I not surprised?" he muttered. Gripping the suitcase handle with one hand, he placed the other at the small of her back, turning her toward the bank of elevators and one that stood alone, separate from the rest.

"Anyway," she said, turning her head to take in the expansive casino behind them, "I'd have been here sooner, but there was a lot to do. I had to put in for a leave of absence at my job, get my car checked to make sure it was safe for the drive—"

"You drove?" He interrupted the flow of words because he was pretty sure that was the only chance he'd have to speak at all. "If you had called to let us know you were coming, I'd have sent the jet for you."

"You have your own jet?" she asked, goggling at him.

"*We* do."

"*We* have a jet. Right. Who doesn't?" Shaking her head, she took a breath and said, "Anyway, I drove so I could stop off in St. George to see my mom and my aunt. Tell them what had happened and get them to babysit my dog for me because I didn't know how long I'd be gone and I couldn't ask my friend to watch her for who knows how many days—"

"You have a dog?" Cooper didn't know why that hit him, but it did. It was something that hadn't come up in Dave's research, either. Cooper'd never had a dog. Or a cat. Or hell, even a hamster. Growing up in a hotel didn't lend itself to pets. As a kid, that had bothered him. Apparently, it still did.

She grinned. "Yes. Daisy's a cute mix of about a hundred and fifty different breeds, and she thinks she's a Great Dane, so she needs a lot of attention and really doesn't like being left alone. My mom loves her, so Daisy's happy and—"

"What did your mom say about all of this?" Another interruption and he didn't feel the slightest bit guilty about it. Until she spoke.

"You keep interrupting me. That's rude, you know, but it's okay for now."

"Thanks so much," he said wryly, but she apparently didn't catch the sarcasm.

"Mom's as freaked out by this as I am," Terri continued. "Neither of us knew anything about my biological parents so we're kind of shocked to find out my birth father even knew who I was, let alone *where* I was. Sorry. Rambling. The point is, I had a few things to take care of before I could come to Vegas."

That bright, brilliant smile had knocked him back for a second but thankfully she hadn't noticed. He felt off his game and that was something Cooper couldn't afford. With that firmly in mind, he brushed aside her rambling. "Doesn't matter. You're here now." Nodding, he slid a card into the slot of the stand-alone elevator. "This is a private elevator. It's the one you'll use to get to and from your suite. The other elevators stop at the nineteenth floor. This one goes directly to the top five floors and the roof."

"Okay…" Another deep breath and he refused to notice how her breasts lifted with the action.

Focusing had never been an issue for Cooper. Until today, apparently.

"The waitstaff and housekeeping have their own elevators that will take them to the top floors for business purposes. The general public can't access the higher floors."

"Sounds very…secure."

If she was joking he let her know by his tone that he didn't find it funny. "As secure as technology can make it. Hayes Corporation offices are on the twentieth floor," he said, turning his focus from her to the matter at hand. "And on twenty-one, two and three we have suites for special guests, dignitaries, celebrities…anyone whose security issues demand a safe, impregnable, luxury suite."

"Impregnable. Right. Sounds cozy." She nodded as the elevator doors whisked open.

"Our guests don't come here for 'cozy.'"

"Good thing," she murmured.

He took that as a direct insult. "A cozy hotel is a B and B. A Hayes hotel offers luxury. Exclusivity."

She blinked at him. "Wow. That sounds terrible."

Surprised again, he said, "What about that is terrible?"

"Oh, just everything, but never mind…"

Cooper thought about arguing her ridiculous point but buried his irritation instead. Unknowingly, she was proving that he was right to want to buy her out of this partnership. If she didn't understand the basics of the hotel industry, then she had no business being a partner. Certainly not *his* partner.

He took a breath. "The owners' suites are on the twenty-fourth floor." Cooper steered her inside the open elevator, slid his card into the slot again, pushed the right button and stood back, looking at her. With the mirrored wall behind her, he was able to take her all in at once. And he had to admit, every damn view he got of her was a good one.

Too bad she was such a pain in the ass.

The elevator swept up in a rush and she laughed, a rich, deep bubble of sound that whipped through the small, enclosed space and wrapped itself around his throat until Cooper felt like he couldn't breathe. Pure enjoyment wreathed her features, when only a moment or two before, she'd been irritated, and damned if he wasn't...captivated. Most women he knew were more guarded about their emotions. But Terri was honest and open and he found that intriguing.

She grabbed hold of the brass rail at her side, tossed her hair back and slanted him a delighted glance. "Well, that's faster than I expected."

"Express elevator." His own voice sounded as tight as he felt. Cooper watched her staring up at the elevator roof and realized she was the first woman he'd been with in this elevator who didn't turn and check herself out in the mirror. Every female he knew would fluff her hair or smooth her lipstick or simply give her appearance a mental thumbs-up. Terri Ferguson, though, was looking up at the digital midnight sky.

"That's so fabulous. Like the lobby." She shook her head. "I love the shooting stars. It looks so real."

"I wouldn't know. Living in a city with this much ambient light, you don't see many stars."

She leveled her gaze on him. "Now, that's a shame."

"I've never thought so."

"Then you don't know what you're missing," she said, looking at him with what could only be sympathy.

Well, Cooper Hayes didn't need anyone to feel sorry for him. Especially over something as minor as not being a stargazer. Watching her, he figured this was just one example of how the two of them were from different worlds. She looked at the stars in the sky, and the only stars he was interested in were the celebrities who came to his hotels. Yeah, a partnership between them would be doomed. Best to end it as soon as possible.

She turned her gaze back to the ceiling, a soft smile on

her face, when falling stars left trails of gold dust across a digital sky. Cooper didn't bother looking at the illusion. Instead, he watched her pleased smile and wondered why the hell he was enjoying it.

Deliberately, he brushed it off and started talking. "We work with a company who designs and installs illusionist skies in the hallways, casino, the lobby. StarFire can follow you all over the hotel."

"That's amazing. I'm a little technologically challenged, so imagining people who can do that? Wow." She looked at him. "It's really great. I mean, everything I've seen since I walked in the door has been just beautiful."

Her face was open and easy to read. So he saw her excitement, the touch of nerves in the way her teeth tugged at her bottom lip. The easy curve of that smile did things to him he really didn't want to think about. Irritated, he snapped, "Glad you approve."

And just like that, her smile wobbled and her eyes lost that sparkle.

Idiot.

Being charming with a beautiful woman had never been difficult for him. Before Terri Ferguson, apparently.

He spoke up again quickly. "The illusions are relatively new. Installed just a couple years ago, but everyone seems to like them."

"I can see why." She relaxed again, but her eyes still looked wary, as if she had walls up because she'd wandered into a hotbed of enemies. Which he really didn't want her to be thinking. He needed her to see him not as an enemy, but rather as a man who was going to do her the favor of sparing her all the work necessary to keep a company like Hayes Corporation running.

"You said yourself this was a strange situation to be in,"

he reminded her with a deliberately casual shrug. "Well, I only found out about *you* a few days ago, too."

She blinked at him. "Jacob never said anything about me?"

"No. I didn't find out the truth until a few hours before you did. So now we're both surprised." He tapped one finger on the key card folder she held. "Anyway, your card will take you to any of the top floors. Right now I'm showing you to your owner's suite."

She dragged in another breath, tossed her hair back over her shoulder and tightened her grip on the cold, brass rail. "Is that where my father stayed?"

"Only when he was in town. He mainly lived in New York."

Even to him, his voice sounded cool, disinterested—and that wasn't good. If Cooper's plan was to smooth the way for her to become an in-name-only partner, then he needed to be a hell of a lot more amiable than he'd managed to be so far. It shouldn't have been difficult at all, but his attraction to her was throwing him off balance. Not something Cooper enjoyed. "Jacob wasn't in Vegas often over the last couple of years, so I didn't see much of him. And I would have, since I live here in the hotel."

Her gaze snapped to his. "You do?"

He'd surprised her and he supposed he could understand it. In her world, people probably lived in neat little houses with backyards and dogs and kids. People *visited* hotels; they didn't live there.

"I practically grew up here," he told her. "Always figured to move out eventually. Get a place away from the Strip, but I realized I like the Strip. And living here is easy. My office is right downstairs. Twenty-four-hour room service, and housekeeping."

"Sure. Of course. Well, housekeeping I really understand. That would be handy." She laughed a little and he heard the nerves in it. "Sorry." She held up one hand and shook her head, smiling wryly. "This is hard to take in. Last week I juggled bills so I could pay to have my car fixed and now..."

"Now you can buy any car you want."

She blew out a breath. "That hasn't really settled in yet."

"Get used to it," Cooper advised quietly.

This was good. He wanted her to realize that the money she'd inherited could change her life. He wanted her to go out and play, explore the world. Hell, do *anything* but stay in Vegas and try to help him run *his* company.

"Your old world is over." When the elevator doors opened with a whoosh, he added, "Welcome to your new one."

A wide hallway where the sun shone through several skylights plugged into the ceiling stretched out on either side of the elevator. Pale blue carpet covered the floor, and the soft gray walls held framed photos of different hotels in the Hayes chain. Cooper watched her take it all in and felt a flush of pride. He was so used to his surroundings, he rarely noticed any of it. But her reaction to the place made him pause briefly to enjoy what he'd built.

"So many different hotels," she murmured, walking up to the closest painting. It was the villa in Tuscany that boasted views from every room and a world-class spa.

"We're in hundreds of countries," he said, not without a touch of pride.

She turned her head to look up at him. "I hate to keep using the word *amazing*, but it's the only one that seems to fit." Then she looked up and down the sunlit hall. "Well, this is different. I'm used to narrow, dark hotel hallways."

"None of our hotels have dark hallways," he said and saw a flash in her eyes at his use of the word *our*. "Not good for business. Makes guests nervous."

"But no StarFire skies up here? The illusions, I mean?"

"The illusions are for the tourists. Our guests. I pre-fer reality." He glanced at the skylights and the sunlight pouring through. "I wanted real light up here. Feels less closed in this way."

Pushing her hair back from her face, she asked, "Do you always speak in short sentences?"

"What?"

She smirked and he ground his teeth together. Fine. He did tend to speak with as few words as possible. Saved time. But no one had ever called him on it before. "Are you always so blunt?"

"Usually," she said, turning to look up and down the hallway. "It's easier to just be up front and honest. Lies tend to get all tangled and twisted."

Now it was his turn to smirk. "Honesty may be best in Utah, but it's not really popular in Vegas. Not exactly the way most business deals are made."

"That's too bad," she said, then tipped her head to one side, her long, blond hair sliding off her shoulders to shine in the sun pouring through the skylight above. "Don't you think?"

"Never thought about it."

"Maybe you should." She squared her shoulders again. She was still preparing for battle. "So, which way?"

He pointed down the hall behind her. "Your suite's to the left of the elevator."

She inhaled sharply and he took a moment to enjoy the lift of her breasts. Damn, he really was spending way too much time thinking about her body and wanting to see more of it. Preferably naked, spread across his bed with moonlight streaming through the windows. But he got a grip on the daydreams and deliberately pushed them aside. Yes, she was gorgeous, but he wasn't going to get involved with the woman he was trying to get rid of. That would only complicate things further.

When Cooper had heard Jacob's daughter was from Utah, Cooper had made the stupid assumption that she'd be some unsophisticated farm girl or something. And for that, he wanted to kick himself. He should have known better than to make assumptions. Maybe he should get out of Vegas once in a while.

As she walked down the hall in front of him, Cooper enjoyed the view. Her long legs made him wish they were wrapped around his hips, and her butt was a work of art. Her hair swung from side to side with every step she took, and her hips swayed in a silent invitation he was more than ready to accept. She flipped him a look over her shoulder and he saw how the dark blue dress she wore reflected in her eyes, making them a startling, crystal blue. Then she smiled and he felt the jolt of it slam home.

She was fascinating. More so than he'd thought she'd be. More than he could afford to acknowledge.

Whatever he wanted to do to her, with her, he had to remember, she didn't belong here and if he had his way, she wouldn't be staying.

He thought of what little information Dave had found on her—only child, father deceased. Well, they shared that, anyway. She'd graduated from Weber State College with a degree in archaeology—as if that would come in handy in the hotel business. She lived alone in a condo she made regular payments on and worked at a bank as a teller and new accounts executive.

That was it. No dirt. No gossip. No angry ex-lover who made threats. No arrests, not even for jaywalking. She was so good it was almost eerie.

This kind of woman was not made for Vegas.

Which meant she wasn't for him, either.

At the suite door, she took one of her midnight blue key cards from the folder and pushed it into the slot. Cooper stayed back, wanting to watch her reaction as she stepped into the luxurious owner's suite.

He wasn't disappointed.

She gave an audible sigh at her first sight of the place and stopped so suddenly to take it all in that he almost ran into her. "This is…"

"Amazing?"

She turned and gave him a quick grin. "Yes. Absolutely."

Cooper walked around her and left her pink—of course it was pink—suitcase against the wall. He edged his suit jacket back and tucked both hands into his pockets.

Still watching her expression, he said, "It's a three-bedroom, three-bath suite. There's no kitchen, but there is a coffee bar that's restocked every evening and a bar fridge with soft drinks, water and wine. The wet bar is across the room and if there's a type of liquor you prefer and can't find it, call downstairs and they'll bring it to you."

"Of course they will."

He wasn't sure what she meant by that, but ignored it and moved on. "There are snacks in the fridge, too, but room service will bring you anything you want any time of day."

"Right." She nodded, letting her gaze slide around the room.

He did the same. The suites had been updated and redecorated only a year ago. Jacob's decorator had gone with shades of gray and smoky blue. There was plenty of chrome, lots of glass and wide-planked hardwood floors dotted with plush throw rugs. The balcony outside a pair of French doors ran the width of the building, affording both Terri and Cooper access.

"This is amazing," she whispered.

"There's that word again," he mused with a chuckle. If she was this blown away by her own suite, it shouldn't take long at all to convince her that she was completely out of her depth as a partner in this business. That was good, wasn't' it? Get rid of her quickly—especially because of what she was doing to him. "Follow me. I'll show you the rest of the place."

"Oh." She spun around to look at him and her eyes were wide. "You don't have to do that. You probably have more important things to do."

He did. But he wanted to get a better feel for her and what she was thinking, feeling. And, as long as he was being honest with himself, he could silently admit that he liked looking at her. "Not at the moment."

"Okay, then."

Cooper closed the roller handle and simply carried her suitcase down a hall to the first of three bedrooms. He opened the door, stepped inside, then moved back to watch her again. Really, he'd never known anyone with such an expressive face. Her delight was clearly stamped on her features, and her eyes were sparkling. Maybe it was growing up in the business world. Or maybe it was Vegas itself, but it seemed that everyone constantly hid what they were thinking or feeling. As if letting anyone in meant giving away their edge.

And truth be told, that was how Cooper operated, as well. He'd spent most of his life building the walls that surrounded him. As a businessman, he kept what he was thinking, what he was after, under lock and key. The only one he truly felt he could be honest with was Dave. Everyone else was kept at a safe distance.

A woman as open and honest as Terri Ferguson was a risk to the walls Cooper had spent a lifetime building.

"This is amazing. Really." She spun around to face him

and pleasure was stamped on her features. "I swear I'm going to find another word to use. Once I get used to—" she waved her arms to encompass the lovely room "—all of this. Shouldn't take more than a year or two."

You won't be here that long.

Yet, even as he thought it, he responded to the shine in her eyes, the wide smile on her face and he thought of things they could do together that would get the same reactions from her. Hell, he could practically taste that mouth of hers. She did a quick spin in place and the hem of her dress lifted higher above her knees, giving him one brief glimpse of smooth, strong thighs.

Instantly, he shut those thoughts down. He didn't need them. Didn't want them. And, he half resented that not only had she arrived to stick her nose in his business, but she was, without even trying, turning his dick to stone.

"Settle in. We'll talk later." His voice sounded gruff even to him. And a part of his brain quietly whispered, *Charming, remember?*

But screw that. He'd used up his daily quota of charm. He looked into her eyes and felt his world tip and he didn't like it. Best to leave now. He wanted to get out of there while he could still walk.

"Okay, then," she said, already turning away from him to wander into the adjoining bath. "I'll see you later."

"Right." Fine. Hell.

She didn't even watch him leave.

Three

Terri didn't stay in the beautiful room for long. Sure, if she'd been on vacation, she would have indulged herself in the luxury of it all for hours. But then again, if she was on vacation, she wouldn't have a room like this. The place she could afford would be a motel somewhere off the Strip probably sandwiched between a liquor store and a pawn shop.

But today, instead, she was staying at the top of a palace.

Her mother had made her promise to take pictures of the hotel so Terri had already documented most of the suite. Now she took some pictures in the grand bathroom.

"Wow. Just…*wow*," she murmured as she moved her phone around to catch the whole thing. From the seafoam-colored tiles to the shower that took up one end of the room with multiple nozzles and a bench—she supposed it was there for when you got exhausted just walking back and forth to the shampoo alcove.

The pale green marble counter was stocked with shampoos and lotions and towels so fluffy and huge they almost qualified as blankets. She still could hardly believe this was happening to her.

"I've never even seen a tub that big," she muttered, taking a picture of the deep soaker tub almost as big as a pool and complete with jets. She couldn't wait to try it out.

"Later," she promised herself and gave a quick look at the mirror, checking her reflection.

Her heart was beating a little fast; her eyes looked wider than normal with a sheen of excitement in them she hadn't seen in a long time. Was it for this place, what was happening in her life?

Or was it, she wondered, because of Cooper Hayes himself?

As if in answer, her heartbeat sped up even faster and her breath caught in her throat.

It was more than just the way he looked, which was off-the-charts gorgeous—but there was an aura of power about him that fascinated her. He was steely and strong and the way he bit words off made her long to hear more of that deep voice. Not to mention the fact that when he touched her, she felt a kind of heat she'd never experienced before.

Not a good thing right now, she reminded herself. She needed to get used to this new world. To see if she could make it her own. Getting involved with her new partner wasn't a smart plan. Then you were tangling up business and need and something was bound to go wrong.

Wow, this was not something she'd expected. Of course, here she was in a plush suite with a lap-pool bathtub and a view of Las Vegas that usually only birds saw. So what about this *was* expected? Then she remembered the flash of something dangerous in Cooper's eyes as he looked at her and told herself that this was a man she had no idea how to handle. But she'd love the chance to *try* handling him.

"Okay, get a grip," she told the woman in the mirror. "You're not here for a romance. You're here because—" She stopped.

Because her old life wasn't enough. Yes, she'd been happy, but now there was a chance at adventure. At something bigger than she'd ever dreamed. She wanted to make this work, she realized. And once her mind was made up, as her Dad used to say, there was just no stopping Terri Ferguson.

Grabbing her black leather bag, she slung it over her left shoulder and headed for the door. The elevator ride was fast. She was still wearing the dark blue dress she'd arrived in and thought she looked pretty good for taking her first self-guided tour of the casino. When the doors swished open, a wall of noise erupted that shocked Terri even as it drew her in.

Stepping off the elevator, she was instantly pulled into the humming pulse of the crowd. It wasn't the first time Terri had been to a casino, of course. Wendover, Nevada, was only a two-hour drive from Ogden so she and Jan often made the drive to see a show or spend the weekend at slot machines, trying to win a fortune that would change their lives.

Well, now her life *had* been changed and so she was looking at this immense adult playground with new eyes, hoping it would give her some kind of insight into her new *partner*.

The place was beautiful, of course. Like the rest of the hotel, the StarFire theme wended its way through the casino, as well. There were slot machines with flashing images of stars sailing through a night sky, and the illusion ceiling stretched across the entire room. The carpet was a deep, midnight blue with silver threads peppering it so that it looked like a night sky, as well. Mirrors dotted the walls and row after row of beeping, clanging machines with eager tourists perched in front of them stood on the carpet like soldiers. Table games formed a huge circle in the center of the casino, and overhead there was another illusion sky, this one with planets and shooting stars making a dramatic statement.

Terri wandered, wanting to see it all—not just the hotel and casino itself, but the guests—how they were being treated, if they looked happy. Like at her Dad's restaurant, the best way to tell if a business was in good shape was to judge it from the customer's point of view. From what she could see, everyone seemed to be having a great time. It was late afternoon, though there were no clocks in the casino to announce that fact.

Music streamed from a lounge bar where the night theme included black-topped tables and pinpoint lights on the walls. Powerful fans ensured there was only a faint hint of cigarette smoke in the air. Cocktail waitresses in impossibly high heels and body-hugging black and silver costumes hurried through the crowd, balancing trays holding full drinks and empties. Somewhere close by, a woman shrieked in excitement and bells and whistles went off at shrill levels that had Terri quickening her steps. She was still smiling as she walked away from the crowds toward what looked like a circle of peace in the madness.

A glassed-in area held sofas, chairs and pots and pots of flowers, blooms bursting in every color imaginable. There were two women inside, each of them working on their phones. Terri walked past, promising herself she'd check it out personally later. She was a little surprised the enclosed area wasn't more crowded with people looking to take a break from the noise.

For more than an hour, Terri wandered through the hotel

and the surrounding grounds. She watched valets laughing with customers and then racing off to get their cars. She saw the bellmen loading carts with luggage. Hotel guests were a steady stream, coming and going. Just beyond the front of the hotel lay the famous Strip, bustling with thousands of tourists.

Her self-guided tour ended when her black heels finally began to make her feet pay. They were beautiful shoes and she loved them, but they had not been designed for hiking. She took a seat at the bar in the main casino and smiled at the bartender.

Glancing at his name tag, she said, "Brandon, I would love a glass of chardonnay."

"Right away." He was gorgeous—just like every other employee she'd noticed—and Terri wondered if good looks were a requirement to work here. He had short blond hair, kind green eyes and wore a midnight-black vest shot through with silver thread over a white button-down shirt and black slacks. As he poured, he gave her a wide smile. "Your first stay at StarFire?"

"How could you tell?" she asked. "Am I that obvious?"

He shrugged, set her glass down on the gleaming black bar top and said, "It's the way you're looking around. As if you're afraid you're going to miss something."

"In my defense, there's a lot to see." Terri took a sip and set the glass back down with a satisfied sigh. "Oh, that's good, thanks. And yes, it's my first time here. It's a beautiful place. Do you like working here?"

It wasn't just small talk; she really wanted to know how people felt about their jobs. And if she was now part owner, shouldn't she?

He shrugged, wiped down a nonexistent spot on the bar top. "No real complaints. Good pay, meet nice people—" He winked.

She smiled and had another sip of the great, icy-cold wine. "Really. I'm curious."

He planted both hands on the edge of the bar, tipped his head to one side and gave it some thought. "On the whole, sure. It's a great hotel. Classy guests. Being a bartender, you see some really weird stuff, but not so much here. It's absolutely the best place I've worked."

She was glad to hear it.

"But," he added, "it'd be nice if they were more flexible with the shifts."

"What do you mean?"

He shrugged and gave a quick look around as if to make sure no one could overhear him complaining. "They don't like us trading shifts if something comes up—like, I had to take my wife to the baby doctor for an ultrasound last week—"

"Congratulations."

"Thanks!" He gave her a wide grin and a thumbs-up. "It's our first. A girl. Anyway, I work afternoons, but I needed the late shift that day. Couldn't switch with the night bartender, so I had to lose a day of pay." He shrugged. "Things like that. It's not bad, necessarily, but it'd be good if they were more willing to work with us."

"Seems like it would make sense," she said. Terri wondered why the hotel was so rigid. As long as the shifts were covered, did it matter *which* bartender was on duty?

"Anything else?" Now that she'd gotten him talking, she wanted to hear more. Customers were a good ruler of how a business fulfilled its duties. But employees were the heartbeat of the place. If she was now a partner in this hotel—and all the others—she wanted to know what was working…and even more important, what *wasn't*.

He laughed a little. "Writing a book?"

"No, just nosy."

All around them the casino was hopping, and at the end of the bar, two men sat sipping beers and playing video poker.

"Okay, why not? This almost feels therapeutic." He had to think about it again. "Well, why can't there be cocktail *waiters* as well as waitresses? Guys could do the job, too."

"Good point," she said, wondering why no one, including her, had ever thought about it.

"And the employee break room?" He shook his head as he warmed to his theme. "Sad. One little fridge and a coffeepot. Oh, and a vending machine with cookies and chips."

"That does sound sad," she said, laughing. "Actually, it sounds like the employee break room at the bank where I work."

"Hey," Brandon said, holding out a hand. "We are survivors of mediocre food and lumpy couches."

She shook his hand and made a mental note to write down everything he'd told her. She could talk to Cooper about this next time she saw him. Wow. Was this what it felt like to be in charge? To have power?

At that thought, she nearly laughed out loud. She didn't have any power. She was a stranger in a strange land and didn't know what to do first.

"Terri Ferguson?"

Turning at the voice right behind her, Terri smiled at the man watching her. He had short blond hair, brown eyes and was wearing an exceptionally well-cut suit. "Yes, I'm Terri Ferguson."

"Nice to meet you," he said, holding out one hand. "I'm Dave Carey, Cooper's executive assistant."

"Oh." She smiled wider and shook his hand. "Nice to meet you, too."

When he released her hand, Dave looked at the bartender and said, "So, what are you and the new owner of the StarFire talking about?"

"New owner?" Brandon's voice was soft, worried. "Terri Ferguson. They told us you'd be arriving soon. I'm sorry, I didn't know—"

"There's no way you could have known, Brandon," she said, trying to ease the panic in his eyes.

"Is there a problem?" Dave asked, shifting his gaze back and forth as if sensing the sudden tension.

"No, of course not," Terri said quickly. No doubt Brandon was frantically rethinking their conversation and wondering if he'd said something that was going to turn around and bite him. His gaze shifted briefly to Dave then back to her with a silent plea in his eyes and she knew he'd rather she didn't mention what they'd been talking about.

Smiling, she turned to Dave. "Brandon's been really helpful. He was just telling me about the movie theater on the third floor." She shook her head. "Apparently, I didn't get far enough in my wandering. I couldn't believe you have your own theater."

"It's not my theater now, Ms. Ferguson. It's yours."

"Terri, please," she said and ignored what he'd said. Until she got accustomed to all of this it was easier on her to not really acknowledge that she was an owner of this fabulous place. "So, how did you know where to find me?"

Dave eased onto a bar stool, then pointed to several spots along the ceiling. "Wasn't difficult. Surveillance cameras. They're all over the hotel and casino."

Cameras. Of course. She hadn't considered that and she should have. Honestly, even the bank in Ogden had security cams everywhere but the bathrooms. Naturally, a luxury hotel with a crowded casino would have cameras everywhere. Why hadn't she considered that earlier? She'd thought it was her secret that she'd wandered all over the hotel. Now she knew Dave had seen her. Had Cooper watched her, too? Had he bothered to look?

Perfect. A minute ago she'd hated the idea of Dave watching her every move and now she was disappointed thinking that Cooper hadn't? She didn't need to be thinking about Cooper right now.

"So you have been observing me the whole time? That's a little creepy."

Brandon moved off to serve another customer, but not before sending Terri a quiet *thank you* with his eyes.

"You make it sound like I'm a stalker," Dave said with a disarming smile. "You can relax on that score. I happened to be going over a security issue and saw you sitting here at the main bar. Thought I'd take the opportunity to meet you in person."

Okay, that made sense and eased that deer-in-the-headlights feel that had briefly gripped her. Terri laughed. "I guess you are a little busy to be watching me meander through the casino."

"Never too busy to watch a pretty woman," he said, then quickly added, "in a nonstalker way."

Smiling, and relaxing in his company, Terri picked up her wine and took a sip. "I appreciate that. But it's still a little creepy to have so many cameras documenting everything that happens. I mean, I get why they're needed, it's just…"

Dave nodded sagely. "I understand. It seems these days that there are always tiny incursions on privacy."

"Exactly." It was a shame Cooper Hayes wasn't as easy to talk to as his assistant. And it was a shame that Dave Carey didn't give her the same tingles that Cooper did.

"Still, I think most people are willing to put up with creepy if it means they feel safer."

"I suppose," Terri agreed. "Or maybe it's because they

don't really look up and notice those cameras focused down on them."

"Maybe you're right." He gave a shrug then changed the subject. "We'll have to have a long conversation about the pros and cons sometime. But for right now, what do you think of the StarFire?"

"It's beautiful," she admitted shamelessly. "I took a little tour of it by myself. There's way too much to see in an hour or two, but I wanted to try to get a feel for it."

"And did you? Get a feel?"

His tone was almost flirtatious and she wanted to tell him that her body was too busy burning for Cooper to be interested in someone else. Dave seemed nice, but he didn't give her the same zip of interest that Cooper had.

Terri laughed and shook her head. "I don't think that's even possible right now."

"I get it." Dave signaled to Brandon and when the bartender came back, ordered a draft beer. "It must be hard for you, coming into all of this so unexpectedly."

Was that sympathetic or patronizing? Hard to tell. But he'd been so nice, Terri gave him the benefit of the doubt. "It's very strange. In so many ways I can't even count them all. I think my mom's in even deeper shock than I am."

"Your adoptive mother didn't know who your birth father was?"

"Nope. There weren't a lot of open adoptions twenty-eight years ago. She and my dad were just glad to get me." Terri thought about that for a long second or two, then smiled at Dave. "I have a wonderful family. Jacob Evans did me a big favor by putting me up for adoption."

Reaching out, he gave her hand a quick squeeze, then released her. *Nope, no zip of heat. Too bad, she thought. An attraction to Dave would have been much easier to deal with.*

"I'm sure he would have been glad to know it."

A pang of regret for the man she'd never know echoed inside her. "Did you know Jacob well?"

"Oh, yes. For more than a decade." Dave took a sip of his beer. "He wasn't an easy man, but he was a brilliant businessman. I think Cooper will miss his input." He paused then said, "But you'll be able to step into your father's shoes there, won't you? I mean, taking on his responsibilities in the company."

Nerve wracking words, but Terri was up for it. She was a fast learner. Stepping into upper management position at such a well-established company wouldn't be easy. But it wasn't impossible, either.

"It's a lot," she said, lifting her wineglass for another sip. "But I'll catch on."

"Oh, of course you will," Dave said. "No one expects you to know everything right away. And I'm happy to help any way I can."

"Thanks. I appreciate that." Terri took another sip and studied Dave over the rim of her glass. He was handsome, polished, friendly, but she didn't get the same *surge* of something hot and tempting from him as she did from Cooper. It would probably be much easier working with Dave, since her hormones wouldn't be distracted, so if he was willing to help her out, she'd be grateful.

"You've met Cooper, I know."

"Yes, he showed me to my suite."

"I'm impressed," he said, laughing. "Getting Cooper to take ten minutes away from the company is a real accomplishment. He gets busy, wrapped up in his work. With a corporation this size, there's always something to be handled. Some problem or challenge that has to be met. He's constantly talking about just how much work there is to do and he never stops. Which means I don't, either. Cooper expects the same kind of commitment he makes, from everyone around him." Dave glanced down the bar to where Brandon was filling a cocktail waitress's tray. "He doesn't have much time for anything but the job. So if he seems to be ignoring you, try not to take it personally." He turned back to Terri and she read sympathy in his eyes. "I'll be here, ready to stand in for Cooper whenever I can. Help ease you into your new position."

"Thank you." A workaholic partner who would expect the same from her. Well, Terri wasn't afraid of work. True, she didn't know anything at all about the hotel business, but she was smart and capable. She would learn.

And, she would prove to Cooper Hayes that she was more than just Jacob Evans's surprise daughter. If Cooper was too busy to be bothered with her, then she'd take Dave's help to find her feet here. She'd been given the chance at something wonderful—she'd be crazy to turn away from it.

Bells erupted. A woman in her sixties with short, graying blond hair and a T-shirt that read *Don't bother me, I'm reading*, shrieked and a crowd of people surrounded her as she shouted, "I won! I won! Oh, my God!"

Terri smiled at the woman's excitement and just beneath the thunderous noise, she heard Dave say, "People come from all over the world, hoping to get lucky in Las Vegas. But *you* got lucky before you even arrived, didn't you?"

She smiled at him and gave a quick look at the casino and the thousands of people milling around. It was all so new. All so promising. All she had to do was work with a man who turned her knees to jelly and carve out a role for herself in this company.

Lucky? That's how it looked, she admitted silently. But she wondered if that was really true.

* * *

Two days later Terri was alone on the balcony of her suite, watching the sun begin to set. She kept a safe distance between herself and the railing where a sheet of Plexiglas provided protection from the wind, and still she had a spectacular view. A palace of a suite. Anything she wanted with a simple phone call to room service or the concierge. And yet she couldn't settle. Couldn't make herself relax on the couch, lose herself in a movie, relax in that glory of a tub. Heck, she couldn't even call Jan. Her insides were jumpy; her mind was racing. And nothing was going to ease it.

For two days she'd immersed herself in the hotel business. There was so much she didn't know, it was staggering. Dave had been as good as his word. He'd taken her to the office floor and introduced her to so many people, their faces became a blur and their names forgotten almost as soon as she heard them.

She'd sat in on a planning meeting and tried to keep her mind on what was being discussed while meeting Cooper's icy gaze. He had studied her as if trying to figure her out, then as soon as the meeting was over, he disappeared rather than spend any one-on-one time with her. Which irritated her on so many levels Terri couldn't begin to count them all. If not for Dave Carey, Terri would still be wandering aimlessly through her new life.

Her brain was filled with things she'd never be able to keep straight. Plans for new hotels and scheduled board meetings on expansion of a company that was already global. And she knew that she'd only seen the tip of the iceberg that was Hayes Corporation.

Nerves rattled her in spite of how kind Dave had been. Why wasn't Cooper the one to help her adjust to all of this? She was *his* partner, after all.

Why was he avoiding her?

"And more important," she murmured, "why is it bothering you that he is?"

Was he deliberately ignoring her, trying to make her so uncomfortable that she'd simply leave without learning more about her legacy? Or did he think her so unimportant she didn't rate any extra time?

"Well, either way, it's insulting," she mumbled. Curling her fingers around the wide iron railing, she let the residual heat from the metal slide into her skin while the cool October wind rushed through her hair like cold fingers. "Whether he likes it or not—heck, whether I like it or not—I'm his partner now. I think I deserve better than being ignored."

The more she thought of it, the higher the flames of her indignation flared. Had Cooper assigned Dave to her? As if she were some long lost relative to be bought off with a tour and a nice glass of wine? Was Dave patronizing her on Cooper's behalf? If that was it, Cooper was in for a surprise.

"Okay, sure, I'm not a tycoon. I don't know anything about the hotel business," she admitted, squeezing that railing. Asking herself why she hadn't gotten a degree in business instead. At least that would have served her better in this situation. Staring off at the distant mountains, watching them go purple with the sunset, she shook her head. "I'm here, though. And my...*father*...wanted me here."

Okay, that really wasn't the reason she'd come. She hadn't known her father so it felt hypocritical somehow to mourn him or to do something she didn't want to do simply to honor his wishes. She was here for herself. She hadn't really known that she was unsatisfied with her life before, because it was all she'd known and she'd accepted it. But now, out of the blue, she'd been handed the opportunity to completely shake up her life. How could she not at least *try*?

"I'm going to be the best partner ever and Cooper is just going to have to get used to having me around."

When a knock on the door sounded, she practically raced through the living room, desperate for *anything* to focus on besides her own whirling thoughts.

She opened the door and stopped dead. Cooper Hayes, big as life and twice as gorgeous, stood there, looking down at her. Instantly, she wished she were wearing her high heels instead of slip-on flats. Being several inches shorter than he was made her feel at a disadvantage. Of course, so did the fact that she was happy to see him—in spite of being so irritated with him only moments before—and he looked as though he wished he were anywhere but there.

"Cooper."

His black suit was tailored to perfection and he wore a midnight-blue tie shot through with silver over a white dress shirt. The tie had been loosened and the top collar button undone. For Cooper, she figured this was casual wear.

One hand braced on the door frame, he pushed the other through his hair and, fascinated, Terri watched those thick strands fall perfectly into place. She almost sighed and then wanted to kick herself for it.

"What're you doing here?"

He scrubbed one hand across his face. "I wanted to talk to you."

"Why the change? You've ignored me for two days."

He scowled. "I was working."

"Right. And now all of a sudden you're not?"

"Look, it's time we talked. That's all. Are you going to argue with me about it or just let me in?"

She considered it.

"Well?" he asked.

"I'm thinking."

Shaking his head, he snorted. "We can argue later, okay? Let's talk now."

Her eyes narrowed in suspicion. "About what, specifically?"

Instead of answering, he said, "You held your own in the planning meeting today."

That was a lie and she knew it. With so many facts and figures being tossed around, Terri had been too humbled to say much at all. Oh, when asked directly, she'd given her opinion, but that hadn't happened often. Most of the employees were taking their cues from Cooper, and he hadn't exactly been hanging on her every word.

"Not really," she said. "I just didn't stumble on my words."

"It was more than that." He pushed away from the doorjamb. "Have you eaten?"

"Not yet. It's a little early and…"

He looked as irritated as he sounded. And yet, there was something about the energy bristling around him that made him even hotter than before. His jaw was shadowed with whiskers, those ice-blue eyes were narrowed on her and with that carefully shaggy haircut, he looked like a well-dressed pirate.

With that thought firmly in mind, it didn't take much for Terri's brain to imagine him in tight leather pants, shirtless, swinging a cutlass through the air as he held her pinned tightly to his side. Okay, fine. Maybe she was reading too many romance novels if she was mentally putting Cooper Hayes onto the cover of one.

He snapped his fingers in front of her face and Terri jolted. "Excuse me?"

He shrugged. "You zoned out."

Okay, yes, she had and she didn't want to think about why. "Right. Anyway, it's early. I was going to call room service in a while."

"No need." He held one hand out to her. "Come with me. I want to show you something."

Why was he suddenly paying attention to her? Her mind wanted to know why he'd decided to stop ignoring her existence. What had changed that all of a sudden he was seeking her out? It was a good thing, right? They had to get to know each other. To work together.

But it wasn't work she was thinking about. The gleam in his eyes was a challenge. One she wouldn't turn her back on. Terri put her hand in his and when his fingers closed around hers, she felt a sizzling jolt of electricity that shot up her arm to rattle around in her chest like a crazed ping-pong ball.

He'd felt it, too. She saw a flicker of surprise come and go from his features—so briefly, maybe no one else would have noticed. But Terri could recognize in him what she was feeling.

Was he fighting it as hard as she was?

Four

Cooper's grip on her hand was gentle, but strong enough to tug her along behind him as he stalked down the hall. She hurried to keep up. "Where are we going?"

"You'll see in a minute."

Back down the elegant hall to the private elevator. "Oh, no, thanks. I just left the offices an hour ago. Not really interested in going back right now."

"We're not going to the office." The doors opened and he tugged her inside. He hit the roof button and Terri's eyes widened.

"The roof?" She looked up at him, confused. "Should I be worried?" she asked, only half joking.

"About what?"

"'Accidentally' falling off?"

Cooper snorted. "I'd never throw you off my own roof. Too obvious."

"Well, I feel better." Since she was watching him, she

caught the fleeting smile that was gone almost before it was there.

"You've seen way too many movies."

"I'm not a movie person. I'm a book person."

"You can be both," he pointed out.

"No," she assured him, "you really can't."

"Books, movies, doesn't matter," he said as the elevator stopped. "There are no bad guys here. You don't need to worry. We're not enemies."

Weren't they? Hadn't Dave made a point of letting her know that Cooper wasn't exactly thrilled with having a new partner thrust on him? And really, looking at it from his point of view, why would he be happy about it?

"If we're not enemies, what exactly are we, then?" she asked. She really was interested in what his answer would be.

"That's a good question." Which wasn't an answer at all.

The elevator doors slid open and he stepped outside. He stopped, looked at her and then held out his hand to her again. Silently, he waited and Terri's mind raced. She could refuse. Go back down to her suite and never know why he'd wanted to take her to the roof. She could turn away from this opportunity to talk to him, away from everyone else, to maybe find common ground that could help them both. Or she could fight her fear of heights and go with him.

Not a hard decision at all, because she'd never been one to back away from what scared her. But that wasn't all of it, either. He was so gorgeous, so intense, and when he looked at her, Terri felt heat simmer inside her bones.

She slipped her hand into his and his ice-blue eyes warmed briefly. His fingers closed over hers and her heartbeat galloped in response.

Then she stepped out of the elevator and stopped dead. "Oh, my God."

She let go of his hand, took a deep breath and simply stared. Terri knew Cooper was right behind her, probably watching her reaction, and she didn't care. This was all so…*amazing*. Turning in a slow circle, she tried to take everything in at once. Surprise wasn't a strong enough word for what she was feeling. *Stunned* was pretty close and yet, even that word wasn't enough.

She walked past Cooper, feeling the heat of his body as she brushed against him. It was incredible. She never would have expected to find this in the middle of a desert city. On the roof of a building. But here it was. A fantasy of flowers, potted trees and flowering vines. Polished stones set in patterns along pathways that snaked through the most beautiful garden she'd ever seen.

"This is…wonderful," she whispered almost reverently.

"Yeah, it is." Cooper moved close and stayed at her side as she continued to walk along the smooth stone path. "My dad started it when I was a kid. We lived here a lot of the time and he wanted me to be able to be outside."

"Seriously?" Well, that piece of information jolted her out of the magic of the place. "He let a *child* come out to the roof?"

He laughed shortly. "If you look close enough, you'll see the Plexiglas barrier. Unless you deliberately try to climb the three feet of concrete and then the five feet of Plexiglas wall, you're not going to fall off."

"Good to know." Still, she deliberately gave the transparent wall—which now that it had been pointed out to her, she could see—a wide berth.

Walking along the polished stone pathway, she followed it through a magical garden with hanging plants, trailing ivy and pots of flowers that tumbled to the ground in brilliant colors.

"When I was a kid, my father had a putting green up here," Cooper mused.

"Really?" She turned her head to look at him, enjoying that he was sharing something of himself. Maybe this was the first step in their getting to know each other.

"Everybody needs a place to relax. This was his." Cooper looked around, taking in the trees, the wooden decking, the raised boxes where chrysanthemums in their brilliant fall colors gave off a spicy scent that flavored the air. "When he died, I kept it all and added to it." He shrugged. "We spent a lot of time together here. I don't come here often now. Not enough time."

"You should make time." She stopped again beside a pergola with climbing, flowering vines dripping from its roofline like a living curtain.

The scene was set for seduction.

There were chairs, couches, a gas fire pit where flames danced and swayed in the wind sweeping across the roof. A small waterfall tumbled over stones into a weathered brass bowl filled with shining stones, and the splash of the water was as soothing as a touch. But it was the cloth-covered table set with fine china and crystal that drew her attention. It was private. Beautiful.

Romantic.

Seduction.

A ripple of anticipation swirled through her at the thought. She hadn't spent much time with Cooper, but every time she *did* see him, there was a near magnetic attraction that buzzed between them, promising all sorts of…interesting things. Another ripple rolled through her body, and Terri took a shallow breath to steady herself. Really didn't work. How could it? With Cooper standing so close to her, it was a wonder there weren't actual flames licking at her.

She was new here. She was going to be working with this man. Giving into what she was feeling could be a big mistake.

Swallowing hard, she asked, "What's going on?"

Another casual shrug. "An early dinner. We both have to eat. Why not here?"

Because they were alone in the growing darkness but for the twinkling white lights strung through potted trees, flowers and entwined through the vine-covered pergola roof. It was magical. And here she stood next to Tall, Dark and Tempting. She felt a quick twist of nerves.

Just a few days ago she'd been at home in her own little condo and today she was on top of the world in Las Vegas, about to step into an exciting new life with a man who could start fires in her blood just by looking at her. She'd be weird if she *wasn't* a little nervous.

He tipped his head to one side and studied her. "Problem?"

"No," she said quickly. "No problem."

She might be a little shaky, but she wasn't going to let him see it. He wasn't the first man to give her a look that said he was thinking about devouring her. Of course, he *was* the first man who made her feel the same way in return.

But this wasn't a date. This was dinner with her new business "partner." Though it seemed like he'd gone out of his way to make the setting lush and anything but businesslike. Still, Terri wanted Cooper Hayes to see her not only as desirable, but also as competent and ready for whatever challenges came her way. Nothing wrong with a good facade.

"Good." He held out one hand to her again. "Before dinner arrives, come with me. I want you to see something."

"There's more?" She put her hand in his and told herself to completely disregard that jolt of heat. The cold wind whipping past them didn't stand a chance against the kind of burn he could prompt, and trying to ignore it was a useless endeavor.

His grip on her hand tightened. God, what was it about a strong, quiet man that was so damn sexy? And why couldn't she stop noticing?

Cooper didn't speak, just walked toward the far end of the roof, drawing her with him. As they went, she idly noticed the walkways, the grass, planted in artistic swirls and waves, the fairy lights strung through bushes and plants. There was redwood decking laid out and on it sat a small café table and chairs. It would be a lovely spot to sit and watch the night sky. Then he stopped and she looked up at him. He was staring off into the distance and when Terri turned her head to look, too, her eyebrows rose as she realized they were standing right at the edge of the building.

The only thing between them and a fall to nearly thirty floors below was a thin sheet of Plexiglas tucked into a three foot tall concrete barrier. Instinctively, she tightened her grip on his hand. "Well, this is unsettling."

He laughed shortly. "Still worried about getting tossed off?"

"No." She whipped her hair back out of her face, but the wind simply picked it up and threw it across her eyes again. "And with the way I'm holding on to you, if I go, you're going with me."

He grinned and pulled her close to his side. "Good to know."

"Wow," she said, mesmerized by his amused, unguarded expression. "You should smile more often."

"I'll make a note. So," he asked, "you have a problem with heights, is that it?"

"No," she said, "just a problem with falling."

A short burst of laughter rolled from his chest and settled over her like a warm blanket. Really, Terri knew she
was getting pulled deeper and deeper into this attraction
she felt for him. That should worry her—and maybe later,
she'd take the time to consider it. For right now she decided to enjoy the heat.

"No danger there," he said and his eyes locked with
hers. "You won't fall, Terri. But if you did, I'd catch you."

"That shouldn't make me feel better," she admitted,
still staring up into eyes that looked both shuttered and
open, "but it does."

He smiled at her again, then waved one hand, encompassing the city lights just bursting out of the darkness.
"This is what I wanted you to see."

Already the streetlights were blinking on and there
were a few headlights shining from the cars streaming
down the street. But the real magic slowly began to take
shape. Seconds ticked into minutes as they stood there
in the growing darkness watching a desert erupt into a
neon dream.

As if in a choreographed dance, bright lights decorating
the casinos surged into life. Electric signs in every color
imaginable lit up the night like an earthbound rainbow
and Terri was so fascinated, she forgot all about her fear
of falling and took a step closer to the wall.

"It's so beautiful."

"It is," he agreed. "I like standing here at sunset, watching the whole city come to life."

She turned her head to look at him. The wind whipped
through his hair and tugged at the edges of his jacket. His
gaze held hers and Terri felt that rush of temptation again.
He was a man comfortable with his place, sure of himself
and who he was, and that was undeniably appealing. His

confidence, his surety, was almost palpable and she could see that he would be a formidable enemy.

But wouldn't that also make him an unfaltering friend—or lover?

Deliberately, she turned away from both him and her thoughts and focused on the view. Brilliant lights marched along the Strip like an invading army, lighting up every shadow, outlining every sight in dancing color.

"There's a gigantic Ferris wheel." How had she not noticed it in the daylight?

"It's the High Roller. Caesar's owns it," he said with a touch of pride in his voice he couldn't quite disguise. "Five hundred fifty feet tall."

"I'll take your word for it." She shuddered at the thought of being so high and *moving* at the same time.

"You can see for miles from the top," he said. "It's higher than the London Eye or the Singapore Flyer. Takes a half an hour to make one circle so you can really enjoy the views."

Terri wondered if he realized just how proud he was of his city or how much he loved it. Whenever she'd thought of Las Vegas in the past, it was as a vacation spot. She'd never really considered people who lived here. Who were a part of this electrified piece of desert. Now she did.

She looked up at his profile as he stared out over the bright lights and thought he looked like an ancient king, standing on the battlements to survey his realm. When he turned his head to meet her gaze, that image remained. He was impossibly good-looking and he wore that aura of strength and power as comfortably as he did the elegantly tailored suit. Cooper Hayes was a nerve-racking man.

Why did she find that so appealing?

Hurriedly, she took a breath and looked toward the lights again. "The Eiffel Tower."

"At the Paris Hotel," he said quietly. "One half scale of the original in France. Have you seen it?"

"No, I've never been out of the country."

"How about New York? The Statue of Liberty here is a one-third scale of the one in New York Harbor."

"I haven't seen that, either."

"You should go. It's damn impressive."

Nodding to herself, she said, "I'll put it on the list."

He chuckled. "You have a list?"

"Of course. The wish list," she said, shifting her gaze to him. "Places I want to see."

"Like…?"

"Oh." She took a breath, thought about it for a minute, then said, "New York, obviously. And I'd like to see the Liberty Bell."

"Really?"

Terri shrugged. "I like history. In fact, there are lots of places right here in the US I want to visit. But I also want to see Paris, London, Venice, for starters."

"Quite the list."

She tipped her head to one side and studied him. The October wind was cold, but the clear wall in front of them cut most of it. He looked completely at home here on top of the world and she wondered if he'd been *born* with that confidence or if he'd worked to gain it.

"I suppose you've been to all of those places," she said softly.

"And more." He crossed his arms over his chest and stared out at the bright lights. "We've got hotels all over the world, so the business requires me to go."

"You went for *business*?" She shook her head. "That's just sad."

"No, it's not," he argued. "That's life. Work."

"Well, when you see something beautiful, you should take the time to admire it. Enjoy it."

His gaze shifted to hers. "Oh," he said meaningfully, "I am."

Terri swallowed hard against the quickening flames inside her. A single look. A simple sentence. And he turned her inside out.

This was probably not a good sign.

"Well, until you can make that list work for you," he said, the abrupt change in subject making her head swim a bit, "Las Vegas can give you New York, the Eiffel Tower and a trip down the Venice canals."

She smiled, steadier now that she'd had a second to catch her breath. "Plus, no long flights."

"You should do it, you know," Cooper told her. "Take the damn trips. See what you want to see."

"Easy to say," she said, laughing. "But trips cost money and I haven't been able to afford—" Terri broke off because that excuse didn't work anymore. Now she was rich. Rich enough to fly first class. Or maybe charter a jet.

That thought was still mind-boggling.

"Just sinking in, is it?" He nodded thoughtfully. "You can go wherever, whenever you want. Nothing holding you here, is there?"

Interesting way of putting it. "Trying to get rid of me?"

"Oh, if that's what I was doing right now, I'd find a better way."

"Is that right?" She walked with him when he took her arm and steered her back through the garden toward the seating area. "And how would you do it?"

He let go of her arm only to place his hand at the small of her back in a move that was both gentlemanly and enticing. She felt that slight touch as a ribbon of heat across her nerve endings. It was as if there was a live flame against her skin. It was unsettling. And exciting.

Then he spoke. "I could offer to buy you out."

She stopped dead and looked up at him. "Buy me out?"

"Why so offended?" He looked genuinely curious. "It's a hell of an offer and Terri, this isn't your world."

She stiffened a little at the implication. Did he think she *couldn't* fit in, was that it? That was insulting—although, hadn't she been telling herself the same thing since all of this started? But it was one thing to think it privately and quite another to have someone else point it out. Squaring her shoulders, she stiffened her spine and lifted her chin.

Well, Terri told herself, he was wrong. Was she a little nervous? Sure. But damned if she'd quit just a few days in. "It's my world *now*."

"Is it?" They stood alongside the seating area. Beneath the white twinkling lights, he looked down at her, and his beautiful eyes were in shadow. "Is it really? Or is your life still in Utah? This isn't an adventure, Terri. Not to me. Not to my employees."

"*Our* employees," she corrected and had the satisfaction of seeing him grit his teeth.

"For now, yes. Jacob left you his half of the company, but do you really think he meant for you to do the job? Are you even sure you want to?"

"I won't know until I try, will I?"

A muscle in his jaw twitched. "Hayes Corporation *is* my world and I'll protect it."

"From me?" she asked, all innocence. "Do I look that dangerous to you?"

A slow, tantalizing smile curved one corner of his mouth, and his eyes seemed to darken in the shadows. "Oh, yeah. You're plenty dangerous."

She'd never thought of herself that way, and Terri had to

admit that a part of her liked hearing him say it. A swirl of something unexpected rose up from the pit of her stomach, danced around her chest, then reached up and closed her throat. Terri had to force herself to breathe. She was way out of her depth here. This man was unlike any other she'd ever known and she had the distinct feeling that if she put one foot wrong on this new path she was walking, the fall would feel like she was dropping from the roof of the StarFire.

"My father wanted me here." It felt good to say it aloud. To remind them both that she had a right to be there.

"He did." Cooper nodded. "But I wonder if he wanted you to *stay*."

She didn't know. Had no way of *ever* knowing. But whether Jacob Evans had intended for her to stay in Vegas and make the corporation her life or not, she felt that she owed it to herself to give it a chance. Jan had told her to grab the brass ring and that was just what she was going to do.

"It's my decision, not Jacob's."

"Is it?" he countered. "Or are you thinking you owe something to the father you never knew?"

Heat that had nothing to do with arousal swept through her. "Are you deliberately trying to get me to leave?"

"If I was trying," he said, "you wouldn't know I was trying."

"Well, that's ambiguous enough."

"Just honest," he countered.

"And confusing as well as not very welcoming."

"Blunt again." He smiled. "I like it."

That smile was lethal. Note to self: remember that. He used that oh-so-rare smile like a weapon—to disarm and distract. And she couldn't afford to be distracted. She was going to build a life here and she had to keep on her toes around Cooper Hayes.

As she stood there, Cooper walked to the table, set with

fine china, crystal glassware and heavy silver, poured each of them a glass of straw-colored wine, then handed her one of the glasses. Grateful, she took a sip to ease the tightness in her throat. Naturally, it tasted wonderful. She'd already learned that Cooper Hayes did nothing by half measure.

"Look," he said, "we're both in a situation we didn't expect."

"That's fair," she murmured.

That half smile erupted again. "All I'm saying is that we take a few days. See what happens. You learn what you can about the business…"

"What I *can*?" she repeated.

"There's a steep learning curve. No offense intended."

"Hmm." She wasn't sure about that no offense thing. Studying the wine in her glass, she mused, "You know, Utah actually has television now. And the internet. We're still learning how to use it, of course, but we're pretty quick."

His lips twitched and tugged at something inside her. "Point taken. Fine. Sit in on meetings. Ask questions. Get familiar with the place."

"I've talked to a few employees already," she said, accepting his unsaid apology for expecting her to be stupid or something.

"That's not what I meant," Cooper told her. "You won't learn about the company by talking with random employees."

"You're wrong about that," she said. "Who better to tell me what working here is like? The higher-ups sitting in offices? I don't think so."

Cooper considered that for a second and realized she might be onto something.

"You're…unexpected," he mused.

"What a nice thing to say." She practically beamed at him and Cooper felt the punch of that wide, delighted smile slam into him again.

"Is it?"

"Well, sure." She walked a little closer to the Plexiglas wall, but stopped well clear of it. "I've always done the expected thing, you know? A's in school to please my parents. Business courses in college because it was the right thing to do in spite of my major. My job at the bank. Dating nice, boring guys." She sighed a little. "I'm a rule follower with a rebel soul."

He laughed at that and she gave him a narrow-eyed look over her shoulder. He held up one hand. Couldn't afford to piss her off, could he? He was here to pour on the charm. Making her mad just defeated his whole plan. "Didn't mean to laugh. But if you've got a rebel soul, why don't you let it out once in a while?"

"In a way, I do." She set her wineglass down onto the table. "I say what I think, even when it gets me in trouble."

She intrigued him in spite of how he tried to keep her at a distance. "If it gets you in trouble, then why do it?"

"Because lies come too easy to people and that's annoying. I'd rather know the truth, hard or not, than some comfortable lie."

"And how's that working for you?"

She actually winced. "Sometimes, not so great. Not that I try to deliberately hurt anyone..."

Yeah, he was getting that. She seemed genuinely concerned with...hell. Everything. So no, if *he* was being brutally honest, he couldn't see her out in a flame war. In his world, lies were the currency of the realm.

Business deals were always smoothed over with exaggeration. Dates were ended with promises of another even when he knew there would never be one. Partnerships were announced when nothing had ever been said about it before. Hadn't Jacob lied to Cooper for years? In *not* telling anyone about the daughter he would leave everything to, he'd lied. He'd let that lie grow. Allowed Cooper to make plans based on the lie.

So maybe she had a point about the power of the truth. Too bad the truth wouldn't help him any.

A bell sounded and Cooper set his wineglass down then strolled to a door behind a huge potted tree. He opened it and a waiter pushing a room service cart came through. "You don't have to serve it, James. We'll take care of that."

"Yes, sir. Good night, sir. Ma'am."

When he was gone, Terri murmured, "I'm not sure I like being a ma'am."

"You don't look like one, if that helps."

She whirled around to meet his gaze and Cooper saw the flash of pleasure in her eyes. He'd like to see more of it.

"What do I look like?"

"Trouble."

She grinned. "Unexpected *and* trouble. Good for me. You know, those short sentences of yours are starting to be appealing."

"Why waste time on words?" he asked, moving in on her.

"No idea," she said, and he swore he could see the pulse point in her neck throbbing.

He hadn't planned to have a taste of her; in fact, he knew the idea could scuttle all his plans, but now that was all he could think of. Here, under the night sky with the city lights glimmering all around them.

"What're you doing?" she asked, her voice a soft hush of sound.

"Thinking about kissing you."

"How much longer are you going to think about it?"

That was all the invitation he needed. He grinned and pulled her in close, threading one hand through her hair to hold her head in place as he closed his mouth over hers. The taste of her seared him. It was more than he'd expected. More than he'd found before with anyone else. Instant heat. Instant need swamping him. He parted her lips, and his tongue swept into her mouth to tangle with hers. She sighed and her breath slid inside him, adding even more intimacy to this stolen moment.

He'd been thinking about her for days. Thinking about doing just this, which is why he'd been avoiding her. Catching glimpses of her in the office or on the casino floor was one thing. Now he had his hands on her at last and he reveled in it.

He slid one hand up beneath the hem of her red silk shirt to cup her breast over the lace of her bra. She trembled and his body responded in a flash. He wanted to feel *her.* Wanted to explore every inch of her and take his time doing it.

She sighed and leaned into him as his thumb stroked across the tip of her nipple. Cooper swallowed a groan and dropped his hand down to her butt, cupping, squeezing, pressing her up against his aching groin.

Deepening the kiss even further, he shifted his hold on her so he could cup her center. She jolted in his arms and instinctively spread her legs farther apart. It was good, but it wasn't enough. Not nearly. He needed to touch her. *Now.*

"Don't let me interrupt." A voice sounded out from somewhere behind them. "No, wait. Yes, let me interrupt."

Five

Cooper broke the kiss and rested his forehead against Terri's. Dammit. He knew that voice. He hadn't heard it in almost two years, but he wasn't likely to forget it. "Celeste."

Terri looked past his shoulder and her mouth dropped open. "You're *Vega.*"

Cooper turned in time to see Celeste Vega's gorgeous features brighten into a pleased smile.

"Ah, you know me. Isn't that lovely?" She stalked toward them, slid the gold chain of her bag off her shoulder and dropped it onto a chair. Picking up Cooper's wineglass, she took a long drink and smiled at Terri again. "Yes, I am Vega. I always loved to come to Las Vegas. The headlines would read, *Vega in Vegas.* Such symmetry," she cooed.

Cooper buried the groan building in his chest. His body ached, his temper was quickly on the rise and he was fresh out of patience for his former lover. "What're you doing here, Celeste?"

Rather than answer, she finished off his wine, handed him the empty glass and said, "I wanted to see you, of course. And how delicious that I find you here, on the roof, where we share so many lovely memories."

Cooper felt Terri stiffen beside him and he could have cheerfully tossed Celeste out of his hotel on her beautiful ass.

Reluctantly, Cooper gave the intruder his full attention because anything less would be dangerous. She was still beautiful. Celeste Vega's striking face had graced the covers of hundreds of magazines. She'd walked the runways in Paris and New York and remained the toast of Europe.

Almost six feet tall, Celeste had short, dark brown hair, shot through with strands of gold and red, cut into a style that hugged her jawline. Her caramel-colored skin seemed to glow against the white silk shirt and slacks she wore. Her almond-shaped, golden-brown eyes could tempt a man into just about anything and in the past, her sultry gaze had worked on him. But as he still had the taste of Terri in his mouth and the memory of her lush body pressed against his fresh in his mind, Celeste's surprise arrival did nothing for him.

Besides, why would he be glad to see her? Nearly two years ago, Celeste had walked out on him in favor of a much older man with a title and a few billion more than Cooper.

"Again. What're you doing here, Celeste?"

She pouted. It was an expression meant to seduce and it had actually worked on him, once upon a time. He was wiser now.

"Why, I almost feel that you're not happy to see me," she said, pout still in place.

"And how did you get up to the roof?" he demanded.

"Ah, one of your lovely minions opened the elevator

to me and before you ask, no, I won't tell you who. You would no doubt torture them for their kindness." Brushing past him, one hand to his chest, she continued, "Cooper, introduce me to your new playmate."

"I'm Terri. Terri Ferguson." She held out one hand that Celeste ignored in favor of air kissing both of Terri's cheeks.

"Well, aren't you adorable? I can see why our Cooper was so eager to get you on the rooftop for one of his famous private dinners." She tossed a sly smile at Cooper, then dropped one arm around Terri's shoulders and steered her toward the table where dinner waited. "Oh. Dinner for two. We'll share, yes?"

Cooper swallowed back the rush of irritation that was nearly choking him. But on the other hand, maybe it was a good thing she'd crashed the party. She'd kept him from going too far too fast with Terri. Celeste was a force of nature. There was no point in trying to get rid of her. She wouldn't go, short of having security escort her out.

She was beautiful and treacherous and Cooper wondered what the hell she was up to.

The following morning Terri sat at her birth father's desk and looked at the stacks of files piled up in front of her. She'd asked for information on the Hayes hotels and now she had enough reading material to last her a year. But to understand this company, she had to immerse herself in it.

She still felt like an impostor. Even more so now, after meeting Celeste Vega the night before. Clearly, the world-famous model and Cooper had had a relationship. And just as clearly, he wasn't happy that the woman had dropped in on him.

Famous rooftop dinners.

Those words echoed in Terri's mind. Last night she'd thought he'd done something special. Just for her. Was she really no more than one more link in a chain of Cooper's women? But as soon as she thought it, she let it go. She *wasn't* one of his women. She was half-owner of this hotel—this corporation. Whatever else went on between her and Cooper, that one fact wouldn't change.

One kiss was hardly a relationship. Though granted, that one kiss was pretty spectacular.

She shivered just remembering the feel of his mouth on hers. Of his hands sweeping up and down her body, the breath-stealing, soul-shaking response that had clattered through her.

Yeah. Okay. Maybe it wasn't a relationship, but it was definitely *something*. But a better question would be: Did she *want* more from Cooper than simple respect and acceptance of her right to be there? She didn't know. Oh, her body knew exactly what it wanted, but that didn't mean it was going to get it.

"Doesn't matter," Terri murmured, while her mind ran an obstacle course of scattered thoughts. "I'm here now. That's what matters."

Sitting in her birth father's office she tried not to feel intimidated by what Jacob had left her. That was a useless endeavor, though. Beyond the closed door of *her* office, people were busy, running the company she'd stumbled into. And she…was trying to catch up.

Resolute, she snatched the top folder off the stack and looked at the photo on the front. *Hayes London*. The hotel looked like a small castle and she had no doubt at all that on the inside, it was a true palace. As good a place as any to start, she told herself.

Then her phone rang, signaling a video chat, and Terri

reached for it like it was a rope tossed to her in a raging river. As soon as she answered, Terri smiled. "Hi, Mom."

"Hi, baby girl." Carol Ferguson looked great. At sixty-five, she was fit and pretty with short, stylish blond hair that would never give in to gray. "How's it going?"

"I don't know." Terri held her phone and sat back in her chair. "How's Daisy?"

"Really?" Carol asked, both eyebrows rising high on her forehead. "You want to talk about your dog?" She shrugged. "Okay, we'll start there. Daisy's great. She's taken over the couch completely, bullied the neighbor's beagle, dug up your aunt Connie's tulip bulbs and is, right now, snoring." She turned the phone so that Terri could see her adorable mutt spread-eagled on her mom's brown leather couch.

"So, now that you know Daisy's fine, how about you tell me how you are?"

"First," Terri said, wincing a little, "tell Aunt Connie I'm sorry about the bulbs."

Her mother waved her hand. "Don't worry about it. Connie can't grow weeds. Those bulbs never would have bloomed. She'll do what she always does. Buy plants in pots, bury the pots and then take credit for growing the flowers."

Terri laughed, delighted at the description because it really was *so* Connie. And wow, it felt good to relax and laugh with someone who loved her. Who understood what she was going through.

"Now, talk to me, sweetie." Her mom's face held the I'm-not-taking-no-for-an-answer expression Terri was all too familiar with.

"Okay, then. This hotel is amazing," she said and chuckled at the use of that word again. Seriously, she was going to have to buy a thesaurus or something. "Mostly, everyone's been very nice. I'm staying in Jacob's suite at the very top of the hotel and—"

"Ouch." Her mom winced. "Too bad they didn't have suites on the ground floor for you."

She grinned. It was good to have people who knew you that well. "I'm dealing. I even went out on the roof last night with Cooper."

"Is that right?" Carol made a *hmmmm* of interest. "Cooper, huh? Is he as pretty in person?"

"Prettier, though he wouldn't love that description."

"Men so rarely do. On the roof? Why?"

Well, now, that was the question, wasn't it? She'd thought it was to share the view. And a romantic dinner. Now she wondered. "He wanted to show me the view and it's beautiful, if scary, to be looking down from about a million feet in the air."

"Uh-huh. Anything else?"

"Well, Celeste Vega showed up."

"*The* Vega?" Her mom's eyebrows rose even higher. Not surprising. Terri's mother was practically addicted to those magazines at checkout counters. She bought them every week and was up-to-date on all the celebrities. She could tell you who was married, getting divorced, going into rehab. Her celebrity love was wide and vast. "Is she as beautiful in person or is it all airbrushing? I've wondered about that. You know you can't trust pictures. These days they could make a troll look like a beauty queen."

Terri laughed. "She's definitely not a troll. Actually, she's even more beautiful in real life. Tall, elegant. Intimidating."

"Why?" Carol argued. "You're very pretty yourself."

"Thanks, *Mom*. No bias there." Still smiling, Terri continued. "She seems very nice…" Her voice trailed off.

"I hear a *but* coming…?"

"But nothing, really." Terri recovered quickly. She didn't want to tell her mother about the romance of the night that Cooper had arranged. About the kiss, about Vega's interruption and then finding out that Terri had only been one of a crowd of women who'd been given that "special" night.

She flipped open the folder in front of her and idly glanced at the photos of the interior of the London Hayes hotel. Just as she'd assumed. Gorgeous. Old world elegance. Sighing, she said, "I'm trying to find my feet here, Mom, but honestly, I'm a little lost, still. I'm going to make this work, though. This is an incredible chance for me, so I'll figure it out."

"Why isn't your new partner helping you?" Carol's eyes flashed and her mouth turned down into what Terri recognized as her going into battle scowl.

"He's a little busy, running the whole company." Terri got up out of the desk chair, walked to the couch and sat down again, curling her legs beneath her. Across the room there were wide windows giving her an extensive view of a bright blue desert sky.

"Cooper's got his hands on everything. He's running this whole company. He can't really hold my hand and walk me through all of this." All true, but what she wasn't adding was that Cooper didn't seem to really *want* her to succeed. Oh, he'd never come right out and said it, but he'd made it plain he'd be fine with it if she gave up and went away. And that would be easier, she told herself.

But she wasn't going to quit. There was a beautiful door open for her and she planned on walking through it.

Taking a breath, she said, "His assistant, Dave Carey, has been helpful, though. He's the one who showed me around the offices, and he's offered to help any way he can."

"I suppose that's fine, then. At least someone there is

helping you. But if everything's going so nicely, why aren't you happy?" Before Terri could speak, her mother said, "Don't bother denying it. I can see it on your face. You're feeling out of place and useless."

Terri laughed and pushed one hand through her hair. "Are you psychic?"

"No, just your mother." Carol turned her head and shouted, "I'll be there in a minute, Connie!" Shaking her head, she looked at Terri again. "Sorry, sweetie. Your aunt Connie and I are off to play tennis with some friends in a minute and you know how crazed my sister is about punctuality."

Good to know that at least *one* of them had their life in order, Terri thought. "I'm not sure what to do here, Mom."

"Well, of course you don't. You haven't even been there a week. Give yourself a chance, honey."

A chance. But only last night Cooper had pretty much told her that trying was a waste of time. That she couldn't do it. But that just meant he didn't know her very well. Terri could do it. Her father had left it to her. Her Dad had taught her to believe in herself and her Mom had taught her to dream. No way was she backing out.

"You're thinking too much," her mother said with a dramatic sigh. "You always do this. You question, rethink and reevaluate way too much. Feel your way through instead. You have good instincts, sweetie. Trust them. You're smart. Capable." She took a breath and huffed it out. "What was it your dad used to say to you all the time?"

A reluctant smile curved Terri's mouth as she remembered. She lowered her voice in imitation and said, "Terri, honey, there is *nothing* you can't do."

"Exactly." Her mother nodded sharply. "Now, stop doubting yourself and get out there and show them what a Ferguson can do when she makes up her mind."

Her mom had a point. She was sitting here going over and over everything she'd said and done in the past few days and getting exactly nowhere. Time to jump in with both feet, so to speak. "Okay, Mom, I will."

"I'm going to say it again, just for emphasis. Feel your way through, Terri. Go with your gut. It's a good one. Trust it."

A wave of affection rolled over her as she smiled at the woman who had raised her, loved her and taught her to stand up for herself. "I really love you."

"Of course you do!" Carol blew her a kiss. "I love you, too. Oh, for God's sake, now your aunt Connie's in the driveway honking the horn. The neighbors are going to have a fit."

Terri laughed. "You'd better go, Mom. And thanks. For everything."

"Love you!"

Once she hung up, Terri walked back to the desk, sat down and picked up the London hotel folder. The pictures were beautiful and reports from hotel managers would be informative. But she really wanted to know what their *guests* had to say about their stays at a Hayes hotel.

She dropped the folder and booted up the computer on her desk instead. She'd learn everything she could about the Hayes Corporation. She'd read customer reviews, check out travel bloggers and— "Oh, no."

Headlines covered the web browser page and right at the top she read *Shakeup at Hayes Corporation—Jacob Evans's daughter to take over half the company. How will this affect stock prices? Does Cooper Hayes know how to share?*

"Oh, God." She scanned the brief article, wondering what her mom and everyone she knew would think about it. Her mind raced even as her mother's advice echoed in the back of her brain.

And of course there were pictures along with the article. Cooper looked fantastic of course—all steely-eyed and tough in a zillion-dollar suit. But it looked as though they'd dug up a picture of Terri from her college years. She was wearing holey jeans, her hair was pulled into a ponytail jutting from the side of her head and the guy beside her—Tom? Micah?—was wearing a kilt.

"Very nice," she murmured, sinking back into her chair. Great. Even the media doesn't think she can do this But, look how surprised everyone will be when she did. "Upside? At least only a few million people will see it."

Dave looked up at the woman in his office and knew he'd done the right thing in calling her. With Celeste Vega around, no heterosexual male would be able to think of anyone else.

"She's nothing," Celeste said, walking the perimeter of Dave's office like an exotic cat. "I don't know why you were worried. She's boring and her breasts are too big."

Personally, Dave thought Terri had a great body, but that wasn't what Celeste wanted to hear. Like most incredibly beautiful women, she preferred thinking that only *she* could snag a man's attention. And to be honest, he reminded himself, that was usually true. In fact, just looking at Celeste from across the room had Dave's pulse pounding. Hell, he was no more immune than any other man when it came to this stunning woman.

When Celeste Vega walked into a room, every other female there seemed to fade into the background. Usually. Once upon a time, Cooper had been completely under her spell. All Dave had to do was arrange for that to happen again.

"Terri's large breasts don't seem to matter to Cooper," Dave pointed out and had the satisfaction of seeing a snap of temper spark in those golden eyes. Good. Even if she didn't actually *want* Cooper back, her ego would never allow her to lose to another woman.

Celeste took a deep breath, then released it slowly as she nodded. "That's because I hurt him terribly when I walked away from him. He must have been bereft."

Dave looked down so he could roll his eyes without being spotted. Celeste might have hurt Cooper but he hadn't exactly locked himself away to recover. Instead, he'd screwed half of Vegas. But whatever.

"I'm sure that's it," Dave soothed. "The point is, we need him to stop wanting Terri long enough that he'll remember she doesn't belong here."

She waved one hand and sunlight flashed off the gold bangles on her wrist, nearly blinding Dave. "Please. I've come back. Cooper won't be interested in her much longer."

"You might have to work at it, Celeste." Dave leaned back in his chair, propped one foot on his knee and folded his hands over his abdomen. "He's not really fond of you, and Terri's got his attention now."

"It's her homebody appeal, I think," she mused, unbuttoning one of the buttons on the forest green silk shirt she wore. It hung partially off her shoulders and with yet another button undone, gave a tantalizing glimpse of golden-brown skin.

"Do you know up on the roof last night, she was wearing plain black cotton slacks? Can you imagine?" She shook her head as if still stunned. *"Cotton."*

From what Dave had seen, Cooper didn't much care what Terri was wearing. He seemed to be more interested in getting her out of her clothes altogether.

Celeste set both hands at her hips. "She's different, that's all. And I can fix that."

Intrigued, Dave asked, "How?"

"How *all* of life's problems are solved, David. Shopping." She smiled to herself and it was so cat-like, Dave thought she might purr. "I'll take her to the Venetian's shops. We'll deck her out in silks and then Cooper will see that she *still* doesn't fit in."

"What?" That made zero sense.

She sighed. "Right now he's overlooking how unsuitable she is, because she's dressed like a farm girl. So he gives her the benefit of the doubt. But once she has appropriate clothing, he'll see that the farm girl is still there. Don't you understand? He excuses the way she doesn't belong because she doesn't look as though she should. But once she's dressed properly, Cooper will acknowledge that she'll never fit into his world."

"Sounds convoluted to me." Shaking his head, he pointed out, "Making her even more attractive isn't going to make him *stop* wanting her."

"Nothing will," she said. "Until he's ready. Right now she's new. She's a fascination. Even though he knows he doesn't want her here, in the company, he wants her in his bed."

"Yeah. I know. That's the problem."

"No, that's the solution. If they have sex, all the better for us."

"What the hell are you talking about?"

"It's sad, really," she said with a dramatic sigh. "You men think sex solves everything. A woman can tell you that sex only creates different problems."

"How's that?" He was not convinced.

"Cooper doesn't want a partner. But he wants *her*." She frowned at that admission. "Once he has her, he has new problems. She'll dig in. Get stars in her eyes. And that will be enough to convince Cooper to send her packing."

Dave stood up, pushed the edges of his jacket back and stuffed his hands into his pockets. He hated to admit it, but she had a point. "You might be onto something."

"Might be?" Celeste laughed shortly. "Trust me, David. If there is one thing I know, it's *men.*"

She stopped walking, set both hands at her hips and gave him a glare that should have coated his body in ice. "You called me here to help you get rid of her, right?"

"Yes." No matter what, they had to get rid of Terri.

"Then you should probably leave it to me."

He shook his head. "This is too important, Celeste. For both of us. Your old Count Whoever died before he could marry you and you want Cooper back. I want Terri out of here so I can get the reward I was promised for more than a damn decade. So if you think I'm going to take a step back and give you carte blanche, you're out of your damn mind."

"Fine." She inhaled sharply. "But stay out of my way, David, or I'll let Cooper know what you're up to."

"That's not a smart play, Celeste, and no matter what, you've always been smart."

"So true." She smiled at him and Dave felt a slam of pure appreciation hit him. "Very well. We're on the same side in this."

Partners. Just like Cooper and Terri.

And with any luck, neither partnership would last very long.

Six

The following day Terri sat in on a meeting and listened to everyone talking. This was the second time she'd attended one of these summits and she was feeling a little better than she had the first time. Maybe it was the pep talk from her mother, or maybe it was simply that she was getting used to the idea of her new life. But either way, Terri was determined to have her say this time. She had an idea that she was sure was a good one and whatever it took, she would be heard.

Ten people sat around a conference table, with Cooper at one end and Terri at the other. She caught him looking at her more than once, but then he would turn that icy focus on one of the others and she could breathe again. Even in a business situation, Cooper stirred something inside her that wouldn't be ignored. He was obviously the king of the room, with the men and women gathered around the table all jostling for his attention.

With all of the opinions being argued, voices raised to

talk over each other, Terri tried to follow it all. But more important, she waited for her chance to speak up herself. This was her chance to get not only Cooper's attention, but everyone else's, as well. She'd looked through a lot of the specs on the Hayes hotels all over the world and she knew that expansion was in the works again.

While most of the members of the board were interested in going into new, untested markets, Cooper wanted more than one Hayes hotel in the major cities where they were already a force to be reckoned with. She could see both points of view, but her idea might bridge them. She hadn't heard anyone else bring up what she was thinking, but for all she knew this idea had been discussed and dismissed in some earlier meeting. So she was taking a risk, but if she was going to make this her new life, then she had to step up and take a stand.

She tapped her fingers against the cover of the file on the Hayes London hotel. She'd gone over it, front to back. Terri knew it was a five-star—she'd expected nothing less—and that the hotel restaurant had two Michelin stars. She knew it was in the center of Hyde Park and that the rich and famous regularly stayed there. What she didn't know was why Hayes Corporation needed *another* five-star hotel in the same city.

"I'm saying simply that moving the corporation into an area completely lacking in five-star accommodation puts us at the top of the mountain." A gray-haired man in a black suit fixed his gaze on the woman in a cherry-red suit sitting opposite him.

This would be so much easier on her, Terri thought, if she could remember their names. But there were so many of them and she hadn't been there very long.

"My point, that you seem to overlook time and again,"

the woman said, "is that if there are no five-star resorts in those areas, then there may be a reason for that."

"*May* be?" he countered. "What kind of research did you have to do to come up with that?"

"My research is impeccable as always," the woman retorted. "When the wealthy go off to play, they expect more than a view to entertain them. And most of these locations you're suggesting are so isolated, we might as well build a five-star monastery."

That statement got everyone talking. Agreement, argument, voices erupted around the table and Cooper caught Terri's gaze. He looked irritated and almost out of patience.

This was a perfect time for her to speak up.

"Excuse me." When no one quieted, she said it again, louder. "Excuse me."

Her insides were jumping but her voice was steady as she met the eyes of everyone who turned to look at her in turn. They were all surprised, as if a kitten had suddenly morphed into a tiger. Well, Terri couldn't blame them for that, could she? The few times she'd met them, she'd been too nervous to talk at all. Too convinced she didn't have the right to an opinion.

But her mom had been correct. And her dad's advice echoed in her mind. *There's nothing you can't do.*

Today she was going to prove him right.

"You have something to add, Terri?" Cooper's gaze locked on her. She read neither encouragement nor condemnation on his face and realized she didn't need either one to make her point.

"Actually, yes," she said, "I do."

A couple of the older men sighed audibly and fell back in their leather chairs as if they'd been shot. Even the women didn't look happy to hear from her. No doubt because they'd had to work for years to earn a spot at this table and Terri had simply been born into it. Well, that wasn't her fault, was it? She hadn't asked for any of this, but now that it was here, she wouldn't run from it, either. At least, not without trying to make it work.

"I was looking at the Hayes London—"

"We're talking about a location in Prague," the older man in black said, not bothering to hide his impatience.

"I realize that." Terri nodded, ignoring his rudeness.

"We don't need a hotel in Prague and we've already got one in London," the blonde in red announced.

A rumble of voices began and Terri knew she would lose them all if she didn't speak up fast. It seemed she would have to fight to be heard. Well, she was ready.

"I'm talking about London," she said, loud enough that she commanded everyone's attention. "I agree that we should have a second hotel there—"

"Of course you do," the older man said with a snort of derision. "You're going to agree with Cooper because you're new here and you want to show him he can count on your vote."

"Eli…" Cooper's voice was a low-pitched warning.

The man disregarded it and slapped one hand against the table. "Cooper, we've been over this already and—"

"If you'd let me finish," Terri interrupted. Eli looked at her, stunned that she would so effortlessly put him in his place. When he was quiet again, she said, "Thank you."

Shifting her gaze to Cooper, she saw a flicker of admiration in his eyes. But she couldn't think about that at the moment. Instead, she focused on the notes she'd brought with her to the meeting.

"In looking at some of our top hotels—" Yes, she'd said *our* and that was a stretch for her. But Terri thought it was important to remind everyone here that whether they approved or not, she was a full partner in the Hayes Corporation.

While she had their attention, she continued. "The main thing I noticed was that the hotels are exclusive to the point that ordinary mortals could never afford to stay there."

The blonde in red gave a dramatic sigh and tapped her long, red nails against the table top. "That is rather the point of a five-star luxury getaway."

"Agreed." Terri barely looked at her, thus dismissing her. "And my point is that we're cutting ourselves off from most of the population."

"And your suggestion is, to what," another man farther down the table asked, "hold a half-off sale every other week?"

Cooper's features remained blank. He remained silent. And Terri knew it was because he was waiting to see how she'd handle herself.

"No, that's not the idea," Terri said, giving the rude man a bright smile just to make him feel lousy. "But we'll save that for later, okay?" Looking from face to face, she said, "My idea is to build a second Hayes Hotel in London—as a test case of sorts. We can call it Hayes 2. With a stylized number two to differentiate between this one and the five-star."

"To what purpose?" Eli asked with a sigh.

"Affordable luxury," Terri said and every head in the room turned to look at her. She wasn't cowed. "We offer this affordable luxury to families. To honeymooners. To seniors off exploring the world."

A few mutters, but no one stopped her. Success of a sort, Terri decided, and kept going.

"At Hayes 2, we still give the A-plus service we're known for, but we also make it family friendly." She took a breath. "At the London hotel, we could work with the tourism industry already there. With every visit we can offer double-decker tours of London in the famous red buses. Or half off tickets on the London Eye—"

A couple of people were watching her with interest now and Terri deliberately avoided looking at Cooper. She didn't want to know what he thought of any of this before she'd had time to finish.

"We're not known for family vacations," Eli said tightly.

"Doesn't mean we can't be," Terri told him, then shifted her gaze around the table, avoiding Cooper. Some of them looked interested; others not so much. But she hadn't lost them completely. And now that she was talking about her idea, she warmed to it and her voice and body language helped sell it.

"If we offer families a safe, beautiful place to stay, they'll come. The adults will get that taste of luxury, but in a safe place that welcomes their children. Seniors would enjoy a plush vacation site without draining their retirement accounts. And if London works out, and I think it will, we can do this all over the world."

She splayed her hands on the folder in front of her. "Everywhere there's a Hayes hotel, we build a Hayes 2. We become the premium place to stay for everyone, not just the uber-wealthy."

Silence. That could be good. Or bad. It was hard to tell, just looking at the faces around her, what they were thinking. But no one had shrieked *that's ridiculous* and stomped off.

That had to be a plus.

"We've never considered this before," Eli mused, tapping his index finger against his upper lip.

"Maybe we should have." Cooper spoke up and instantly, everyone's attention was on him. "It's an interesting idea," he continued. "We'll need some hard numbers, though. I want to know just how many families vacation together in big cities. What they do, how much they spend." He swiveled his head and pinned a man in his forties. "Ethan, get me as much as you can by tomorrow."

"On it."

"I want location suggestions. In London." He gave the blonde in red a nod. "Sharon, you're on that."

"By tomorrow," she promised.

"And we meet again tomorrow afternoon to discuss the findings. Three o'clock here."

Murmurs of agreement blended with the soft scrape of chair legs against carpeted floors. Cooper kept his gaze locked with Terri's as everyone else filed out of the meeting room.

"You surprise me."

"Good. That's almost as nice to hear as 'unexpected' and 'honest.'"

He snorted, shook his head and leaned back in the black leather chair. "How'd you come up with this family thing?"

She tipped her head to one side and looked at him for a long second or two. "In the real world, 'family' isn't a 'thing.' It just is."

"Uh-huh." His gaze pinned her. "So what made you come up with it?"

Sighing a little, she stood up, walked to the end of the table and took a seat beside him. "You know I've been wandering through the hotel, looking around, talking to people."

He nodded.

"Well, I was at the pool, talking to Travis the lifeguard—"

"The lifeguard."

"That's right. Anyway, he was saying how the pool was rarely busy because the guests don't really want to get their hair wet or something——" What she didn't say was, she'd seen it for herself. Yes, October was cool, even in the desert, but warm enough for the "beautiful people" to stretch out on chaises beside the pool. When she was there, a sole man had been swimming laps.

"Travis has a lot to say…"

"Don't get all huffy," she said quickly. "I asked him."

He frowned. "What the hell is huffy? Never mind. Go on."

"Anyway, there are some kids here, but the pool's so deep it's really not child friendly."

"We have a kid's pool," he argued.

"Please." Shaking her head sadly, she said, "It's like the size of a hot tub. Kids need room to play. With slides and water toys and——"

He held up one hand. "I get it. So from this, you decided we should go into the family hotel business?"

Terri shrugged. "I'm from Utah. People there have lots of kids. And they take vacations. People with kids like nice hotels, too. But if the kids are bored, no fun for anyone."

"I didn't say it was a bad idea."

"You didn't say it was a good one, either."

"Does it matter to you what I think of it?"

"Well, yes." She leaned back in the chair and slowly swiveled it back and forth. "We're partners, right?"

He studied her and those cool-as-ice eyes gave nothing away. All Terri knew for sure was that she'd survived the meeting, and that Cooper was still making her feel things she probably shouldn't. But oh, the burn and sizzle in her blood felt good anyway. And on that score…she needed to know something. "Vega seems nice."

He snorted, pushed out of his chair and walked across the room to the small refrigerator installed in a wet bar/

coffee station. "No. Celeste is many things but I wouldn't say 'nice' was in the mix."

"She's beautiful." Terri watched him and her gaze dropped unerringly to his butt. A really excellent behind.

"Absolutely."

"You know her well?" *None of your business, Terri*. But she couldn't help herself.

He glanced at her over his shoulder. "Are you asking if we're lovers?"

Well, she preferred *blunt*. "I guess I am."

"We used to be. Now we're not."

"Okay. Good to know." *Really good*. Because there was just no way Terri Ferguson from Ogden, Utah, could compete with Celeste Vega, supermodel. Not that a single kiss meant that anything was going on between them. Although the fact that she wanted more than that one kiss might. But the point was, Celeste Vega was out of the picture.

Okay, back to what they'd been talking about. "So did you think it was a good idea or not?"

"It's interesting," he allowed thoughtfully. "We've never focused on families as guests."

"I know. I looked at about a hundred of the files." She stood up and walked around the corner of the table. "Hayes Paris is lovely. Really. But if you had a Hayes 2 there, you could tie it in with Paris Disney. Give the families that visit a real experience. And gondola rides in Venice and skiing lessons in Switzerland and—" His mouth tightened. "You hate it."

"No. I don't."

"And yet, you don't look happy about it."

"I'm not a big smiler, in case you hadn't noticed."

"Why not? You should be happy."

"Is that right?" He tipped his head to one side and gave her a cool stare that didn't even slow her down.

"Well, yeah. You're a bazillionaire, you're gorgeous, you live on top of a palace, probably have hot and cold running women. Why aren't you happy?"

If anything, his frown deepened, so maybe she'd struck a nerve. And she wasn't sure how she felt about that.

"I don't have hot and cold running women," he muttered.

She was glad to hear it. "Okay…but the rest is true."

"Is there a reason why you're concerned about my level of happiness?"

"I'm a humanitarian?"

His lips twitched briefly. "Yeah, that must be it."

The conversation had shifted from business to personal and Terri knew she shouldn't, but she wanted more. "When did you lose your father?"

He blinked. "Well, that came out of left field."

"I'm sorry." She pushed her hair back from her face. "I don't even know why I asked that. But I've been thinking a lot lately about fathers—my dad and Jacob Evans. So I was wondering about your father."

He nodded and bent down to open the fridge. After another second or two of admiring his behind, Terri deliberately shifted her gaze to avoid the chance of drooling. So instead, she looked around the room. As meeting rooms went, it was, of course, palatial. With gray walls, navy blue trim and a table big enough to comfortably sit twenty people.

When Cooper stood up again, he was holding two water bottles. He carried them back and handed one to her. Twisting the cap off his, he said, "My dad died ten years ago."

"I'm sorry."

"Yeah, me, too." He looked up to a row of pictures on the wall opposite them. "My dad bought this hotel forty years ago."

"Really?" She took a sip of her water and set it down just before Cooper took her hand and led her close to the framed black-and-white photos.

"There it is. Or was," Cooper amended wryly. "The StarFire. Six floors of average rooms and a casino the size of my living room." He smiled looking at the photo and Terri studied it with him.

In the grainy image she saw a man in his thirties, hands in his pockets, grinning at the photographer with a look of pride on his face. The hotel was nothing like its current incarnation. There was no dancing fountain out front to dazzle tourists. No wide, fancy entryway hustling with bellhops. But, looking at Cooper's father, she could see the promise of what would come shining in his eyes.

"A year after he bought it, Dad was deep into remodeling—" He paused. "Not into *this*, but updating, improving the casino. Anyway, he needed an investor. Jacob had money and wanted in on the ground floor. So he and Dad became partners in Hayes Corporation and the rest is history, I guess."

"It's come a long way."

"Really has," he agreed. "And now we're worldwide. At least Dad lived long enough to see that happen."

She turned her head to look at his profile as he stared at his father's picture. "You miss him."

"Every damn day." His voice was low and filled with more emotion than Terri had ever heard from him.

She gave his hand a squeeze in solidarity. "I know just how that feels. My dad was smart and wickedly funny and sometimes I ache to hear his voice again. To hear 'Hi, Princess,' when I call. To get a hug. To hear him laugh."

Cooper looked down at her as his grip on her hand tightened. For a second or two they simply stared at each other. Survivors of a loss that still haunted each of them.

"My dad would have liked you," Cooper finally said.

"Why?"

"Because you don't play games. There's no BS with you and that's what he was like, too."

Terri smiled. "You keep complimenting me."

He grinned briefly. "I don't know that most women would call that a compliment."

"I do."

"I know you do," he murmured, staring down into her eyes. "I'm trying to sort that out."

Terri smiled up at him. "Are you saying I'm not only unexpected, but a mystery?"

One corner of his mouth tilted up. "I suppose I am."

"What a nice thing to say." Terri felt that flutter of something warm and oh so nice fill her chest. He not only looked great, he smelled wonderful. And the longer she stood here next to him, the more of a temptation he became.

He admitted quietly, "You're making me think things I shouldn't."

"Why shouldn't you?"

"It would make things even more complicated than they already are."

"And we don't need more complications," she finished for him.

"Might be worth it, though," he mused, tugging her a little closer.

"We should probably find out," Terri said, moving into his arms, tipping her face up to his.

"Research, research," he muttered and smiled briefly before claiming her mouth in a kiss that was instantly soul-searing.

Terri wrapped her arms around his neck and held on tightly as his tongue tangled with hers. Every cell in her body was putting on a party hat and hanging streamers. Her stomach did a wild spin and tumble and it felt as though her blood was heating, thickening in her veins. Complications be damned. Her mind shut down and her body happily took over.

His hands roamed up and down her back and Terri loved the rush of warmth that he left in his wake. Then she was grateful—grateful that she'd worn a simple yellow dress with a full skirt and a tight waist. Cooper swept the hem of her skirt up and then slid his hand beneath the thin elastic band of her lace panties.

She tore her mouth from his and her head fell back as he cupped the center of her, stroking that one *wonderful* spot where sensations gathered expectantly. Again and again, his thumb moved over that hard, tight spot and she trembled in response. She held on to him as she rode the waves of what he was making her feel. He dropped his head to kiss her neck, the line of her throat, the tip of his tongue stroking her skin.

"Cooper..."

"Come," he whispered against her throat as he pushed her higher, both of them breathing hard and fast. "Just let go, Terri."

A moment later she did. She couldn't have stopped the flash of release even if she'd tried. Her body quaked helplessly; her hips rocked into his hand and her fingers dug into his shoulder as she looked for purchase in a suddenly spinning world.

The climax seemed to roll on and on and Cooper kept it going, his fingers, pushing her along, not giving her time to breathe as jolt after jolt rippled through her until she finally slumped bonelessly against him.

He pulled his hand free, smoothed her skirt back into place, then cradled her tightly to him, lowering his face to hers for another kiss. This one was as hungry as the last, telling Terri that what was simmering between them was far from over.

"Okay," she whispered at last, "that was...worth a complication or two."

"Good," he said. "Because I've got more complications in mind."

She looked up at him and saw the need flashing in his eyes. Saw the tightness in his jaw and felt tension radiating from his body. She felt it, too. Now that she'd had a small sample of what he could do to her with a touch, she wanted more.

The ornate clock hanging on the far wall began to chime softly and Terri gasped. "I have to go."

Wryly, he said, "Not the reaction I was hoping for."

"No." She laughed, smoothed her hair and tried to ignore the fact that her body was still humming. "Would you ask someone to put those files I brought with me back in my office?" *My* office. Funny how naturally that had come out. She picked up her bottle of water and took a long drink. Wow. Orgasms—and irresistible men—could really make your throat dry. "I'd do it, but I don't want to be late."

"Sure. And late where?"

"I told Debra down at reception that I would be there at two." Terri moved for the door quickly. "She's going to show me around, walk me through the reservation process."

"Why?"

She stopped. "Why what?"

"Why do you need to know how reservations work?"

"Well, if I'm going to do this, I want to learn as much as I can." She threw a quick look at the clock again. "Really have to go. Bye."

She stopped when he called her name. Looking back at him from the door, she waited.

"Dinner tonight. At the Sky restaurant. Then we'll take in Darci Ryan's show in the Shooting Star amphitheater."

Her heart jumped. "That sounds suspiciously like a date. What about complications?"

"Think we've already proven we're ready to take the risk, don't you?"

That hum inside her grew brighter, hotter. "We're in Las Vegas. What better place for a gamble?"

That amazing smile flashed briefly again. "I'll pick you up at seven."

"Okay." Nodding, she went through the door, closed it behind her and for a couple of fast seconds, leaned back against it to catch her breath. Her legs were still trembling, her heartbeat thundering in her chest and her breath was uneven.

Terri's body was lit up like the neon night in Vegas. She felt the buzz of expectation and knew that she wanted Cooper more now than she had before and that was really saying something.

She'd never been much of a gambler, so maybe here, with Cooper, she'd have a little beginner's luck.

Seven

In all the times Terri had checked into hotels over the years, she'd never really thought about the whole process. She'd never make that mistake again.

Debra Vitale was the assistant manager, a woman in her fifties who'd been with the StarFire hotel for twenty years. She knew everything there was to know about her job and was patient enough to explain it all to Terri.

Debra even walked her through signing in a couple of guests on her own and Terri laughed with the incoming guests, explaining that she was new. And, with the helpful champagne served to those in line, people were, on the most part, patient. When her last guest left the counter, Terri turned to Debra.

"This is a lot more complicated than I ever realized."

"It really is," Debra said, smiling. "But you did a great job."

"I don't know about that, but—"

Two desks down from Terri, Brent, the reservations clerk who had checked *her* into the hotel just a few days ago, was talking to a young couple.

"I'm very sorry," he said apologetically. "We simply don't have a record of your reservation."

Terri's gaze shifted to the couple, each of them holding an untouched glass of champagne. The woman was desperately trying not to cry while her husband—Terri assumed he was her husband—looked frustrated with just a touch of helplessness.

Curious now, Terri started walking over, not surprised when Debra went with her. "Is there a problem?"

"Ms. Ferguson." He said her name like a prayer of gratitude. "There seems to be a mistake here somewhere."

"Who are you?" the man on the other side of the counter asked.

"I'm Terri Ferguson, one of the owners of the StarFire." Wow, she hadn't stumbled on those words at all. "How can I help?"

Almost at the end of his rope, the young man said, "We have a reservation here for a junior suite for two nights." He handed over a printout of his confirmation. While Terri read it, he kept talking. "We're on our honeymoon. Staying here two nights before we fly to Hawaii…" He took a breath and said, "I don't know why you don't have a record of it, but—"

Terri looked from him to the bride at his side and back again. Honeymooners. A twinge of sympathy grabbed her, then she asked Brent, "Have you checked *everywhere*?"

"Yes, ma'am, I have," he said and Terri still didn't like the sound of *ma'am*. "There's no record of it and—" he lowered his voice "—we don't have any junior suites available. They're all booked."

The lobby and casino were loud, as usual, but all Terri

could hear was the quiet sniff of the bride as she fought back tears of disappointment. She knew that Brent and Debra were both watching her, to see how she handled this crisis, so Terri jumped right in.

"Okay," she said, "have we got suites available on the VIP floors?"

Brent's eyes widened, then as he understood where she was going with this, a slow smile curved his mouth until he was grinning at her. "Yes, ma'am, we do."

Terri shot a quick look at Debra and saw the approval in the other woman's eyes. That felt good. It would have convinced her, if she'd had any doubt at all, that she was doing the right thing. What good was owning a couple thousand hotels if you couldn't give away a room now and then?

Brent turned to the computer, hit the keys like a concert pianist and a moment later confirmed, "We've got a two-bedroom suite ready on the twenty-second floor. It's open for the next week."

"Perfect," Terri said and gave his hand a pat. "Print out some keys, will you? Oh, and refund their room deposit, as well. And, we're not charging them for anything."

His eyebrows shot up. "You want their entire stay comped?"

"Is that the word?" She smiled. "Then, yes. Comped. I think when your honeymoon starts off that badly, it takes a little magic to turn things around."

He laughed to himself, shook his head and printed out a set of keys. Then he tucked them into a folder and handed it to her.

"While we're at it," Terri said, "have room service send up a dozen roses and a bottle of champagne. Oh, and good tickets to Darci's show tonight."

"I'll take care of that," Debra said, then murmured, "Well done, *boss.*"

Terri grinned.

Brent looked at her, approval clear on his features. "You are a great boss."

"Thank you. Now, let's get this new couple settled." She motioned for the newlyweds to follow her down the length of the counter to the bell stand. There, she signaled one of the bellmen and said, "Please take Mr. and Mrs. Hunter to the twenty-second floor. Suite 2205."

"Yes, ma'am."

Terri sighed. She was clearly going to have to get used to the ma'am thing. Turning to the Hunters, she handed the key packet to the brand-new husband. "We've given you a suite on the VIP floor—"

"We can't afford that," his wife said quickly.

"You don't have to afford it," Terri told her as the noise level around her rose and fell like waves. "Your stay is on the house."

"What?" The new husband looked down at the folder in his hand, then lifted his gaze to Terri's. "I don't understand."

"It's simple." Terri smiled at both of them, knowing exactly how they felt. It was almost impossible to compute when something completely out of the blue crashed down on you. "The StarFire wants to make it up to you for the reservation problem."

He stared at her, clearly stunned. "I don't know what to say."

"Oh, my God," his bride whispered.

"You don't have to say anything. The StarFire is happy to make this right." At least she was pretty sure Cooper would be good with it. And if he wasn't, well, she *was* a partner, wasn't she? "We wish you a long and happy marriage and a fabulous honeymoon."

"Thank you," the man said and held out one hand. "I can't tell you how much we appreciate this."

"You don't have to try. Be sure to catch the show, too," Terri said. "Darci Ryan is playing in the main theater tonight. The concierge will send your tickets up to the room."

"Tickets to her concert, too?" The bride took a gulp of her champagne.

"This is—" Jack Hunter shook his head, lost for words.

Terri took advantage of his stunned silence. "While you're here, we want you to enjoy yourselves and not worry about a thing." Terri grinned at both of them and loved watching the succession of emotions that crossed their faces.

"I don't know how to thank you," the bride said softly. "You saved the honeymoon."

Terri grinned. "We're happy to help. Be sure to check out our restaurants. They're pretty fabulous. Or room service if you prefer privacy. Just pay as a room charge and you're set. Now, if you'll go with the bellman, he'll show you to your suite."

The bride laughed in delight, threw herself at Terri and gave her a huge hug. "This is amazing. You're amazing. And when we get back home, we're going to tell everyone we've ever met to come to the StarFire. Thank you so much!"

Terri hugged her back, then released her. "You're welcome. Enjoy your stay with us."

"We absolutely will," the groom assured her.

"If you'll follow me…" The bellman took their luggage and started off across the lobby, headed for the private elevator.

Once they were gone, Terri headed back to reservations. She still had plenty to learn, but today was a good start.

Celeste watched the whole performance.

That's how she thought of it. The eager young lovers,

saddened and disappointed, and Terri Ferguson riding to the rescue. She hated that she admired what Terri had done.

Something she had noticed over the years: most people in positions of wealth and power lost all sense of the other people around them.

But Terri had seen the problem and solved it in a lovely way. The honeymooners were cooing at each other and laughing all the way across the lobby and Terri had given that to them. Maybe she was more than Celeste had assumed her to be. And maybe, once she became accustomed to this life, Terri would stop noticing people like the young couple she had just helped.

Celeste wondered, and found herself hoping Terri wouldn't change. Looking at the couple again, she bit back a wave of envy so thick she could hardly draw a breath. She'd wanted that once. A shining kind of love that would last and grow warm as the first flash of heat dissipated. But the world in which she lived didn't *do* love.

Instead, there were quick "relationships" that flamed out as spectacularly as they began. She'd had plenty of those over the years, and Celeste was forced to admit that the closest she'd ever come to more was when she'd been involved with Cooper. Maybe she'd have had a real chance there. But she'd tossed him and the idea of *more* away in favor of an old man with a title and a few more zeroes in his bank accounts. For all the good that had done her.

Her count had died two months before their wedding and his grown children hadn't even waited until after the funeral to show her the door. And since he hadn't changed his will, she'd been left nothing.

Now she was an aging supermodel with a limited number of years to build up her own bank accounts—or to find a man who could give her all of that and more. Was that man Cooper? She couldn't be sure, but until she got rid of Terri, she'd never know.

Terri was younger than Celeste and it was a barb in the throat to realize that she looked it, as well. In her sunshine-yellow dress, Terri looked fresh, innocent almost. While only that morning, Celeste had found a few tiny lines at the corners of her eyes. Lines. Not wrinkles. She would never be wrinkled and lines could be dealt with.

But it was lowering to admit that time was finally catching up with her. Since she'd begun her modeling career fifteen years ago at seventeen, Celeste had been a star. People around the world knew her name and face. Feeling that power slowly coming to an end was something she hated to think about, let alone acknowledge. Men around the world had thrown themselves at her feet and she'd walked across them like rocks in a river, to get where she wanted to be.

Which was one reason she'd come back to Vegas.

Soon, her modeling career would end—either that or she'd be relegated to B-list jobs, which she wouldn't tolerate. So she'd come to Vegas to take Cooper back. She'd planned to come in another month or so, but when Dave called to tell her about the new woman Cooper was interested in, Celeste had advanced her arrival.

Now it was time to make Cooper see that Terri would never truly belong in his world. Forcing a smile, she walked across the lobby, loving the slide of her black silk pants across her skin.

At the long, marble-topped counter, she caught Terri's eye and motioned for her to come over.

"Celeste, hi. What're you doing here?"

Around them, people noticed her, whispering, and Celeste instinctively posed for them, tossing her hair back from her face.

"I've come to take you shopping," she said. "The hotel limo is waiting for us outside."

"Oh. I can't go now. I'm really busy here and—"

"Terri," Celeste sighed a little. Was the woman really this earnest? "You are the owner. You may come and go as you please. And as the owner, you need to go shopping. You have a responsibility to look the part you're living."

Terri looked down at her simple yellow dress and then to Celeste. "I could use some new things, I suppose. I'm going to dinner with Cooper tonight and—"

Celeste used every ounce of her legendary self-control to hide the irritation she felt at Terri's statement. A dinner date with Cooper. To be followed, no doubt, by simple Utah sex.

All the better, she told herself. This was the plan. Celeste Vega was an experienced, wildly inventive lover. Once Cooper had slept with Terri, and indulged in vanilla sex, the pretty blonde would never hold up in comparison to Celeste.

"Excellent. Let's go, then." Celeste started walking, fully expecting Terri to follow her. The quick click of heels against the glimmering floor tiles behind her, told Celeste she was right. "I thought we'd start at the Grand Canal Shoppes at the Venetian."

"We have shops here in the StarFire, too."

"Yes, but we can't ride in the limo to these shops. Or drink the champagne waiting for us."

Terri laughed a little at that, then said, "But I need my purse. My credit cards…"

"You must start thinking like the owner of the StarFire," Celeste ordered, threading her arm through Terri's just to keep her walking. "You'll charge everything to the hotel and have it delivered to your suite."

"Oh, but—"

"In this," Celeste commanded, *"trust me."*

Two hours later Celeste had to admit that she'd enjoyed herself more than she had expected to. Usually, the people Celeste was with had their own agendas. Terri didn't. She didn't want anything from her. Wasn't trying to use her to advance her career. She was…nice. Sweet, even.

And that in itself was enough to make Celeste feel off balance.

"Is it always like this for you?" Terri asked.

"What do you mean?" Leaving the Grand Canal Shoppes, where cobblestone paths wended past tidy shops where flowers spilled in bright splashes of color, they walked across one of the stone bridges that spanned a canal where gondolas sailed. October sunshine was warm, but not hot, and a soft wind blew in from the desert.

"People have been taking pictures of you for the past couple of hours."

"Oh." Strange, she'd hardly noticed. Was it that Celeste was just so used to the attention? Or had she been having such a good time, it hadn't registered? "Yes, it's one of the downsides of celebrity. You can't even leave your house without makeup on or you're on the front page of a tabloid looking like the wrath of God."

"It's gotta be weird to live like that, isn't it? You can't even go shopping without being watched." Terri smiled tightly at a woman aiming her phone at them. "It's like you're never really alone."

"You get used to it."

"I don't think I could."

"I didn't either, once," Celeste admitted, remembering a younger version of herself who had railed against every tiny dig into her privacy. "And now I don't remember what it was like to be invisible."

Terri shifted one of her shopping bags to her right hand.

Celeste noticed. "You could have had those bags delivered to the hotel along with the rest."

Smiling, Terri said, "I know, but I just wanted to carry the red dress and shoes with me. I've never owned anything so gorgeous and you know, I wouldn't have bought that dress if you weren't there. Incredible how expensive it was considering there's so little fabric to it."

Celeste laughed. "It looked wonderful on you." Too good, actually, but if she was to get Cooper's attention back on *her*, then she needed him to get Terri into his bed so he could be bored.

Hmm. Perhaps Dave was right after all. Her plan did sound wildly convoluted. But she was committed now.

"Do you like it?" Terri asked. "The attention?"

Celeste looked at her and saw genuine interest in Terri's eyes. She couldn't remember the last time she and one of her "friends" had had a real conversation. Usually, it was about this man or that party. But Terri had been talking to her for two solid hours, asking questions and actually listening to the answers.

And Celeste wasn't sure what to do with that. Terri wasn't really her friend. Celeste didn't *have* friends anymore. She had air-kissed strangers flitting in and out of her life and she'd become so accustomed to that superficial life, Celeste hardly knew how to respond to reality.

"If I didn't like being noticed," she finally said, "I went into the wrong business."

"I suppose." Terri lifted the bags she held and changed the subject. "Anyway, I appreciate you taking me shopping."

"It was fun," Celeste said, again surprising herself with the admission. In fact, she couldn't remember the last time she'd enjoyed herself so much. Terri talked to everyone. Salespeople, tourists, other shoppers. The barista who'd prepared their cappuccinos had been half in love with her by the time they left.

Celeste had signed autographs for a couple of people and then laughed with Terri over some truly hideous fashion offerings in the shops. She'd told her about growing up in San Diego, California, and how she'd been "discovered" by a modeling agent while she was playing volleyball at the beach. Terri had told her all about growing up in Utah and had made it sound lovely enough that Celeste was tempted to go and see it for herself.

All in all, it had been a very different kind of afternoon for Celeste. Spending time with another woman without the inherent jealousy and backbiting of her profession had been…fun. And there was that word again.

Yes. She was definitely unsettled.

The StarFire limo was waiting for them and within fifteen minutes, the two women had been whisked back to the hotel. In the lobby, Terri gave her a tight hug. "Thanks so much, Celeste. It was good to get out of the hotel and feel a little normal—even if this is a brand-new kind of normal. I'm still sort of having a heart attack over the prices of these things."

"Terri," Celeste said with a sigh, "you're half owner of a company worth billions. It's time you started dressing the part."

Nodding, Terri said, "I know you're right, but I still feel a little guilty. Without you along, I would have headed to the mall, not the Grand Canal."

With high drama, Celeste clutched her heart. "Now you're going to give *me* an attack. The *mall*? Never." Giving her a smile, Celeste said briskly, "Oh, and thanks to *you*, I have several new things that I'm going to look spectacular in."

Terri laughed. "I know you will. Now, I think I'll go upstairs. I'll see you later?"

"Of course." Celeste watched the other woman hurry across the crowded lobby toward the private elevator. And she was surprised to realize that a part of her was sad to see Terri go.

Up in Cooper's office, Dave Carey was frustrated and furious.

"Thousands," Dave said, holding out the stack of receipts. "The two of them spent *thousands* at the Grand Canal Shoppes and charged it all to the hotel."

Cooper took the receipts and idly flipped through them. "I'm guessing Celeste is behind the more expensive items," he murmured.

"Does it matter whose is whose?" Dave threw both hands high. Accounting had sent him the stack of receipts from some of Las Vegas's finest shops and he'd been riding on fury ever since. Yeah, Celeste had told him her plans, but she hadn't said they were going to go through nearly fifty thousand dollars. *Most* of it spent on Celeste herself.

Her "plan" clearly wasn't working. Terri Ferguson was supposed to be feeling out of place here. Instead, it seemed to Dave as though she was settling in. Getting pretty damn cozy with the idea of being a billionaire. In fact, it was starting to look like they were all going to be stuck with Terri.

"Your new 'partner' doesn't seem to have any trouble living it up on the company's dime. She didn't *earn* this, but she's got no problem spending like she did." Dave looked at Cooper and waited for the flash of fury he was sure would be coming.

But Cooper only shrugged and tossed the stack of papers onto his desk. "She didn't buy a damn jet, Dave. It's some clothes."

"Celeste went shopping, too—"

"Celeste *always* shops." Shaking his head, Cooper said, "A few thousand to keep her out of my hair seems like a good deal to me."

"Seriously?" Dave whirled around, walked a few paces away, then stomped right back to the edge of Cooper's desk. "You're actually okay with this? What happened to *get the new partner out of town as fast as possible*? Buy her out? What happened to *that* plan?"

Cooper gave him a cool stare, but Dave wasn't fooled. He saw the fire behind the ice in Cooper's eyes, and Dave took a mental step back. If he pushed his old friend too hard at the wrong moment, he could ruin the whole thing for himself. He had to handle this carefully, keep reminding Cooper that the two of them were on the same side.

"I don't answer to you, Dave," Cooper said softly.

"I know that." Dave held up both hands in a peace-making gesture. He eased back in his tone and body language. "I'm just thinking about the future, Cooper. This is your company she's trying to horn in on."

"She's half owner whether either one of us likes it or not."

Dave didn't. "She's trying to change too much too soon."

Cooper leaned back in his desk chair and stared up at him. "How long should she wait?"

"You know what I mean," Dave countered and felt himself losing this particular battle. "Hell, I thought we were on the same page on this."

"We are."

"Then why are you okay with family-style hotels and thousands spent at boutiques?"

"You ever hear of a long game, Dave?" Cooper stood up. Eye to eye with his old friend, he continued, "I'm giving her time to see that this isn't what she wants. Shopping doesn't bother me. The family hotel thing might be a good idea. But one good idea doesn't mean she's going to make this her career. Her life. Once she realizes that, she'll take the offer of a buyout more easily."

"Seems to me she's having too good a time to give it all up now." Dave pushed one hand through his hair and fought a fresh wave of frustration. Had Cooper so completely let his own desires take hold that he didn't notice when the woman was entrenching herself?

"A few thousand dollars on clothes isn't going to make a difference here, Dave. She'll leave. Eventually."

Eventually.

Dave gritted his teeth to keep from saying more. Friends or not, Cooper was the boss and there was only so much he would be willing to put up with.

"Take the receipts back to accounting." Cooper walked across the office to the window affording an incredible view of the Vegas Strip. "Make sure they know to approve any purchases made by Terri."

"Right." Dave swept up the papers and curled them in one tight fist. At the door, he paused and turned when Cooper called his name. "Yeah?"

His gaze was hard, cool. "Leave Terri to me, Dave. Is that clear?"

"Couldn't be clearer," he said and walked out. With the door closed behind him, Dave swallowed back a rising fury. His plans were crumbling because Cooper had a hard-on for the woman currently screwing them all over.

Damned if he'd leave it to the man who couldn't see past his own dick.

Eight

Several hours later Cooper couldn't find it in him to be mad about the thousands of dollars Terri had spent at the Venetian. At least, not when she was wearing the smallest, tightest, sexiest red dress he'd ever seen. It was strapless, exposing the tops of her breasts to his hungry eyes. It was tight, skimming her figure like a lover's hands. And it was so damn short, it was just barely legal. Her long, tanned legs looked silky smooth, and the red heels she wore seemed designed to keep a man's gaze fixed on those legs.

They'd been to dinner at the hotel's best restaurant, attended Darci Ryan's concert and now they were having a drink in the hotel's top bar. All very civilized. Except he felt more like a man on the edge of a precipice. Slipping over that edge could make for a long, dangerous fall. If he got involved with Terri wouldn't that throw a wrench into his plans? Did he care?

He had a sip of his scotch and said, "So I hear you gave away a two-night stay in a VIP suite?"

She went perfectly still and actually looked guilty. "Is that a problem?"

Cooper stared at her as she took a sip of her wine. "Problem? I don't know. You realize those suites go for five thousand a night."

Terri choked on her wine and fought for breath, slapping at her own chest. "*Dollars? Five thousand dollars?* Really? How do we justify charging so much money for basically a place to sleep?"

Wryly, Cooper said, "It's a little more than a cot with a single wool blanket."

"Well, sure, but seriously?"

"Views that can't be beat, top-notch security and twenty-four-hour butler service? Media rooms? VIP seats at concerts, in-house massages…"

She took another sip of her wine and Cooper watched her throat work as she swallowed. It shouldn't have been sexy, but it was. Hell, he was discovering that everything about Terri Ferguson was sexy. Even just *thinking* about her could make him as hard and eager as a damn horny teenager. Being this close to her was a kind of torture.

"Wow." She whispered the word and shook her head as if she still couldn't believe the cost of the room she'd comped. "Okay, well the room was going to be empty all week, anyway. So let's just say that we're letting the Hunters stay there to check it out. Make sure the suite is in good shape."

"Yeah," he said, mouth twitching as he listened to her try to justify the comp. "We already know that."

She grinned. "Now we'll be sure."

When he didn't say anything, simply continued to watch her, Terri sighed. "Okay. They were on their honeymoon.

Their reservation got lost. The bride was crying and nobody should cry on their honeymoon and—"

"It was a nice thing to do," he said. He'd have probably
done the same thing himself ten years ago. These days,
though, he was too involved upstairs to spend much time
in the heart of the hotel.

She beamed at him. "Really?"

"Great PR, too. They'll tell everyone they know about
the StarFire and the owner who saved their honeymoon."

"We sent them champagne and roses, too," she told him.

He actually laughed. "Naturally."

She tossed her long blond hair behind her shoulders,
and he watched the bosom of that dress like a hawk, half
expecting her breasts to pop out the next time she took a
deep breath. Even as he thought it, though, he smiled to
himself. Never gonna happen, but a man could dream.

"I like the dress."

"What? Oh." She laughed a little uneasily and ran her fingers across the bodice as if checking to make sure it was in
place. "Thanks. It's gorgeous, isn't it? Celeste picked it out."

"Of course she did," he mused. Celeste settled for nothing less than the best—especially when someone else was
paying for it. "Did you like the show?"

Her eyes lit up. "It was wonderful. And going backstage
to meet Darci? Amazing. She's so nice, too. I didn't expect
that, but maybe I should have." She shrugged. "Just because someone's famous doesn't mean they're unfriendly.
Celeste has been really nice to me even though you and
she used to—"

Her voice trailed off so he finished the sentence for
her. "Be lovers." He watched her teeth tug at her lower lip
while she thought of something to say.

Finally, she asked, "How long ago?"

"She left almost two years ago. Why?"

"*She* left you?"

"Yeah. Again. Why?"

"Just…" She paused, took a breath that brought those breasts closer to spilling out of the red, silky fabric. "I guess I wanted to know if you were done with her before—"

"Before I take you upstairs to bed?"

"Before we take each other." Her gaze met his and he had to admit, he still liked her style of being blunt. Cutting right to the point.

"It's not her I'm thinking about," he said.

"That's good." She shifted in her chair, sliding those long legs against each other until he had to make a fist to keep from reaching out and stroking her skin.

They were in the StarBar on the nineteenth floor. The views out the three hundred sixty-degree windows were incredible, and the crowd mobbing the place showed Cooper just how popular this spot was. No loud music making conversations impossible. There was a gleaming black piano in one corner and one talented pianist keeping waves of notes rolling through the crowd. And suddenly, he was wishing he'd taken her to the roof instead. Where they could have a private drink. Where he could touch her as he wanted to.

They had a booth at the back of the room and still there was a wide view of the night sky and the echoes of neon from far below.

"So what *are* you thinking right now?" she asked.

"All kinds of interesting things." His gaze locked with hers and he saw the flash of response in her eyes.

Another deep breath and all Cooper could think was he was another quarter inch of fabric away from having her breasts tumble free.

And into those delicious thoughts came Dave's voice, his warning, the reminder of what this was all about. But,

Cooper assured himself, as he silenced his friend's cautionary words, he had lost sight of nothing.

Terri was here, so he'd deal with her until she wasn't.

Sooner or later she would go. Once she realized she was out of her depth and wouldn't be able to tread water indefinitely. Which was perfect for him. He liked his relationships as temporary as a jackpot win. But for now, everything else had to take a backseat to what was happening between them.

For days the tension between them had been tightening. Every touch, every glance, was filled with enough sexual heat to start a bonfire.

And tonight they'd feel the flames.

She finished off her glass of white wine, licked her top lip in a deliberately slow, sensuous manner, then said, "Show me."

He stood up, took her hand and pulled her from her chair. Even as tall as she was, despite the amazing heels she wore, he looked down into her eyes and Cooper felt a jolt of heat so vicious, it stole his breath. "Let's go."

He kept a tight grip on her hand and Terri's fingers were curled just as tightly around his. She kept up with his hurried strides across the bar and that told him she was as eager as he to finally sate the hunger.

They were almost to the private elevator when Cooper heard it.

"Mr. Hayes!"

"Dammit." He gritted his teeth and drew Terri to a stop before turning to face a security guard walking toward him. He read the man's name badge and asked, "What is it, Guthrie?"

"Sorry to interrupt, sir." In his forties, he was ex-military and kept his blond hair in the buzz cut he must prefer. "We've got a couple cheats, boss."

"Someone's *cheating*?" Terri looked from one to the other of them and Cooper almost laughed at her shocked expression.

"Yeah, we get them." He frowned at the admission. "It's not easy cheating the system in Vegas, and we've got plenty of security and surveillance that cuts it down, but there's always *someone* who thinks he's got it figured out."

Guthrie nodded at Terri before turning back to Cooper. "The twenty-one dealer alerted the pit boss about the card counter. Guy wasn't even trying to hide it. Can't figure if he's ballsy or just stupid. Anyway, we've got him locked down. Security will grab him when he tries to leave the floor."

In a weird way, Cooper almost admired card counters. At least they were willing to work for it. Though it wasn't strictly cheating, most casinos didn't allow card counters because it was too easy for them to judge the odds on betting.

"Okay, and…" Cooper tightened his grip on Terri's hand. He really didn't need all of this right now.

"The other cheat? Looks like he's using a new technique on a video poker machine. Guy's hit four jackpots in the last two hours."

Cooper frowned. "Same machine?"

"Same jackpots, too." Guthrie nodded. "The guy's hit four deuces with a three kicker twice."

"That's impossible," Terri whispered. "The odds are—"

"How do you know that?" Cooper watched her.

"I like math. And that's way out of the realm of possible."

"We think so, too, ma'am," Guthrie said. "We've got the guy pinned under the eye in the sky, but if he bolts, he's leaving with a lot of cash and the secret to his success."

Irritated as hell, Cooper turned to Terri. "I've got to handle this."

"Should I come?"

Tempting, but— "No. You go on up. I'll let you know what happens as soon as I can."

"Okay." Terri gave his hand a hard squeeze before taking the private elevator to the owner's floor.

Cooper and Guthrie took another elevator to the third floor, where the surveillance room and a wall full of computer monitors waited for them. This was *not* how he'd planned on spending his night.

"I want this handled fast," Cooper muttered as they walked into the heartbeat of the StarFire. Damned if he'd let Fate interrupt he and Terri again.

"Don't blame you, boss," Guthrie murmured and quickly led the way to where they were watching the cheat.

An hour later a card counter had been escorted out of the casino and a brilliant cheat with an electro-magnet had been arrested. Cooper was done dealing with people. He'd had enough of the noise and the crowds. All he wanted now was to get back to Terri. To finish what they'd been promising each other for days.

He'd brought a bottle of champagne and a pocketful of condoms with him, but Terri didn't answer her door. He knocked again with the same result and wondered if she'd gone to bed. Then he remembered the look in her eyes and told himself no way. Shaking his head, he walked back to his own apartment, then out onto the balcony. A cold, sharp wind blew at him, easing over the edge of the Plexiglas to ruffle his hair. But it didn't do a damn thing to the fires burning inside him.

Her balcony doors were open, so Cooper walked into the living room of her suite. Lamplight created puddles of gold in the darkness as if she'd left them burning for him in welcome. He went down the hall to her bedroom, found another lamp burning there. Light and the muffled purr of tub jets drifted through the open bathroom door and Cooper headed for it.

He shrugged out of his suit jacket and tossed it onto the nearest chair. Setting the champagne bottle down on the dresser, he tore his tie off and opened his collar button. He could breathe easier now, but his heart was pounding and his body felt hard and heavy.

Scent reached him first. It was light, airy, like a summer morning. Then he saw the billowing steam lifting off the bathtub and finally, he saw *her*. She had her hair bundled up high on her head and she was stretched out in the tub while powerful jets hummed and frothed the bubble bath she'd added to the water into a mountain of soap bubbles. She looked like a damn fairy. Unreal. Mystical.

And he wanted her so badly, he was choking on the need.

Her eyes were closed, until he said simply, "Terri."

She didn't jolt in surprise. Instead, she slowly turned her head and opened her eyes to look at him. "I wondered when you'd get here."

"Sorry I'm late," he said, smiling in spite of the tension gripping him.

She pushed up a little higher in the tub, finally giving him a good look at those breasts of hers, dotted now with bubbles.

"I figured you'd find the open doors…"

"Good guess."

"So why are you still dressed?"

"Good question," he muttered and tore his shirt off. While she watched, he undressed quickly, then stepped into the tub and hissed. "You *like* boiling?"

She grinned up at him. "I like it hot."

"Now that, I take as a direct challenge."

"Excellent." She smiled and the fairy-like image intensified. Covered in bubbles, strands of blond hair falling out of the topknot on her head and those big blue eyes watching him, she was, at the moment, *everything*.

Lowering into the water, Cooper felt the jets blast against his back as he levered himself over her, taking her mouth with a hunger that surprised even him. She reached up and encircled his neck, pulling him down to her, parting her legs and wrapping them around his hips.

The wet glide of his skin against hers set his nerve endings on fire. He'd waited. Wanted. And now he would have.

Cooper filled his hands with her breasts, stroking his thumbs across her hardened nipples until she was writhing beneath him and the hot water churned and splashed up both sides of the tub. She tipped her head back against the edge and stared blankly up at the ceiling. Running her hands up and down his back, fingernails dragging along his spine, she groaned his name. Cooper dipped his head, took one of those perfect pink nipples into his mouth and rolled his tongue across the tip. She gasped and arched high, her legs still locked around his hips.

Cooper fought the urge to slide into her heat right then. But damned if he'd complicate things further with an unintended pregnancy. They'd have to wait for a bed to complete this, but for now he could torment them both even further.

He lifted his head and shifted quickly, spinning her around until he was behind her—her back to his front. Her butt was a temptation he ignored. For now. Hot water pulsed against his back as the jets, on high, pummeled the water and their bodies.

Cooper kissed her neck, ran his hands across her breasts and down her sides, sliding across her abdomen, to her center, then to those long, lovely legs.

"Cooper…" Her head against his chest, she turned her

face up to his. Her eyes were glassy, her lips parted into a hungry pout that tore at him. "Cooper, what're you—"

"You'll see…" He held her thighs open and slid closer to one of the tub's jets. As soon as that rushing hot water hit her center, Terri jolted in his arms.

"Cooper!" His name came out as a helpless shriek. The water pulsed, her body moved and she breathed, heavy, fast, rocking her hips into the source of her torment. And he watched it all. Watched her strain and reach for the orgasm that was inching closer and closer. He'd never seen anything as totally sexual as Terri moving in the bubble-filled water, finding pleasure in the swirling heat.

Lifting her arms, she reached back and brought his head down to hers. While the water pounded against her core, she dragged his mouth to hers and kissed him breathlessly, desperately. He held her, their mouths fused, their breaths mingling and when the hot, frothy water finally pushed her over the edge, he tasted her surrender and had never known anything sweeter.

When her body finally stopped trembling, Cooper spun her around in his arms again, lifting her legs to hook them around his hips. With one quick move, he could be inside her, buried so deep within that it might possibly ease the incredible ache that had been tearing at him for days. And because he was no more than a breath away from doing just that, Cooper muttered, "That's it."

"What? What's it?" She threw her head back and looked at him through passion-glazed eyes.

He stood up, still holding her to him, her legs around his waist. "We stay here another second, I'm going to take you in this tub."

"And that's bad?" she asked dreamily.

"Without a condom it is," he snapped, really close to saying *screw it* and getting on with things.

That registered fast. "Right. You have one? A condom? Or two?"

"I do." He stepped out of the tub and a wave of water sloshed out behind them.

"We're making a hideous mess," she complained, glancing down at the water pooling on the green tile.

"Housekeeping," he muttered, and snatched up his slacks on the way to the bedroom.

"Right. Good point."

The French doors were still open to the night and a soft wind slipped inside, brushing across their wet skin, making them both shiver. But Cooper was past caring. There was only so much torture a man could take. Only so much waiting. He walked to the wide bed, dropped Terri onto the mattress where she bounced with a laugh that rippled through the lamp-lit shadows and made him smile in spite of everything. He grabbed a condom from his pocket, tore it open and sheathed himself faster than he ever had before.

And then finally he was where he'd wanted to be almost from the first moment he saw her. Cooper covered her body with his and when she lifted her legs to pull him in, he followed. He pushed himself deep inside her and as she gasped, he sighed at the sense of completion that swamped him. Tightly inside her heat, he held perfectly still for a long moment or two, just to savor the sensation.

Then his body took over and he moved within her, creating a rhythm that she eagerly matched. Their bodies sliding together in perfect harmony, their harsh breaths echoing in the stillness. Desperation fueled desire, and desire flashed into an almost unbearable heat.

He watched her face, saw everything she was feeling written there and knew that he would never tire of seeing her like this. Of knowing what they could build together.

Days of wanting, thinking, needing, combined to bring them both rushing toward climax. It was going too fast and he knew it. Sensed it. He wanted to make it all last longer, to drag this out forever, but he couldn't wait another second. And the sounds of her moans and gasps told him she felt the same. There would be time again for slow and torturous. Tonight they needed satisfaction.

Faster, higher, they chased each other up the mountain until the peak was within reach and then, locked together, they flew over the top and held on to each other all the way down.

A couple of minutes later Cooper's head cleared of the lust-driven fog he'd been living under for days. He was staggered. Shaken. Nothing he'd ever known had prepared him for what had just happened and damn, if that didn't put the fear of God into a man. His control of any given situation was what he prided himself on. But with Terri, his instinct was to throw control out the closest window.

What the hell was he supposed to do with that?

But in the next second he reassured himself that what he was feeling was only because Terri was new to his life. She was at once an innocent and wildly receptive. She was different from every other woman he knew. She was open, kind, funny and didn't really care about the money or power she now commanded.

What he had to do was get used to having her, being with her. Then these...*feelings* would fade and he could send her back to Utah with a smile on his face. He congratulated himself silently on once again taking the reins in the situation. He felt a little better about everything.

When he was fairly certain he could move without collapsing, he rolled to one side and draped one hand across his belly.

Next to him, Terri went up on her elbow and looked down at him. "That was amazing."

"You really like that word, don't you?" He gave her a quick smile, because what else could he do? Her hair was a tumble of waves and curls, her lips were swollen from so many hungry kisses and the curve of her mouth hit him hard.

"Sometimes, it's the only one that fits." She licked her lips and sent a jolt of fire to his belly and Cooper knew he was still in dangerous territory.

"This one time, I'll agree with you." But he wouldn't stay lying there beside her. If he did, he'd take her again and that wasn't going to help him get his head on straight. He pushed off the bed and stalked to the bathroom. Cleaned up, he tossed a few towels onto the floor to soak up the flood, then reached down to turn off the tub jets.

On his way back into the bedroom, he snatched his slacks and pulled them on.

Terri sat up in the bed and looked even more fairy-like now. The bed was huge and she looked so small in it. A single lamp tossed just enough light to make the shadows deeper and to somehow highlight her. Her blond hair tumbled down over her shoulders and onto her breasts, and his hands itched to cup them again.

Danger, his mind shouted. *Get out while you can.*

"You're leaving already?"

"Yeah." He was leaving now, while he could still convince himself to go. But he had to say something. To head off at the pass any thoughts that this might be more than what it was—satisfying sex. "Look, Terri, I don't want you to—"

She tipped her head to one side, her long hair sliding off her shoulders to swing free like a golden curtain. Holding up one hand for quiet, she finished his sentence for him.

"Get stars in my eyes? Hire a wedding planner and pick out a sweet little bungalow built for two?"

He stopped pulling his clothes on, leaving his dress shirt hanging open. Staring at her, he tried to figure out what she was thinking. Feeling. Was he somehow completely wrong about what was rushing through her mind? Usually about now, whatever woman he was with started sighing romantically and hinting that if they were so good together they should *stay* together. Be a couple. Be engaged. Then married. But he'd already discovered Terri was like no one he'd ever known.

Hell, for all he knew, she hadn't enjoyed any of this. No. Bull. He knew when a woman had a damn orgasm, and hers had rocked both of them. So what was she up to?

"Yeah," he said. "I didn't say that."

"You didn't have to." She scooted off the bed and naked, she walked right up to him. His mouth watered. He wanted her again. Now. "God, Cooper, do you really think you're completely unreadable? Panic was shining in your eyes so brightly I could have read a book by it."

No one had ever seen through him so easily before. "I don't panic."

"Not about much, probably, but this, yes." She slid her hands up his chest, her fingers defining every ridge of every muscle. Heat spiraled from her touch, soaking through his skin to burn up his bones. Then her thumbs moved over his flat nipples and he hissed in a breath as he fought for control.

"But you don't have to worry," she continued, sliding his shirt down off his arms to let it fall to the floor. "I didn't fall madly in love in an instant."

"I didn't say you did."

"And, if I promise not to propose, will you stay?"

Well, didn't he feel like an idiot? Cooper was used to

being the one to hand out the after-sex cautionary tale. Felt weird to be on the receiving end and he didn't much like it. But damned if he didn't admire her for it. "Blunt. No BS. I still like that about you."

"Here's more blunt," she said, going up on her toes to slant her mouth over his in an all too brief kiss. "How many condoms did you bring?"

Nine

A slow smile curved his mouth as he dipped into one of his pockets and came up with a handful of gold foil packets.

"I do like a man who comes prepared." Terri felt the rush of pure, feminine power as she saw the flash of heat in his eyes. Taking one of the packets, she opened it, then unzipped his slacks, found him hard and ready and slowly slid the thin layer of latex along his length.

She watched his silent battle for control and loved that she had been able to bring this strong man to a place of vulnerability. While her fingers curled around him, he pushed his slacks down and kicked them aside. Smiling to herself, she knew he wasn't going anywhere. Not yet, anyway.

"I've got to have you again," he muttered.

"Just what I wanted to hear," she whispered.

He scooped her up into his arms and stalked across the bedroom. She could really get used to being carried by Cooper Hayes. At the bed he sat down and settled her on his lap. Instantly, Terri sighed at the feel of him rubbing against a tender spot, still trembling with her last climax. She was greedy and she was okay with that. She wanted more and wasn't afraid to show him how much.

Moving on him, she swiveled her hips, teasing, almost taking him inside, then pulling back, torturing them both with the hunger that gnawed at their souls. His ice-blue eyes were swimming with heat and she knew hers looked the same. There was something vibrant and powerful between them. She'd never known that sex could be this good. Always before, it had been a soft, almost sweet experience, with a muffled ripple of pleasure to cap it off.

But with Cooper, there was magic. There was an explosion of sensation that left her trembling even as she ached to feel it all again.

His hands closed on her hips; his gaze pinned hers. "No more playing, Terri." He tipped her over onto her back and loomed over her.

But before he could, Terri rolled over onto her belly and lifted her hips off the mattress. Looking back at him over her shoulder, she whispered brokenly, "Be inside me, Cooper."

"You're killing me," he admitted.

She grinned and wiggled her hips. "That is so not the plan."

Cooper moved to kneel behind her and closed his hands over her butt. She groaned as his strong fingers kneaded her flesh, then he slipped one hand down to stroke that hot, desperate core of hers. Her hips moved of their own accord, rocking, swaying, as her body looked for what only he could give her.

Curling her fingers into the meadow-green duvet, Terri lifted her hips higher and held her breath until he pushed himself deeply into her body. He moved with long, sure strokes, pushing her along the path to completion at a breathless pace. She moved into him, taking him so deep, she thought he almost became a part of her. Again and again, he took her, pushing her, claiming her. His hands held her steady and still the world rocked around her.

She tipped her head back and moaned, hearing the hunger in her own voice. Her body coiled tightly. Anticipation heightened every thrust he made because she was that much closer to the explosion she was reaching for. This was more than just physical, her mind whispered. He wasn't simply taking over her body, but he was sliding into her heart, as well. She felt something deep, something overwhelming for him. But she just couldn't think about that now. At this moment, all she wanted in her mind was what he was doing to her body. What he was making her feel. But one day soon, she was going to have to deal with this new development.

He breathed fast and hard, and Terri heard his desperation as clearly as she felt her own. When the first ripple began deep inside her, she quivered in response, pushed back against him and shouted his name. In reaction, Cooper pushed himself even deeper into her heat and Terri's vision went dark under the strength of the orgasm that hit her. She called his name again and rode the waves that crashed inside her.

Her body was still trembling when she felt him stiffen, heard him shout and then his body, too, was shattering and the world tipped crazily one more time.

Terri could hardly look at Cooper over the conference table the next afternoon. If she did, she was sure everyone at the meeting would see what she was thinking. And she couldn't *stop* thinking about the night before.

It had been magical. Incredible. They'd gone through

every one of the condoms he'd brought to her room and they'd finally given in to exhaustion as dawn touched the sky. When she woke up, Terri was alone with her memories and rumpled sheets. She hadn't heard from Cooper all day and now they were here, in the conference room, sitting at opposite ends of the table from each other as if they were strangers.

Her stomach spun; her mind kept replaying the things he had done to her and with her all night and yet, in his eyes, she saw a cool indifference that she didn't understand.

"So," Cooper demanded, his voice shattering her thoughts and bringing her back to the moment at hand. She was about to find out if her family vacation idea would be approved or not. "Ethan. What'd you find out?"

The man shot Terri an apologetic look before saying, "Surprisingly enough, I found that the numbers bear out the family vacation angle. I wouldn't have thought so many people were dragging their children to Europe, but they are. And it's not just families." He paused, checked his notes, then continued. "As Terri suggested, there are more and more seniors doing extensive traveling. Most of them seem to prefer organized tour groups where reservations and luggage and itinerary are taken care of for them.

"If we work in tandem with those tour organizations, it would be a profitable angle for a Hayes 2. Heck, we could even offer our own tours—maybe offer a stay at two or more of our hotels. They'd come flocking to us for, as Terri put it, 'affordable luxury.'"

Terri let out a breath she hadn't realized she'd been holding. Then Cooper asked, "Sharon?"

"Ethan's right. He brought the numbers to me and together, we dug deeper. There is a demand for the kind of thing Terri suggested. Actually," she added apologetically, "I can't believe none of us considered this before. You asked me to look for locations and I've found several possibilities in Chelsea, Kensington or Knightsbridge for the first Hayes 2." She turned to look at Terri with a new respect in her gaze. "How do you feel about it, Terri?"

Delighted with how this had gone, Terri spoke with more confidence than she'd had the day before. She'd also done some research on family-friendly areas, so she said, "Any of those options sound great, but I'd prefer Kensington. Why don't you see what properties are available and we can go forward from there?"

"I'll get right on it," Sharon said. "And if it's okay with you, I'll bring what I find to your office tomorrow."

Again, Terri felt a rush of pleasure and now it was mixed with pride and a terrific sense of accomplishment. Whatever else happened, she'd at least earned the respect of the people at this table.

"That would be great, thanks. Around two?"

"Perfect," Sharon said.

"All right," Cooper spoke up then. "Is there anything else to cover?"

Everyone began to gather their things, but Terri's voice stopped them in their tracks.

"Actually," she said and every head in the room turned to look at her. Cooper raised one eyebrow as he waited for what she had to say.

"With all of the research I've been doing on European hotels, I noticed that they all offer tea and coffee services in their rooms. This includes a small hot pot along with instant coffee, a variety of tea bags and packages of a few cookies."

"Yes…" Cooper drew that one word out until it was almost three.

"I know we do that here, too, in the more expensive

rooms. Why not carry it through to all the rooms?" Terri looked from one face to the other, waiting for a reaction. She didn't have to wait long.

"Because," Eli pointed out, "our guests now order room service coffee. Or go down to the coffee station in the casino where they'll spend even more money."

"True," Terri argued, because she'd already considered that. "But if they had enough in their rooms to make one cup of coffee, they'd still need room service. I checked with hospitality and the coffee most usually ordered is a full pot, which is six cups. No one who wants that much coffee will be dissuaded by the offer of one free one. And, they'll have coffee to get them through the wait for more."

Eli's mouth worked as if he wanted to disagree, but couldn't find a way to do it.

"And," Terri pointed out, "a couple of cookies won't be breakfast, so they'll still go downstairs to the coffee station. Still stop to throw money into a slot machine. They'll just be in a better mood when they get there."

Someone snorted a laugh.

"It's a good idea," Cooper said.

"Thanks." Terri looked directly at him. His gaze locked with hers even as he spoke in general to the room at large.

"Ethan, put someone on this. I know we've got a lot of the supplies on site now, so I'd like hospitality to work with housekeeping to take care of this."

"Today?" Ethan asked, surprised at the sudden decision.

"Why not today?" Terri asked.

"Exactly," Cooper declared. "Why hesitate on a good idea? I want coffee and tea setups in every room by the end of the week." Cooper stood up and looked at Ethan. "We'll need more hot pots, so contact the restaurant supply companies. Go outside Vegas for supplies if you have to. Work with housekeeping to get this taken care of ASAP."

"Yes, sir." Ethan shot Terri a look of respect, then stood up. "I'm on it."

Everyone else stood, too, and one by one, they left the room, until it was just Cooper and Terri alone again. His gaze was locked on hers, but he didn't speak. Didn't give away any indication of where his thoughts were.

Didn't he feel anything after last night? Had he deliberately shut it all down? Why?

Diffused sunlight poured through the tinted windows lining the conference room. Silence stretched between them until she simply couldn't take it anymore. "You should have woken me when you left."

He shook his head, but he never broke eye contact. "No point in you being awake, too."

Sounded reasonable, but Terri thought there was more to it. "Are you sure that's the reason?"

"What else would it be?" He stood up, shoved his hands in his pockets and kept the ice in his eyes as he looked at her.

What the heck had happened? Where was the heat? Where was the man who'd shown her exactly what her body was capable of? She'd gone her whole life thinking sex was a nice pastime. Now she knew it was so much more when you were with the right man. Was he regretting what they'd shared? And again, *why*?

Terri walked toward him and he didn't back up. He didn't have to. The distance in his eyes was powerful enough.

"I think you were just trying to avoid me."

He snorted and shook his head. "No."

"Cooper—" She reached out to touch his arm, and this time, he did pull back.

"Terri," he ground out, "this isn't the time. We've both got things to do. Last night's over. This is today."

"Wow. And you think *I'm* blunt." She was hurt, sure,

but she was angry, too. She'd thought they'd found a new connection last night. Now it was as if he was setting fire to the bridge linking them. "Why are you so cold? I told you I wasn't looking for a proposal or a proclamation of undying love…"

"Yet," he bit off.

"Excuse me?" She choked out a laugh and didn't know whether she was surprised or insulted.

He sighed. "Terri, if we keep doing this, it's only going to get more complicated."

Nodding to herself, she asked, "And complications are bad?"

"They are for us," he snapped, irritation sparking around him like a firework show run amok. "We're already trying to figure out this business partner thing and if it's going to work."

"I thought it was working," she said and felt the flush of pleasure she'd experienced at the meeting slowly drain away. "You liked my ideas. Ethan and Sharon both discovered they'd work. We're moving forward on them…"

He pushed one hand through his hair, then took hold of her upper arms, pulling her in close. Terri tipped her head back to look up at him and didn't feel any better when she met his gaze.

"You had a couple of good ideas, yeah. And I'm not taking anything away from you. But Terri, running this company is more than that. And I don't know that you're ready for it."

She'd been feeling pretty confident about it all until just now. "Well, we can't know until I try."

"Trying might cost us too much."

"Again. Won't know until we try."

"And the complications be damned?"

"They're only complications if we allow them to be."

Deliberately, she ignored the ice in his eyes and the rigid tension in his body. Going up on her toes, she slanted her mouth over his and it took less than five seconds for him to kiss her back. To wrap his arms around her, hold her tightly to him and devour her mouth with all the passion they'd shared the night before.

Her heart leaped into a gallop and her blood simmered into a fast boil. Would it always feel like this when he touched her? Kissed her? She really wanted to know the answer. Would they be simply business partners? Or lovers as well? When Terri finally pulled back, breaking the kiss, she looked up into his eyes and smiled. "So I'll see you later?"

He took a breath and nodded and she saw heat in his eyes again. "Yeah. You will."

Dave wasn't happy.

Everyone in that meeting had come out singing Terri's praises. How could it have come to this? She was supposed to be a fish out of water here. Supposed to be embarrassing herself and irritating everyone who worked with her. Instead, she was the golden girl. She'd talked the head chef out of quitting when he was furious with a sous-chef. She'd promoted Debra in reservations to assistant manager. And the rest of the employees were deliriously happy at their newly instated right to switch shifts on their own. How was she doing all of this?

And even if she had made some inroads in this one hotel and casino, what the hell did a bank teller from Utah know about running a multibillion-dollar company? Why were they letting her make suggestions on expansion? And how the hell had she come up with a winning idea?

Somehow, she'd managed to pull off what everyone was saying was the next big thing. *Luxury hotels for families?*

Hayes was going to be catering to kids now? And they thought that was *good*? Plus, what was this crap about a coffee setup in the rooms? Since when was that a great idea? Hell, she'd had Cooper moving on that one so fast, Dave heard that housekeeping was scrambling to buy up every damn hot pot in Vegas.

She was entrenching herself in the Hayes Corporation. Digging in deeper with Cooper himself.

Dave's future was disappearing in front of his eyes.

He had to get rid of her. Fast.

Terri saw the picture on the internet as soon as she got back to her office. She and Celeste, crossing the little stone bridge outside the Venetian. And the headline read, *Ex-lover and current lover of Cooper Hayes. Comparing notes?*

"Oh, God." Terri slumped in her chair. Celeste might be used to having her privacy compromised, but Terri wasn't. "What's next? I'm giving birth to alien babies?" She grabbed her phone and called her mother.

"Well, hi, sweetie," her mom said. "If you're calling about the picture, yes, I saw it."

Of course she'd seen it. The Celebrity Watcher missed nothing.

"This is so embarrassing," Terri muttered and thought about her friends and neighbors in Utah seeing the same headline. Closing her eyes, she imagined Jan's reaction and could almost hear her friend laughing hysterically.

"Why are you embarrassed?" her mother asked. "You're a grown woman. You're allowed to have a lover—as long as he's not married, involved or pining away for someone else."

"He's not." Well, not the first two, anyway. Terri really couldn't be sure he didn't still have some feelings for

Celeste. What man wouldn't? And she was the one who'd walked away from him. But if he still cared, he was hiding it well.

"Then there's no problem. How's everything else, honey?"

"Crazy, but better, I think." Cooper still had doubts, but Terri was on her way to proving herself. To him. To everyone.

When she'd first arrived in Las Vegas, she'd felt overwhelmed and unsure of herself. But she was learning the job, the company. She was making friends and fitting into this new life a lot easier than she'd thought she would when she arrived. But most important, Terri was learning that she wanted this more than she'd expected to. Meeting the employees, making sure their guests were happy, it was all…fun. And isn't that what work should be?.

"It sounds to me like you've made up your mind about this new life," her mother said a little wistfully. "You like it, don't you?"

"I do. And before you ask, it's not just Cooper," she said, "though I admit, he's a big part of it all. But I like the challenge, Mom. I love knowing that I can have an idea that will change the way we do things."

"*We*. That's a statement right there."

"Yeah, I guess it is. Am I crazy to decide to change my whole life after hardly a couple of weeks?"

"Sweetie, you've never been crazy. Your aunt Connie, *she's* crazy."

Terri laughed as her mother had meant her to.

"You're a smart, capable woman, Terri. You know what you want and when you make a decision, it's the right one for you."

"Thanks, Mom and oh, I promise to come and collect Daisy soon."

"Daisy's fine, don't worry about that." She paused, then

said, "I just poured myself a glass of wine and got down a bag of chips. Tell me everything."

While Terri talked, her mind was working. Now that her decision was made, she'd have to go back to Utah and put her house up for sale. If she was going to commit to this life, then she was going all in.

Over the next week Terri threw herself into her new life. She had meetings with Sharon and Ethan about the new London hotel, which would be in Kensington. They'd found the perfect property—a beautiful old hotel that desperately needed some loving attention. Once it was purchased, they'd start the renovations, and the hope was to have the first Hayes 2 open for business by next summer.

She'd also spent a lot of time working with housekeeping and hospitality on the tea and coffee services. With a selection of herbal and caffeinated teas, not to mention cookies, granola bars and biscuits, the feedback from their guests was overwhelmingly positive. And to soothe Eli's worries, the coffee station in the lobby *and* room service were reporting that people were still ordering their coffees and breakfasts.

Every day brought a new challenge that she was happy to meet. Between working with the bartenders to devise a way to shift-change that wouldn't inconvenience anyone, and helping out at registration when one of the clerks had to go home sick, Terri was busy—and enjoying herself far more than she once had on the teller line at the bank.

And every night, she was with Cooper. Her heart was happy, but her mind kept warning her about possible problems. Cooper was still holding a part of himself back from her, though it did feel as though she was chipping away at his emotional walls bit by bit.

It was important. She had to make him realize that there

was more between them than heat. She had to find a way to let him know she was falling in love with him. Not something she'd planned on, but how could she help it? He was sexy and kind and warm and standoffish and altogether a man who would keep her intrigued and attracted forever. She liked the way his mind worked. She liked the flash of respect for her she saw in his eyes.

And she knew it wouldn't take much for her to finish that beautiful slide into a love so deep and rich that it would kill her if she lost it.

All she had to do was prove to him that she was here to stay. Then he'd be able to drop the shields surrounding his heart and see what she already did. That they made a great team.

So late one afternoon, when Dave came to her with an opportunity, she grabbed it.

"He's an elusive investor," Dave said as he took the elevator with her down to the StarBar for a private meeting. "Honestly, Cooper's been trying to convince the man to invest in Hayes Corporation for years. If you could pull this off, it would completely convince Cooper that you can do this job."

Terri gave him a quick hug. "Thanks, Dave. I appreciate your confidence in me."

"You've earned it," Dave said with a quick grin. "Just convince Simon you're interested and the rest will take care of itself."

"I can do that." And once she did, it would prove to Cooper once and for all that she was serious about being a part of StarFire. That she could be the partner he needed—not just in the business, but in his life. And once he relaxed about all of it, she could tell him that she was falling in love with him. Terri slapped one hand to her belly at the swirl of nerves nestled there. Dave didn't notice the sudden shock she felt, thank God. *Love.* Funny how that one word could color everything around you. She saw Dave's loyalty. Celeste's friendship. This hotel and the employees who were becoming her friends. She saw the business started by a father she'd never known but who had trusted her with what he'd built.

Mostly, though, she saw Cooper.

The man who had swept her off her feet right from the first. He was icy and warm, cut off and vulnerable. He was all business and then tender. He was, in short, everything she wanted. And maybe, Terri told herself, she'd loved him all along. Or maybe it had awakened in the middle of the night when she woke to find herself in the circle of his arms. But it didn't really matter *when* she began to love him. It was enough to know that she did and she always would.

Dave winked. "I know you can do it."

Terri was going to make sure of it.

By the time Terri finished her meeting with Simon Baxter of TravelOn and got back up to the offices to tell Cooper all about it, most everyone on the business floor had gone home for the day. The desks were empty and her footsteps echoed in the silence. The quiet in the normally busy room was so absolute, it was a little spooky.

But that unsettled feeling disappeared when she opened Cooper's door and saw him sitting at his desk. Through the window behind him, the soft glow of neon shone against the glass. Cooper's jacket was off, tie loosened and the top collar button of his shirt undone.

The love she'd only just acknowledged filled her heart and spilled over into warmth that slid through her bloodstream. How could she not have recognized what she felt for Cooper before now? Because they hadn't known each

other very long? What did time have to do with anything?
Her adoptive parents had fallen in love over a weekend,
gotten married three weeks later and had had forty-two
years together before her dad died.

And she wanted that with Cooper. Wanted this life she'd
just discovered. Wanted him. Wanted the family they could
build together. Just looking at him made her heart race.
Then he looked up and the smile that flashed briefly across
his face when he saw her, left Terri pretty much a goner.
Love rose up inside her and opened like a spring tulip. It
was lovely and so necessary, she didn't know how she'd
lived this long without it.

Now she would show him that she loved him. That they
were great together. That she could be his partner, personally and in business. Even though the office was empty, she
closed his door behind her, wanting to ensure their privacy.

"Hi," he said. "I was just going to head upstairs.
Where've you been?"

"I was at a meeting," she said, walking toward him.

Frowning a little, he pulled her down onto his lap. "With
who?"

"That's the surprise," she said, squirming around on his
lap until she could face him. Wrapping her arms around his
neck, she leaned in and kissed him hard. Excitement was
still fluttering inside her. She'd done it. She'd struck a deal
with Simon and now all it needed was Cooper's approval.
Terri couldn't wait to see his face when she told him.

"I was talking with Simon Baxter."

"What?"

She grinned at the shock in his eyes. And it was about
to get even better. "Simon has agreed to invest in Hayes
Corporation. I think it's a really good deal, but of course,
none of it will go forward until I get your agreement."

"My *agreement*?" He pulled her arms down from his

neck and stared at her as if he'd never seen her before. "What the hell did you do?"

Confused, Terri just blinked at him. "I told you. I talked to Simon and we agreed on an investment level. But Cooper, nothing's set in stone until you approve it, too."

"And I never will." He lifted her off his lap, set her on her feet, then jumped out of his chair as if he couldn't stay still a moment longer. "Why would you do that?"

Terri didn't understand why he was so furious, but he definitely was. His eyes were flashing, his jaw was tight and he practically vibrated with outrage.

"He's an investor," she said. "I thought that was a good thing."

"If it was, I'd have taken him up on his offer ten years ago when I lost my dad." Jamming both hands through his hair, he shook his head. "Simon Baxter, the motel king. God. I can't believe you went behind my back on this."

"I didn't go behind your back, Cooper." Terri was stunned. He was looking at her as if she'd stabbed him through the heart. How had this all gone so wrong so quickly?

"That's what it looks like from here," he countered and walked away from her as if needing the distance. "I don't *want* outside investors, Terri. Never have. Hell, I didn't want *you*."

Shock punched her and she watched him through eyes suddenly blurred by unexpected tears. She blinked frantically. Damned if she'd cry.

"This is *my* company, Terri," he raged. "I'm the one who took it over from my dad and built it up into what it is now. And I did it without anyone's help."

"What about my father? What about Jacob?" she countered. "He was your partner. You weren't all alone in this, Cooper."

"Jacob came in and out, but he didn't stick his nose into the running of the business. Which is more than I can say for *you*. The running of the company, the building it into what it is now? That was me. I did it my damn self." He paused, jerked his head back and gave her a hard look. "Is this why you really came here?"

He started pacing in long, fast strides. "Have you been playing me all along? Setting me up for a takeover? You're all innocence and sex, getting past my guard, easing me into a situation that you set up? How the hell much is Simon promising you to betray me?"

"Betray?" She took a step toward him and stopped. "I only did this as a surprise for you."

He laughed shortly but there was no amusement in the sound. "Surprise? Well, congratulations. You pulled it off. I thought you didn't play games."

"Play games? I *don't*." How had it come to this? Why was she defending herself to a man who had already tried and convicted her? "Aren't you the one who keeps telling me that there's no BS with me? That I'm blunt? To the point?"

She didn't know why he was so angry, but she hadn't done anything to be ashamed of. She'd only talked to Simon with the best of intentions. "Now all of a sudden you think I'm scheming? Well, you're *wrong*."

He snorted. "Of course you'd say that."

"Well yeah, because it's *true*." Terri shook her head and tried to figure out where she'd zigged when she should have zagged.

Maybe she should have talked to Cooper about the meeting first, but Dave had assured her this was something Cooper wanted. And when that thought settled in her mind, she began to wonder if it wasn't someone else pulling the strings here. Was it Dave, leading her into this very confrontation for reasons of his own? She'd trusted him. *Cooper* trusted him.

"I don't play games, Cooper. I don't lie. And I wasn't working against you. I was trying to do this *for* you."

He snorted again. She was really getting tired of that sound.

She took a breath and tried again. "I'd never even heard of Simon Baxter until Dave told me he was here and wanted to meet."

"Dave?" His head whipped up and his cold, cold eyes met hers.

"Yes," she insisted. She had to make him understand that she never would have done anything to hurt him. "Dave told me that you'd be happy about this. That I could finally prove to you that I can be your partner. That's the only reason I went to the meeting in the first place."

Seconds ticked past quietly while he stared at her. Terri felt sick that it had come to this. She hated seeing the repulsed look in his eyes but couldn't think of a way to get past it.

Finally, he spoke. "You expect me to believe that my oldest friend is the one who turned on me? Dave and I have worked together for more than ten years. You've been here a few weeks. I'm supposed to take your word over his?"

Her chest hurt. Her eyes stung. Her breath was like knives moving in and out of her lungs. She wouldn't have believed it possible for everything in her life to turn so quickly to trash. But the look in Cooper's eyes told the story. He didn't believe her. He'd even said out loud that he hadn't even *wanted* her there.

"So you'd rather believe it was me, is that it?"

"I didn't say that."

"You didn't have to. I don't care who you believe, Cooper," she said, voice tight, but steady. She did care, of course. Desperately. But she wouldn't give him the satisfaction of seeing how much his words had torn at her. "But if you think so little of me, after all we've shared, then I have to wonder if you're the one who's been playing me all this time."

When he didn't say anything, just kept looking at her with those icy-blue eyes, Terri sighed and felt her soul shrivel into a ball of pain. "You have, haven't you?"

He shifted his gaze away from hers. "No."

"Don't lie to me," she murmured, waiting for him to look at her again. "You kept waiting for me to fail. You *wanted* me to fail so I'd leave and you could have your precious company all to yourself again."

"Terri…" He ground his teeth together and scowled tightly. But he didn't deny a thing.

"Congratulations. I never saw it. Didn't even consider you were just biding your time before buying me out. It must have been really frustrating for you when I succeeded."

"Damn it, Terri—"

"Don't curse at me, either." She took a breath, squared her shoulders and lifted her chin. Her gaze burned into his as she said, "I didn't fail, Cooper. *You* did."

She turned to leave but stopped when he spoke again.

"Got another meeting?" Cooper taunted.

"No." She looked back at him, the man she loved. The man who didn't trust her. Didn't want her. "I just don't want to be here anymore."

Ten

In her suite, Terri gave in to the tumult inside and allowed the first tears to fall. She couldn't believe what had happened. Why had Dave done that to her? Why would he deliberately set her up? Had Cooper's reaction been an act? Had he and Dave done this together?

"No," she muttered. "He wasn't acting. He was surprised. Furious."

She dropped her black bag on the long, slim dining table and only then noticed a brown envelope with her name typed efficiently on the front. She swiped tears out of her eyes, picked up the envelope and tore it open. With her luck it would be an eviction notice signed by Cooper himself.

Sniffing, she sat down at the dining table and pulled the papers free. First, there was a typewritten letter from Mr. Seaton, Jacob Evans's lawyer. The man who'd come to see her in Ogden and started all of this.

Ms. Ferguson, as per your late father's wishes, this letter from him is delivered three weeks following his death.

A letter. From the father she would never know. Terri was almost afraid to read it. With everything else going on right now, could she take one more buffeting? But even as she considered ignoring it, she unfolded the letter and read…

My dear Terri,

Though I've not been a part of your life, I have kept a fatherly, if distant, eye on you all these years. Your parents were good people and I am grateful to them for loving you the way I couldn't.

But I want you to know that your mother and I were very young and very much in love. She became pregnant and we made plans to run away together after your birth. But I lost my love the night you were born. She died and you lived. I knew that alone, I couldn't give you the life you deserved, so I allowed your adoption. It was the hardest thing I have ever done.

Terri's eyes filled with tears that spilled over and ran, unheeded, down her cheeks.

I want you to know that you were loved even before you were born.

And though you rightly loved your parents, I hope that sometimes, you might spare a thought for the parents who loved you and let you go.

Be happy, Terri.
Your father,
Jacob Evans.

Terri's tears blurred the page as she carefully folded it again. Too many emotions in one night, she thought as her throat closed up with a wave of sympathy, regret and loss rising up to settle in the center of her chest.

"It's too much," she whispered. "All of it. I feel like I can't breathe." She looked around the lavish suite—four thousand square feet of emptiness—and felt as barren as the room in which she sat. She needed comfort. So she stood up, walked to the closest phone and dialed room service.

"Hi," she said, hoping she didn't sound as pitiful as she felt. "I need you to send up the biggest hot fudge sundae we have. And a slice of chocolate cake. Twenty minutes? That's great. Thank you."

While she waited, she opened a bottle of white wine, poured herself a glass and muttered, "Wine and chocolate. Perfect."

Jacob Evans had loved her. She'd never know him.

Terri loved Cooper Hayes. She'd never have him.

Her heart was torn, her insides felt as if they'd been sliced to ribbons and the flush of success she'd been feeling only hours ago had completely dissipated.

"He hadn't wanted me to succeed. That's why he kept looking surprised at everything I did." Shaking her head, she sat down at the dining table, dug into her purse and pulled out her cell phone. "I need a friend. A *real* friend." And there was only one person who came to mind.

Texting her, she wrote:

Can you take some sick days starting tomorrow? I need the cavalry.

Sure. What's wrong? What happened? What do you need?

Terri grinned. God, it was good to have someone you could count on no matter what.

I'll tell all when you get here. Buying you a ticket, will email it to you.

Okay, bazillionaire, I'll let you.

Terri laughed and it sounded broken, even to her.

Thanks, Jan.

Just tell me who you want me to slap.
See you tomorrow.

Flipping open the laptop on the table, Terri hurriedly checked into Jan's favorite airline's site, bought a ticket for first thing in the morning, then emailed it to her.

Then she sat back, took another sip of wine and swallowed past the knot of emotion lodged in her throat. Terri felt lost. It was as if everything she'd believed since coming here had all been a lie. Had she ever really had a shot at this? Or had it all been a play acted out by really convincing actors?

A knock on the door sounded and she opened it to room service. The young guy carried a tray holding a gigantic sundae and the biggest slice of chocolate cake she'd ever seen.

"Anything else, Ms. Ferguson?"

"No," she said, handing him a ten dollar tip. "That's it, Rory. Thank you."

"Yes, ma'am."

She winced, but laughed as she locked the door. Funny, now being called ma'am was the least of her problems.

* * *

By morning Cooper was ready to kick some ass.

All night long he'd been awake, thinking about the confrontation with Terri. What he'd said to her. What Terri had said back. The look on her face when he'd accused her of betraying him. He couldn't forget it. The pain in her eyes. The way her mouth had dropped open in complete shock. She'd folded her arms over her middle as if in a futile attempt to shield herself from more verbal attacks. *He'd* done that to her.

Shaking his head, he dismissed her response as irrelevant. He couldn't worry about her hurt feelings when the rug had just been pulled out from beneath his feet.

Terri turning on him was one thing. Hell, until her he'd never really known a woman he could learn to trust. But to know that it was Dave—his best friend—the one man he had always trusted over all others, who was behind it all, was too much to swallow.

Naturally, he hadn't taken Terri's word for a damn thing. He'd told himself that she was covering up, trying to make herself appear innocent while tossing Dave to the dogs. So Cooper had done the only thing he could to try to get to the truth. He'd called Simon Baxter. Just remembering that brief conversation ripped him open again.

Maybe he should have believed Terri. She'd always been nothing but honest with him. He'd held himself back from her to protect himself and in doing so had really screwed everything up. But who could blame him for not wanting to admit that it was his oldest friend who had betrayed him.

"Simon," he'd said, clenching the phone to his ear while he stalked up and down the balcony at his end of the owner's floor. He avoided even looking at the French doors to

Terri's suite. "I hear you had an investment meeting tonight with my new partner."

Keep it friendly, open. Get him to spill what he knew.

"I did," Simon confirmed jovially. "That's a smart young woman you've got there, Hayes. She drives a tough bargain. Yes, you're a lucky man."

"Yeah. Sure I am." He felt as lucky as a man climbing the steps to his own gallows, but that was beside the point at the moment. "Terri tells me it was really Dave who got the ball rolling this time around."

In the background, Cooper heard the click of a lighter and knew the older man was lighting up one of his beloved cigars. Celebrating what he thought was a coup?

"That's right," Simon said. "Ol' Dave has been assuring me for a year now that you'd come around eventually. See the sense in us joining forces."

Cooper's heart sank even as his fury roared into life. It was a struggle to keep his voice steady. "Is that so?"

"Well, hell, you know that boy is really ambitious—got yourself a live wire there, Hayes. But he's loyal to you. Got your best interests at heart. He sees that the two of us merging would be good for both our houses."

Sure. Because a five-star hotel company merging with a roadside motel outfit couldn't be anything but great. What the hell had Dave been thinking? A year? A year, he'd been working on this behind Cooper's back? What the hell else had he been up to?

Cooper had gotten what he needed, so he wrapped it up.

"Well, Simon, I hate to disappoint you again," he said tightly. "But my company's going to stay privately held. No outside investments. No mergers."

"Well, here now, that's not what Dave's been feeding me for a damn year. It's not what that girl had to say last night, either!" Outrage colored the older man's voice but he had nothing on how Cooper was feeling.

"Dave doesn't have the power to make deals, Simon. You know that. As for Terri," he muttered, rubbing one hand across his forehead as if to ease the ache pounding there. A cold wind slapped at him and it felt as if the universe itself was trying to push him around. "She's new here and doesn't understand." Though apparently, she'd understood Dave in a way Cooper hadn't. What was he supposed to make of that?

"Dave said this was all for you. That you'd okayed it."

"He lied." God, those words tasted bitter. But damn if he didn't have to swallow them. His friend had betrayed him. Tried to sell him out. Working deals and using Terri to do it.

"Now, see here," Simon blustered.

"We're done, Simon," Cooper said and hung up. It took all his control not to throw his damn cell phone against the wall just to watch it shatter.

Terri has been telling the truth. But did that change anything, really? She was still the partner he hadn't wanted. She'd done some good work in the last couple of weeks, had come up with some fresh ideas that were already panning out. But she still didn't belong, did she? Even as he thought it, he told himself that of course she did. She'd proven herself there to him. To all of them.

And he'd never wanted a damn partner, so why should he be expected to just welcome her with open arms? If she stayed, they'd get drawn deeper and deeper into what had already grown into something far more than temporary. Was he ready for that? Hell, was he even capable of it?

Shoving the memory of that phone call and the long, lonely, miserable night that followed to the back of his mind, Cooper stood up when Dave knocked, then walked into the room with all of his usual, casual flair.

"Come on in."

Grinning, Dave said, "You wanted to see me?"

"Yeah." Cooper came around his desk, perched on the edge of it and watched his friend come closer. More than ten years they'd worked together, played together, had each other's backs—or so Cooper had thought. Now he had to wonder if Dave had been working against him all along. How much of their relationship had been a lie right from the beginning?

"Terri told me she met with Simon Baxter last night."

Wincing, Dave shrugged. "Yeah, she told me she wanted to meet him. I didn't want to introduce them, Cooper." He lifted both hands in a helpless shrug. "But she *is* a partner here so I didn't feel I could refuse."

Clearly, Dave was going to ride this horse right into the ground. Nodding, Cooper said, "Plus, it would have been hard to refuse when you're the one who set it all up to begin with."

"What?" He laughed, but the sound was nervous.

"You've been working for a year to get something going with Simon," Cooper continued, watching his friend's eyes, seeing the flash of guilt before it disappeared again.

"Oh, come on. Really?"

Ignoring the halfhearted denials, Cooper asked, "If Jacob hadn't died—if Terri hadn't shown up—how were you going to work it?"

"Are you nuts?"

"No. I'm pissed." Cooper saw it in his eyes. Dave was realizing that there was no point in denying anything anymore. "How the hell could you do this, Dave? We're *friends*. We've worked together for years."

"Together?" Dave choked out a laugh and shook his head. "No, Cooper, you're my *boss*. I work for you."

"So the hell what?" Stunned, confused, Cooper countered, "You're my assistant. That's a bad thing?"

"You still don't get it." He laughed again. "A bad thing? I hate every minute of it." Every semblance of a smile, of friendship, drained from his expression and his eyes were fiery. "Everything about it. I jump when you say, go where you say, do what you say. My God, I do most of the damn work around here and I'm still just an employee. I'll never be *more*."

"If you believe all of that, you're the one who's nuts. Yeah, you do a good job, but we all do." Outraged, Cooper said, "Oh and yeah. Poor you. Sorry about the six-figure salary and the five weeks of vacation every year—at whatever Hayes hotel you want to stay in. Yeah, it's rough to be you."

Dave sneered at him. "What the hell do you know about anything? You're the golden boy. Everything goes your way. You've got money falling out of your pockets. Your ex charges a ten thousand dollar dress to your account and you shrug it off as a cheap way to keep her occupied.

"You want to know how I would have handled Simon if that *simpleton* hadn't shown up to take over? I'd have gotten the shares you promised me and I'd have sold them all to Simon for a damn fortune. Then *finally*, I could have lived the way I want to. Hell. The way I deserve to."

The viciousness pouring out of the man shook Cooper. How could he not have seen any of this in all this time? Hell, he'd never even guessed that Dave was so eaten up by jealousy that it had soured him completely. Ten years with this man and it turned out Cooper didn't know him at all. What did that say about his judgment? He wanted to trust Terri but how the hell could he let himself? What if the face Terri showed him was as false as the one Dave had been wearing for years?

"Man, you should be an actor. You kept up the best friend role all these years and never let a damn thing slip."

"Please." Dave waved one hand. "You see what you want to see. Always have. God, you looked at Terri and saw a mastermind trying to sell you out?" He laughed. "Seriously? *Her?*"

"She's no simpleton," Cooper said tightly. "In the short time she's been here, she's turned quite a few things around. Plus, she's not a liar. That's something you wouldn't understand."

"Really? And you do?" Dave sneered and shook his head. "Didn't you just chase her off, accusing her of back-stabbing you?"

He had. Pain jabbed at him at the reminder of how she'd looked at him. How she'd turned and walked away. How he hadn't stopped her. And he'd deal with the guilt of that later. For now, though… "Time for you to go, Dave."

"Oh, I'm going. Don't worry. I'll be hired at another hotel chain before the week's out."

"I wish them luck." Cooper folded his arms across his chest. "We were friends once, so I won't have you tossed out…"

Dave held up one hand. "Spare me the speeches."

"Fine. No speech. Just two more words. You're fired."

Even after this confrontation, Cooper could see that the finality of those words slapped at Dave. But he recovered quickly. "Fine. I'll take my severance package in lieu of notice. And I won't miss any of this one damn bit."

When he left, Cooper stared at the door for a long time, wondering if Dave was right about at least one thing. Did

Cooper only see what he wanted to? Was he blind to anything that might shake up his view of the world?

Okay, two things. He *had* assumed that Terri was the betrayer. Even knowing her inherent honesty and the fact that she could be as blunt as a sledgehammer, he'd believed it. Or at least a part of him had.

Because it was easier that way. It would have given him an excuse to get rid of her. To buy her out and make her leave. It would have given him a reason to stop this connection with her before his feelings grew even more than they already had.

And now that the damage was done, the question was, did he try to undo it? Or did he leave it alone for both their sakes? He wanted to go to her. To hold her, tell her he was wrong. Tell her that what he felt for her was so damn startling he didn't know what to do with it. But he didn't. Because if she left now, he didn't want to watch her go.

Terri opened the door and Jan rushed in. Her short, spiky black hair was perfect and her bright green eyes sparkled. She wore black leggings, a sapphire-blue tunic sweater and flat black boots.

"Wow! First class plane ticket, a limo with champagne to pick me up and a gorgeous bellman to wheel my bag. I could get used to this." Jan dropped her purse onto the dining table and pulled Terri into a hug.

Terri hugged her back, more relieved than she could say that Jan, with her outsized personality and fierce loyalty, was there with her. Then she looked past her friend and saw Jake, the bellman, waiting.

"Oh, hey," Jan turned and reached for her purse. "I need to tip you and—"

"No, you don't," Jake said with a wink and a wicked grin. "It's on the house."

When he left, Jan fanned herself. "Boy, he's a cutie, huh?" When she looked at Terri, Jan must have read the misery on her friend's face because she instantly went feral. "Okay, who hurt you? Just point me at them."

"God, it's good to see you," Terri said softly. "Everything's just a mess."

"Messes can be cleaned up," Jan told her and threaded her arm through Terri's walking into the living room. "Let me have one minute to have a small orgasm over this suite, then you can tell me all about it."

Terri laughed, dropped onto the couch and started talking. Jan's features displayed every emotion in the book as Terri went through what had been happening in the past couple of weeks. She told her everything, didn't hold back, and by the time she was finished, Jan was furious.

"What is the matter with this Cooper? Can't he see you were set up?"

"I don't know," Terri said, still hurt from the night before. "Maybe he doesn't want to know it. He said himself he never wanted me here."

Jan gave her a gentle shove. "Well, it wasn't up to him, was it?"

"No, but maybe it is now."

"Why?" Irritated, Jan jumped to her feet, walked away a few steps, then came right back. "You're a partner in this business, Terri. He doesn't have the right to bitch about it. Well, okay, he can bitch, but he can't change it."

"No, but I can," Terri admitted. Leading the way over to the wet bar, she opened the fridge, pulled out a bottle of wine and uncorked it. As she poured two glasses, she said, "I wanted you to come because I needed the company on my drive back to Ogden."

"What?" Jan took her glass and had a sip.

"I want to stop by my mom's and pick up Daisy, but then I'm going back home. I don't belong here, Jan. And Cooper doesn't *want* me here."

"So you quit?" Jan set her glass down, propped both hands on her hips and gave Terri a hard look. "Really? Your birth father wanted you to have what he spent a lifetime achieving and you're going to walk away because Cooper's bent out of shape? You came here for you, remember? Because it was finally your time to do something that you wanted to do."

Put like that, leaving, giving up, sounded like a terrible idea. But Terri had been haunted all night by these and a million other thoughts. And alone in the dark, she'd decided that this was the best way. Just leave the situation. Let Cooper have his business. She'd proven to him and to herself that she was up to the task. That she could do anything. Maybe that was enough.

"It's easier this way," she argued. "I sell him my shares and we never have to see each other again."

"Uh-huh." Jan shook her head and dropped into one of the chairs, waving a hand at Terri to get her to do the same. "And the fact that you love him is what—going to be ignored?"

"It has to be. He doesn't want me here, Jan."

"Because you're dangerous to him, Terri."

She laughed. "Me? Dangerous?"

"Yeah, you." Jan took a breath and let it out again. "He's had everything his own way for so long, he doesn't know how to share."

"He's not a kindergartner," Terri said.

"*All* men are kindergartners," Jan countered.

"So I should stay and be miserable waiting for him to

come to his senses?" Terri shook her head firmly. "That doesn't sound like a good time to me."

"Well, hell, of course not," Jan said. "But why should you be miserable? You said yourself that until this blowup with Cooper, you were having a great time. You've got a knack for this and you know it." Terri's. "You have just as much right to be here as Cooper, yes?"

"Yeah…"

"You've come up with a few great ideas already, right?"

"True, but—"

"You've got friends here, don't you?"

"I don't know," Terri admitted, thinking about all of the people she'd met and worked with over the past couple of weeks. Yesterday, she would have said she did have friends. She would have counted Dave among them. Now how could she be sure about any of them?

"Well, I do. You're *you*, Terri. You've got friends. People who are on your side. Are you really going to walk away? Show them all that you can be defeated this easily?"

"Easy?"

"Okay, bad word, but you know what I mean." Jan gave her hand a squeeze and sat back. "Don't give it up, Terri. Don't let him take this from you. You wanted this. For yourself. Why should you leave because he's being a giant pain in the ass?"

Jan had a point. Heck, she had *lots* of points. Terri felt her balance reassert itself. Jan was right. About a lot of things. And this is exactly why Terri had needed to talk to Jan. Her friend saw through layers to the bottom line better than anyone she'd ever known. And she knew she could trust Jan. With anything. Terri only wished that Jan were here all the time instead of all the way in Ogden… Terri actually *felt* the lightbulb go off in her head as a brilliant idea occurred to her.

"I'll stay," she said quietly. "I've made something here. Something I love. That I'm good at. You're right. I shouldn't have to leave to make Cooper feel better, so I'll stay."

"Atta girl!" Jan grinned, toasted her with the wine and took a big gulp.

"If you will," Terri finished.

"What?" Confused, Jan looked at her and waited.

"How would you like to move to Vegas and work at Hayes Corporation as my executive assistant?"

"Are you serious?" Jan asked, her eyes flashing excitement.

"Oh, yeah. Very serious. I really need you here, Jan. I can trust you to always be honest with me. To tell me when I'm being stupid or about to make a huge mistake—to come up with fabulous ideas to shake up both the company and Cooper—" The more she said, the more Terri knew this was the right thing to do. She could have her best friend with her, and Jan would be making more than twice as much as she had in Ogden.

"Well, sure, but you don't have to *hire* me for that."

"Just hear me out," Terri said quickly and this time it was she reaching for her friend's hand. "You can live here with me. This suite is four thousand square feet."

"Holy God!" Jan's gaze whipped around the room, then back to Terri. "That's bigger than both our condos put together!"

"I know! We'll have plenty of room. And you'd work for me. I'll pay you a huge salary and you'll get great vacations in any of our hotels every year and—"

"Stop the sales pitch," Jan said, scrambling up to rush around the table. "You had me as soon as you said you needed me. I really missed you the past couple of weeks,

Terri. And I'd love to live here. Hello? Jake the bellman for one..."

Terri gave her a tight hug and for the first time since she came to Vegas she felt good about facing the future. Even if that meant working with a man who didn't trust her—and would never love her.

Eleven

God, it was good to laugh again. After an hour with Jan, Terri felt better than she had in a long time. It was going to be brilliant, having Jan in Vegas with her, working with her.

When a knock on her door sounded, Terri's laughter ended abruptly and she had a wild thought that maybe it was Cooper, coming to apologize. To tell her that he'd been wrong from the beginning and that he understood now that he loved her and trusted her and—

"Wow," she muttered, pushing up from the couch. "I lead a rich and full fantasy life."

"Cool," Jan said with a grin. "When you get back, tell me all about it."

"I don't think so," Terri said. Her tiny, hopeless fantasies were better off staying private. Then she looked through the peephole and felt fury rise up inside her.

Yanking the door open, she looked at Dave and demanded, "What're you doing here?"

All apology, Dave squeezed past her before she could close the door on him and shut him out. Holding up both hands, he said, "Just listen to me for a minute, Terri, then I'll go."

She closed the door, crossed her arms over her chest and stood hipshot, tapping the toe of one boot against the tile floor. Behind her, she felt more than heard Jan walk up to join them.

"Who are you?" Dave asked.

"Is this Dave?" Jan asked.

"Yes, this is him. What do you want, Dave? Haven't you already done more than enough?"

Jan lined up beside her and mimicked Terri's stance. "Why are you listening to him, Terri? Let's just toss his ass out."

"Now, just a minute," he argued, flashing a furious glance at Jan.

"No, you wait," Terri interrupted and stepped into his space. Poking him in the chest with her index finger, she demanded, "Why did you do it, Dave? Why did you set me up? Let me think Cooper wanted a merger with Simon Baxter?"

His gaze shifted between Jan and Terri like a cornered dog, before settling on Terri. "It wasn't my idea."

"Really…" Jan wasn't asking a question.

He huffed out an impatient breath and ignored Jan completely. "Terri, Cooper wanted me to do that. He set it all up so you'd fail miserably. He wanted an excuse to finally get rid of you."

"Bastard," Jan murmured.

Terri had to agree. If it was true.

But she remembered the look of shock and anger on Cooper's face and she was willing to bet it had been real. If he'd been acting, he deserved an award. Shaking her head so hard, her blond ponytail swung from side to side behind her, she said, "That makes no sense at all."

"Sure it does," Dave argued quickly. "He figured you'd be so upset at your 'mistake' that you'd sell him your shares and he'd have what he always wanted. The company all in his name."

"What a crappy thing to do," Jan said.

Terri could feel her friend's anger, but she still wasn't convinced. Not entirely, anyway. "Why are you telling me this? If you were willing to set me up for Cooper's sake, why turn on him now?"

"Because he fired me," Dave said and lifted his chin. "He doesn't want any loose ends. Didn't want to risk you finding out he's been using you all along. For the past couple of weeks, he's been softening you up, placating you by accepting your ideas, sleeping with you to keep you off balance—all to eventually convince you to leave."

Terri felt cold all over. Funny, but anger could be ice as well as fire. Was Cooper really that underhanded and vicious? Or was Dave playing her again for his own reasons? How could she know? She'd cried enough. She'd been furious. Now she was just cold and calm. Cooper had gone through a lot to get rid of her. Why? Why not be up front and honest in the first place? Why not just offer to buy her out right from the beginning?

Because, her mind whispered, *he'd known you wouldn't walk away then. It was too new. Too important for you to try. So he let you. Encouraged you. All with the plan of making you quit in the end.*

"He doesn't give a damn about you, Terri," Dave was saying. "Or me, for that matter. We've been best friends since college and he just tossed me out. He's incapable of caring, Terri. Cooper Hayes is an empty shell."

She wouldn't have thought so. But she'd seen a side of

Cooper after the Simon blowup that she never had before. And still, she knew a Cooper that Dave didn't. Passionate and warm and funny. He didn't seem empty to her—just… guarded. Cooper had to know that Dave would come running to her to spill his guts, wouldn't he? Why would he be loyal to the man who fired him? So again, Terri was left feeling at sea, not knowing which way to turn or who to believe.

He left shortly after and the quiet in the suite was overwhelming. Terri got herself a bottle of water and took a long drink while Jan watched her as if she were an unexploded bomb. Which was what she felt like. Everything inside her was so tension-filled it was a wonder she hadn't already burst.

"Okay." Jan looked at her. "Do we believe him? I mean yeah, we're already mad at Cooper because he's a jerk. But Dave set you up. Why should we believe him now?"

"Good points," Terri murmured as she thought it all through. Dave could have warned her privately last night before that meeting with Simon Baxter. He could have confessed the truth about Cooper's plan and then sworn her to secrecy. But he hadn't. So no matter how Dave tried to paint himself, he wasn't a good guy. Terri looked at Jan. "Either Dave's lying or Cooper was last night—and for the past couple of weeks."

"How do we tell?"

"I don't know that we can." Terri was disgusted, disappointed and so damn tired of feeling hurt. Had he really been lying to her all this time? Had she trusted, loved a man who had never intended to care?

"So," her friend finally said, "what's next? What do you want to do?"

What she *wanted* to do was face Cooper. To tell him

he'd lost. To tell him that she loved him, but he'd lost that, too. And she would.

But first, "Would you call downstairs, Jan? Get the valets to bring my car around?"

"You're leaving?" Surprise flickered in Jan's eyes. "What happened to you not letting Cooper chase you away? What happened to my great new job?"

"I'm not leaving. Well, not for long. I'm going to find Cooper, and then you and I are driving to St. George to see my mom and pick up my dog."

"Okay…"

"Then we're coming back here." Terri's gaze was clear and sharp. "And we're both going to get to work."

"Wahoo!"

Fifteen minutes later Jan was downstairs and Terri was knocking on the door to Cooper's suite right down the hall. Mentally, she rehearsed just what she would say to him when he opened it. She would stare him down, tell him that she loved him but was determined to get over it. She'd tell him that she was staying in Vegas, no matter what he did to try to make her leave. She would look into his blue eyes and try not to wish that everything was different. But everything in her mind dried up and blew away when the door swung open to show her that Cooper had already moved on.

Celeste Vega, wearing nothing more than a towel, gave her an awkward smile.

Celeste lifted one hand to her mouth in a dramatic fashion, and used her free hand to hold the thick, navy blue towel to her breasts. "Terri! Oh, this is so embarrassing…"

And well thought out, she added silently. Dave had given her his pass key to Cooper's suite. Celeste's plan had been to surprise Cooper with her naked self—ready and willing to resume the relationship she'd turned from nearly two years ago.

But having Terri catch her here? That was hard. She hated to see the look of stunned hurt on the other woman's face, and regret was a new sensation for Celeste. She was used to taking care of herself, no one else. So why did she feel guilty?

"Celeste?" Terri blinked, shook her head and said, "I was looking for Cooper..."

"This is so uncomfortable," Celeste said, tossing a look toward the hallway over her shoulder as if expecting Cooper to walk into the room any second. She was in so deep now, she had to keep going. Had to make Terri give up on Cooper so Celeste could have another shot at him, So she steeled herself and said, "He's in the shower, sweetie. I'm just about to join him."

Nodding, Terri said, "I see. Okay. Well." She took a deep breath and tried to hide the pain in her eyes. But Celeste saw it and felt another sharp blade of regret slice her heart.

She'd come to Las Vegas to win Cooper back no matter how she had to do it. But hurting Terri was harder than it should have been. Celeste hadn't expected to care for the other woman. To enjoy the budding friendship that was dying miserably at the moment. But she'd come too far to stop now.

Cooper and Terri were already estranged—Dave had told her that much. This, then, would be the driving wedge that would keep them apart. And that was what Celeste wanted, wasn't it?

Meeting Terri's gaze was the hardest thing Celeste had ever done. She felt terrible. A dog. A snake. A worm. And Terri's simple dignity made her feel even worse.

"I'll go, then," Terri said, "and leave you two alone."

"Terri—" Celeste didn't want her to be hurt. But this is how it had to be. Still, she wanted to say something to ease Terri's pain. What, she had no idea. As it turned out, it didn't matter.

"It's all right, Celeste," Terri said softly. "Cooper's made his choice. Would you tell him that I'm leaving? I'm driving to St. George."

She frowned. "Where is that?"

"In Utah. My mom lives there. So…" She took another breath. "Just tell him, okay?"

Celeste reached out and took Terri's arm as she turned to leave. Her gaze fixed on Terri's, Celeste said, "You really love him, don't you?"

Inhaling sharply, she answered, "Yes. But don't hold it against me. I'm sure I'll get over it."

Cooper was done. He'd been dealing with the fallout of Dave's treachery all day—a couple more of his employees were now looking for jobs thanks to being involved with Dave's plans. Plus, he'd had to handle all the things Terri had taken on.

After last night he wasn't surprised that she wasn't in her office, but he was shocked to realize that she had become so important to the simple running of the business. When had she taken on so much of the day-to-day drivel that went with running a huge company?

"And how the hell does she get anything done with everyone running to her every five minutes with some petty complaint?" He shook his head and looked down the hall toward her suite.

She was in there, no doubt still furious with him, and he really couldn't blame her. He'd been a bastard. Worse, a *blind* bastard. Dave had worked her, Cooper had used her and all she'd done was work her ass off.

"And damn it, I *miss* her." It wasn't just his own busy mind keeping him awake the night before. It was being without her. He'd reached for her countless times and found only an empty bed and cold sheets.

He missed her laugh, the shine in her eyes when she was excited by something. He missed hearing her stories about what was happening in his own damn casino and mostly, he just missed her. Her smile. Her scent. Her taste. God. Cooper suddenly felt like he'd been hit over the head with a two-by-four.

He *loved* Terri Ferguson. When the hell had that happened?

He didn't want to buy her out. He didn't want her to leave. He wanted her here. With him. His partner. And so much more. So, just exactly how could he fix this?

He unlocked his door, walked into the suite and stopped at the sound of a familiar voice.

"You're late."

Cooper jolted and looked to the couch where Celeste sat, wrapped in one of his bath towels. "Oh, no. Not today. What the hell are you doing here, Celeste?"

"I came to seduce you," she admitted, rising to her feet with the grace of a ballet dancer.

"Thanks, but no, thanks," he ground out. He didn't want her.

He wanted Terri.

Damn it, why hadn't he gone to her earlier?

"I've lost, then, haven't I?" Celeste dropped the towel to the floor.

Cooper got a full frontal look at one of the most beautiful women in the world—his own ex-lover—and didn't feel a thing. All he could think was, *She's not Terri.* He wondered how the hell she'd gotten in, then figured it had to be *Dave*.

Celeste picked up her short black dress from where she'd tossed it earlier and shimmied into it. Then she backed up to Cooper and said, "Zip?"

He sighed, zipped her dress and took a step back. "Go away, Celeste. Seriously. I'm not in the mood for whatever you're playing."

Turning around to face him, she looked him dead in the eye to say, "Before I go, you should know that Terri was here."

"What?" He grabbed her upper arms. "When?"

"About a half hour ago." She bent down, picked up the towel and handed it to him. "She found me wearing this. I told her you were in the shower, waiting for me to join you."

A hot jolt of anger erupted. At her. At himself for letting it come to this. "Damn you, Celeste. Why the hell would you do that to her? She *likes* you."

"Because I wanted you back," she said, fluffing her hair then smoothing her palms over her hips. "I decided that I could get rid of Terri and have you to myself."

"No, you can't," he said tightly. "What we had is long dead, Celeste. Not interested in a replay."

Her eyebrows arched. "Not kind, but sadly a truth I'm forced to accept. I don't like it. Comfortable lies are so much easier to live with than hard truths.

"Do you know, until I met Terri, I hadn't told the truth to people in years. Somehow, I think she infected me with her honesty." Smiling wryly, she said, "She was my friend and I've ruined that now. I'm sorry for it."

"You've ruined a hell of a lot more than that."

"No. More truth for you, Cooper. The ruin between you and Terri, you've done yourself. She's not like us, Cooper," Celeste said. "She's real. When she offers her heart, it has no strings. No expectation for reward. It simply *is*."

Cooper scrubbed both hands across his face. She was right and he knew it. Hell, he'd known it all along. Terri was different. Terri said what she thought and didn't have a dishonest bone in her body. And he hadn't trusted her. Because he'd lived for so long looking cynically at everything, he hadn't recognized *honest* when it finally showed up.

Damn it. He'd let her get away. He'd had something real. Something most people never found and he'd let it go.

"I'm leaving," Celeste said. "If you see Terri again—"

"If?"

"—please tell her I'm sorry for hurting her."

"What do you mean *if* I see her?" Cooper demanded.

"Didn't I tell you? She left."

Panic nearly blinded him. "Left? Left for where?"

"She said to St. George, in Utah somewhere. Her mother's house." Celeste swung her black leather bag across her shoulder, opened the door, then stopped. "She loves you, you know."

"How do you know?" Cooper's gaze snapped to hers. "Did she tell you that?"

"Yes."

"Well, she didn't tell *me*!" And why the hell not? In the midst of that fight they'd had, why hadn't she thrown those words at him? Looking for sympathy or an edge into wheedling him around to her way of thinking and—that was exactly why she hadn't told him.

Terri didn't play games.

Celeste shook her head at him and asked sadly, "Can you blame her? Don't be foolish, Cooper. Go after her. I once walked away from you. I don't recommend it."

* * *

"Who does this?" Terri demanded as they barreled down the highway toward St. George in her brand-new, shiny red convertible.

Jan stroked the leather dashboard as she would a lover. "Who cares? He bought you a car before he turned into Jerk Of The Year. Call it a win and let it go."

"It's not that easy." Of course Cooper would do something like this. When she'd joined Jan at the valet stand, the car was waiting for her.

"That's not my car," she'd said.

"Yes, ma'am, it is," the valet said. "Mr. Hayes bought it for you a week ago. Said you needed to drive something decent."

When her eyes fired, the young valet backed up fast and hid in the valet booth. She couldn't blame him. Naturally, Jan was thrilled with the new car and had hopped right in.

Terri, though, turned and shot a hard look at the top of the hotel as if she could glare at Cooper from there. He just tossed her car aside and got her a new one without bothering to tell her? What kind of person did that?

Cooper had bought this car for her a week ago, back when he was supposedly still softening her up to get rid of her. Why would he do it? And why hadn't he said anything to her about the car, just waiting to let her discover it on her own? Why wouldn't he have told her?

But even as she mentally did gymnastics trying to convince herself that Cooper wasn't really the bastard Jan had named him, Terri remembered Celeste. In his suite. Wearing a towel. About to join said bastard in the shower.

Nothing could have been clearer than that, right? The sting of tears hit her eyes again and she was grateful for the sunglasses she wore. Terri didn't want Jan to see her cry over him. Heck, she didn't want to see *herself* cry any more tears over Cooper. She'd cried a river and it hadn't helped. Hadn't changed a thing.

"Come on, Terri, admit it." Jan shouted to be heard over the roar of the wind. "Your car was on its last legs—wheels. It wasn't going to last another winter."

"It didn't have to make it through snow. It lived in Las Vegas now."

"And now you have a Vegas car." Shaking her head and throwing her arms high to feel the wind rushing at them, Jan said, "A shiny, showgirl car! Red convertible, girl! Look on the bright side. You have this great car that had to cost him a fortune. *And,* you're not going anywhere, so you're going to totally ruin his day. Every day."

Slowly, Terri smiled and stepped harder on the gas. "You have a point. How fast can we get to Mom's house, do you think?"

Jan grinned. "Let's find out."

Terri didn't bother to knock. She just walked into the small, lovely house her mother and aunt shared. It was a two-bedroom, two-bath Spanish-style patio home on the golf course. Connie spent most days out on the patio, checking out the retired golfers, looking for her fourth husband.

Terri's mom spent most days laughing at Connie.

"Mom?" She stepped into the entryway, with Jan right behind her. She'd expected to have her mom and aunt running to greet her. And if not that, at least she had thought her *dog* would be glad to see her.

"Seems awfully quiet. Maybe they're not home," Jan said, peeking into the living room as Terri closed the door. "Uh-oh."

"What? What's wrong?" Terri pushed past her and

stopped dead when she spotted Cooper, comfortably seated on her mother's couch, the traitorous Daisy stretched out across his lap. "Cooper—"

"Terri, honey!" Her mother rushed in from the kitchen, carrying a wooden tray holding a frosted pitcher of iced tea, three glasses and a plate of cookies. "You made wonderful time. That new car Cooper gave you must be a wonder to drive."

"I. He. What?" Terri shook her head, stared from Cooper to her mother and back again. "How do you know about the car?"

"Well, Cooper told me, of course." Carol Ferguson shook her head, then smoothed her perfect blond hair. "It was a relief to me, I'll admit it. Your poor old car was running on prayers."

"A relief," Cooper repeated softly.

Terri glared at him.

"You should have seen his arrival," her mother said, practically glowing as she looked at Cooper. "Do you know, his helicopter landed right on the golf course? People will be talking about it for months!"

"Helicopter?"

He shrugged and continued petting Daisy. "My pilot put down quickly, then took off again. I don't think it did any harm to the course itself."

"Oh, I'm sure it didn't," Carol said. "It was so exciting."

"I bet," Terri said.

"Your mom's been very nice, letting me stay to wait for you," Cooper said, his long, clever fingers rubbing Daisy's belly until the dog was a quivering bowl of jelly.

"Your dog's a traitor," Jan whispered and walked over to give Terri's mom a big hug.

"So good to see you, sweetheart," Mom said. "I love your hair."

Jan grinned, then shifted a hard-eyed look on Cooper. "I'm glad to see you, too, Mom. But I sort of question your taste in guests."

"Now, Jan…"

"Nice to meet you, too," Cooper said wryly.

"Why don't I just go and get a few more glasses for the tea," Carol said, taking Jan's arm and dragging her off, too. She called back over her shoulder, "Connie's assaulting one of the golfers but she should be along soon…"

In the quiet of the living room, Terri felt completely off balance. In a million years, she never would have expected to find Cooper here. With her mom. And her dog. All comfy and cozy.

The living room was bright and cheerful, with a vase of fall flowers in the center of the coffee table. The furniture was plain but good quality and thanks to her mother, the room was tidy, tables polished, the scent of the flowers flavoring the air. The blinds were open, allowing the fall sun to slant into the room and paint gold stripes on the floor.

And while she stalled, looking at a room that she knew as well as her own home, Cooper watched her. She couldn't tell what he was thinking and she wished she could. But she knew very well what she was *feeling*, so she went with that.

"Why are you here?"

"Because you are."

"Cooper—"

"I needed to talk to you, Terri," he said, "and you'd already left the hotel."

She shot a dirty look at Daisy who was now doing the dog version of a purr. "I suppose I should thank you for the car."

"But you don't want to."

"No, I don't." She shifted her glare to him. "You got rid of my car without so much as asking me."

"Your car was a disgrace to all cars everywhere."

She took a breath. Hard to argue that point, but she tried. "It wasn't any of your business."

"You're welcome."

Daisy sighed and opened one eye to look at Terri as if to say, *Don't ruin this for me.*

"I like your dog."

"She's apparently a shameless tramp with very low standards in men."

He winced at that barb. "I also like your mom and her sister. Though your mom warned me to watch out for your aunt Connie."

Terri brushed that aside. Why were they talking about this? About things that didn't matter. "You're not Connie's type. She likes them rich and old enough to not last long."

He laughed shortly and the sound tore at her. How could he be acting like nothing was wrong?

"I'm so sorry you had to cut your shower with Celeste short," she said. "That must have been painful for both of you."

He scowled at her. "I know what she told you. Damn it. I wasn't even there when you stopped by my room. Celeste set the whole thing up to get me back, to chase you off."

Terri swayed from the impact of his words. She'd liked Celeste. And somehow the fact that she had lied to Terri was almost worse than the thought that she'd been showering with Cooper. Almost. "Seems there was a lot of that going on. Dave, Celeste, *you*, all working overtime to get rid of me."

"Seems like it worked, too." Cooper gave Daisy one last stroke, then set her aside and stood up. Shoving both hands into the pockets of his slacks, he said, "Celeste told me you left. That you came here."

"It *didn't* work," Terri countered, taking a step farther

into the room. "I'm not leaving Las Vegas, Cooper. I only came here to get my dog. Then I'm going back to the StarFire. You can't force me out. I won't go."

"Good."

"Just because you think— What?"

"I said good." He walked closer in a few long, determined strides. "I don't want you to go."

"Well, that's news to me," she said, because she couldn't believe him. Not anymore. "You told me just last night that the plan had always been to get rid of me. To buy me out."

"Yeah, it was." He yanked one hand free, rubbed the back of his neck, then pinned her with an ice-blue gaze she couldn't look away from. "Hell, Jacob sprung you on me. I didn't even know you existed and suddenly I acquired a partner. One who didn't know anything about the business. I was pissed. But then, things changed."

"Really? Last night you accused me of backstabbing you."

"Yeah, see, this is why I had to talk to you. I was wrong."

Terri blinked at him and shook her head as if she hadn't heard him right. "Well, there's something I never thought I'd hear from you."

"If you need me to say it again, I will," Cooper ground out. "I won't enjoy it, but I'll do it." He came closer and Terri stood her ground, not giving an inch. "Dave told me everything. How he was working against me all these years. How he used you. How even if his plan with you had failed, he was prepared to sell me out once he got what he thought he deserved. And I never saw it in him.

"But even if he hadn't confessed, I never should have thought it was you. It's just not your style, Terri. You're so damn honest it's a shock to most people. Apparently, even to me."

She heard the pain in his voice and her instinct was to soothe. To offer comfort. But she didn't. Because he'd hurt *her*. But that sounded so damn petty, she had to say, "I'm sorry about your friend."

"You really are, aren't you?" Shaking his head, he reached for her but she moved away. His hands fell to his sides. "Even after everything he did. Everything I did. I was a complete ass last night."

"No argument here."

A wry smile curved his mouth briefly. "I didn't expect one. But I am so damn sorry. I've spent so many years dealing with people who always have an agenda, I forgot what it was like to be around someone who didn't."

"As apologies go, that was pretty good," she admitted. Her heart hurt, just looking at him. Everything in her wanted to go into his arms and feel him hold her. But she didn't, because they still had more to say.

"I'm just getting started," he said and this time when he reached out to cup her shoulders, she didn't slide out of his grasp. "You're the best thing that ever happened to me and I don't want to lose you. I want to start each day looking into your eyes. I want to hold you while we fall asleep together. You're everything I need, Terri. That's why I'm here."

"I thought you came to talk to me."

"Well, yeah, and to ask you to marry me."

"Marry you?"

He grinned. "Yes. I want us to be together. Always. A team. Terri, we're great together and I want it to be permanent. A commitment. From each of us."

Terri didn't even know how to react.

"We can build a house because I know you want kids and so do I and maybe a hotel isn't the best place to raise them—"

"Kids?" Her heart picked up speed and her breath got short and fast.

"Yes, a family. " He pulled her in close enough that she had to tip her head back to look into ice-blue eyes that were suddenly as warm as a summer lake. "You love me," he said. "Celeste told me."

"Celeste had a lot to say," Terri muttered.

"And I love you," Cooper said softly.

"You do?" she whispered.

"Of course I do. Why do you think I'm here? Why do you think I bought you that car so you wouldn't end up broken down on the side of the road in the middle of the desert? I loved you even then. I just didn't want to."

"And now you do."

"Now I have no choice," he muttered. "I want you. I need you. I love you. One night without you and I was going nuts. I kept reaching for you during the night and you weren't there. Damned if I'll spend another night like last night."

"I missed you, too," she said. "But after last night, I thought it was over."

"It's never going to be over for us, Terri," he said, his gaze moving over her features like a gentle touch. "We're supposed to be together. I get that now. And we'll build the damn house wherever you want it—"

"No."

"No? What do you mean *no*?" His brow furrowed, he stared at her through narrowed eyes.

"I mean, we'll live at the hotel. My suite is huge, so I'm sure yours is big enough for a family…"

"Six thousand square feet," he told her. "Five bedrooms, six bathrooms."

"Oh, my God." She laughed up at him. "Yeah, that's big enough. And we have the roof garden—we can make the Plexiglas higher…"

"If that's what you want, sure."

"And Jan's going to be living in my suite so—"

His eyebrows went high on his forehead. "You mean your friend who hates me?"

Terri grinned. "I hired her as my executive assistant."

He grinned back at her. "Of course you did. And you'll probably have better luck with your best friend than I had with mine."

"I'm sorry about Dave."

"Yeah," he said. "Me, too. Well, if we're going to be neighbors, I'll buy Jan a car so she'll like me."

"No, you won't—"

"I like red, too," Jan called from the kitchen.

"Perfect." Terri laughed and leaned her forehead against his chest.

"See?" Cooper grinned and he looked so wildly happy that Terri's heart fluttered. "She likes me already. So does your mom. And your aunt. And you love me, Terri. Tell me you love me."

She looked up at him. "I love you. And yes, I'll marry you."

"Damn straight." He kissed her hard and fast, then let her go long enough to dig into his pocket for a small, black velvet jewelry box. He flipped the lid open and Terri gasped. "It's a star sapphire. Like the StarFire. And the diamonds around it are just for show."

Shaken, she held her left hand out and he slid the ring onto her finger. The stone was huge, with a blast of color at the heart of it, looking just like a star. The setting was gorgeous and it fit as if made for her. "It's a beautiful show."

"Are you sure you want to live at the hotel?" he asked. "What about your fear of heights?"

Sighing, she said, "As it turns out, the only thing I'm afraid of is losing you."

His thumbs smoothed over her cheeks. "Never gonna happen. You and I are a hell of a team, Terri. And that's how it's going to stay."

"I do love you so much, Cooper."

"I'll never get tired of hearing it."

"Can we come out now?" Carol Ferguson called. "We'd love to see the ring!"

"In a minute," Cooper shouted, then whispered to only Terri. "First things first."

He kissed her and Terri gave herself up to him. To the man she would build dreams with.

And together, they'd watch those dreams come true.

* * * * *

HOT CHRISTMAS KISSES

JOSS WOOD

Prologue

Christmas, the year before

In a rural part of Devon, three thousand miles from her home in Boston, Massachusetts, DJ Winston smoothed her hands over the maroon-and-silver dress and turned to face her computer screen.

Her two best friends, twins Darby and Jules Brogan, lounged on Jules's couch in her office back in Massachusetts, coffee cups on the table in front of them. As was their custom, they'd shortly be closing their business for the Christmas break, ending the year by treating their staff to lunch.

"Send everybody my love and tell them I hope they have a lovely minivacation."

DJ ignored Darby rolling her eyes at DJ's inability to wish anyone a merry Christmas. She tried, she really did, but the words always got stuck in her throat.

*Merry Christmas! Happy holidays! Ho, ho, ho…*nope, she couldn't do it. She could talk interest rates and contract terms, equity and cash flow, but she stuttered and stammered her way through December. The festive—hah!—season made her feel like she was eight again, alone, frightened and wondering why neither of her parents loved her.

DJ knew the twins would like to discuss her antipathy toward Christmas, but it was, like so many other subjects, off-limits.

DJ adored the twins, but she believed in keeping some distance between her and the people she loved. Distance was her safety net, her belay rope, her life vest. Distance was how she'd always protected herself. And since it had worked for her as a child and as a teen, what was the point of changing her strategy now?

Darby cocked her head to one side. "That dress looks fantastic with your dark hair and eyes, DJ."

Jules nodded her agreement. "Vibrant colors suit you. But with your height and build, anything looks good on you, you know that."

She didn't, though.

While the twins saw her as attractive, she still saw herself as the gangly, dark-haired teenager who embarrassed her blond, blue-eyed mother. DJ was smart enough, Fenella reluctantly admitted, but she was too tall, too lanky, with not enough charm. So Fenella said when she was in a good mood.

DJ tried not to remember the words Fenella let fly when she was angry.

"What shoes are you wearing?" Darby asked.

"My Jimmy Choos, the ones you made me buy last week." DJ nodded to the sexy silver shoes on the bed.

"So…" Darby drawled. "When is Matt arriving?"

DJ released an irritated sigh. "He's not."

"He stood you up? Nice Christmas present." Jules was sarcasm personified.

DJ sighed. Darby and Jules didn't understand that her and Matt Edwards's ad hoc arrangement worked for them, as it had for the past six years. Depending on their schedules, she and Matt met for a night or a weekend. That was when DJ stepped out of her life, pushing aside numbers and profit margins, cash-flow issues and cost projections. When she was with Matt, she allowed herself the freedom to be another version of herself—fun-loving, exuberant and sensuous.

Neither she nor Matt had any expectations, and DJ was very conscious of the fact that, despite making this unusual situation last for many years, their arrangement was a temporary thing.

They had no ties to each other, nothing to bind them except for the expectation of good sex, a few laughs and a relaxing time spent in undemanding company. She didn't need more. A partner, boyfriend or permanent lover wasn't something she wanted for herself; after being abandoned by her father and rejected by Fenella, DJ wasn't prepared to hand over her battered heart to another human to kick around. She was keeping possession of that fragile organ.

Spontaneous weekends spent with Matt worked well for her, but yesterday he'd blown her off, saying that he, despite it being Christmas, needed to stay in the Netherlands, to consult with a client who was in a world of hurt. Because Matt was a fantastically successful human-rights lawyer, *hurt* could mean his client was a political refugee ducking prison time, or a tribe of aboriginal people who'd been kicked off their ancestral land and were facing the imminent loss of their culture and way of life.

The fact that his on-and-off lover needed to escape Christmas and was horny as hell didn't nudge the needle of his what-international-laws-did-this-violate? scale.

DJ had considered missing her friend's wedding but that meant *doing* Christmas in Boston. Ugh. Attending this Christmas Eve wedding was the lesser of two evils.

Her friends on the screen were still waiting for her response. Right, they'd been discussing Matt's non-arrival. "We have an understanding that work always comes first. He's tied up doing something terribly important."

What he wasn't doing was her.

DJ pulled a face, glanced at the corner clock on her laptop screen and sighed. "I'd better slap on some makeup or else I'm going to be late for the church service."

Darby frowned and waved at DJ's dress. "Take that off first. You do not want to get makeup on that dress."

Good point. Friends since kindergarten, she was superbly comfortable disrobing in front of them. Allowing them to see her messed-up inner world was what she found difficult. DJ gently pulled the dress over her head and laid it on the bed.

Jules whistled. "Push-up bra, tiny thong, heels. Edwards has no idea what he's missing out on."

"I agree."

That voice.

DJ whipped her head up and looked toward the doorway. Her heart, stupid thing, did cartwheels in her chest.

Matt, a shoulder pressed to the doorframe, looked as effortlessly sexy as he always did. A tall blond with deep green eyes and a surfer's tan, he had the face and body to advertise sun, sea and sex. He didn't look like what he was: a brilliant international lawyer with a steel-trap mind.

The moisture in DJ's mouth disappeared and it took all her willpower not to run to him and start removing his clothes. She desperately wanted to slide the cream linen jacket down his arms and rip apart his navy button-down shirt. The leather belt would be next, and she'd soon have the buttons of his designer jeans undone. In her hand he'd be hot and hard...

It had always been this way. Matt just had to look at her with those incredibly green eyes and she went from cool and collected to crazy in ten seconds flat. She didn't love him—hell, she barely knew him—but, damn, she craved his mouth, his hands on all her long neglected and secret places.

Okay, try to hold it together. For God's sake, be cool.

"I thought you couldn't make it," DJ said, wincing at the happy note in her voice. *Yeah, opposite of cool, Winston.*

She glanced at her dress lying on the bed, considered slipping it on and then shrugged. Why bother? Matt had seen everything she had, more than once.

Matt stepped into the room, walking with a grace not many big men possessed. "My client was delayed."

Matt crossed the room to her and his hand lifted to cradle her face, his thumb brushing across her lower lip. He looked down, and she felt the heat of his gaze on the tiny triangle low on her hips and her equally frivolous bra. She was, in turn, both entranced and brutally turned on by the passion flaring in his eyes. Being wanted by this sexy man always shot a ray of enhanced sunshine through her veins.

"Nice outfit, Dylan-Jane," Matt said when their eyes locked again, his voice extra growly.

He was the only person, apart from her mother, who'd ever called her by her full name, and on Matt's lips it was a caress rather than a curse.

"Hi."

The single-syllable greeting was all her tangled tongue could manage.

"Hi back." Matt lowered his mouth to hers and as their lips touched they both hesitated, as they always did. DJ had no idea why Matt waited but she enjoyed stretching out the moment, ramping up the anticipation. Yes, she was desperate for his touch, but she also wanted to make the moment last. The first kiss, after so long apart, was always exceptional.

Finally, Matt's clever mouth touched hers and it was, as always, sweet and sexy—a little rediscovery and a whole bunch of familiarity. The kisses they'd exchange later would be out of control, like a wildfire, but this one was tender and, in its way, as soul-deep sexy as what would come later.

Talking about later...

It took everything DJ had to pull her mouth off his, to drop her hands from that wide, warm chest. "If we don't get dressed we're going to be late for the wedding."

"Yeah, you have about fifteen minutes to get out of that room to beat the bride to the church."

DJ yelped at Darby's dry voice. DJ took a step to the side to look past Matt's arm to the computer screen. Her friends were still there, both looking worried. DJ was thankful that they'd only had a view of Matt's broad back and truly excellent butt during that kiss.

"Hey, Matt," Darby said.

Matt pinched the bridge of his nose, shook his head

and rolled his eyes at DJ. With a rueful smile he turned around and looked at the screen. "Ladies."

"Well done for arriving in the nick of time," Jules said, her voice tart.

Matt just raised one sandy, arrogant eyebrow. Then he stepped up to the desk, looked down at the screen and smiled. "'Bye, ladies." He closed the lid to the laptop and turned back to face DJ.

"I've missed you."

DJ tipped back her head to look into his eyes, her cynical side wondering if he said that as a way to talk her into bed. But the look on his face was sincere, his eyes radiating honesty. Besides, Matt didn't use coercion. She was either fully on board or he backed off; Matt did not whine or beg or force.

Besides, they both knew she was going to slide into bed with him the moment she saw him standing in the doorway. She was putty in his hands.

"You, half-naked in sexy lingerie, is my early Christmas present." Matt lifted a curl off her forehead and tucked it behind her ear. His mouth curled up into a deprecating half smile. "But I'm embarrassed to tell you that I hightailed it out of my office to make my flight and I've been rushing ever since. I didn't want to be late, so I didn't stop to buy condoms. You wouldn't happen to have any, would you?"

DJ shook her head. Well, crap. Matt never, ever made love to her without one.

"So, damn. No condoms. Maybe we should go to the church and pick this up later."

Oh, hell, no.

"Or we could just carry on…" DJ ran her finger down his hard erection before fumbling with the snap on his pants.

Matt groaned. "Dylan-Jane, oral isn't enough. I need to be inside you. I'll go pick up some condoms and come back. We'll miss the service, but we could still make the reception."

Hearing his rough, growly, frustrated voice, DJ melted. "I'm on the pill, Matt. I'm clean, there hasn't been anyone since we last hooked up, and if you can tell me you are…"

Matt nodded. "Yeah, I am." He kissed her lips before pulling back again. "Can I trust you with this, Dylan-Jane? There won't be any unexpected surprises?"

If he knew her better, he wouldn't have to ask. Sure, the time they spent together was a fantasy, hot and wild, but that wasn't the person she was in real life. In Boston, she didn't do the unexpected and she hated surprises. Her life was planned, regulated, controlled.

And a baby was Darby's dream, not DJ's.

"I've got this, Matt." DJ pushed his pants and boxers down his hips, wound her arms around his strong neck and lowered her mouth onto his, whispering her words against his lips. "Come inside me, Matt, it's been too damn long."

Matt didn't hesitate, quickly pushing her panties to the side. He slid inside her, held her there and then lowered her to the bed. Gathering her to him, DJ knew that he'd try to be a gentleman—he always tried to make their first encounter together slow and reverential. She didn't need either—she needed hot and hard and fast.

"Matt, I need to burn," DJ told him in a tortured whisper.

Matt pushed himself up and slowly rolled his hips. When she released a low moan, he smiled.

He had a repertoire of smiles, from distracted to

dozy, but this one was her favorite: part pirate, part choirboy, all wicked.

"Well, then, let's light a match, Dylan-Jane."

Matt slid his hands under her hips, lifted her up, slammed into her and catapulted her into that white-hot, delicious fire she'd longed for.

She was almost, but not quite, tempted to murmur "Merry Christmas to me."

One

Nearly a year later...

In the public area at Logan International Airport, Matt Edwards ignored the crowds and maneuvered his way around the flower bearers and card holders. He'd mastered the art of walking and working his smartphone: there were ten messages from his office and a few text messages. None, dammit, were from Dylan-Jane.

Despite reaching out over a week ago, she'd yet to give him a definitive answer about them getting together in Boston.

Maybe she was making him wait because he'd been out of touch for so long. But he'd been busy and it just happened that they'd had less contact this year than usual. A lot less. But he was here now, and he was hopeful they could recapture some of their old magic.

"Matt!"

Matt turned, saw the tall frame of his old friend Noah Lockwood striding toward him and smiled. Well, this was a pleasant surprise.

Matt pushed his phone into the inside pocket of his black jacket before shaking Noah's hand. "It's great to see you, but what are you doing here?"

Noah fell into step beside him. "I've just dropped Jules off. She's flying to New York to meet a client. I knew you were coming in today, saw the flight times and thought I'd buy you a beer."

An excellent plan. It had been months, maybe even more than a year, since he and Noah had exchanged anything other than a brief phone call or a catch-up email. At college, they'd been tight, and despite their busy lives, he still considered Noah a friend.

Noah had also introduced Matt to DJ, and for that he'd always be grateful.

"I'd love a beer."

They walked to the nearest bar and Matt headed to two empty seats at the far end of the joint, tucking his suitcase between him and the wall before he slid onto the barstool. Within minutes he had a glass of an expensive microbrew in front of him.

Noah raised his glass and an enquiring eyebrow. "What brings you back to Boston?"

How to answer? Matt ignored the ache in that triangle where his ribs met. This visit, unlike those quick visits to see his grandfather, was going to be…difficult.

Emotional. Draining. Challenging.

All the things he most tried to avoid.

"I'm moving my grandfather into an assisted-living facility." Stock answer.

Noah looked surprised. "The judge is moving out of his home? Why?"

Matt took a sip of his beer before rubbing his eyes. "He's showing signs of dementia and Alzheimer's. He can't live on his own anymore."

"I'm sorry to hear that," Noah said. "How long are you going to be in town for?"

Matt tapped his finger against his glass. "I'm not sure, but since I don't have any court appearances scheduled until the New Year, probably until after Christmas. So, for the next three weeks at least."

Noah's eyes were steady on his face and Matt felt the vague urge to tell his friend the other reason he was in Boston. But talking wasn't something he found easy to do.

Noah didn't push, but changed the subject by asking another question. "So, are you going to contact DJ while you're in town?"

Matt sent Noah a sour look. "Who's asking, you or your fiancée?"

Noah grinned. "Jules's last words to me weren't 'I love you, you're such a stud,' but 'get Matt to tell you why he and DJ haven't spoken for nearly a year.'"

Matt shook his head. "You are so whipped, man."

Noah just grinned.

"I thought Jules and Darby would be happy to hear that DJ and I drifted apart. They aren't my biggest fans."

Noah rubbed the back of his neck. "Look, I'm in the middle here. I introduced you to DJ but I never expected your no-strings affair to last for years. I've told the twins to leave you two alone. You are adults and you both know what you are doing.

"But they love her and they are worried about her," Noah added.

Matt's head shot up. "Why are they worried about her?"

Noah released a soft curse. "You've got to know how much I love Jules, because if I didn't, I wouldn't ever consider broaching this subject."

Yep, whipped. If Matt wasn't the subject of the conversation, he'd find Noah's dilemma amusing. "The twins are worried because she hasn't been the same this past year. She's been quieter, more reserved, less… happy," Noah told him.

Matt filled in the blanks. "And they are blaming me for that?"

"Not so much blaming as looking for an explanation. DJ isn't talking, so my fiancée, damn her, asked me to ask you. Man, I sound like a teenager."

"So you didn't just accost me to have a beer?"

"The beer was an added incentive," Noah said, obviously uncomfortable. "Look, forget it, Matt. It's not my or Jules's business and I feel like a dick raising the subject."

Matt wanted to be annoyed but he wasn't. He'd always envied the friendship Dylan-Jane and the twins shared. They were a tight unit and would go to war for each other. He'd been self-sufficient for as long as he could remember, and his busy career didn't allow time for close friendships. It certainly didn't allow time for a relationship.

Matt carefully picked his words. "DJ and I have an understanding. Neither of us are looking for something permanent. I'm sorry if she's had a tough year but I don't think it's related to me. We were very clear about our expectations and we agreed there would be no hard feelings if life, or other people, got in the way of us seeing each other."

"Other people? Are you seeing someone else?"

Was Noah kidding? It had been a hell of a year and

he hadn't needed the added aggravation of dating some-one new. He'd had a slew of tough cases and he'd been sideswiped by explosive news and saddened by an ex's untimely death. And he was now required to make life-changing decisions for his once brilliant grandfather.

Starting something new with someone new when he was feeling emotionally battered wasn't the solution to anything. As a teenager he'd learned the hard lesson that emotion and need were a dangerous combination.

He'd fallen in love at sixteen and he'd walked around drunk on emotion. His ex, Gemma, and he had made their plans: they'd graduate, go to college, get married, have kids…and they'd feel like this forever. She was the one, his everything…

At seventeen she'd informed him she was pregnant. A part of him had been ecstatic at the news of them hav-ing a baby—this would be the family he'd never really had, his to protect, his to love. *His*. All his…

After ten days of secret planning, and heart-to-heart discussions, Gemma flipped on him, telling him she'd miscarried and was moving across town and chang-ing schools.

She didn't love him, she never really had…

He'd vowed then that love was a myth, that it was a manipulative tactic, that it didn't really exist. His par-ents, his grandparents, Gemma—they all proved his point. At seventeen, he'd dismissed love and forever as a fabrication and nothing since had changed his mind.

He now believed in sex, and having lots of it safely, but love? Not a chance.

And sex, in his mind, meant DJ.

DJ didn't want anything permanent, either. Just like him, she was allergic to commitment. They spent just enough time together to enjoy each other but not enough to become close. It was the perfect setup...

Or it had been.

He was back in Boston, in her city, and he saw no reason not to meet. It had been too long since he'd held her, since he'd tasted her skin, inhaled her fruity scent, heard her laugh. DJ, fun-loving, exuberant and sensuous, was exactly the medicine he needed. She'd be a distraction from thinking about how to handle the bombshell news he still hadn't wrapped his head around.

Matt looked at Noah. "I really don't know what's going on in DJ's life, but I doubt it has anything to do with me."

Noah drained his beer. "Are you going to see her while you're in Boston?"

Of course he was. "Yeah."

"Then I've been told to tell you that if you hurt her, they'll stab you with a broken beer bottle."

Matt rolled his eyes. DJ's friends were fierce. "Understood. But, as I said, we have a solid understanding."

Noah lifted his hands. "Just the messenger here." He pulled some cash out of his wallet and ignored Matt's offer to contribute. "If you don't want to spend the next month or so in a hotel, you're welcome to use the carriage house at Lockwood House. When we are home, Jules and I live in the main house."

Noah's property was, if Matt remembered correctly, the cornerstone of a very upmarket, expensive golfing community north of Boston. It was a generous offer and Matt appreciated it. "Thank you. That would be great."

"It was Jules's idea. That way she can keep an eye on you." Noah smiled. "And you do know that our house is directly opposite where Darby, DJ and Levi Brogan live? The same Levi Brogan who is superprotective and has no idea that you've been sleeping with the woman he loves like a sister for the last five-plus years?"

Oh, crap.

"It's going to be fun watching you tap-dance around him," Noah said before he clapped Matt on the shoulder and walked out of the bar.

Matt looked down at his phone and automatically stabbed his finger on the gallery icon. He flicked through the images of Dylan-Jane, memories sliding over him, and stopped when he came to a topless photo he'd snapped of her lying on the sand on a private beach in St. Barts. She was facing the sea but had turned her head back to look at him and the camera, her sable hair skimming the sand. She was all golden gorgeousness— flashing dark eyes, flushed cheeks, rosy nipples on her perky, tanned breasts.

Unable to resist her, he'd picked her up and carried her to the water, where they'd had amazing sea sex.

He had lots of great memories of DJ but, hell, making love to her in the sea and later on the sand was one of his favorites.

He desperately wanted to make more memories…

Shaking his head, Matt pulled up his last chat with DJ and quickly skimmed over the words they'd exchanged over the past week. He'd told her that he'd be in Boston the following week and asked if they could meet. DJ had sent him a surprised-face emoji as a reply…

Matt frowned. A surprised face wasn't a yes…

Neither was it a no…

What it was, was a strange way for DJ to respond.

She'd always been up-front and honest about telling him her plans, whether she could meet him or not. They didn't play games, didn't lie. They either wanted to be together, for a day or three or four, or they didn't. They could either make time for each other, or they couldn't. This year they hadn't managed to meet and that was just the way life went. He presumed she was busy managing her rapidly expanding design firm and he'd had his all-consuming work and the additional personal dramas to deal with...

But could she be dating someone else?

Matt's stomach tightened and he told himself to get a grip. He had no right to be jealous. They'd both agreed they couldn't expect to be monogamous when they were so far apart. He had been for the past year but that was more through circumstances than choice. They'd agreed to be honest with each other, to tell each other if someone else was on the scene. He hadn't had a text or phone call or email from DJ saying that. In fact, since late March, she hadn't reached out to him once. Previously, he'd received the odd email from her, funny memes that made him laugh, silly selfies she took.

Matt frowned, remembering that her friends were worried about her, that they thought something was wrong. Was she sick? Busy? Annoyed?

Or, worse, done with him, with what they had?

His phone beeped again and this time it was a text message. The distinct tone told him who it was from.

Hi. I'm not ready. Can I take some more time?

Sure, he replied. No pressure. I'm in town until after Christmas, unless something urgent comes up.

Right, he had no choice now but to wait until the daughter Gemma had never told him about decided to contact him again. And he wasn't visiting his grandfather until tomorrow.

So, what could he do with the rest of his day?

Mmm, maybe he could drop in to see Dylan-Jane. See whether there was a chance of them taking up where they'd last left off...

And, he admitted, he could see for himself whether she was happy or not.

In the coffee shop on the Lockwood Estate, Mason James delivered an espresso to the student sitting at the table in the corner and glanced at the complex math equation the kid was solving.

Because math had once been his thing, Mason scanned the guy's rough notes and immediately saw where he'd gone wrong. Mason opened his mouth to point out the mistake before pulling back.

Three years ago, complex situations and equations, troubleshooting and problem-solving, was what he'd done for a living and he'd made a stupid amount of money from it. The responsibility of the problems he'd been given to solve—some of them with life-and-death outcomes—had generated enough stress to elevate his blood pressure to dangerous levels and burn a hole in his stomach. It had also ended his marriage and threatened his relationships with his sons.

So Mason got out of the think-tank business, buying a chic coffee shop to keep himself busy. He attended his boys' ice hockey and baseball games, played video games with them and helped them with their homework. He delivered coffee, muffins and pastries and told himself it was good to be bored.

Boredom didn't place a strain on his heart, or burn that hole deeper into his stomach.

Mason turned away and then heard the low curse. He looked around to see the student putting his head in his hands, tugging his hair in obvious frustration. It was, for him, simple math. What harm could it do to help?

Mason turned back, scanned the equation and tapped a line. "Rework this line."

Blue eyes flew up to meet his and Mason saw the doubt.

"With respect, I'm in the doctorate program at MIT..."

Mason shrugged and waited him out. He didn't bother to tell the guy that he'd been through that program and many more. He just tapped the line again until the kid finally turned his attention back to the equation. His brow furrowed and then he released a long sigh. Yep, the light had dawned.

"Hey, thanks so much."

Mason smiled briefly before retracing his steps back to his small kitchen. Before he reached his destination, he heard the muted ping that indicated he had a customer. He didn't need to see who was pulling the door open—his heart was way ahead of his eyes and it was already picking up speed.

Mason leaned his shoulder onto the nearest wall and watched his current obsession walk into his coffee shop, followed by a brunette clutching a stack of bridal magazines. The older of Callie's twin daughters, he remembered—Jules. Callie had her arm around Jules's waist and love for her child on her face.

Callie Brogan was a beautiful mom.

Mason ran his hand over his face. The last thing he was looking for when he opened Coffee Connection was to be attracted to a stunning, ebullient, charming widow. Yeah, she was older than him but who the hell cared? He could date younger woman, *had* dated many of them, and none of them captured his interest like Cal-

lie Brogan did. It was unexplainable and not something
he could wish away.

God knew he'd tried.

Callie's head shot up and her eyes locked on his.
Electricity arced between them and his pants, as they
always did when she was in the room, tightened. Even
though he was across the room, he could see her nipples
respond—God, her breasts were fantastic. A flush appeared on her throat, down her chest. Despite her pro-
tests, Callie was as aware of him, as attracted to him,
as he was to her...

Why hadn't they ended up in bed already?

Oh, because she wasn't ready and because she was
still in love with her dead husband.

Mason looked up at the ceiling and shook his head.
His was said to be one of the most brilliant minds of
his generation, yet he was flummoxed by how to get
this woman to sleep with him.

That's all he wanted, some fantastic sex with an attractive, interesting woman. He wasn't looking for love
or forever—as a scientist, he didn't believe in either.
The human species simply wasn't that evolved. But sex,
a few hot nights? Yeah, he most certainly believed in
man's most primal urge.

Mason started toward her—he couldn't stay away
if he tried—but the infinitesimal shake of her head
stopped him.

Right, he wasn't wanted. He should go and count
stock or take out the trash or do his taxes.

Simple, stress-free jobs he could do with his eyes
closed. But so blah and boring. Looking through the
huge windows of his shop, he wished he could go cave-
man on Callie. He'd toss her over his shoulder and put
her behind him on his Ducati—in his fantasy it was

spring or summer—and ride away. When he reached the first isolated area, he'd stop.

He had this fantasy of stripping her down, bending her over his bike and taking her from behind, his hands on her amazing breasts, his lips on her neck, sliding into her wet, warm...

"Sorry, sir? I'm stuck again. Could you help me?"

Mason rubbed his face before squinting at the messy calculations.

Since bike sex, or even warm weather, wasn't in his immediate future, he could do math. And while he mathed, he could also keep an eye on Callie, which was his latest and greatest pleasure.

Two

Matt walked into Brogan and Winston's showroom on Charles Street and looked around.

A counter ran along an exposed brick wall and to the right of it was a waiting area with a striped green-and-white sofa and a white chair, both with perfectly placed orange cushions. Funky art hung on the walls and a vase brimming with fresh flowers sat on the coffee table. He liked what he saw, immediately understanding why Winston and Brogan had such an excellent reputation and were booked solid for months.

DJ, as the CFO, worked behind the scenes, but Matt knew how important her work was to the company's overall success. He couldn't do what he did without Greta, his office manager, who took care of the paperwork, the staff and the billing. Greta was as indispensable to him as DJ was to Winston and Brogan. Her name, after all, was on the door.

Matt heard footsteps on the iron staircase to the left and he turned to see a pair of knee-high boots and sexy knees coming down the stairs. He knew those legs, the shape of them. He'd tasted the backs of those knees, nibbled those pretty toes. The rest of DJ appeared: short skirt over black leggings, a white blouse, that gorgeous long neck. As she hit the bottom stair, he finally got to see her face for the first time in too many months and, as always, her beauty smacked him in the gut.

Her thick hair, as dark as a sable coat, was pulled back into a soft roll, tendrils falling down the sides of her face. Black-rimmed glasses covered her extraordinary brown-black eyes and her lips were covered in a soft pink gloss. She looked both beautiful and bossy, efficient and exciting.

Two steps and she could be in his arms—he'd duck his head and he'd be tasting her.

"Matt."

No excitement, no throwing herself into his arms, God, he didn't even rate a smile? What the hell had happened between last Christmas and now?

Matt took a closer look at her eyes and saw wariness, a healthy dose of I-don't-need-this-today. Well, tough. He didn't like unresolved situations. When he'd left DJ in the UK everything had been fine. Yeah, many months had passed but, unless she now had a boyfriend and had moved on, nothing should've changed. And if she had found someone—a thought that froze the blood in his veins—then why the hell hadn't she just said so? That was their deal, dammit.

"Got someone else, Dylan-Jane?"

It took her a little time to make sense of his words, but when she did, her eyes widened and she quickly shook her head. Yep, that was answer enough. So, no boyfriend. "Then what's the problem?"

DJ glared at him, sent the young receptionist a cool smile and jerked her head toward the stairway. "Can we discuss this in private?"

Matt jammed his hands into the pockets of his pants as he followed DJ up the stairs and down a short passageway to a corner office. He stepped inside the brutally neat room and watched her stride toward her wide desk.

She wanted to put a physical barrier between them but he had no intention of letting that happen. One long step allowed him to capture her wrist. He swung her around and pulled her to him so that her breasts touched his chest and the top of her head brushed his chin. He looked down at her, his mouth quirking at her shocked expression. "So, no new guy, then?"

"No."

Thank God. Matt dropped his gaze from her eyes to her mouth and after a couple of beats, looked her in the eyes again. She immediately understood what he wanted…and yeah, it was what she wanted, too. The attraction between them had always been a living, breathing thing. A year ago, he would've dived into the kiss and been sure of his welcome, but too much time and distance had created a barrier between them. It was hell to wait for her to make the first move, to wait for her to rise onto her toes and fit her mouth against his. It took a minute, maybe more, but then her lips were on his and the world suddenly made sense again.

Matt immediately took control of the kiss, covering her mouth with his, sliding his hands over her hips and bringing her flush against him. His pants immediately shrunk a size as he filled the empty places of his soul by kissing Dylan-Jane. Spice, sex, heat, heaven...

It took less than a heartbeat for Dylan-Jane to open her mouth up to his tongue, and a second later her arms were looped around his neck and her fingers were in his hair. Potent relief ran through him: she still, thank God, wanted him as much as he craved her.

Matt wound his tongue around hers, tasting her spiciness and sweetness, and sighed. Yeah, he'd missed this, missed her breathy moans and the purrs of appreciation she made in the back of her throat.

When DJ's fingers pushed into his hair, when she held his head to keep his mouth on hers, he knew she was fully, completely in the moment with him.

Matt pushed aside his urge to strip her, telling himself that he wasn't going to make love to her on her office couch in the middle of the day. But he could kiss her, let her fill up those hollow spaces in his soul. He needed nothing as much as he needed to hold her...

Soft, sweet and still sexy—Matt felt like he'd conquered the world when she quivered under his touch. He needed to taste more of her, kiss a place more intimate than her mouth, so he flipped open the top buttons of her designer silk shirt and pushed aside the fabric to reveal her lace-and-satin bra. Unable to wait, he pulled aside the cup and there she was, pretty and plump. Ducking his head, he touched his lips to her, swiping his tongue across her nipple, feeling the shudder run through her.

He loved that he could make her feel like this, that he could take her from mad and sad to pleasure, that he could put those purrs in her throat, make her arch her back in eagerness. Her fingers in his hair tightened as he blew air over her nipple and his name on her lips was both a plea and a demand for more.

He moved to her other breast, loving the taste and texture of her. His hand traveled down her hip. Matt slid his other hand over her ass, kneading her under the fabric of her skirt before inching the material up so his fingers brushed the back of her thighs. He wanted those legs around his hips, her breasts in his mouth. He needed to be inside her as soon as possible.

He wanted them naked; he needed *her*. Matt's hand slid between her legs, wishing away the fabric barriers between her secret places and his fingers…

Then Matt was touching air and DJ was…gone.

Matt looked at the empty space between them and shook his head. One minute she was in his arms and the next she was halfway across the room, staring at him, her mouth wet from his kisses and her eyes blurry with desire. She wanted him, so why the hell was she six feet away and he was here? Matt took a step toward her and DJ held up her hands.

"This is my office, Edwards. I'm not about to get naked with you here."

Fair point. How soon could they leave? It had been a hell of a long time since he'd seen her naked, kissed her senseless, heard her moan as she fell apart in his arms.

"I'm not about to get naked with you at all."

Matt blinked. What?

There wasn't anyone else. They'd just shared a kiss hot enough to melt glass. They'd been sleeping together for many years. He was going to be around for the foreseeable future and she was cutting him off?

What was happening here?

What was he missing?

DJ gestured to the sofa. "Take a seat, let's talk."

He'd rather be making love, but since that was out of the question Matt sat down, adjusting his still rock-hard erection and begging it to calm the hell down because it wasn't needed at this precise moment.

"Coffee?" DJ asked.

Matt nodded, stretched out his legs and ordered himself to get a grip. He watched DJ with narrowed eyes as she popped a pod into her fancy machine, powered it up and, when the mug was full, added a dash of milk. Ignoring the sugar dispenser, she walked over, placing the mug on the coffee table in front of him. Then she took the seat opposite him and draped one slim leg over her bouncing knee.

DJ was nervous. Now, that was interesting.

"What are you doing back in Boston, Matt, and how long do you intend to stay?"

"I have some personal business that necessitates me sticking around for a few weeks. One part of that personal business is persuading my grandfather to move into an assisted-living facility."

DJ's eyes turned warm with sympathy and his heart stuttered. He loved her expressive eyes, the way emotions swam through them, the way they resembled luxurious chocolate.

"Is he sick?"

Matt shook his head. "Alzheimer's."

"I'm so sorry, Matt." DJ tipped her head to the side, curiosity all over her face. "And your other personal business?"

He wasn't ready to talk to her, or anyone, about his daughter, Emily.

Besides, he wasn't here to *talk*. He wanted to *feel*. He wanted to touch the skin on the inside of DJ's thighs, pull her tasty nipples into his mouth, nibble her toes.

In her arms, while he loved her, he could forget about the complications of this past year.

Dylan-Jane was his escape, his fantasy woman, the perfect relationship because it was all surface. Because she didn't demand anything more than he was prepared to give.

But instead of falling into him and losing herself in the pleasure he could give her, she was retreating. Hell, if she had "back off, buster" tattooed across her forehead, her message couldn't be any clearer. DJ uncrossed her legs, leaned forward and rested her forearms on her bended knees. She stared at her hands for a long time before looking up at Matt. "Cards on the table, Matt?"

He didn't expect a good hand but nodded anyway.

"Your being back in Boston, even on a short-term basis, doesn't work for me."

Well, hell. Not what he wanted to hear. In his mind, reality crashed into fantasy and he felt a little sick. And a lot disappointed. He'd been relying on having some time with DJ as a way to step out of his head and regroup.

"I have a life here and that life doesn't have room for a hot lawyer who wants to share my bed." DJ glanced at her desk and lifted her eyebrows. "But maybe we can go somewhere in the New Year, see if the magic is still there."

Matt didn't know if she was being serious, and not knowing where he stood pissed him off. And there was something in her tone…something he couldn't put his finger on. Behind her tough-girl words, he could see vulnerability and…was that guilt?

"What aren't you telling me, DJ?"

DJ arched an eyebrow. "I don't know what you're referring to."

Damn if that prissy voice didn't make him harder than he already was, if that was possible. "Spill it, DJ."

Irritation flashed in her eyes and she shook her head, looking weary. "Lawyers. If you weren't so damn hot I wouldn't have hooked up with you." She sighed. "I don't have space in my life for an affair with you, Matt. I work long hours, I like my space. Also, I tend to get cranky around this time of year, so I prefer to be alone."

She didn't like Christmas? Why not? There was a story there. Another one. And why was he suddenly so curious? For seven years, he'd managed not to ask her questions, not to dig deeper, but now his first reaction to new information was to find a spade and start shoveling?

Get a grip, Edwards!

"Apart from a weekend of great sex with you here and there, I like being alone. Seeing you a couple of times a year is enough for me."

Matt leaned back, placed his ankle on his opposite knee and held DJ's gaze. She was trying so hard to remain calm, to persuade him that she was a cold woman who didn't feel anything, but she needed to become a lot better at lying before he bought into her BS. She wasn't cold, or sophisticated, or tough. What she was, was bone-deep scared of having him in Boston.

Why? Why could she easily handle a few days with him but seeing him regularly scared the pants off her?

And why did he care?

And why wasn't he saying to hell with this drama and walking out her door? He could leave, walk down the block and into a bar and, after a couple of cocktails and an hour or two of small talk, he was pretty sure he could score. But he didn't want sex with some random stranger.

There was only one woman he wanted…

Matt leaned forward and swiped his thumb across DJ's lower lip, his fingers lightly stroking her jaw. Desire burned in her eyes and under his fingers her skin heated. Glancing down, he noticed her nipples beading, pushing against the thin fabric of her silk shirt.

She'd never been able to hide her attraction to him, thank God. Because he saw her need for him, could feel her heat, could almost taste her…he pushed.

He kept his voice low, but his tone was resolute. "So here's what's going to happen, Dylan-Jane. I'm going to be living across the road from you and we're going to run into each other often. Your friends are mine and our paths *will* cross. And even if they don't, I'll make damn sure they do. It's been too damn long since I've had you and I want you under me as soon as possible. Yeah, this year has been unusual, I accept that. What I don't accept is this barrier you've flung up between us. But know this, I will pull it down and I will find out why you put it up in the first place."

"Matt—"

"Not done." He narrowed his eyes at her. "We've always been honest with each other and you're not being honest now. While I think part of what you said is true—you like being alone and Christmas sucks— that's not the whole truth."

"You haven't told me the whole truth about why you are back in Boston," DJ pointed out.

He hadn't, he had to give her that. "But that has nothing to do with you, nothing at all, and I know, don't ask me how, that your stay-away-from-me attitude is all about me, about us."

He saw agreement flash in her eyes and sighed. God, what was going on with her? And why couldn't she just spit it out? Matt closed his eyes and released a long breath.

"Jesus, DJ, just tell me already."

DJ stood up, walked over to the window and folded her arms across her stomach. She bowed her head and he could see her shoulders shaking. God, he hoped she wasn't crying. Tears were his Kryptonite. He stood up, went over to her and stood behind her, not touching her but silently offering his support. "You can tell me, Dylan-Jane."

DJ remained silent for a long time and when she finally turned, he saw the capitulation in her eyes. Finally!

"We made love on Christmas Eve and I got pregnant." Her words were a series of punches in his solar plexus. He battled to find air, to make sense of her words. Then DJ took another deep breath and spoke again. "I lost the baby in February."

It took a minute, an hour—a decade—for his brain to restart, his mouth to work. He thought he was calm but when the words flew out of his mouth, they emerged as a roar. "Why the hell didn't you tell me? As soon as you knew?"

DJ's face drained of color and she retreated a step so that her back was flush against the window.

"I tried—"

"Not that hard," Matt shouted, unable to control the volume of his voice. "I had a right to know, dammit! How dare you take that away from me? You lied to me! You let me believe one thing when the exact opposite was true. Jesus, Gemma!"

Gemma? Had he really said that?

Matt stared at DJ, noting her dark eyes dominating her face. She was edging her way to the door, needing to walk away from him. He didn't blame her. In his anger and shock, he'd overlapped Gemma's and DJ's actions and he wasn't sure which situation he was reacting to. He needed to leave, to get his head on straight, to think about what she'd said, what had happened.

To find distance and control.

Matt whirled around, walked to the door and yanked it open. Stepping into the hallway, he saw Jules and Darby jogging down the hallway toward him with Amazonian warrior-woman expressions on their faces. They blocked his path, momma bears protecting their cub.

"What happened?" Jules demanded, her expression fierce.

"Did you hurt her?" Darby asked, equally ferocious. "If you hurt her, we will make her press charges."

God, what did they take him for? "She's fine. We just had an argument," Matt wearily replied.

Air, he needed air.

"If she's hurt, Edwards, I swear to God we'll string you up," Darby told him before she and Jules pushed past him and rushed down the hallway to their friend's office.

Matt watched them rush away, his heart trying to claw its way out of his chest. He rubbed his hand over his breastbone, trying to ease the ache, a part of him still not believing DJ's declaration. For the second time in his life, he'd heard that a woman had miscarried his baby. Unlike the last time he'd experienced this news, the baby he'd briefly given DJ would not, like Emily had earlier this year, write him a letter and tell him that he, or she, was his biological child and ask if they could meet.

He didn't want a family, wasn't cut out to be a dad, but, *man*, that thought made him feel profoundly sad.

Three

So wow. That happened.

DJ stared at her office door, flabbergasted by Matt's off-the-wall reaction. She'd spent hours imagining the conversation they'd just had, and she'd never once thought Matt—cool, calm, *controlled* Matt—would lose it.

And lose it loudly.

DJ dropped to the edge of her couch and placed her head in her hands. After trying to reach him a few times in March and failing to connect with him, she concluded that there was simply no point in telling Matt that she'd conceived and then miscarried. It had happened so quickly, he'd been so far away and, really, what impact would it have on his life? Zip. Zero.

If anything, she'd expected him to be thankful she wasn't still pregnant because, hell, a part of her was grateful for that.

There were many reasons why she felt relieved about losing the baby—and even more reasons why she felt guilty for feeling relieved. Not having to tell her own mother that she was going to be a single mom was high on the list. DJ hadn't had any contact with her father since she was a child, so telling him wasn't a factor.

Her parents were, in fact, the reason she'd never wanted to have kids. She was terrified that she, like them, would turn out to be as horrible at raising a child as they were.

She lived with the memories of her father walking away—at Christmas, for the love of God!—to move in with another woman and her child, a girl he adopted as his own shortly after leaving. He'd left DJ with Fenella, who wielded her tongue like a scalpel. DJ's goal in life had been to have an awesome career and enough money so she could be free from her mother's checkbook and caustic tongue. No stranger, DJ knew, could hurt you as much as someone you loved.

DJ's office door banged open and her best friends rushed inside. DJ stood, and Darby grabbed her biceps and gave her a tip-to-toe scan.

"We heard shouting. Did he hurt you? Are you okay?"

"What? No!" DJ frowned at them. "Matt would never hurt me."

Jules arched her eyebrows. "We heard him yelling."

DJ wrinkled her nose. Fair point.

"You don't fight, DJ, so what's going on?" Jules asked.

And there it was.

While she didn't volunteer information, she didn't lie to her friends. As Darby stepped back, DJ gestured

for them to sit on the sofa. She'd dropped one bombshell today, she might as well drop another.

A year was a long time to keep this secret and now
that she'd shared it with Matt, she didn't want to keep
it to herself anymore. Darby and Jules were her friends,
she should be able to tell them stuff. She *wanted* to tell
them, even if it would be hard to say and, for Darby,
hard to hear.

DJ looked at the twins, thinking that they couldn't
be more different if they tried. Jules was dark-haired
and blue-eyed, Darby a silver-and-steel-eyed blonde.
The only thing they had in common was their stylish
dress sense and the worried expressions on their faces.
They sat down on the couch and Darby gestured to the
chair opposite, silently suggesting that DJ join them.

DJ wanted to stay exactly where she was.

"Sit down," Jules suggested.

DJ touched her fingertips to her forehead, conscious of a monstrous headache. She sucked in some
air, waited for her knees to lock and walked over to the
empty chair, sending a wishful glance toward her coffee machine. Damn, she needed caffeine, preferably
intravenously injected. And if it was laced with a stiff
shot of whiskey, she wouldn't complain.

"Talk to us, DJ," Darby said, sounding worried.

DJ linked her fingers around her knees and tried
to calm her racing heart. As a child, every time she'd
tried to communicate with her mother, she'd been cas-
tigated, shamed or ridiculed. If she could avoid talking, she would. Because, when she tried to explain her
thoughts and feelings, more often than not, she made
a hash of things.

Look what a mess she'd made of talking to Matt.
He'd stormed out, mad as hell.

Prior experience told her that this conversation wouldn't go well, either. DJ fiddled with her hair and sent a longing look toward her computer. This was why she liked numbers and spreadsheets and data. They didn't require her to form words.

"DJ, we're worried about you," Jules said.

"I'm f—"

"If you say you are fine, I swear I'm going to slap you!" Darby said, her words and expression fierce. "We know something is wrong, it has been for months and months!"

Hearing the fear and worry in her voice made DJ feel like a worm. And because she was already overly emotional, tears rolled out of her eyes and down her cheeks.

Jules dropped to her knees in front of DJ. "For God's sake, just tell us already! Is your mom being a super bitch? Is it Matt? Did he do something to you?"

"No, that's not it." DJ ran her hand around the back of her neck and looked for her courage. Lifting her head, she looked past Jules to Darby. "This is so damn difficult for me, Darby, I don't know how to tell you this—"

"Just say it, DJ." Darby ground the words out.

"When Matt and I got together last Christmas, I got pregnant. I miscarried about six weeks later, in February. I never told Matt. I never told anybody."

Jules gasped, but DJ was most concerned about Darby. Color leached from her face and her bright eyes looked like moonlight in her face. DJ saw her friend's hands shaking. Just like she'd anticipated, Darby was taking the news badly.

DJ needed to apologize. "It was an accident. I didn't plan it. I knew it would upset you, so I didn't tell you.

And I felt so damn guilty because I didn't want to be pregnant when you want a child so badly. And then I felt—still feel—sad, and guilty, for losing that child."

Darby rocketed up and slapped her hands on her hips. She shook her head and looked at Jules. "Can you believe this?"

Jules stood, too, and took a step closer to Darby, showing that they were a unit, a team of two, and that DJ was on the outside of their group.

"So, judging by his shouting, Matt is furious because you didn't share this news with him, either?" When DJ didn't answer, Jules threw up her hands. "We don't blame him. He has a right to be as mad as all hell, Dylan-Jane."

DJ bit her lip. Okay, their reaction was worse than she'd expected. She lifted her hands and quietly murmured, "I'm sorry."

Tears turned Darby's eyes a lighter shade of silver. "I'm sorry that you had so little faith in us that you couldn't tell us sooner, DJ. I'm sorry that you think I am petty enough to only think about myself when you are faced with one of the most difficult situations of your life. I'm sorry that you think so little of our friendship, so little of yourself." Darby's soft words were loaded with sadness. They burned DJ like acid-coated hail.

"When are you going to realize that you can mess up, DJ, that you can be human?" Darby asked.

The hailstones turned into hot bullets that pushed through skin and bone to lodge in her heart.

"Dammit, DJ, for months we waited for you to talk to us, to ask us to share your burden. But you shut us out! Then you started looking and sounding better and you slowly started coming back to yourself, so we decided not to bug you, to let you be. But now we find out that you were pregnant and that you had a miscarriage and you chose to deal with all that alone?" Darby cried.

"Everyone was worried about you, DJ. Callie, Levi, the Lockwood boys," Jules added. "When are you going to realize that you are as valuable, as much a part of this family, as the rest of us? When are you going to start leaning, start accepting that we are here for you?"

DJ should trust them. She wished she could. They'd never, not once, let her down. But she was terrified that someday they might.

At eight, she'd believed she was the center of her dad's world, but he walked away without looking back. Her father had been the first, but Fenella continued the rejection. Every time she dismissed or denigrated DJ, played her mind games, DJ felt as alone, as abandoned, as she had the day her dad left.

It was easier to believe the people she loved would abandon her when she needed them most rather than face that kind of hurt again.

Darby rubbed her hands over her face. "Dammit, DJ, I am so sick of you trying to be perfect, of you standing alone and apart. I cannot believe I am saying this, but you have to make a decision. Either you are part of our lives in every way, prepared to lean on us, or you go your own way. Whatever you choose, we are never going through this again!"

This was the reason she didn't talk, why she kept her own counsel. Once again, she'd cracked open her shell only to have a knife shoved into her exposed belly. She talked to Matt; he'd exploded. She opened up to the twins, and they issued her an ultimatum.

"We need you to talk to us!" Darby said, her expression now determined. "We want to know about the big and the little things, the good and bad. And stop trying to find every excuse you possibly can for avoiding Christmas family functions. Enjoy being with us over the next few weeks. For the first time in your life, properly embrace what being part of our family means. If you can't do that, if you won't do that, then I think it's time we all move on. We love you too much to only have access to a facade. And frankly, we damn well deserve more!" Darby didn't raise her voice, but DJ was left in no doubt that she meant every word.

DJ looked at Jules, hoping to find her as shocked at this ultimatum as DJ. But Jules just looked sad. "Let us know what you decide, Dylan-Jane."

God.

Jules followed Darby to the door and when it closed behind them, DJ dropped to her chair and stared at the floor.

Yep, it was official. Having heart-to-heart conversations really wasn't what she did best.

The following evening, Matt walked across the road to Levi Brogan's house. Like most of the houses in the gated community, and like Lockwood House itself, it was Georgian-inspired with its portico and columns. But instead of redbrick, the cladding was painted a pale gray and the white-framed windows were free of shutters. Ivy climbed up the side of the three-story building and across the front of the three-car garage, on top of which was what looked to be a guest apartment.

Matt rested his hand on the gate and looked around. He liked this exclusive community, liked the amount of space between the houses, the big trees and the quiet streets. He was used to the bustle of city living in The Hague, but this golfing community held a serenity that appealed. He'd never visited here before.

This was Dylan-Jane's world, her people.

For years they'd met on neutral territory, places where neither of them had friends or acquaintances. They could focus on each other with no distractions. Their trips to unfamiliar places subconsciously reminded them that their time together wasn't real life.

But being in Boston, in her town, and living across the road changed that.

He couldn't get on a plane and distance himself. His obligations to his grandfather and the meeting he hoped to have with Emily were happening side by side with his need for DJ.

He wanted her—of course he did. He didn't think there would ever be a time when he didn't want her. But here, in Boston, he'd started wondering about more than the attraction between them. Which house was her childhood home? Had she climbed that magnificent maple down the street? Had she been a tomboy or a girlie girl, naughty or nice?

Matt rubbed his forehead with his fingertips, trying to push away the curiosity. He was asking for trouble if he looked at DJ as anything other than a no-strings, uncomplicated affair.

He didn't do complications. He avoided risk. For the past eighteen years, he'd forced himself not to think about having a family, reinforcing the belief that marriage and having kids wasn't for him. He'd been at the mercy of unpredictable parents and then unyielding grandparents and neither set of parental figures gave him anything near what he needed. He didn't want to perpetuate that dysfunctional cycle...

For eighteen years, he'd managed to stand apart, to not get involved, to be self-sufficient...but being in Boston made him think of family and those childish shattered dreams.

It had to stop. He was not an insecure kid anymore. Enough of the past...

Matt jammed his hands into the pockets of his pants and rocked on his heels, still not walking through the gate. There could never be anything more between him and DJ, he knew that, but he was also certain that he owed her an apology. By losing his temper, he'd reacted badly. She'd shared a horrible experience with him and he'd seen the pain in her eyes, but he'd pushed her feelings aside to indulge in his life-wasn't-fair moment. He should've listened, tried to understand before reacting.

Yeah, not his proudest moment.

Irritated and ashamed, Matt pushed through the gate and walked up the steps to the ornate wooden door. He knocked and when a female voice answered, "We're in here," he stepped into the hall.

Matt followed the sound of the voice to a large sitting room filled with sofas covered in a mishmash of fabrics and colors. It shouldn't work, but it did. It was luxurious and comfortable and homey and chic all at the same time, and he immediately felt at home.

Glancing around, he saw Jules and Darby sitting on a flame-orange sofa, holding on to wineglasses like they were lifelines, tension radiating off both of them. Shoulders hunched, mouths tight, eyes bright. Matt frowned, looking for DJ. Where was she?

His big boots hitting the hardwood floor had them lifting their heads and he saw the misery in their eyes. Yeah, this wasn't good.

"What's happened? Where's DJ?"

Darby exchanged a long look with Jules and she released the breath she was holding. "Matt. Perfect."

A shed-load of sarcasm in two words. "Is DJ okay?"

"DJ is always fine, Matt, didn't you know that?" Darby said, her words bitter. But beneath the sarcasm, Matt heard pain and worry.

"She's in her apartment, Matt," Jules finally answered. "Yesterday and today were tough for her. If you were planning to keep fighting with her, please don't."

So Jules still felt protective of her friend. Her statement lessened one of the many coils squeezing his heart.

"Are you still mad at her?" Jules demanded, obviously curious.

No, his anger now had a different target—himself.

Matt shrugged. He wasn't in the habit of discussing his personal life, but these women were DJ's best friends, the people who knew her best. He kept his explanation short. "I've been calling her since last night. Messaging her, emailing. She isn't responding."

Darby shook her head, disappointed. "Join the club. God, I could just strangle her right now!"

Okay, so he'd obviously walked into some additional drama. Maybe he should come back later, when they were all a little more even-keeled. He was an expert at reading body language, but he didn't like dealing with drama anywhere other than in court, where he used it to get the result he wanted.

"What happened?" he asked, forcing a gentle note into his voice.

"I— She— DJ…grrr."

Matt lifted his eyebrows at Darby's actual growl. DJ had really managed to annoy the crap out of Darby.

Darby shoved a hand through her hair, looked from

Jules to him and her chin wobbled. "Yesterday we gave her an ultimatum. It wasn't pretty." Darby threw up her hands and rapidly blinked. Yep, definitely tears. And damn, if she was in tears then DJ was more than likely crying, too.

Such fun. Matt sent a longing look to the door.

"I need to get out of here," Darby muttered, pulling at the collar on her white polo-neck sweater. Since she made no effort to move, Matt figured she wasn't going anywhere.

But leaving sounded damn good and Matt wished he was anywhere else. Someplace that didn't have about-to-cry women, best friends fighting, a crap load of emotion. Nailing a bad guy using facts and words sounded like heaven right now.

"Maybe I should be the one to go."

"Yeah, you don't get to be that lucky," Jules told him, standing up. "The easiest way to get to her apartment is to leave the house via the kitchen door, turn right and the stairs to her apartment are there. Tell her that she's expected to join us ice-skating tomorrow evening. It's the first of our get-into-the-spirit events."

"Get into the spirit of what?"

A touch of amusement flickered in Jules eyes. "In the weeks leading up to Christmas, we all do fun things together. It's a tradition my dad started, and we've kept it going. DJ always finds an excuse to avoid any of our Christmas get-togethers."

"She does? I thought she loved hanging with you guys," Matt replied, confused.

Jules started to speak then looked at Darby, who shrugged. Some sort of twin-communication thing happened and Jules continued, "DJ gives a lot more than she takes. Despite a quarter of a century in our lives, she still doesn't talk to us. Maybe you being here can change that."

Matt saw hope flicker in her eyes and didn't like where her thoughts were taking her. It was better to shut down that line of thinking right now. "Please don't hop aboard the happy-ever-after train, ladies. DJ and I have an understanding that neither of us are going to go hearts and flowers on each other. That's not who we are, what we do."

Two sets of eyes were fixed on his face and Matt felt a bead of sweat roll down his temple. God, these women were tough. He tried again to get his point across. "Seriously, it's not going to happen."

Still nothing but intense stares.

Matt tested the words on his tongue, constructing sentences to convince them that there wasn't anything more between him and DJ than an inability to keep their hands off each other.

This isn't difficult, Edwards. Tell them you like DJ, you respect the hell out of her, but you have no intention of settling down with her, or anybody, ever.

DJ wasn't the problem—he was.

He opened his mouth to speak, but no words passed his lips. Great. He'd never, ever been tongue-tied before.

Another Boston first.

Mason saw, and ignored, the quizzical glances Callie sent his way as he sat at Eric's table, trying to help him grasp some of the trickier elements of partial differential equations. Judging by Eric's heavy sighs, Mason either wasn't explaining properly, or PhD-level math was a step too far.

Mason saw Eric's eyes flick to the intricate tattoo

covering the lower part of Mason's left arm and knew the kid was trying to reconcile his big brain with his hard-core tat. Eric would probably feel more comfortable taking instructions from someone not wearing cargo pants, biker boots and a black V-necked sweater, but...

Screw that. Mason had always marched to the beat of his own drum and it had been a long, long time since he'd felt the need to impress anybody, never mind a pimply-faced grad student. Cutting the kid loose with a suggestion that he take his problems to his math professor, Mason left Eric and focused on something far more pleasant. And difficult.

Callie Brogan was in the house and, as such, his day was made. Yep, it was official: he might look tough but his middle name was *pathetic*.

Callie saw him approach and looked from him to Eric and back again. He could see the wheels turning in her agile brain.

"What are you doing with Eric?"

Mason barely resisted running a quick hand over her bright blond hair. It would be soft and silky and he wanted it falling over his fingers as he plundered her mouth. But judging by Callie's inquisitive eyes, he was alone in that fantasy world. "Helping him with math."

"I've known Eric since he was a toddler and he's never needed help in anything academic." Callie frowned. "He's one of the top math scholars at MIT, so how can you help him?"

Thank God his ego was in decent shape or she'd have him whimpering. "I did have a life before this place, Callie."

"Doing what?"

"You haven't Googled me?"

"I prefer to get my information directly from the horse's, or in this case, the ass's mouth."

God, he loved her sass. "Come on a date with me and I might tell you."

Callie narrowed her gorgeous eyes and he fell into all that blue. He could easily imagine her naked on a deck chair on a golden beach, blue in her eyes, in the sea and in the sky. And wasn't that one of the items on her bucket list, to fall asleep naked in the sun? He could help her with that, but only after he spent an hour or two rocketing her to three or four of the most intense orgasms of her life.

Seeing that Callie was about to pepper him with more questions, he lobbed one of his own. "How far along are you with completing your bucket list?"

He'd heard that she went out on a date—not with him, dammit—and he was still pissed about it. "Had a one-night stand or phone sex yet?"

Callie flushed with either anger or embarrassment, possibly both. "That has nothing to do with you."

He saw the denial in her eyes and felt sweet relief. He was about to push for another date when Callie nodded to his arm.

"Did that hurt?"

Like a bitch but he couldn't admit that, so he shrugged. Callie leaned forward to inspect the intricate Polynesian design. Her finger traced a raised vein on the outside of his arm and he felt a bolt of lust skitter along his spine.

Callie lifted her eyes and they slammed into his. "Do you have more?"

Oh, this was too easy. He grinned. "Maybe. Get naked with me and find out for yourself."

Callie made that sound that was half an embarrassed snort and half a laugh. He loved it.

Callie lifted her finger off his skin and he immediately missed her touch. Leaning back, she folded her arms and raised an eyebrow. "Are you doing anything on Friday evening? Around seven?" Callie asked him.

Mason didn't try to hide his surprise. "No, why? If you're about to ask me to a movie followed by dinner followed by sex, then my answer is yes, yes and hell, yes."

Callie rolled her eyes and Mason's mouth twitched. God, he loved annoying her.

"It's not, repeat, *not* a date but—"

He held his breath.

"—my clan goes ice-skating on the first Friday of December. Why don't you and your boys come along?" Callie suddenly looked doubtful. "Can you skate?"

It was his turn for an eye roll, but because he was trying to act his age, he resisted. "Sure, I can skate. Can I hold your hand on the ice?"

Callie frowned. "No, but you can tell me why you are so good at math."

"That knowledge is worth a kiss," he countered.

"On the cheek."

"With tongue."

"You're not that good and I'm not that curious!"

Mason leaned across the table, his eyes locked on hers. "Yeah, I am. And yeah, you are."

He was so close he could smell her coffee-and-mint breath, see the panic in her eyes. He looked down at her full, wide mouth before looking back into all that blue. Unable to resist, he dropped a kiss to the side of her mouth, not trusting himself to touch her lips. "See you on Friday, gorgeous."

"You are the most annoying, irritating, frustrating man alive."

Mason grinned and made himself walk away, knowing that Callie was watching his ass.

Yep, day definitely made.

Four

Matt tapped on DJ's door and when she didn't answer, he tested the lock, not surprised to find it open. Slipping inside her apartment, Matt waited for his eyes to adjust to the low light of the room. DJ took tidiness to the extreme.

The apartment was a showpiece, beautifully and expensively decorated, with cushions perfectly placed on the sofa facing him. The coffee table held a low vase with floating flowers, and a stack of magazines on the shelf under the glass top was expertly aligned. The desk in the far corner of the room was clean except for a slim, closed laptop and a black paper folder. The shelf behind her desk held a row of matching black files, each label immaculately printed. Nothing looked out of place—in fact, it barely looked like anyone lived in this showroom.

It was a far cry from the messy hotel rooms they'd

shared over the past few years. Clothes were usually scattered over various surfaces—normally left where they tossed them—and towels ended up on the floor, with shoes where they could be tripped over. DJ had said she wasn't the same person at home as she was with him, and her apartment was the first evidence he had to back up that statement.

Matt made his way to a sofa facing a bay window that looked onto an icy pond next to a putting green. Nice view, he thought as he reached the back of the couch and looked down. DJ's eyes were closed and her even breathing told him she was asleep. Matt noticed the blotches on her face, the tear tracks on her cheeks, and sighed. He walked around the couch, looked down at another coffee table and decided that it looked sturdy enough to hold his weight. Sitting down, he rested his forearms on his thighs and looked at DJ. Really looked.

This was a stripped-down version of DJ, as natural and as beautiful as he'd ever seen her. Her hair was longer than before, her cheekbones more pronounced. The top button of her tailored white shirt had popped open, revealing the lacy edge of her bra and the swell of her breasts. Always so sexy…

Matt forced his eyes back up to her face. Beautiful, but even in sleep, she looked sad. God, had he done this? Her friends? Most likely it was a combination of both.

As if sensing him sitting there, DJ slowly opened her eyes. When he saw all that rich, deep, sad brown, his heart lurched. DJ lifted her hand and her fingers grazed his cheek.

"Matt."

Because he couldn't resist, he leaned forward and placed his mouth on hers, pushing his tongue between her lips. He tasted tears and wanted to burn them away, to remind her of the passion they shared that made everything else recede, if not disappear.

"Matt."

His name was a plea and a benediction, a cry and a hope. Matt kissed her again. This was what they were good at, what they needed. They weren't good at talking or connecting. But giving each other pleasure?

They excelled at that.

Sex was the best way to rebalance the scales, to take them back to that place where they felt comfortable with each other, to a time when their relationship was simple.

DJ placed her arms around his neck, lifting herself up so she was kneeling, her breasts pushing into his chest, her mouth nuzzling his neck.

Gripping her shoulders, he gently pushed her back, wanting to look into her face, into her eyes. Her gaze sharpened from sleepy to sexy and her voice, when she spoke, was rough with need.

"Kiss me, Matt."

It was the affirmation he'd been waiting for and Matt capitulated. His hands came up to tunnel into her hair, holding her head so he could thoroughly explore her mouth. His tongue twisted around hers and then he changed the angle of her head, looking to take the kiss deeper. He dialed up the passion from fiery to ferocious. DJ whimpered, held on to his shirt and made that low, growly, sweet sound that told him she was utterly turned on. When Matt pulled back to kiss her jaw, to suck her earlobe into his mouth, his hands got busy undoing her shirt.

"Hurry, Matt, I want you inside me."

"I haven't had you in nearly a year, there's no chance I'm rushing this." Matt's hands covered her breasts as he touched her through her silky bra.

Matt pushed aside the fabric and pulled one nipple into his mouth. He felt DJ's nails dig into his shoulders, the slight pain keeping him focused on his task of driving her insane before he pushed her over the edge.

Matt stood, banded his arm around her waist, lifted her off her feet and held her flush against his erection. How was he going to last? If she so much as brushed him with her hand, there was a good chance of it being over before he got to the fun stuff.

This woman made him lose control.

"Get naked," DJ panted, pushing his jacket off his shoulders. "I need to get my hands on your skin."

She yanked his shirt from his pants, pulling it up his torso. While she explored his broad chest and dropped kisses on his hot skin, he reached behind and grabbed the collar of his shirt to pull it up and over his head. While he toed off his shoes and socks, DJ pulled off his belt and opened his pants. And finally, clothes gone, he was in her hot, soft hands. She circled him and rested her forehead on his chest, looking down. Matt gritted his teeth—he was so damn close—and dropped a kiss onto her dark head.

She was the only woman who could make him lose control. Needing her as mindless with sensation as he was, Matt got rid of her clothes, sighing at the little froth of red lace covering her mound. So feminine, so pretty, so DJ.

Matt pushed his hand beneath the tiny triangle to find her bead, blown away by how wet she was.

"You want me," he stated, his words coated with awe.

"I missed this, I missed you." DJ pushed her hips up, riding his fingers. "Come inside me, Matt. Fill me. It's been too damn long."

Matt knew she was close. Hell, he was, too, so he

bent down to pick up his jacket, yanking his wallet out of the inside pocket. He found a condom, ripped open the packet and, with DJ's help, rolled it down his aching shaft.

Banding one arm around her narrow waist, Matt spread her legs so that her hips gripped his. He lowered them to the couch and she immediately slid over him, skin to sizzling skin.

DJ swiped her core over him before pulling him back with a gentle hand and positioning herself over his tip. He braced himself for the torture of entering her inch by inch, but DJ didn't wait, she just pushed down as fast and hard as she could.

She gasped, rocked once, twice, and he felt her insides contract, felt the rush of wet heat engulf him. Released by her orgasm, he launched his hips up, gritting his teeth as that familiar, white-hot sensation ran along his nerves.

He'd wanted to make it last, wanted to make DJ come again. He'd wanted to look into her eyes as she did...

He tried to hold on but when DJ ground down on him again, when he felt another tremor pass through her, he rocketed upward, his fingers digging into her butt, his mouth on her shoulder.

For a moment, for one single second as he shattered, he understood the way the universe worked, saw all the galaxies, rode a comet.

For one brief, blinding second everything made sense, and nothing was impossible.

As his heart slowed and his brain returned to its place between his ears, he heard DJ's ragged breathing, inhaled the intoxicating scent of her light perfume, soap and sex. His hand drifted up her spine, marveling at her soft, warm skin.

DJ slid her arms around his neck and pushed her nose into the underside of his jaw, her breath warming him. Matt started to speak but then realized that, once again, his tongue was tied.

How could he tell her that was the best sex they'd ever shared? That he felt more connected to her than ever before? That he couldn't imagine doing this with anyone else…?

Matt placed his hands on DJ's hips, easily lifting her off him and placing her on the sofa next to him. As he stood up, he felt her eyes on him, knew she was wondering why he so abruptly dislodged her.

Without looking at her—he couldn't afford to—he snatched up his clothes and stalked across the apartment to the guest bathroom. Closing the door behind him, he disposed of the condom, flushed and gripped the small basin.

He forced himself to look at his reflection, grimacing at the panic he saw in his eyes.

He *should* be panicked.

That wasn't fun sex or no-strings sex. It wasn't sex he could walk away from. That was crazy, want-to-do-it-again, want-to-do-it-again-for-the-rest-of-his-life sex.

Oh, God, he was in so much trouble. No.

They'd had sex. It wasn't a big deal. They'd had sex many, many times before. Nothing had changed.

Nothing. Had. Changed.

Everything had changed.

What the hell had she been thinking?

DJ kept her eye on the bathroom door as she pulled on her clothes with jerky movements. She'd been half-asleep when she first became aware of Matt's presence and she wished she could blame her actions on her sleepy state, but that would be disingenuous, if not an outright lie. Matt had asked her whether sex was what she wanted and she'd been quick to agree.

It had, after all, been a very long time.

Sure, months and months had passed without any relief, but that wasn't why she'd said yes. No, her agreement was partly because she kind of, sort of, hoped that making love—no, having sex—would hit their reset button, that they'd magically be transported back to a time when getting naked didn't feel fraught with tension.

This time last year her relationship with Matt had been uncomplicated. They met, they made love, they left. Apart from a few days, a handful of times a year, their lives didn't intersect.

But now he was in Boston, in her life, living across the road. And, because she had terrible luck, he was here during December, which had to be her least favorite month, by a million miles.

DJ walked over to the window and looked down the road, noticing that most of the houses on the street were strung with Christmas lights. Levi intended to do theirs sometime soon and she'd heard Noah and Jules discussing how they intended to illuminate Lockwood House.

Every bulb, every colored light, every wreath on every door reminded DJ of her father walking down the path to the sidewalk while she stood on the porch under twinkling lights and stupid mistletoe, sobbing while she begged him not to go.

She was rapidly approaching thirty. She should be over her antipathy to Christmas. It wasn't, after all, the holiday's fault that her father was a jerk. But as the lights went up and the nativity scenes, snowmen and reindeers appeared on front lawns, she felt her tension level ratchet up. By Christmas day, she felt ready to snap.

By adding a sexy human-rights lawyer who made her body sing, her heart sigh and her brain stutter to her Christmas angst, life was not playing fair.

DJ heard the door to the bathroom open and she turned to look at Matt. Like her, he'd dressed but his button-down shirt was open and untucked, and his feet were bare under the hems of his designer jeans.

He looked at home in her apartment. It felt right to see him here amongst her carefully collected possessions. DJ wondered what his place looked like, wondered if they shared the same taste, whether his furniture and art would jibe with hers.

Why was she even entertaining thoughts like these?

Matt was a fly-in-and-fly-out guy. And she liked that about him. She accepted that he wasn't the stay-still type and she knew she wouldn't be blindsided when he left her.

Because people always left.

Except the Brogans. And the Lockwoods.

DJ sighed. She'd spent most of her life protecting herself against the slim possibility that they might leave someday, too. But keeping herself apart had landed her in a heap of trouble and was at the heart of the current tension between her and the twins.

"Why the frown?" Matt asked her.

DJ jerked up her head to find him looking at her. Ignoring his question, she tipped her head to the side. "Why are you here? Why didn't you call before you came over?"

"I tried. Once or thirty times."

DJ remembered she'd turned off her phone after fighting with Matt and the twins, in an effort to find some much-needed solitude. She should turn it back on. "After you left, the twins and I had a disagreement about business, so I took some time to recharge."

Matt sent her a steady look. "I saw your friends on the way in. An argument over business wouldn't cause all of you to have red noses and wet eyes."

Dammit. He wasn't just a pretty face.

"Whatever you are fighting about is deep and personal and while a part of me wants to kick ass and take names, I'm going to assume you know how to fight your own battles.

"Besides, I'm nobody's white knight," Matt added, his voice rough. "Unless it involves statutes and penal codes and a check at the end of it, I'm not interested in saving anyone."

Yeah, she got the message: don't expect him to run to her rescue. If she hadn't learned, a long time ago, that the only person she could fully trust was herself, she'd be disappointed.

DJ pushed her hair back from her face. "You never answered my question—why did you come by, Matt?"

She wouldn't insult him by suggesting that he'd only come over for sex because it seemed like he'd been as caught off guard at that happening as she'd been.

It was Matt's turn to ignore her question. "Have you got a beer?"

A drink sounded like a great idea. Why hadn't she thought of that? "Sure."

Matt followed her across the room, past the designer dining table to the kitchen area. He leaned his elbows on the counter and looked at her. "I never imagined your place to look like this, Dylan-Jane."

DJ frowned as she took a beer from her fridge and reached for a glass. "Like what?"

Matt shook his head at the glass she offered and took the bottle. "Minimalistic. So very luxurious but so damn tidy. I'm a bit of a slob but I thought you were even messier than me."

DJ leaned back against the counter and folded her arms. "I was on holiday, taking a break from being tidy. I told you, my time away from Boston with you was fantasy, and in my fantasy I don't have to be perfect."

"Who demands perfection from you?"

DJ turned back to the fridge, opened it and took her time removing a bottle of wine before reaching for a glass. She had no intention of answering that loaded question. When he didn't push, DJ turned around and poured herself some wine.

DJ looked up and met his eyes. "I suppose you want to talk about what happened."

"I'll listen to anything you want to tell me, DJ."

DJ gestured for him to follow her, leading him back to the sofa by the bay window. She tucked herself into the corner, bare feet under her butt, and gestured for him to take the other corner. Matt pushed the coffee table toward the window and stretched out his long legs. Moving down, he rested the back of his head on the sofa and they watched night shadows dance across the pond and putting green.

DJ kept it simple, briefly detailing the facts. A homeopathic medicine that, apparently, interfered with the efficacy of the pill. Initially thinking that she had food poisoning, followed by the dawning realization that she hadn't had a period for a couple of months. That carrying a baby was the emotional equivalent of being kicked by a horse.

"Why didn't you call me, DJ? Why go through that yourself?"

"I was taking it all in. I knew I should tell you but how to do that, what to say? There was nothing between us but a couple of weekends and some very hot sex and I suddenly had this child growing inside me, a child neither of us wanted, or was ready for. Then said child went away. End of story."

"Not hardly." Matt scoffed. "I would've listened, DJ."

But she didn't confide in others. She never had talked, not about her past or her childhood. What was the point of whining? Her childhood was over. She'd survived her father leaving and she'd survived being replaced when he adopted his new wife's daughter not even a year later. All communication between them ceased and DJ was down to one parent, Fenella, who possessed a brilliant mind and the personality of a honey badger.

Nobody saw the easily angered, frustrated and self-absorbed woman who'd raised DJ. In public, Fenella was affectionate and solicitous, but back home, she reverted to being mean and critical, constantly reminding DJ that she was nowhere near as bright, talented or accomplished as she needed to be. In Fenella's eyes, DJ was her only failure.

DJ lifted her eyes to look at him and when their gazes connected, attraction flared. Matt brushed his lips across hers and DJ sighed. The past faded, her tears were a dim memory and the argument with Jules and Darby, and their ultimatum, was forgotten. There was just Matt and the way he made her feel.

Physical contact was so much easier than an emotional connection. She felt his low curse on her lips before he pulled back, lifting his hand to push it through his thick hair. He took a long sip from his bottle while looking out the window into the dark, cold night.

"While kissing you is always a pleasure, I don't think it's a great idea right now. We both know we're not going to stop there and we'd be using sex as a distraction from this talk. Our attraction is still there, Dylan-Jane."

"As evidenced by crazy couch sex," DJ agreed. "Why can't we keep our hands off each other, Matt?"

"Possibly because we use sex to put a whole bunch of space between us, to avoid having deep, tough conversations."

DJ opened her mouth to argue before realizing that he was right. Deep conversation and swirling emotions weren't part of what they shared, who they were. She and Matt tumbled into bed, laughed through their love making, enjoyed each other's body. Their encounters had been laughter and tequila shots, room service and perfumed sheets.

They could never go back to that. Never again would she be able to call up Matt or send him an email with a link to an inn in Vermont or a castle in Scotland suggesting they meet. She'd never again meet him in a hotel lobby or wait for him at an airport, laughing as they rushed to make a connecting flight. She'd never sink into a Jacuzzi naked, her back to his chest, his leg wrapped around hers holding them in place.

The distance and events of the last eleven months had changed their relationship and they were now in no-man's-land. Despite the crazy couch sex, they couldn't be lovers again, but neither, despite this first meaningful conversation, were they friends. They were undefined, nebulous.

DJ didn't like undefined. Everything in her real life was carefully thought through, understood, slotted into boxes. At work she was brutally efficient, meticulous and detail-oriented. Even, as Darby and Jules frequently groused, anal. But the books were always balanced to the last cent, their returns were always submitted early, their creditors paid on time. She exercised regularly, had health and dental checkups every six months. Like her office, her apartment was ruthlessly organized, and her car was squeaky clean.

She had control over things but people baffled her.

Matt, the Brogans—they wanted her to communicate. They simply didn't understand that she didn't have it in her to exchange emotions on a deeper level. It was easier, safer, to retreat.

Or it had been.

Over the past year, things had changed. She'd changed. And now it was a few weeks off Christmas and Matt was here and suddenly she was feeling emotional connections she hadn't felt before.

She didn't know what to do with that.

DJ turned her head to look at Matt, watching as he rubbed the back of his neck. She wanted to replace his fingers with hers, tug his head down and kiss him. But she couldn't. They'd done it once, broken the drought, and they couldn't drink from that well again. Not here. This was the real world and in her real world she didn't get to kiss sexy men who weren't leaving town anytime soon. Because when her lover wasn't flying out the door, kisses led to dinners and sleepovers and breakfasts and more dinners and soon she'd be rearranging her entire life to keep him happy, to do anything to make him love her. She'd squash her own needs and feelings in the hope he'd love her like her mother never did.

So, no matter what she thought she was feeling, it was better to stay emotionally distant than to put herself in that position. She'd acknowledged and accepted that her parents had given her a warped view of love, but that wasn't something she could change. She simply sucked at relationships…evidenced by the fact that she might've messed up a twenty-five-year friendship.

"And the reason for that big sigh?" Matt asked, looking at her.

DJ shrugged and went for the easiest answer. "I'm trying to figure out how to mend my relationship with my two best friends. They are so mad at me."

"If it helps, I don't think they've totally given up on you. I was told to tell you they expect to see you at the rink tomorrow evening."

DJ groaned. "That's just cruel. They know I'm hopeless at skating." She was hopeless because she always made an excuse not to join the Brogans at the rink, to avoid their Christmas festivities and the memories that seemed to feed off carols and mistletoe, cookies and eggnog.

"I'm tagging along, too," Matt told her, his eyes glinting with amusement.

She wanted to smile, to lose herself in that warm green gaze, but she made herself take a mental step back. "Maybe it's better if we keep our distance from each other, Matt."

Matt held her eyes for a long minute, his gaze steady. DJ felt like he was looking into her soul, carefully taking her apart, piece by piece. When he eventually spoke, his tone was soft but full of purpose. "You and I are going to find a new way of dealing with each other and that starts now. I'm going to hold your hand and teach you to skate and we're going to try and be something we've never managed to be—friends."

Five

After Matt left, DJ sat cross-legged on her couch in the dark, her head in her hands. Damn, people confused her.

After years of wickedly hot sex and fun, uncomplicated weekends, Matt thought they should try and be friends... What the hell did that mean? That she should forget that he could send heat to her core with one smoldering look, a small brush of his hand against her skin? How could she be his friend when all she wanted to do was slap her mouth against his and run her hands over his broad shoulders? After all they'd done to each other, how could she be expected to shut off her attraction, to forget how he made her feel?

Yet, despite wanting to jump him whenever he walked into a room, she couldn't allow herself to indulge. They'd taken the edge off, yes, but he wasn't here for just a night or a weekend. He would be here the next morning, the next day, the week after next. He was no longer her fantasy—he was here, part of her daily life, and she didn't know how to deal with that.

Matt's answer was to try something different: he wanted to be friends. But before she could make a new friendship, she had to fix the mess she'd made with her old friends.

After finding her phone, she quickly sent them a message.

Can we talk? Fifteen minutes, in the kitchen?

They both responded in the affirmative and DJ sucked in a panicked breath, feeling her heart rate accelerate at the thought of opening up. She told herself she didn't need to fear their reaction. If they got angry, they wouldn't disparage or demean her. They'd only ever shown her love...

She could do this. She *had* to do this.

Not giving herself any more time to think, she picked up her phone and dialed Callie's number.

"Baby girl." Callie answered the call the same way she'd done all her life. DJ felt her heart stammer, then settle. This woman had been, in so many ways, her rock and her sounding board, an untapped source of unconditional love.

"Hey, Cal."

"What's wrong?" Callie demanded, her voice sharpening. DJ could imagine her leaning forward, her mommy instincts on high alert. They'd never been able to get anything past Callie.

"Nothing is wrong but I do need to talk to you. And the twins."

Callie hesitated. "Scale of one to ten?"

It was a throwback to her childhood. Callie was the

mom all the kids gravitated to for advice. She'd developed a system to filter teenage nonsense—one to three meant the news wouldn't matter in three months' time, four to seven meant it was marginally important and eight to ten was life-changing.

DJ sighed. "Twelve?"

Callie was silent for ten seconds before speaking again. "I'll be there in five."

Just like that, no questions asked. DJ disconnected the call. She slipped on her coat, shoved her feet into the old boots she kept by her front door and stepped into the night. Frigid air burned her throat and made her eyes water as she walked down the stairs to cross the lawn and head up the broad steps that led to the kitchen door of their magnificent house.

While she'd grown up in a house possibly even more luxurious than this one, this Georgian-inspired building was home. DJ looked left, saw Levi's SUV parked to the side of the garage, knowing that their expensive sports cars and Levi's imported superbike were tucked behind doors of the four-door garage. They lived a privileged, wealthy life—they had all the tech and toys— and she was grateful.

But as she'd learned, money just helped paper the cracks on a life; it didn't plug them. Money didn't shield you from pain.

DJ left her coat and boots in the mudroom and slipped into the lavish gourmet kitchen to see the twins entering the large, airy space from the hallway. Without saying a word, Jules reached for three wineglasses and Darby selected a bottle of French wine. DJ watched them, thinking that a warm glass of red would go some way to soothing her jitters.

"Your mom is on her way," DJ quietly told them and

saw their eyes sharpen. Neither of them spoke. Jules just retrieved another glass and Darby poured wine into crystal goblets. Silence prevailed until Callie burst through the back door, shrugging off her cashmere coat and pulling her gloves from her fingers with her teeth.

"What's going on and what did I miss?" she demanded, flinging herself into a chair and reaching for a glass.

Looking at Callie, DJ wondered how the woman could ever call herself old or fat. Yeah, she wasn't stick-thin, and neither did she look like she was in her thirties, but she was still one of the most attractive women DJ had ever laid eyes on. Fenella was coldly beautiful, her features perfectly aligned, but Callie was arresting in a way that Fenella was not. Callie was warmth and charisma, a big, bold personality who oozed love and natural charm.

No wonder Hot Coffee Guy was, as DJ had heard, flirting with her.

Jules tapped DJ's hand to pull her back to the present, a place where she really didn't want to be. *Suck it up, cupcake.* Yeah, it might feel like a root canal but what was the alternative? Losing the twins? Not an option.

Ever.

Three sets of amazing eyes looked at her and DJ pulled in a big breath. Releasing the air, she looked at Callie. "I've been keeping quite a big secret from all of you." Right. Another big breath. "At the beginning of the year, I miscarried Matt's baby."

Callie's eyes radiated sympathy. "Oh, baby. I'm so sorry."

"I'm sorry I didn't tell you what I was going through," DJ said, keeping it simple. "I should've." DJ pushed her hair behind her ears. "I didn't tell you because I was trying to protect Darby—" she saw Darby wanting to interject but DJ held up her hand, asking for patience "—but I know that was just an excuse."

"And what does that mean, DJ?" Jules asked.

DJ bit the inside of her lip. "It's easier to keep things inside, to bury them deep. I'm not good at…exposing myself. I'm not good at friendships." DJ saw that they were all about to protest and raised her hand again to keep them from interrupting. "I'm not, but I'm going to try and do better. I have to get a handle on this friend thing, partly because you said so."

Jules raised an arched eyebrow. "Only partly?"

DJ pulled a face. "And also because that's what Matt and I are trying to be."

"He friend-zoned you?" Darby asked, amused.

"It was a mutual decision." DJ darted an embarrassed look at Callie. "After this last year, things just feel *different*. We couldn't go back to what we were, so we thought we'd try something new."

Jules laughed. "That is too funny. You can't possibly be friends with someone who sets your panties on fire. But it'll be fun watching you try."

Then Jules touched DJ's hand with the tips of her fingers, her expression turning serious. "We'll talk about that man again—and dear Lord, he's so much sexier than I remember!—but I have something to say first."

Oh, dear. They were going to let her off the hook, of that DJ was reasonably certain, but not without a hell of a lecture first.

"DJ, you are the most independent woman we know, and that's saying something because we're pretty damn independent, too," Jules said quietly. "Your loyalty to us is absolute. Whenever we've needed you, you've moved mountains to be there. You are happy to give, but it's

time you realize that you have to take, too. You not leaning on us, not reaching out to us—it had us worried.
But you also hurt us."

"We know that you find it difficult to talk—"

Difficult? No, impossible!

"—but you cannot keep isolating yourself, pulling
back into your shell when life slaps at you. Life is a series of ups and downs but your I-can-manage-on-my-
own streak stops here and it stops today." Jules's gaze
pinned DJ to her seat. "Are we clear?"

DJ nodded. "Does your ultimatum still stand?"

She needed to know. She couldn't live her life with
that over her head.

Callie frowned as Darby and Jules exchanged long,
guilty, remorseful looks. "We were mad at you and we
wanted to get your attention. We would never really
walk away from you, I hope you know that," Darby
admitted.

Callie's eyes narrowed. "You threatened to walk
away from her?"

Jules and Darby squirmed in their seats at their
mom's displeasure. Jules wrinkled her nose as she explained, "As Darby said, we were mad at her."

Callie's eyes were ice-cold. "The problem with
knowing each other so long and so well is that you
know exactly what buttons to push to inflict the most
hurt. Threatening to walk away from DJ was cruel and
I am *not* happy."

DJ wriggled, feeling uncomfortable. She never imagined this conversation would turn into Callie fighting
with her daughters. Dammit! Look what happened when
she talked.

"Mom, DJ knows it was just a way to make her see
the light!" Darby protested.

"By threatening her with her greatest fear? Her dad walked away at Christmastime and Fenella frequently threatened to do the same thing! She often told DJ that her father had the right idea, that DJ wasn't good enough or smart enough or pretty enough for her father, or Fenella, to want to stick around."

Darby pushed her chair back and ran around the table to wrap her arms around DJ, resting her head against DJ's. "I'm sorry, DJ, I didn't think!"

DJ patted the arm that was choking her and when Darby released the pressure against DJ's throat, she sucked in some air. When she felt like she could breathe again, she kept one hand on Darby's arm and, with the other, took Jules's hand. "It's okay. And you were right to be mad. I should've opened up to you. I really should've."

"Damn right you should've," Callie tartly retorted.

DJ nodded. Underneath Callie's frustration was a lifetime's worth of love and DJ knew how lucky she was to have these amazing women in her life, standing in her corner.

It was hard to say the words, but she needed to…

"I love you," she said, her voice cracking. She waited a beat before speaking again. "That being said, do I still have to do the Christmas thing?"

"Yes!" Callie and Jules and Darby said in unison.

Well, crap. It had been worth a shot. Darby released DJ and went back to her chair as Jules replenished their glasses. A comfortable silence fell over the table for a few minutes before Darby spoke again, lifting her eyes to meet DJ's. "Can I be honest?"

"When are you ever not?" Jules murmured.

"Am I jealous that you got pregnant accidentally? Hell, yes. Did I have a moment of 'it's not fair'? Absolutely, I did. And I think that's normal," Darby stated, her voice low.

DJ couldn't think of a response so she remained quiet as Darby continued. "But those are *my* emotions, what I have to deal with. I know that you two will have babies eventually. Sometime in the future, one of you will carry a child and I'll be grateful to walk beside you, experiencing it, even if it's only secondhand. When it happens, I want to be involved. Please don't shut me out."

DJ leaned across the table to wipe Darby's tears off her cheek, unaware that her own tears were flowing as freely.

The back door opened and they turned tearstained faces to see Levi walking into the room, his T-shirt streaked with grease. He stopped, looked from one face to another and then walked across the room, yanking sheets off the roll of paper towels. Having grown up with their tears, he didn't bat an eyelash as he tipped up chins and wiped away their tears.

When he was done, he tossed the soggy sheets in the trash can and placed his hands on his hips. "Wine, tears, holding hands. Whose ass needs kicking?"

Matt had faced down hardened criminals and sly lawyers, hard-assed judges and tough police officers, and not once had he felt nervous or out of his depth. He had the law on his side and he knew how to bend it to get the outcome he wanted. And, not to blow his own horn, he was damn good at it.

But now, as he lifted his hand up to knock on the Brogans' wide wooden door, he felt jittery.

He'd received a message from Dylan-Jane, inviting him over for dinner, and he was still deciding whether to knock. Matt wasn't good at family occasions; his experience with family meals had been an extreme of opposites. Meals with his parents had been people sitting around makeshift tables drunk or stoned or both, with little to eat. Meals with his grandparents had been filled with food, but were stilted, boring affairs, where nothing but law and politics were discussed.

His daughter, the one he still hadn't met, had grown up with better family dinners than he had. From her emails, he gathered that Emily's family was close. She had two younger brothers, also adopted, a houseful of pets, a successful dad who adored her and a stay-at-home mom. Matt was so grateful that she'd had a stable, loving home to grow up in.

He'd experienced poor and unstable. He'd experienced rich and stable. But in both situations, he'd been only tolerated and mostly ignored.

Yet here he was, standing on another doorstep, about to face another family. And as if that wasn't hard enough, he also had to keep his burning attraction to DJ under wraps.

Yeah, he'd spouted off about being friends, but... God, he was feeling anything *but* friendly. How could he be DJ's friend when all he wanted to do, all he thought about, was exploring that sexy mouth, running his tongue down her neck, over the slope of her perfectly shaped breasts, and pulling her puckered nipple into his mouth? He wanted to hear her gasps of pleasure on his lips, on his skin. He wanted to swallow her whimpers of delight, hear her soft panting after he pushed her over the edge.

Forget being her friend. He'd far prefer, on any day, to be her lover. After many years of phenomenal sex, he now had to stand in the friend zone?

What the hell had he been thinking?

"Matt."

Matt turned and saw that the front door was open, that DJ was waiting for him to step inside. After hanging up his coat, Matt scanned her face. Her olive skin held more color than the last time he'd seen her, but her enormous, brown-black eyes dominated her face.

He'd always loved her eyes. They were the first feature he'd noticed seven years ago. That night she'd had no makeup—she didn't need any—and worn tight jeans and a tighter top. Their eyes had met and his heart, young and stupid, bounded out of his chest and flopped at her feet.

Just like it was doing right now. Dammit.

Tonight, her jeans were designer, with strategic rips, and she wore them with a simple long-sleeved red T-shirt. Simple clothes for a meal at home, but she looked as sexy as a red-carpet diva. Slender bare feet ended in flame-colored toenails and the denim fabric lovingly caressed her long legs and the gentle flare of her hips. He pulled his head back to glance at her ass and...crap. Yeah, fan-friggin'-tastic.

Again, just how was he supposed to keep his hands off her?

DJ held out her hand for him to take. Spontaneous gestures of affection weren't DJ's style, but Matt took her hand and laced his fingers in hers, frowning as a tremor ran from her to him. She looked up at him and smiled hesitantly. "Hi."

Resisting the urge to kiss the hell out of her, he dropped a kiss on her temple and murmured in her ear, "Are you okay?"

"Much better, thanks," DJ replied, her voice soft.

"Did you speak to your friends?"

Her hand rested on his chest and she grabbed his

shirt as if to hold on. Under her hand his heart was beating hard. "Yeah. It went better than I thought. We kissed and made up, but they refuse to let me ignore Christmas."

"One of these days you are going to tell me why you hate Christmas," Matt murmured.

"If you tell me why you're really in Boston," DJ countered.

She looked up at him, her eyes begging him to tell her the truth. He knew it was partly curiosity and partly because she was feeling off balance at having opened up to him. She probably thought that if he told her his own truths, then some of the balance of power between them would be restored. But he couldn't.

He'd promised Emily and, more than that, he couldn't afford to become any more emotionally intertwined with Dylan-Jane than he already was. He was leaving in a few weeks and, God willing, in the New Year they'd go back to fun weekends, hot sex and casual goodbyes. They couldn't move from friends back to lovers if they allowed their thoughts and feelings to bubble forth in Boston.

Hot sex, fun weekends—that was what they did. Matt frowned at the bitterness he tasted in the back of his throat at the thought that he might want more.

What the hell was wrong with him?

"Edwards."

Matt turned around and looked across the hallway to where Levi Brogan stood, arms crossed and a serious look on his face. He had rich brown hair, and his stubble held a hint of red. With cold eyes and a belligerent attitude, Brogan radiated enough aggression to ignite a turf war. Matt instinctively knew Levi was not a man to be messed with.

Levi walked across the hall and yanked open the front door. Ignoring DJ, he jerked his head toward Matt. "Outside."

Ah, crap. Matt sensed movement behind him and turned to see the three Lockwood men stepping into the hall. Levi's hot glare stopped their progress. Levi held up his hand and shook his head. "Nope, just him and me."

DJ moved in front of Matt. "Levi, stop being a jerk! This has nothing to do with you."

God, she was trying to protect him? Seriously? Matt felt a warm glow in his stomach before he realized that she was putting herself between two big men. Not a place for a small woman to be.

"Move, Dylan-Jane," Matt commanded, holding Levi's hot eyes.

"No! This is insane. You are not Neanderthals!" DJ cried. Frustrated, Matt placed his hands on her waist, easily lifted her and sat her butt on the edge of the hall table, not caring that it was obviously old and very valuable.

"God, you definitely need to eat more," Matt muttered. Ignoring Levi and the sharp eyes of the Lockwoods, Matt placed his hands on either side of her thighs and waited until her eyes, deep brown and worried, met his. When was the last time someone had worried about him? He couldn't remember. And why did he feel like his heart was being warmed by a gentle fire?

"Levi is protective. He might punch you," DJ whispered.

Matt swallowed his smile at her obvious concern. "I know. I can handle him."

"I don't want you to fight," DJ said, biting her lip.

"We're big boys, Dylan-Jane, and hopefully it won't

come to that." His words failed to reassure her so he shrugged and compromised. "I promise I won't throw the first punch."

"You men are ridiculous."

"I know." Matt dropped a kiss on her nose and straightened. Without looking at her again, and ignoring Noah and his brothers, he walked through the open front door and onto the wide porch to face Levi. Matt placed his hands in his pockets and waited for Levi to speak.

"When I got home, the three of them were in tears."

Since Levi failed to ask a question, Matt didn't bother to answer him. It was a lawyer thing.

A minute passed with Levi not saying anything and Matt became tired of waiting. "If you are going to punch me, can you get it over with?"

Levi's head jerked up and Matt caught the smallest flicker of amusement. "I don't know if you could handle me punching you, lawyer boy," Levi taunted.

"Yeah, that's what the last guy I put down said," Matt replied, keeping his tone light.

Levi folded his arms across his big chest and his biceps bulged. Yeah, the guy was bigger than Matt, but not by much, and Matt was fast and sneaky. He'd hold his own.

He hoped.

Levi nodded. "So, what's the plan of action?"

"I'm not sure what you are asking me, Brogan."

Levi looked annoyed, but Matt suspected that annoyed might be his default expression. "I don't like the idea of you dropping in and out of DJ's life."

"What DJ and I do has nothing to do with you or your family."

Levi glared at him. "Of course it does! From what I can work out, for the first couple of years this thing you had seemed to work. She still dated and we met a few of the guys she was seeing—"

A red haze appeared in front of Matt's eyes at the thought of DJ seeing other men. Over the past seven years he'd never once worried about her sleeping with anyone else. Why now?

"But then she stopped. We all flirt and have fun, she doesn't. I feel—we all feel—like you are playing her, stringing her along, keeping her at your beck and call."

It galled Matt to have to explain himself—he wasn't the type—but this was obviously a major concern for DJ's friends. He needed to address it so he could enjoy his meal with them. "I don't know what to say to you, Levi, and I wish I did, because I would love this conversation to end. All I can tell you is that DJ and I have an agreement."

"Great sex and no commitment?"

It was a mutual, adult decision and Matt had nothing to be ashamed of. "Yeah." Frustrated and wanting to go back inside, preferably without a broken nose, Matt sighed. "I like and respect DJ. She knows that. I'm pretty sure you heard about the miscarriage and I'm not discussing that, except to say we are trying to work out how to deal with each other going forward. I don't want to hurt Dylan-Jane and I'll do the best I can to make sure that doesn't happen. That's all I can promise you."

Levi rubbed his hand over his beard, nodded once and held out his hand. "Levi Brogan, protective big brother."

Matt gripped Levi's hand. He assumed the interrogation was over, but then Levi clasped Matt's shoulder and dug his fingers into his muscles. Matt forced himself not to react to the ribbons of pain running down his arm. "Let's go have a beer."

Matt allowed Levi to take a step or two toward the door before shaking his arm out and rolling his shoulder. The man had skills and he was very thankful that big fist hadn't connected with his face.

Not having to deal with protective big brothers and friends was just another reason not to bother with commitment.

But it had felt nice, earlier, to have DJ defending him, and he liked knowing that if he wasn't around, DJ had some good guys looking out for her.

Walking into the hall, Matt ignored the thought that *he* was the guy who should be looking out for her.

Six

Mason James walked between his sons and scanned the familiar sight of Frog Pond, Boston's favorite ice rink.

He'd been bringing Emmet and Teag to skate at the famous landmark since they could stand, and despite their feigned nonchalance, he knew his boys loved the bright Christmas lights and the festive atmosphere at the rink. Mason, skates over his shoulder, looked from one young face to the other. Time passed so damn quickly. Within a year or two, his house would be empty. No shoes on the floor, sports gear in the hall, or messy bedrooms, no having to constantly restock the fridge.

He'd be alone.

He'd miss his boys, of course he would, they'd been a band of three for a long time, but being alone didn't scare him. Being bored did. And while the coffee shop was a nice change of pace, it wasn't what he wanted to do for the rest of his life.

He was still figuring out what that might be.

Helping that kid with math had been a rush, an unexpected pleasure. He'd forgotten how beautiful equations could be.

It was the first time in a long time that he'd admitted that he missed his old life, missed the satisfaction that came with solving complex problems. He didn't want to go back to the stress, but he couldn't see himself making coffee until retirement.

This was his town; MIT had been his playground. His work at the think tank and several patents had paid for a few houses, lots of big-boy toys and a fat bank account. He was fit, healthy, youngish—he could do anything and go anywhere. He needed adventure. And definitely more sex.

Maybe that was why he was so drawn to Callie.

She challenged him on a level he'd never experienced before. Breaking through to her was proving as hard to solve as string theory.

Mason released a long sigh and two heads turned to look at him with bright, inquisitive eyes. "Problem, Dad?" Emmet asked.

"I'm good."

Like he was going to explain to his teenage sons that he was having woman problems. They spent enough time obsessing about girls without adding his own drama to the mix.

Speaking of, he looked around for a curvy blonde, wondering if Callie had conveniently forgotten her invitation to meet him here. Maybe she was running scared again and hiding from their attraction. He was so damn over it.

He wanted her, she wanted him… It shouldn't be complicated.

"Skating would be a lot better with a stick and a puck." Teag was Mason's hockey-mad offspring.

"Yeah, but then there wouldn't be any pretty girls," Emmet replied as they approached the rink.

Mason watched as Emmet made eye contact with a girl a year or two older than him, saw his flirty look and the lift of his head. The blonde nodded to the rink, sent him a see-you-on-the-ice-big-boy look and Mason's stomach tightened. Oh, God, he was going to have to repeat the make-smart-decisions-and-always-wear-a-condom speech. Talking to his oldest about having responsible sex, when he wasn't having any sex at all, was a special type of torture.

"Mason?"

Lust skittered up and down his spine and blood rushed from his head straight to his groin. Not feeling much older than his sons, Mason slowly turned to look into Callie's bright eyes—her blond hair was under a woolen cap that covered her ears. Her nose and cheeks were red, her coat was a bright pink and her tight jeans showed off her great legs. Her skates were a bold, bright green and she looked as at home on the ice as she did on land.

"Hey."

He heard Emmet's snort and knew the kid was rolling his eyes at Mason's greeting. After jamming his elbow into Emmet's side, Mason gestured to his sons. "Meet my monsters, Teag and Emmet. Boys, this is Ms. Brogan."

Teag mumbled a hello but Emmet held out his gloved hand and smiled. "Ms. Brogan. Nice to meet you."

Any other father would've been proud of Emmet's show of manners but Mason knew his son was a born flirt and could charm any female from birth to a hundred and ten. It was his superpower.

Callie shook his hand. "Nice to meet you. You boys skate?"

"Yeah, they skate. I've been bringing them here since they were tots."

"And by middle school he couldn't keep up," Emmet teased.

"Like hell." Mason rolled his eyes at Callie and smiled in response to her grin.

She looked so young standing there, with her unpainted mouth and flushed cheeks. It took all he had not to lean across and cover his mouth with hers, to see if her lips were as cold as he thought.

Mason pulled his wallet out of his jeans pocket, took out some cash and handed it over to the boys. "Go and buy us some tickets. I'll meet you at the entrance."

"Trying to get rid of us, Dad? So we won't embarrass you in front of the pretty lady?" Emmet queried, laughing.

"You embarrass me on a daily basis," Mason responded, knowing his boys wouldn't take his words seriously. He worked damn hard to make sure they knew he loved them and was proud of them. "But yeah, go find someone else to bug."

Teag rolled his eyes and Emmet laughed again. Tossing a quick goodbye to Callie, they melted into the crowd. Mason turned to Callie, putting his hands over Callie's as they gripped the railing. "Will you still be here when I get back?"

Callie lifted a finely arched brow. "Do you want me to be?"

"More than you'd believe," Mason fervently replied. "You don't want to hang with your kids?"

"Even if I did, they don't want to hang with me. And they weren't joking about being able to skate rings around me." Mason ran his finger down Callie's cheek, frustrated at not being able to feel her through his leather glove.

So he pulled off the glove and cupped her cold face in his hand. Better, so much better. His hand covered the side of her face and he pushed the pad of his thumb onto her bottom lip.

He couldn't resist—he needed a taste, just one. He lowered his head but Callie's hand on his chest kept him from connecting. "Mason, your boys might see you kissing me!"

"I'm pretty sure they won't pass out from the shock."

Callie lifted her aristocratic nose. "Public displays of affection are not my thing."

Mason swiped his thumb across her bottom lip again before releasing her with a deliberately loud sigh. "So I guess my fantasy of parking off a side road and taking you from behind as you lean over my Ducati isn't going to happen?"

Callie's mouth fell open. She flushed but Mason didn't miss the way her eyes turned a deeper blue... with lust? Interest? Curiosity? Well, now...

Then Callie narrowed her eyes at him. "What do you want from me, Mason?"

It was a good question and one he could answer honestly. "Sex. A couple of laughs. Some conversation. More sex."

"I'm not looking for a relationship, Mason. That's not what I want. Or need."

Mason dropped an open-mouthed kiss on her temple and whispered in her ear. "I'm not asking you for one, Cal."

With the colored lights and laughter reflected in her eyes, she looked damn perfect, like his own personal Christmas angel. He pulled back, fighting his instinct to brush his lips across hers, to burrow under her bright jacket to cup her breast.

God, she was driving him mad.

Callie pulled away and skated backward. She smiled at him—genuinely—and his heart flipped over in his chest. Mason was surprised that it could still do that.

"Hurry back, Mason, and I'll show you that I can skate rings around you, too."

He released a short burst of laughter. "Big talk, Brogan!"

Callie spun into a pirouette and Mason watched her spin faster and faster until he felt dizzy. When she came to a stop she was neither out of breath nor wobbly.

"Show-off," Mason grumbled, unable to keep an impressed smile off his face.

"Ten minutes, or else I'll find someone else to skate and flirt with," Callie told him, her expression saucy. He loved her laughing eyes, her wide mouth, the energy vibrating off her. Soaking her in, he just stared at her, unable to get his feet to work.

This was the woman he wanted to spend time with, the one he was completely captivated by.

Callie patted her head and touched her face with her gloved hands. "What's wrong?"

"Nothing. You are just so damn beautiful that you take my breath away."

Callie's face softened, her eyes misted over and her lip wobbled. God, he hadn't meant to make her cry. He'd spoken the truth. It had been wrenched from deep inside his soul.

Crap, why was his soul forcing words out of his mouth?

He'd spoken the truth not two minutes ago. This was pure lust. There was nothing here his soul needed to be concerned about.

He'd tried commitment, monogamy, marriage. It wasn't a road he was interested in walking again.

Callie spun around once and when she stopped, her eyes were clear as she tapped her watch. "Eight minutes. You're running out of time."

Mason bolted. There was no way he was missing out on his chance with the most intriguing woman on the ice.

DJ walked onto the ice at Frog Pond and felt her feet slide away from her. Gripping the railing, she swallowed her curse and tried to get her balance under control. DJ lifted her head up and looked around.

Noah and Jules were skating together, hand in hand, while Darby skated in front of them, shamelessly showing off her skill. Levi, Ben and Eli were behind them, looking as at home on the ice as they did on the boats they loved to sail.

Where was Callie? DJ's eyes moved across the pond and she saw her standing on the far side of the rink, talking to… DJ narrowed her eyes. Was that Hot Coffee Guy? *Go, Callie.*

DJ tried to turn around so she could face the skaters—she really wanted to watch Callie flirt with Mason—but her feet wanted to go south instead of east. Cursing, she stayed where she was and continued to look around. Despite her aversion to anything Christmas, the brightly colored lights decorating the trees surrounding the ice rink looked fantastic. Blue, red, green, yellow and pink were draped through the trees and the café was brightly adorned with white.

She could—almost—see the appeal. With one hand DJ tugged her beanie over her ears before pushing her nose into her scarf. She'd left a spreadsheet incomplete at work in her rush to get to the rink. Not because she wanted to skate, but because she knew Matt would be here.

DJ wanted Matt with an intensity that made her breath hitch and threatened to buckle her knees. She had his scent—sandalwood and spice—in her nose and she could easily picture his broad hands, masculine and powerful. Then she imagined those hands on her body, in her hair, between her legs.

Maybe she'd conjured him up, because suddenly Matt was flying across the ice toward her, stopping with pinpoint precision in front of her.

DJ got an impression of dark jeans, a caramel-colored coat and a red beanie before his bare hands cupped her face and his hot mouth covered hers. DJ gripped his coat with one hand, sighing into his mouth when his kiss gentled, exploring, tantalizing. His thumb stroked her cheek and she tasted mint and coffee and sex and sin, a heady combination that had her releasing her grip on the railing.

Her feet shot out and she felt herself falling, her legs flying between Matt's as they both tumbled to the ice. DJ felt air leave her body as her tailbone and then her back collided with the ice. Whatever oxygen she had left whooshed out of her when Matt fell on top of her.

Matt immediately placed his hands on the ice and pushed himself up, his arms holding his weight off her. "DJ? Honey? Are you okay?"

DJ opened her mouth but no sound came out and she snapped it closed. She tried again and…nope. Nothing.

"You're winded, honey," Matt said, rolling off her and kneeling on the ice. "Sit up and take slow, deep breaths. You need to stay calm and relax."

Yeah, easy for him to say when he wasn't the one who couldn't breathe. Matt pulled her up, held her face and looked in her eyes. "Breathe for me, Dylan-Jane. In and out, there you go."

DJ felt air hit her lungs. With every breath she took, she relaxed a little more.

When she could, she spoke. "Ack, talk about sweeping me off my feet, Edwards." DJ held out her hand so Matt could pull her up. He grabbed her hips when her skates went haywire again.

"Technically, you swept me off my feet," Matt said, wrapping a strong arm around her waist. DJ sank against him, knowing he wouldn't let her fall.

DJ looked around for the exit. This skating malarkey wasn't for her. "Can you guide me off the ice, Matt?"

Matt leaned against the side of the rink, pulled her between his legs and gripped her with his knees. With his hands steady on her hips, she felt stable. He was so close, their breaths mingling in the cold night air, and DJ thought about reaching up to kiss him again, but then remembered that was what caused their fall in the first place.

Really, she shouldn't be thinking about kissing him at all. Weren't they supposed to be *friends*?

She groaned and Matt, because he was so in tune with her, sent her a sideways look and a half smile.

"It's hell, isn't it?" he asked.

"What is?"

"Wanting each other so much. I look at your mouth

and remember the way you taste. I keep looking at your hands, wishing they were on me…stroking me."

She had to ask. "Stroking you where?"

Matt pulled her hand under his coat and placed it on his crotch. She felt the beginning of what she knew would turn into a fantastic erection.

A fireball of lust rolled down her spine and lodged between her legs as Matt allowed her hand to drop to her side. One comment! One small innocuous comment, a quick feel and she was turned on.

DJ darted a look at Matt's profile, frowning at his having-a-pleasant-time expression. So unfair that he could look calm and controlled while her face was on fire and her panties were one spark from igniting.

Yeah, some payback was in order.

DJ sent him what she hoped was a seductive smile. "I keep thinking back to St. Barts. You looked mighty good handcuffed to that canopied bed." She felt the tension in Matt's back, heard his ragged intake of air and smiled. "If I recall, I only used my mouth."

Matt muttered something under his breath that sounded like a series of creative curses. DJ smiled at the pained expression on his face.

Scales rebalanced… Now he was as turned on as she was.

"This is our first time out together as *friends* and ten minutes into the conversation we're in the bedroom," Matt complained.

"You started it by kissing me," DJ retorted.

"You started it by looking sexy and confused, trying not to enjoy the Christmas lights and decorations, trying to resist the festive atmosphere."

Dammit, he was so perceptive.

Warmth seemed to radiate off him so she shuffled

her feet forward and gripped the belt loops on his jeans. "And then we kissed and you went up in flames."

His grip tightened on her hips. "What are we going to do about it, Dylan-Jane? I can't help thinking that, after all we've done together, the sexual shenanigans in St. Barts included, trying to be your friend is the most dumb-ass suggestion I've ever made. Tell me you want me as much as I want you."

"Matt—"

"Is that a yes, a no…a hell-I-don't-know?"

"All three," DJ whispered, looking up. "We haven't even *tried* to be friends, Matt!"

Matt sighed. "I know. But I also know that the first time we are truly alone, all our clothes are coming off."

That was the truth.

He met her eyes, both of them oblivious to the fact that kids were chasing each other across the ice, that lovers were gliding arm in arm, that a Santa and his elves were doing figure eights in the center of the rink. DJ lost herself in his gaze and wished they were alone, that they were naked and that he was sliding into her, completing her.

"I want you, DJ. Only you."

Dammit, Matt! DJ wrenched her eyes off him and sucked in some cold air. If she didn't think she'd land on her butt again, she'd skate away.

She had to be sensible, just for a minute. She needed clarity. "Where are you going with this, Matt? Are you saying we should sleep together?"

Matt nodded. "I can't think of you as a friend. I certainly can't treat you like one. So, for as long as I am here, let's do what we do best. We can think of our time together as just being another weekend, but…longer.

And when I leave after Christmas, we kiss each other goodbye and go back to normal."

Could she do this? Could she mix her real life and her fantasy life by having a fling with Matt? Would that be a solution to the yearning and churning, constant craziness she felt whenever he was around?

C'mon, Dylan-Jane.

She was kidding herself if she thought this would be like their weekends away. He was in her town, watching her live her life. Here in Boston, he couldn't be her fantasy man, she couldn't pretend her real life didn't exist. This *was* her life and he was standing smack in the middle of it.

Reality dictated that they couldn't spend every moment together making love, they'd have to talk more, spend nonbed-time together. And that was dangerous. One of the reasons she limited her time with Matt was because she liked him, a lot. He had a wicked sense of humor, a razor-sharp brain and streaks of honor and integrity a mile long.

He could tempt her into wanting more than good sex, into thinking about commitment and relationships and belonging to someone.

And wanting that from a man, looking for love, was a sure way to get her heart diced.

She'd experienced heartbreak when her dad left and knew what it felt like to be left behind. And thanks to her mother, she also knew what it felt like to love someone who didn't love her back. She didn't want to relive either experience.

But most of all, she didn't want to fall in love.

So don't, she told herself. *Just don't.*

"Are you going to put me out of my misery sometime soon?"

She should say no, but she wasn't going to. Going to bed with Matt, having an affair with him, was pretty much all she'd been thinking about since he'd dropped back into her life.

"Yes, okay. Let's have a fling." Not able to look at Matt, DJ sent a longing look toward the café, its lights beckoning her to come in and get warm. "Well, let's go, then. Your place or mine?"

Matt chuckled. "I want you, Dylan-Jane, but a few more hours won't kill us. Let's teach you to skate and then we can join your family out on the ice."

DJ looked to where Matt pointed and she saw Darby and Jules skating together, arm in arm. Noah held Jules's other hand and Callie, sans Hot Coffee Guy, had her hand tucked in Levi's elbow. And they were skating toward DJ.

Jules and Darby were the first to reach her and both sent her a concerned look. "We saw you fall. Are you okay?"

"I'm fine. I just really suck at skating."

"You really do," Matt agreed, his arm still holding her upright. DJ rolled her eyes. She knew that. Hell, they all knew that.

"Let's get off the ice and get a table, then we can all be together," Darby suggested, but DJ heard the reluctance in her voice. They all loved to skate and if it wasn't for her they'd be on the ice for another hour at least.

"No, you guys carry on," DJ told them, tightening her hold on Matt. "Matt's offered to catch me if I fall."

Darby lifted her eyebrows. "You sure?"

DJ nodded. "Very. What about meeting in an hour? I'll buy the first round."

Her clan chorused their approval of that suggestion

and skated off. DJ watched them go, love and affection bubbling in her chest.

God, she loved them. All of them. Feeling a little overemotional, she tipped her head back to look at Matt, whose eyes were on her face, his expression tender. Not ever having seen that look from him before—a combination of pride and affection and lust—DJ bit the inside of her lip. He couldn't—*shouldn't*—look at her like that. It not only made her want to strip him where he stood, but it also coated her heart in warm goo.

No acting gooey, stop with the mushy thoughts.

This would be just a series of sexual encounters over the next month or so. She was not going to let it be more than fantastic sex with someone she liked.

Really liked.

A *lot*.

DJ pushed back her shoulders, ignored her wobbling ankles and tried to put a cheeky smile on her face.

"Let's do this." she said, her tone jaunty.

"Yes, let's."

Instead of helping her with her uncooperative feet, Matt curved his free hand around her neck, placed his thumb under her chin and tipped up her head. His mouth hovered over hers, his words dancing on her lips. "We'll skate, but right now, let's do *this*."

Matt's green eyes scanned hers then lingered on her mouth before he pulled his gaze back up to meet hers. Eye contact, DJ decided as electricity skipped over her skin, was damn sexy. His thumb, slightly cold, grazed the side of her face, across her cheekbone, toward her ear and back again. Anticipation sizzled.

Instead of using his lips, he moved so that his cheekbone skated across hers, skin on skin.

DJ muttered his name before tilting her head so that

her lips brushed his…once, twice…and silently demanded to be kissed. Masculine lips touched her cold ones and DJ was instantly plugged into a source of heat warming her from the inside out. Tongues circled, danced, withdrew and tangled as she and Matt stood on thin blades in the freezing night, oblivious to the background music of Christmas carols and the hoots of skaters.

Maybe December and Christmas—the decorations, the lights and the festivities—weren't as bad as she'd always thought. But honestly, she was kissing Matt, which meant anything and everything was instantly bolder and brighter and better. Even Christmas.

Seven

DJ opened the door to her apartment and stepped inside. The living-room drapes were open, and she immediately noticed the soft white lights strung up over Lockwood House, softening the austere lines of the two-hundred-year-old home.

DJ took off her coat, hung it up on the stand next to the door and walked over to the window facing the street. "Lockwood House looks pretty."

Matt moved to stand behind her, his arms banding her waist, his right hand covering her left breast in an action that was as familiar as it was exciting.

Matt rubbed his chin across her head. "By the way, doesn't anyone in this neighborhood believe in colored lights?"

"Noah's grandfather, and great grandfather, only ever used white lights to decorate Lockwood House, and the tradition has extended to all the houses in the community."

"It seems like a nice place to live," Matt murmured.

"It really is. A community of its own." DJ tipped her head to the side so Matt had better access to her neck. God, she loved the way he used his tongue and teeth.

DJ reached down, found the switch to her lamp and warm, golden light filled the lounge. This wasn't a hotel suite, she suddenly realized. Those were her books on the shelves. She'd chosen the painting above the mantel, the glass bowl on the coffee table.

This wasn't neutral territory, this was her home. And Matt was in it and he was about to make love to her.

He was in her space again…in her very intimate, feminine space. If he left—when he left!—she'd have memories of him here, in her bed, naked in her apartment. She didn't know if she wanted that, but then again, she couldn't stop this…

Well, she could—of course she could. Matt would walk away if she asked him to, but she didn't want to ask him anything.

Except, maybe, to inquire as to when he was planning to strip her down and kiss her in certain feminine, neglected places.

Matt pulled her sweater up and over her head. DJ felt the clasp of her bra spring apart. Then the material was a flash of blue on the floor and Matt's tanned hands were on her pale flesh, kneading and squeezing her breasts, her nipples pushing into the palms of his hands.

DJ felt Matt step away from her and she turned around to watch him pull his shirt and sweater over his head, revealing a wide chest lightly covered with sun-kissed hair. His happy trail, darker and heavier, ran from his belly button and disappeared beneath the band of his jeans.

DJ's hand drifted over his stomach, her fingers exploring the hard ridges of his six-pack. How he managed to maintain his fitness level and physique while working the crazy hours he did, God only knew.

"Bedroom," Matt commanded, holding out his hand.

Darby led him up the stairs into the loft, wondering if he'd like her bedroom, decorated by Jules Brogan in cream and mint.

But Matt only had eyes for her—his gaze moved from her breast to her face and back again as he shucked his shoes and stepped out of his jeans.

Moving around her, he lay down on the bed and tucked his arms behind his head. "I love watching you undress."

The appreciation in his expression, the desire in his eyes, made her feel intensely feminine, extraordinarily powerful. DJ took her time, slowly removing her boots, sliding her leggings down her hips inch by excruciating inch.

When she was finally naked, she sat down on the side of her bed, her hip pressing into Matt's hard thigh. Her thumb skated over his hip bone, and she marveled at how soft his skin was right there. Holding her hair back with her hand, she bent down so her lips could graze his shaft, her tongue could nibble his tip with tiny, sexy touches she knew he loved. She felt him jump, go from simply hard to steel, and wasn't surprised when Matt's hand gripped her head, urging her to take him into her mouth. She did, and twisted her tongue around his tip, curling her fingers at the bottom of his erection.

She used her mouth on him for a few minutes more before sliding up his body, straddling his hips so that her core came into contact with his solid heat. She was so close already, it wouldn't take much...

"This. You." Matt lifted his hands to play with her breasts, then lifted himself with his core muscles—hot, hot, hot—and swiped his tongue across one nipple, then the other. Holding himself in that position, he slid a finger between her and his dick, finding her happy spot with deadly precision.

"Need you, baby," Matt muttered, falling back. His other hand patted the side table and he lifted the foil packet to his teeth, ripped it open and pulled the condom from the packet. Sliding her back, he rolled down the latex, his eyes glinting with desire.

DJ wished they could make love without a condom. She wanted to feel him skin on skin, heat on heat. She thought about suggesting it, but knew he'd never trust her again. She'd failed them once when it came to birth control and he wouldn't take another chance. She didn't blame him, but a part of her wished they had that level of trust.

Matt placed his hands on her hips, pulled her so the tip of his penis rested at her opening. She expected him to slide in—she was wet and ready and he knew it. But Matt just pulled her head down and gave her a long, languid kiss before his eyes, so brilliantly green, looked into hers.

"What are you thinking, DJ?"

She couldn't tell him. It was too personal, far outside the parameters of what they expected from each other. She pulled a smile onto her face and rubbed herself against him, still resenting the thin barrier between them. "Just thinking how much I enjoy this and how much I love being with you."

"A truth but not the whole truth. Tell me, Dylan-Jane."

DJ rolled her head, looking toward the window to

avoid his eyes. Matt gently turned her head to face him
again. DJ saw the determination on his face and knew
he wouldn't let this go. He was going to stay exactly
where he was until she told him the truth. Dammit.

"I was wishing that you trusted me enough to go
without the condom, so we could be together without
a barrier." She saw the flash of panic in his eyes and
shook her head. "I understand why you won't and I
don't blame you… It would've been nice, that's all,"
she quietly added.

Matt didn't say anything but his eyes didn't leave
hers. She felt his hand slide between them, felt him
touch himself before pulling his hand away again.
Before she could comprehend that he'd removed the
condom, he was inside her, skin on skin, his heat and
hardness filling her, touching her without any barrier
between them. Igniting instantly, she surged against
him, blown away by how splendid he felt.

But mostly, she was conscious of her heart swell-
ing, her soul sighing at his display of faith. Tears ran
down her cheeks and she buried her face against his
neck, feeling absolved and trusted. And if she allowed
herself the fantasy, this one action of his might suggest
that she was loved. Just a little.

At the thought, an orgasm slammed her hot and hard.
Her heart and soul detonated simultaneously.

Mason tossed back the comforter on his bed and
sent an uninterested glance at the massive flat-screen
TV on the opposite wall. He sat down on the edge of
his king-size bed and looked at the pile of books on his
bedside table. He didn't want to watch TV; he certainly
didn't want to read. What he most wanted was Callie…

He wanted her here in his cream-and-brown, professionally decorated bedroom, rolling around on his big-enough-for-a-party bed.

He ran his hand over the back of his neck, feeling like his skin was too tight for his body. After skating, he should be tired, but what he needed was a release, an hour or two—or five—of unimaginable pleasure. Mason picked up his phone and scrolled through his contact list, stopping when he hit a name. Kate would be awake; he could call, slip out of the house and be at hers in twenty minutes.

It was very late, his guys were asleep and a nuclear bomb would have trouble waking them up. They would never know he was gone. Mason looked down at his T-shirt and his thin cotton pants, and knew that he wasn't going anywhere. He didn't want Kate.

He didn't want anyone but Callie.

Crap. Mason dropped his head and released a series of f-bombs, cursing his attraction to a woman who filled his thoughts and haunted his dreams. Once he got her out of his system, his life would go back to normal, he was sure of it.

Mason looked down at his phone and scrolled up, stopping on the Cs. Her number was there, big and bold, taunting him to call. If he couldn't see her, taste her, make love to her, then he could hear her voice.

Mason glanced at the time, saw that it was close to midnight and sighed. She'd be asleep and she wouldn't appreciate a midnight call…

But what if she wasn't? What if she was up and thinking about him and feeling lonely and horny and frustrated and…

What if she was feeling even a little of what he was? No guts, no glory.

Mason hit the green icon on his phone and held his breath as the phone dialed out. One ring, two.

Four, five...crap. Mason was at the point of hanging up when Callie's breathless "hello" stopped the incessant ringing.

He was so surprised that, for an instant, he lost his words.

"Mason, if you're trying to do some heavy breathing, you're really bad at it."

Mason chuckled. "Sorry, I didn't expect you to answer so I zoned out from surprise."

"Why wouldn't I answer?" Callie asked.

"Sleeping, annoyed that I phoned you so late," Mason replied, leaning against his leather headboard. He swung his legs onto the bed and closed his eyes, allowing the slight rasp of her voice to slide over him.

"I seldom go to bed before twelve thirty. And I'm happy you called me."

Mason smiled. "Were you thinking of me, Callie?"

"I was. I was looking at my bucket list, wondering how you'd feel if I called you up and asked you to do something with me so that I can cross it off my list."

Mason's heart accelerated into a flat-out gallop and all the moisture in his mouth dried up. "As I recall, there were only two items on your list that you couldn't manage on your own. A one-night stand and phone sex. I'm happy to help with either, darlin'."

Very, very happy to help. He was a good guy that way.

Callie didn't reply and Mason could easily imagine her blushing, staring at the ceiling in mortification. The silence between them widened and Mason was about to back off, to crack a joke to break the tension, when Callie spoke again.

"If I can't even ask you for phone sex how can I actually do it?" Callie whispered.

Thank you, baby Jesus.

Mason closed his eyes, relief seeping out of every pore. He was already rock-hard at the suggestion and he wanted Callie wet and writhing as well.

"I'd love to have phone sex with you, Cal."

Callie's sigh of relief was audible. After a moment, she spoke again. "So, how does this work? Do I just say a whole bunch of sexy stuff?"

Mason was glad she couldn't see his grin. "Why don't you let me make love to you, Cal?"

"You can do that?" Callie asked, skeptically.

Damn straight he could. Mason released a low laugh. He'd start with the easy stuff. "What are you wearing?"

"Uh…um." Callie hesitated. "A short black transparent negligee?"

No, she wasn't. Mason suspected she was wearing something comfortable, something she wore every night. "I think you are wearing a long T-shirt and sleeping shorts, maybe just the shirt. Your hair is down, you have no makeup on and your eyes are that stunning shade I call horny blue."

"God." Callie released her first moan and Mason felt like he'd won a million-dollar lotto ticket. He intended to have her moaning a lot longer. "For your information, Cal, I don't need to see you in negligees or heels. As soon as I see you, no matter what you are wearing, I go instantly hard."

"You…do?"

How could she not have noticed? Mason brushed his hand over his engorged dick, wishing it was Callie touching him. "Are you imagining me there with you? Wishing I was?"

"Yes. So much." Then Callie surprised him by continuing. "I'm thinking about kissing you, your tongue touching mine."

"I love your mouth, Cal." Mason slipped his palm under the band of his pants to take himself in hand. "I'm kissing my way down your neck, Cal, licking my way across your collarbone, sucking the creamy skin on your shoulder. You have such gorgeous skin."

Callie released a quick, sharp sigh and he heard a tiny gasp. Was she as turned on as he was? God, he wished he could see her. He considered suggesting they switch to a video call, but he couldn't risk spooking her so he pushed the idea aside.

"I'm thinking about my arms being around you, pulling you in. Your softness pressing against my hardness and trust me, Cal—" he brushed his thumb over this tip "—I'm hard everywhere."

"Are you touching yourself right now?" he asked.

"Um…no?"

Mason bit the inside of his lip to keep from laughing out loud. "Honey, how am I going to make you come if you don't touch yourself?"

Mason made a few more graphic suggestions and wondered how much longer he could last.

"God, Mace. This is so hot."

They hadn't even gotten to the good part yet. Mason clutched the sheets on his bed, not wanting to finish before she did. This was all about Callie.

Everything was about Callie.

This wasn't some random female he wanted to love and leave, this woman—older than him, requiring more effort than he normally was prepared to put in—was Callie Brogan. Wife, mother, widow, yes, but that wasn't how he saw her. He simply saw a woman comfortable in her own skin, someone who'd loved and lost and wore her scars proudly. Wise, funny, giving…not someone he could play with.

What the hell was she doing?

Despite her brave talk about not wanting a relationship, she wasn't the type who would give herself to any man without some sort of emotional connection.

He didn't do connections, emotional or otherwise. Keeping his boys' heads on straight was hard enough and he didn't want the responsibility of making another person happy.

His skills only extended to making a woman in his bedroom happy—after that they were on their own.

"Mace?"

"Yeah?"

"You stopped talking, I thought I lost you."

He closed his eyes. "Maybe we should stop this, Cal."

Callie released a low wail. "You have got to be kidding me! Why?"

"I can't give you what you want, honey."

"Right now, all I want from you is an orgasm," Callie retorted, her words covered in a layer of fierceness. "I swear, if you leave me hanging, I will disembowel you with a butter knife."

The corners of Mason's mouth lifted at her threat.

"Now, where were we?" Callie demanded. "Are you touching yourself, Mason? Do you wish your hand was mine?"

She had no damn idea how much.

DJ woke up slowly, her eyelids heavy as she fought the urge to snuggle down, to drift off again. It was still dark and she forced her eyes open, looked toward her window to judge the time. Did she still have an hour or three to snooze?

The drapes on her window were closed but she could see a bright sliver of light near the window frame. Why were her drapes closed? They had no neighbors on this side of the house so privacy wasn't a problem and she couldn't remember when last she'd pulled the drapes.

DJ tried to roll out of bed, but then the warmth of a male arm tightened around her and she tensed. Matt was hogging most of her big bed, his head on her pillow, his jaw rough with stubble. His spiky eyelashes lay against his cheek. His mouth, usually pulled into a stern line, looked relaxed and fuller in sleep.

Like her, Matt was naked and DJ was struck by how right it felt to wake up with this big man in her bed. The crisp hair on his chest tickled her nipple and her hip was half on his hard stomach. Under her cheek, she could feel the impressive bulge of his biceps, the smooth male skin.

Her knee rested on his hard-as-steel morning erection.

Somehow this felt more normal than waking up alone. Matt hogging the bed, holding her tight, made her feel secure, content, so very well loved.

Last night had been such fun, far more enjoyable than she ever thought possible. After tugging her around the rink and finally getting her to skate without falling for a few yards—she wasn't ever going to skate for fame or fortune—she and Matt joined the rest of the clan in the Frog Pond Café to warm up. Matt, with his dry sense of humor, had them cracking up with his observations about their fellow skaters. When Levi asked him about his work, he captured their attention by recounting some of his more interesting cases. DJ, who followed his career more closely than they did, immediately realized that he didn't talk about his biggest wins or the high-profile trials he was involved in. Possibly because those cases were filled with despair and tragedy.

It took a strong man to deal with what he did, DJ decided. He delved into a world few people had knowledge of. Political and war refugees, international criminals, the darker side of humanity. She understood his need to detach, to stay uninvolved. If he didn't, he wouldn't be able to do his job. Was his emotional detachment a habit? Was that why he wasn't interested in commitment?

DJ sighed. Why was she suddenly so curious? Why did she suddenly want to know the answers to these questions? They weren't going anywhere serious; they couldn't. In a few weeks, he'd be leaving her and Boston and she didn't know when she'd next see him. She never asked for the details of his life, because she couldn't afford to feel close to him, to create an emotional tie that would make her miss him more than she already did.

They didn't do ties, emotional or otherwise.

What they had was mutual respect and sex. Hot, crazy, wild sex.

Except that…

They hadn't.

They hadn't had sex last night, they'd made—dammit to hell and back—love. Sweet, sexy, soul-on-fire love.

It had been emotional and touching and, God, wonderful. It was fairy-tale sex. Sex like she wanted to have for the rest of her life. It was sex that walked hand in hand with early-morning snuggling, lighthearted arguments over whose turn it was to make coffee, pick up milk and buy takeout.

DJ tensed, annoyed with herself. It had been one

night—*one night!*—and now she was picking out crockery and thinking about a life together? Had amazing sex finally melted her brain?

She and Matt didn't have any type of future except for maybe a stolen weekend here and there. They lived on different continents, in different time zones. They both had careers that demanded enormous amounts of time and energy. There was no way they could have anything more than the next few weeks and, possibly, some hookups in the New Year. That was who they were, what they did.

DJ looked at his closed eyes, his strong profile, and told herself not to be stupid. Besides, neither of them wanted anything more, really. Despite her promise to try and be part of the Brogan clan, she was never going to give another person the chance to hurt her again. Her parents had taught her that lesson well.

This was about sex, fun, a fantasy. Matt was a hookup, not a husband.

Eight

"Morning," Matt muttered, his eyes still closed but his thumb making patterns on the bare skin above her hip. "Question—how long have we been asleep? Where's my coffee? What time is it?"

DJ picked up his wrist, looked at his expensive time-piece and frowned. "Your watch has stopped."

Matt cranked open one eye. "My watch is one of the most iconic brands in the world, it doesn't *stop*."

"Well, it says that it's ten."

Matt lifted his arm, squinted at the steel-blue face and nodded. "That's because it is ten. In the morning." Matt resettled his arm across her waist, her breast in his hand, holding her close.

It took a moment for it to sink in that she was late, very late. "Matthew! I should've been at work three hours ago!"

"Nuh-uh. Apart from the fact that it's Saturday, last night the twins gave you the day off. Remember?" His eyes remained closed but a satisfied smile crossed his face. "They obviously suspected we'd need some time to recover." He waited a beat. "They weren't wrong."

There wasn't anything she wanted more than to lie here with Matt—well, maybe a cup of coffee came close—but she had checks to issue, orders to sign. Contracts to negotiate. And if she was being honest, she really wanted to put some distance between her and all those unwelcome feelings Matt pulled to the surface with his display of trust and his tender treatment of her.

DJ felt like he'd pushed the sharp end of a crowbar into a crack in her soul and was slowly prying her open to reveal the chaotic mess she was inside. She could sleep with him, but it was essential that she stopped confiding in him.

He was her lover who was leaving, not her friend.

She needed coffee. And an additional ten IQ points.

DJ wiggled out from under his arm and sat on the side of the bed. Seeing Matt's long-sleeved shirt lying on the floor by her feet, she pulled it over her head before picking up her phone. She swiped the screen and saw that she had a few text messages on the group she and the twins used to communicate. Maybe there was a problem at the shop; they wanted her to come in; they needed her.

Her hopeful assumptions were way off base. It's nine thirty, guess you got some last night. Darby's message was accompanied by a few high fives and a thumbs-up.

Shop is quiet. Don't want to see you here was Jules's contribution to the conversation.

Dammit. DJ looked over her shoulder to Matt, who was lying on his side, his head propped up on his hand. Jules felt her stomach flip over and heat rushed to that space between her legs. Sexy guy...

She pouted. "I'm not going to work. I've been banished."

Matt's mouth twitched with amusement. "If I didn't have a healthy ego, I'd feel insulted by your disappointed tone." DJ felt his hand skim her hair. It was another tender gesture so DJ stood up and walked over to the window, pulling the drapes aside. Cracking the window an inch, she sucked in freezing air before resting her head against the cold glass. She felt on edge and jittery, as if there were a hundred tabs open in her brain and none were loading properly. What was wrong with her?

"What's going on in your head, Dylan-Jane?"

She couldn't answer him—she'd revealed too much last night and she needed to put a whole lot of space between them and whatever the hell she was feeling. Because it was strange and unfamiliar and she didn't understand any of it. And not understanding scared her...

DJ heard movement behind her. Matt rolled out of bed, stood up and stretched, blissfully unconcerned about his nakedness. And why should he be? He had the muscled, hard body of an athlete and a face that stopped traffic. She admired his long legs—and his butt—as he disappeared into the bathroom. She lightly banged her forehead against her window. *Pull yourself together, Winston. You are acting like a fool...*

Her phone buzzed with an incoming message and this time it was from Callie. Next Christmas event: Christmas tree buying followed by cookie making at my house. Friday. Invite Matt.

Matt walked out of the bathroom, picked up a pair of boxers and slid into them. Pushing his hands through his hair, he arched an eyebrow. "Can I get some coffee?"

"Sure." DJ followed him down the spiral staircase and leaned her forearms on the granite counter as he made himself at home in her kitchen. Having him in her space—wearing only boxers and a spectacular case of bedhead—felt right. She could see them doing this next week, next month, next...

Stop! Distance, Winston. This is your life, not a rom-com.

DJ looked down at the phone in her hand and switched mental gears. "Callie has invited you to go Christmas tree shopping and to make cookies next Friday."

Matt took two mugs from a shelf and dug through her selection of coffee pods. He selected two dark espressos and popped one into the machine. While he waited, he leaned his hip against the counter and smiled. "Why do you make it sound like a root canal?"

"Close. Firstly, Christmas tree shopping with the twins and Callie can go on for hours as they search for the perfect tree. Since all Christmas trees look the same to me, it's torture. And I'm not the cookie-baking type."

"So drink wine and watch."

Matt handed her a cup of coffee, his expression serious. "Why do you hate Christmas so much, Dylan-Jane?"

It was a good opportunity to practice keeping her emotional distance so she trotted out her stock answer. "It's a rip-off. A commercial exercise we're suckered into."

"Cynical," Matt said, preparing his own coffee.

DJ sighed when the rich dark taste hit her tongue. "Truthful. Listen, I know you feel the same way since you're the guy who flew back to The Hague on Christmas day last year to work."

"My client was in trouble. I don't hate Christmas, I just don't have a lot of experience with it." Matt leaned back and crossed his feet. "When I was a kid, there wasn't money for Christmas presents. Hell, there was barely any money for rent." He saw her puzzled look and explained. "My grandparents were richer than God, but they cut my dad off when he got into trouble with alcohol and drugs. When he dropped out of college for the third time, they washed their hands of him."

DJ knew Matt wouldn't appreciate sympathy so she just held his gaze and listened.

"I went to live with my grandparents—lots of money, lots of luxury—but they were atheists so Christmas came and went like any other day in their house. Then I went off to college and Christmas breaks were spent skiing or on the beach—either way I was partying. Baking cookies, ice skating and tree shopping never featured." Matt lifted his mug to his mouth and took a sip. "Sounds nice, though."

Memories, hot but sweet, rushed in. "My dad loved Christmas, far more than my mother. He took me skating, shopping, to see the tree-lighting ceremony on Boston Common. We built snowmen and decorated the house."

"But now you loathe the season. So what happened?"
Don't answer, don't answer...

"He left. A week before Christmas he walked out, leaving me with my mom." DJ winced, aghast that she'd let so much slip. She never spoke about her dad and she hated talking about her mother.

Matt didn't make any false sounds of sympathy or utter any platitudes. "A week before Christmas? That's harsh. Are you still in contact?"

DJ felt the prickle of tears in her throat. "Nope. He dropped out of my life completely the following year. It was around the time he remarried and replaced me with his stepdaughter."

Matt stared down into his coffee mug before shaking his head. "I swear, I think the ability to bear a child should be heavily regulated and subjected to strict application rules."

"I think I want to apply, Matt."

Her words came out of nowhere and Matt looked as shocked as she felt. She bit her lip and closed her eyes, wondering who she was becoming. This new person tolerated Christmas, wanted to move emotionally closer to Matt and kept opening her mouth to allow odd statements to escape.

Original DJ wanted to kick DJ Version Two off the nearest tall building.

Surprise settled onto Matt's handsome face. "Uh… I'm not sure what response you are looking for."

"You don't have to give me one." DJ stared at the V in the base of his throat. She shook her head, suddenly needing to admit the truth to herself. Out loud. "I think I do want a baby, Matt. Sometime in the future, I want someone of my own to love, someone who can't leave me."

DJ stared down at her coffee, wondering how he'd react, what he'd say about that deeply personal revelation. She'd rather him not say anything at all than have him utter a cliché. She was so stepping out of the box they'd drawn around their relationship. This wasn't fun or superficial. This was raw and deep and scary, but it was real. And honest. Maybe she was a little tired of shallow, maybe she was braver than she thought and maybe it was time to look deeper, to be more.

Matt looked poleaxed at her unexpected revelation, and she knew he needed more time to process what she'd said, this new path she'd put herself on. She stood up and patted his shoulder. "Ignore me, I'm just tired, Matt. Christmas makes me emotional. Don't worry, this is just some temporary seasonal craziness. After some food and coffee, I'll be back to my normal, distant, cynical self."

The problem with that statement was that, for the first time in forever, she wasn't sure she was speaking the truth.

And, worse than that, she didn't think Matt believed her.

When DJ walked into the media room of the Brogan house a few days later, Darby looked up from her corner of the massive leather couch and smiled. When DJ reached the fireplace, she held out her hands to the blaze before picking up Darby's glass of red wine and taking a healthy sip.

"Hey! Get your own!" Darby protested.

DJ took another defiant sip before passing the glass back to Darby. "Where's Jules?"

"She and Noah flew to Cancún to see someone about a super yacht. He to design it, she to decorate it."

DJ turned her head to look out the tall windows and sighed at the freezing rain. Cancún sounded awesome. Jules and Noah had the right idea. DJ flopped down onto the seat next to Darby and rested her head on the back of the couch. She sighed and closed her eyes, fighting the urge to doze off. Long days at work and long nights with Matt were taking their toll.

Darby lifted her bare feet—her toes were rocking a bright orange polish—and placed them on DJ's thigh.

DJ looked closer and saw that Darby's big toes sported a butterfly sticker. "Cute."

"Thanks." Darby held her glass against her cheek-bone. DJ felt her friend's eyes on her and turned to look into her beloved face. Knowing that Darby was going to interrogate her about Matt, DJ jumped in first. "Any interesting projects on the horizon?"

Her tactic worked because excitement flashed in Darby's thunderstorm eyes. "I've seen the bid documents for the new art gallery the city wants built, the one close to the MFA? They've placed an open call for submissions for the design. They'll select the best ten concepts and those architects will be allowed to submit their designs for consideration." Darby frowned. "The only problem is that Judah Huntley is throwing his hat into the ring."

"Who?"

"Judah Huntley is one of the world's best architects, described as a tour de force, a visionary, ruthless in his quest for design perfection. And, as I've heard, he's submitting a concept design."

Ah, damn. DJ placed her hand over Darby's knee. "You're a wonderful architect, Darbs."

Darby pouted. "It isn't fair that a man can be that talented, that smart and that hot."

DJ's eyebrows flew up at Darby's comment. "Hot?"

Darby leaned forward and dug her phone out of her pocket, then her fingers danced across the screen. When she handed DJ the phone Darby looked down into the very sexy face of a dark-eyed man in his midthirties. "Holy cupcakes with sprinkles."

"I can show you a photo with his shirt off," Darby offered.

DJ held up her hand. "I don't think my heart can

stand it." She waved her hand in front of her face. "Phew, *hot* is too mild a word. Gorgeous, sex-on-a-stick."

"Let's not forget brilliant and ridiculously talented." Darby released a sigh and placed her phone facedown on the arm of the chair.

A thought occurred to DJ. "Question—why do you have a photo of Judah Huntley with his shirt off?"

Darby couldn't meet DJ's eyes. "I happened to Google him and a picture of him on a beach in Cyprus popped up."

"Just popped up?" DJ asked, skeptical.

"He was there with his opera-singer girlfriend. She has a house there," Darby muttered. "He's hot but I've heard he's an arrogant alpha-hole. Talking about hot men, how is yours?"

Damn, DJ had opened that door and Darby strolled on through. "Matt?"

"You say that as if there are a dozen others. Is he joining you for the cookie-making marathon?"

DJ rolled her eyes. "He's actually looking forward to it." So was she. It sounded like it was going to be fun. She narrowed her eyes at her friend. "Did you sprinkle some of your magic I-love-Christmas dust on him? On us?"

"Maybe," Darby replied, looking smug. "So, what is happening between you and Matt? You're spending every night together."

DJ leaned across Darby, took her empty glass, poured some wine into it and took a sip. When Darby reached for it, DJ held it against her chest. "Mine. Especially if you are going to make me talk."

"Then talk."

DJ pulled her hair to one side and placed her hand

on Darby's foot. How to explain this? "Matt's arrival in Boston has been a catalyst for me."

"How so?"

"Just being with him, in his company, shakes me up, makes me think. It's like he's handed me a pair of glasses and I see the world clearly."

"He's done all that?" Darby had the right to sound skeptical.

"Not directly. But a lot has happened since he arrived, and I've been forced to look at my life and my interactions with people with a more critical eye." DJ shook her head. "I'm suddenly not content to skate on the surface, Darby. It's not all fun and games anymore."

"Do you have feelings for him?" Darby asked carefully.

"I've always had feelings for him, I wouldn't have slept with him for so long if I didn't. If you are asking me if I'm falling deeper into something, then..."

DJ hesitated, not wanting to verbalize her thoughts. It all felt a bit too real.

"Then?" Darby prompted.

"My head tells me I shouldn't want a relationship. I know how emotionally dangerous they can be. He definitely doesn't want one."

"But you're in one, DJ," Darby pointed out. "You've been in each other's lives for a long time and while it might not be the most conventional relationship in the world, it's still a relationship."

DJ released a frustrated sigh. "I know. Relationships are risky."

"Sure, but risk is part of living, part of life. And sometimes—like for twenty-five years—people don't let you down."

DJ groaned. "You just had to take the shot, didn't you?"

"Yeah." Darby grinned. "The point is worth repeating…some people don't let you down, some people are in it for the long haul. Maybe Matt can be that person, *your* person."

DJ would love to believe that, but he wasn't. She knew he wasn't because he kept reminding her he was returning to The Hague—he'd utter seemingly offhand comments designed to remind her not to expect anything more than the fling, with a definite expiration date, they were currently enjoying.

Besides, she'd been protecting herself for so long, how could she be expected to throw caution to the wind and place her heart in someone else's hands?

DJ looked at the bottle of wine and sighed. "There's a little wine left in that bottle. I'm going to be a good person and rescue it."

Darby handed her the bottle. "You make me proud, every day."

Nine

Work had Matt holed up in the study of Lockwood House for two full days, staring at phone records, surveillance footage and reading reams of case notes on his human-trafficking case. He had to make the tough decision on whether the Europol investigators had enough evidence to prosecute. In Matt's opinion, the case was still light and he wanted more.

He only had one chance to nail those bastards to the wall and they couldn't take a chance on circumstantial evidence. They needed solid, stick-like-glue evidence, as he told the lead investigator.

He was not a popular guy at Europol HQ at the moment.

Needing air and a sense of normalcy, he left Lockwood House shortly before lunch and headed downtown, reluctantly admitting that he needed to touch base with DJ. They hadn't connected for the past forty-eight hours and he missed her.

Why?

For years and years, they'd shared only snippets of time and, while he thought about her occasionally, he'd never felt this primal urge to see her face. Missing her had nothing to do with sex and the way they burned up the sheets. This was about making a connection.

He was due to return to Europe after Christmas and he and DJ were supposed to go back to normal, to resume their see-you-when-I-see-you relationship. A year ago, jumping in and out of her life felt normal, sophisticated, modern. Now it…didn't.

He wanted to see more of DJ. He wanted to meet his daughter and he wanted Emily to meet his… What was DJ? His girlfriend, his partner, his significant other? What she wasn't was his on-and-off lover. He definitely wanted them to be more on than off, but how could he juggle his career, Emily and DJ? All while he was living across the world.

Not seeing DJ every day, having an eight-hour flight between them, was a hellish thought.

Matt shook his head, annoyed with himself. He shouldn't be obsessing. Was he using DJ as a way to distract himself because he'd yet to hear from Emily and was worried that he wouldn't? Or to avoid facing the fact that his grandfather's mind was rapidly deteriorating? Over this year, he'd realized he was losing his grandfather, had discovered a daughter he never knew he had and lost a child he'd never met—maybe his biological clock was ticking.

Matt found parking a block from Winston and Brogan's showroom and opened his car door to the frigid, snow-tinged winter air. Buttoning his coat, he stepped onto the sidewalk and frowned. Was having a family—having children, *more children*—something he was considering?

That wasn't a game he'd ever been interested in. He was the product of family dysfunction and he had no idea how to be a husband or a dad. He'd be as much of a dad to Emily as she'd let him be—accepting that she already had a dad and Matt was very late to the game—but more kids and a partner shouldn't be on his agenda.

Besides, even if he decided he wanted a wife, family, kids and a cat, when would he have the time? His work took up everything he had and then some. It had been hard enough trying to carve out time to be with DJ last Christmas. The coming year, with the trial looming, was going to be hell.

As much as he wanted to keep whatever this new thing was with DJ, realistically he didn't have it in him to make space for her in his life. There were too many obstacles—her life was in Boston, his was in The Hague. She couldn't move, neither could he. It was impossible.

So why was he even thinking about her in those terms?

Futile and impossible.

"Are you just going to stand there and hover?"

Matt jerked his head up to see Darby standing outside the showroom, stamping her feet. She looked chic and professional. "Hey." Matt pushed his hand through his hair as he walked up to her. "Where have you been in this horrible weather?"

"I went to a bid presentation for a new art gallery that I'd love to design."

"That sounds exciting," Matt replied, genuinely interested.

"Yeah but I don't have a hope of getting it." Darby pulled a face as Matt opened the door to Winston and Brogan and allowed her to precede him. "Judah Huntley was there and the board of governors was salivating at the thought of getting the amazing Huntley to design their new gallery."

Matt grinned. "I met him once, at a cocktail party at the US embassy in Amsterdam."

"Embassy party? Ooh la la," Darby teased.

"Trust me, embassy parties are as tedious as hell. Judah and I were equally bored and we ended up hitting some clubs in Leidseplein."

"Is that the Dutch word for the red-light district?" Darby's eyes were full of humor.

Matt grinned. "No, funny girl. Is Dylan-Jane in?"

"She was when I left. Are you still joining us for cookie-making night on Friday? We've moved the venue from Mom's house to the coffee shop. Mom needed more production space."

Inside the showroom. Matt hung his coat on the hook next to Darby's. "How many cookies do you guys eat?"

Darby led Matt up the stairs to the offices on the second floor. "They aren't all for us. We send a lot to women's shelters in the city," Darby said, stopping by her office door. "This is me. Go pull DJ from her spreadsheets and take her to lunch. Better, take her Christmas shopping. She knows what I want, I emailed her the list."

Matt laughed, shook his head and walked the few steps to DJ's office. Rapping on the frame of the open door, he watched as she took her time to lift her head, her eyes foggy with concentration. They cleared, she smiled and fireworks went off in his brain.

"Matt, hi. This is a nice surprise." DJ, dressed from head to toe in black, stood up, effortlessly elegant. Her long hair was pulled up into a wispy twist and her eyes were the rich color of bitter chocolate behind her black-framed, hot-as-hell glasses.

Hands off, Edwards. "I've come to take you for an early lunch. And Darby wants me to take you Christmas shopping."

"Okay."

Matt walked over to her and put his hand on her forehead, dramatically checking her temperature. "Are you feeling all right? I'm talking about Christmas shopping, with cheery music and crowds and commercialism."

DJ pushed his hand away. "I'm reconsidering my stance on Christmas. So far this season hasn't been that bad."

"God, you *are* ill. Lie down, take off all your clothes and I'll check you for spots and injuries."

DJ laughed. "Funny."

DJ lifted her mouth to kiss him, then hesitated. To hell with that. Hooking his finger into the low waistband of her pants, he pulled her to him, holding her lovely face in his other hand and lowering his mouth to hers.

The first taste of her was a shock—there was a minor jolt of electricity to his heart and groin before he sighed and settled into the kiss. Slim arms encircled his neck and fingers pushed into his hair, danced across his jaw. Thoughts of trafficked girls and kids, gun runners and drug smugglers—and annoyed lead investigators—fled and there was only DJ...

Always DJ.

The thought rocked Matt and he pulled his mouth from hers, avoiding her puzzled look by holding her head against his chest. He could feel his fingers tingling and his heart pounding out a terrified beat. No, that couldn't be the way he was thinking. His off-the-chain thought was just a reaction to kissing her, to not seeing her for a day or two.

*You normally don't see her for months and you've
never had these thoughts before...*

Shut the hell up, brain.

DJ wiggled out of his tight embrace and stepped
away from him. "Everything okay?"

Matt kept his face blank and prepared to lie his ass
off. He was only looking at his life and feeling like it
was a distorted version of what he thought he wanted.
Only when he put DJ into the picture, did the picture
come into focus.

Really, Edwards? There was no way for them to have
more than they currently did; they lived different lives
on different continents. Besides, except for that one-off
comment about having kids, DJ had never so much as
hinted that she wanted more from him. He didn't have
more! He was giving her all he could.

"Sure, why wouldn't it be?"

Matt walked over to the window and placed his hand
against the cool glass. He felt off-center and weird, thoroughly disconcerted. How had DJ morphed from being
the woman he wanted to occasionally spend time with,
into the woman he wanted to spend *all* his time with?

Was it Boston? Christmas? A brain tumor?

DJ perched on the arm of her sofa and crossed her
legs. "Actually, I was about to call you. Please feel free
to say no but my mom has invited us to supper. She
wants to meet the famous lawyer I'm dating."

Matt frowned. "Yeah, right." He scoffed. "I'm not
famous."

"Apparently you have a bit of a rep for being a great
lawyer. Strange but true."

Matt smiled at her gentle teasing.

"Anyway, Fenella wants to meet you and while I'd
rather get my eyes dug from my skull with a hot tea-

spoon, I can't say no. You can. Say no, Matt. I like you too much to subject you to Fenella Carew."

Matt picked up the conversational hand grenade Darby dropped at his feet. "Carew is your mother? The ex–attorney general of Massachusetts?"

Darby snapped her fingers and pointed her index finger at him. "Yeah. Lucky me."

Matt tipped his head to the side. "Judging by your underwhelming response, I assume she was a better lawyer than she was a mother."

"Much. One of my biggest fears is that I could, one day, be a mom like Fenella. Uninvolved, narcissistic, self-obsessed."

Matt just looked at her, his eyes steady on her face. He arched one eyebrow in a silent request for her to keep talking.

DJ threw her hands up into the air. "Why do I keep telling you stuff? Your eyes are like a truth drug! One look and I'm spilling my soul. It's very annoying," she complained.

Matt felt both proud and worried that this woman, the one who hated to talk, seemed to talk so easily to him.

"As a little girl, I loved pretty dresses, shoes, hair bands, anything that was pink and girlie, the more glitter the better. Every birthday and every Christmas all I wanted was makeup, plastic jewelry, tiaras and princess dresses. But she insisted I wear jeans, plain white shirts, ugly sneakers. Then she'd tell whoever would listen that I dressed like a boy, that she wished I'd act more like a girl. The next time I got ready to go out, I'd wear a dress and she'd tell me I looked dreadful and make me take it off." DJ folded her arms across her chest, her body language defensive. "My entire life was a constant stream of mixed messages."

"Babe." Not knowing what else to say, he hoped his one word would convey sympathy and sorrow and put a little warmth back into her eyes.

Matt reached out to take her hand, but she wouldn't meet his eyes, choosing instead to look out the window behind him. Her honesty made him wonder whether he'd be an uninterested dad like his father, or an autocrat like his grandfather. Neither, he decided, since he was never going to put himself in a place where he needed to raise a kid from scratch.

But he could ease some of DJ's fears now. "That's not you, DJ... She's not you. God, you are her exact opposite."

"I'm not," DJ protested. "Like her, I'm a perfectionist, uptight and anal. I overthink everything. My brain never shuts down."

"You're also honest. You told me about getting pregnant, told me about the miscarriage, you were open and forthright. You might not *like* to open up, but, when you do, you don't play games. You are nothing like your mother."

DJ started to argue but a squeeze of his fingers on her thigh kept her from speaking. "And instead of looking at Fenella as a role model, maybe you should start paying attention to your real mom and what she taught you."

DJ cocked her head, not understanding. One side of Matt's mouth lifted in a half smile. "DJ, Callie has been more your mom than anyone else. You've told me, more than once, that she was the one who bandaged your knees, gave you hugs, picked you up and dusted you off. You don't think you are a part of the Brogan family but you are the only person who thinks that. Callie worries about you as much as she worries about the twins and Levi, the Lockwood crew. Not a day goes by without her touching base with you, and she tells you every day that she loves you. She's your mom, DJ, by choice. And that sometimes means more."

God, he was her lover not her psychologist, her bed buddy not her life coach. DJ had lived on this planet quite successfully for nearly thirty years—she didn't need heartfelt advice from him. This wasn't what he did; this wasn't who they were.

Matt felt like he was standing on quicksand while his world rocked from side to side. Maybe he should book a plane ticket, fly to Europe and get a dose of reality. His grandfather was due to be moved into the assisted-living facility sometime between Christmas and the New Year. Matt could skip the festivities with the Brogans and return sometime before the New Year. If Emily was ready to meet him, they could do it after Christmas. That would give him some distance from DJ and, judging by that hearts-and-flowers speech, he needed some damn space.

Not that he was being insincere—he meant every word—but he didn't need her looking at him with stars in her eyes.

DJ stood on her toes and brushed her lips against his mouth in a tender kiss that rocked him on his emotional heels. He could do rough and wild, hot and fast, but emotion-soaked kisses were his downfall. DJ followed up that bombshell kiss by brushing her thumb against his lower lip.

He watched, discombobulated, as she picked up her phone and tapped out a message. Seconds later his device beeped. "My mom's address, in case one of us runs late. She wants us there by seven. Don't say I didn't warn you."

Matt heard the faint buzz of his phone ringing in his

pocket and pulled it out. With luck it would be his assistant or a colleague, someone who would bring him back down to planet Earth with a little legal-speak. He looked down at the screen and saw Emily's name.

Of course it was. Because, obviously, life didn't think he had enough on his plate right now. He shot a glance at DJ, realizing that he had yet to tell her about his daughter. Should he have told her? The old Matt, the one who just met up with DJ occasionally, wouldn't have bothered. But Boston Matt wanted to. He desperately wanted to ask her advice, to take her hand as he spoke to his daughter for the first time.

He was the person people leaned on, the one who steadied the ship, and yet here he was, looking to someone else—DJ—to do that for him.

No. That didn't work for him.

Matt pushed steel into his spine and turned his back to DJ as he answered his daughter's call.

"Emily? Hi, this is a surprise."

"Hi. I've been up all night thinking. I can't keep jerking you around, so if you want to meet, we can do that now."

Matt looked at DJ, who'd picked up her phone and was scrolling through it, but he knew she was listening to every word he uttered. He'd just invited her out for lunch and shopping, but he was going to bail on her. If he didn't meet Emily now, who knew when she'd find her nerve again?

"Yeah, okay, I can do that. Where are you?"

"I'll send you a GPS pin with the diner's coordinates. Just hurry, okay? I'm scared I'm going to bolt."

A cold hand squeezed his heart. "Please don't, Emily. I really want to see you." Matt looked at his watch. "I'm on my way. Ten minutes, okay?"

Matt turned to Dylan-Jane, not surprised to see her puzzled expression. He knew she was about to ask who Emily was, why he needed to run. He didn't have the time to answer, he just needed to get to his car so he could see his daughter.

He clamped his lips together, not trusting himself to speak.

To spill.

But, crap, he wanted to. He wanted to share this news, his worry and excitement, with DJ. Because the urge rocked him, Matt took a bunch of mental steps backward.

Emily and DJ were two very separate parts of his life. Emily was linked to him, by blood and responsibility, and she was a consequence of actions he'd taken a long time ago. DJ was his fun, a way to step out of his very busy life and relax. These two parts of his life didn't need to merge.

He hadn't promised DJ anything beyond good sex and some laughs.

Running scared, Edwards?

Damn straight he was and he was okay with that.

DJ grabbed his arm as he walked past her. "Matt, what's going on? Who is Emily?"

He jerked his arm away, fighting the urge to hold her, to let her hold him. He needed distance *now*. He needed to sever this connection, and fast, before he caved.

"I don't have the time to deal with your jealousy, Dylan-Jane."

Matt watched pain flare in her eyes as his words struck their target. And, yep, he felt his heart cramp. Well, it was no less than he deserved.

DJ's eyebrows flew upward. "What? Where did that come from?"

Matt felt overwhelmed, not an emotion he was accustomed to experiencing. He ran a hand over his face, wishing the floor would open up and let him slide on through. "I need to go, DJ. Emily isn't relevant to our relationship."

He'd resorted to lawyer-speak, a new low.

DJ nodded once, her eyes blank and her expression wooden. Her voice was cool when she asked her next question. "Do we even have a relationship, Matt?"

They were doing this *now*?

"Yeah, sure. What we have works for us because we don't make demands on each other. Not for time or information." He glanced at his watch, saw seconds ticking by and thought about Emily bolting. "I really do need to go."

DJ nodded once before making an exaggerated gesture toward her office door. "Then, please, don't let me hold you up."

Her voice was bland, but the part of him that wasn't terrified about meeting Emily and confused by the emotions churning inside him realized there was a note of anger in her voice.

"Goodbye, Matt."

That sounded like finality. Okay, maybe he'd overplayed his hand, but Emily was waiting. "I'll see you later, Dylan-Jane. If not at your place, then at your mother's."

"Yay," she muttered to his departing back and her words drifted over to him. "Misery loves company."

Ten

DJ lifted her fist to her mouth and stared at the door Matt slammed shut behind him.

What in the name of all things sweet and holy had just happened? One minute she'd felt like she was the center of his world, like he genuinely cared about her, and the next he was trotting out his we're-only-sleeping-together shtick.

One moment she'd been standing in his spotlight while he chased away the menacing shadows of her childhood. In that moment, it felt like they had one heart, a shared soul. Because words were inadequate, she'd kissed him, reached up to brush her mouth against his lips to try and convey how much she appreciated his insight.

Matt had always seen more of who she really was than she was comfortable with. Maybe that was why she kept him at a distance, why she never allowed their conversations to go very deep. Because she knew that if she did, she could fall for him.

He was the one man she'd allowed to peer into the murky haze that made up her soul. But, because she was so damn scared of getting hurt, of letting any man see her tangled mess of insecurities, she'd tried to keep him at a distance, knowing she could slip into love.

As she was doing now.

Slipping? Was she already there? Probably?

Almost definitely…

Lately, once or twice she'd thought Matt might be feeling more. It was in the way he looked at her, touched her, the way his actions spoke so much louder than words. The way he listened to what she had to say.

She'd genuinely thought something was shifting between them but his words and actions after his strange phone call blew that notion to hell and back. Underneath her confusion, fury rumbled.

How dare he think she was jealous because she asked a simple question? She absolutely knew Matt wasn't talking to another lover. One, she and Matt had an agreement—if they were together then they were *together*. They didn't cheat. But it was obvious that Emily, whoever the hell she was, was important to him. DJ understood that Matt had a life apart from hers, but it wasn't a crime to ask him for a peek inside that world.

Really, it wasn't like she'd asked him to marry her next Tuesday.

What was the big deal?

She released a long, irritated stream of air before realizing that Matt rarely talked about his childhood or, God forbid, his feelings. DJ was the only one spilling her secrets and showing her soul. She'd talked about her father, his abandonment and how that had affected not only her views toward Christmas, but also toward men and relationships in general. She'd spoken about her mixed emotions over the loss of their baby and now, not twenty minutes ago, she'd told him all about Fenella.

Matt now *knew* her. She didn't know him.

DJ heard her door open and her heart lurched—she stupidly thought that Matt had returned, that he'd come back to apologize. But her hopes were dashed when Darby entered DJ's office, her expression concerned.

"Everything okay?" Darby asked. "I saw Matt rushing past like his pants were on fire."

DJ sank down on the arm of her sofa and shook her head. "I have no idea."

Darby frowned, closed the door behind her and sat on the coffee table in front of DJ. "What happened? He looked pretty relaxed when I spoke to him earlier."

DJ held her hands up. "I was talking to him about Fenella—she invited us to supper tonight—and I was explaining that she was hell to live with, how I never knew which way to jump because she was so damn inconsistent—"

"Talking about your mom, another breakthrough," Darby murmured. "When you start talking about your dad, I'll know that your wall is about to tumble."

DJ dropped her eyes and Darby gasped. "You told Matt about your dad? God, DJ, you never speak about him, not even to us."

Yet another way DJ had refused to open up. "I'm sorry, Darby."

Darby waved away her words. "I'm just thrilled that you are speaking to *somebody* about him. Go, Matt!" She frowned when DJ shook her head. "Or not. Tell me what happened, sweetie."

"He got a phone call from a woman. He called her Emily."

"Oh, hell." Darby did the math and added up incorrectly.

"No, it wasn't that type of call," DJ protested. "Emily isn't a girlfriend." DJ held up her hand to silence Darby's protest. "She's *not*, Darby. Trust me on this."

"Okay," Darby said, doubt in her voice.

"I asked who she was and he nearly snapped my head off. He made it very clear that I had no right to question him, that we didn't have that type of relationship."

"The snot-shoveling piece of a rat's—"

DJ interrupted Darby's rapidly escalating tirade. "He's right, though, Darby. We're only bed buddies. Our relationship was based on fun and good food, wine and truly excellent sex. Talking was not part of the fantasy."

"But I'm sensing that's changed?"

"Yes. For me, at least. Him? Not so much."

"How has it changed?"

It was too late to back away now, to switch subjects or to halt this conversation. But why did she need to? Darby was her oldest friend and she trusted her implicitly. "Because he's the only guy I can imagine doing this with."

"Doing what, darling?" Darby softly asked.

Dammit, Darby was going to make DJ verbalize it because Darby knew that articulating these feelings meant they couldn't be easily dismissed or denied. Once DJ said it, it would be out there, a living, breathing, tangible thing.

They both jumped when Jules poked her head through the door, her eyes bright with curiosity. "What's going on?"

Darby waved her in. "DJ is about to tell me that

she's in love with Matt," Darby said, her eyes not leaving DJ's face.

"I'm not, I don't think…" Yep, there she was, backtracking like mad. Ah, crap. DJ closed her eyes and jumped. "I'm in love with Matt, but I don't want to be. We've just had a huge fight, he won't talk to me and we're going to my mother's for dinner!"

"Call it off, DJ. You have enough to deal with without adding Furious Fenella to the mix."

DJ was about to agree with Darby, then she realized that, maybe, this was an opportunity not to be missed. If she pulled out all the stops—fantastic designer dress, do-me shoes, sexy hair and smoky eyes— she could show Matt what he was missing. Make him think about sticking around, trying to make something work between them.

DJ tipped her head and looked at her best friends. "I need your help."

They nodded, almost simultaneously.

"What do we need?" Darby asked. "A getaway van, a shovel, some rope?"

Jules rolled her eyes at her twin. "Seriously, you worry me. What do you need us to do, DJ?"

It warmed DJ to know these were friends who would move a body for her. But she needed something else today, something she'd enjoy less. "Come shopping with me."

DJ stood in her mother's expensively decorated white-on-white-on-whiter living room and clutched a glass of sparkling water to her chest.

As he always did, Jim, Fenella's closest confidant for the past fifteen years, offered DJ a glass of what she was sure would be an utterly delicious red. DJ wasn't brave enough to take the risk. She recognized the upholstery fabric; it was shockingly expensive. And the white carpet under their feet was just as pricey. Red wine, white furniture and nerves were a dangerous combination.

"I thought you said Matt was coming with you," Fenella said, obviously annoyed.

Nice to see you, too, Mom. "I'm sorry he couldn't make it," DJ quietly murmured.

"Did he give you a reason?"

Actually, no, she hadn't spoken to him since he walked out of her office hours before. She'd been too proud to call him and when he failed to make an appearance at her door by seven, she pulled on her coat and gloves and hat and walked the short distance to Fenella's house. He had the address, he'd either rock up or he wouldn't. It was out of her control.

DJ's solo appearance was greeted with as much enthusiasm as an audit visit from the IRS. DJ looked around the room as an awkward silence descended. No tree, no decorations, not even a hint of Christmas anywhere. Funny that she'd never noticed her mother's lack of Christmas spirit before.

The delicate chime of the doorbell catapulted Fenella to her feet. She scuttled to the hallway to yank open the front door. DJ folded her arms and watched Matt step inside, his enigmatic eyes meeting hers over Fenella's blond head. His eyes widened as he took in her body-skimming black dress. She felt his hot gaze like a caress, down her cleavage, over her hips, onto her exposed thighs. His eyes widened when he noticed the fire-engine red works of art on her feet.

DJ half smiled as he had to wrench his gaze upward. Her outfit had put a house-sized dent in her bank account, but his gobsmacked reaction was worth every penny.

She was damned if she'd make it easy for him to walk away, and if he did, she'd wanted to make it hard for him to forget her.

DJ took a sip from her glass of water—she was a little surprised that he was here. Yes, he'd said he would be, but she'd expected him to use their fight as an excuse not to attend.

But then she remembered that this was a man who wasn't afraid of conflict: he took on sovereign governments, warlords and irascible judges for a living. He most certainly would be able to handle her narcissistic mother.

DJ saw Matt hand over a bottle of what she knew to be a phenomenally expensive champagne before he removed his designer coat. His dark gray suit was tailored, his shirt white, his tie the color of old charcoal. He looked urbane and successful and every inch the powerful lawyer he was reputed to be.

But as he stepped into the living room, DJ saw the strain on his face, the banked emotion in his eyes. Whatever happened at his impromptu lunch date had upset him and DJ cursed herself for caring. Why should she, since she was just his bed buddy?

DJ placed her glass of water on the mantel, watching as Matt shook hands with Jim and was handed a glass of red. So, despite his tough day he wasn't nervous and had no worries about Fenella's white furniture and scathing tongue. Matt took a sip and briefly closed his eyes before engaging with Fenella.

DJ lifted her chin and narrowed her eyes. He might be able to ignore what happened between them earlier, but she was still feeling raw and exposed and very off balance. She was no longer the same person she'd been a year ago. She didn't think she could pretend his lack of communication didn't matter. It *did* matter to her. She wanted more, dammit.

She was terrified that she wanted *everything*.

She couldn't do this. It was too risky. She was opening herself up to the possibility of too much pain.

DJ pushed her fist into her sternum and ordered herself to breathe. She'd been so very close to throwing caution to the wind and telling him she wanted him, that she might love him. But what was the point?

They could never have anything more than the stolen weekends they'd had for the past seven years. While lovely, those weekends were like light-as-air chocolate mousse. Terrifically tasty but lacking substance. After spending so much time with him lately—all but living with him, sharing her body with him—there was no way she could go back to two-day weekends in hotel rooms.

Wanting more and never getting it would be slow torture. It would slowly kill the little they had. It was only a matter of time before they split up. They were simply delaying the inevitable. Why not call it quits now? They'd had no contact for nearly a year before Matt came to Boston and they'd survived. They could just pretend the past little while was only slightly longer than a normal weekend and go their separate ways, no harm, no foul.

Okay, maybe a little harm and a little foul. But not nearly as much as there would be if she kept going with this until he finally decided she wasn't what he wanted, until he met the woman he couldn't live without.

She was, as her dad had taught her, easily replaceable. She needed to leave, on her terms this time. She'd be in control. She'd be the one to walk away. She was never letting anyone leave her again.

"Dylan-Jane."

Matt's deep voice had her lifting her head because pride—the same pride that pulled her through years of living with Fenella—refused to show him that he was the one person she'd wanted to choose her.

It was over, it had to be.

The risk was too great, the reward—stolen weekends and nothing more—too small.

"Matt."

Matt bent his head to place a kiss on her cheek and DJ cursed herself because she so badly wanted to step into his arms, lay her head on his chest.

"Damn, you're mad at me."

Well, yeah. "Why are you here?" she asked him, keeping her voice low.

"There was no way I was sending you into battle without backup," Matt softly replied before stepping back.

Damn him for being sweet, and sensitive to how vulnerable she felt around Fenella. Just when DJ felt that she should push him away, he did or said something that made her desperate for him to stay.

"I can handle my mother."

"Why should you have to do it alone?"

Because you are leaving, and I have to? Because I've done it all my life?

DJ, seeing her mother approaching—Fenella could not bear to be left out of a conversation—swallowed her response.

"I'm so glad you're here, Matthew, albeit a little late. Let's go into the dining room. I don't want the pastry on my beef Wellington to get soggy."

Her beef Wellington? Fenella hadn't cooked anything more complicated than scrambled eggs in twenty or more years.

Fenella placed her hand in the crook of Matt's elbow and, ignoring DJ, led Matt away.

Situation normal.

Matt looked across Fenella's exquisitely decorated dinner table to meet DJ's eyes and his stomach tied itself in another knot.

Stop eyeing her like she's a pretty Christmas present you can't wait to unwrap, Edwards.

He took a sip of wine and wondered when this damn day would ever end. He'd had tough days before—in his line of work tough days were a given—but today ranked right up there. It had been a day of emotion, and emotion wasn't something he was accustomed to dealing with. He was very aware that he'd behaved badly toward DJ. Biting her head off when she asked about Emily was a dick move. And insinuating that she was jealous had been a double dick move. Not his finest moment.

The one thing he now knew was that his head and heart were at war. About his life, his career, Emily... Dylan-Jane.

His head and his heart were arguing about everything he most cared about.

Emily had been everything he'd suspected she'd be: smart, funny, confident. While his brain told him to stay aloof, to keep his distance, his heart—idiot organ that it was—flopped at Emily's feet. He liked her and, ten minutes after meeting her, liked that she was in his life. She was a part of him, someone he'd be connected to forever, a commitment he *welcomed*...

He was welcoming commitment into his life. Matt resisted the urge to look for a flying pig.

Maybe he was shaking free of the shackles of his past. Maybe he was, finally, acting like the adult he'd always thought himself to be. Maybe it was a combination of Emily, DJ and being back in Boston, but he felt freer, less constrained, able to look at his circumstances with clarity.

The one thing his heart and head agreed on was that he'd acted like a prize asshat earlier.

And a dishonest one at that.

It wasn't DJ's fault that he'd felt overwhelmed by the realization that she was far more than a casual bed buddy, that he didn't want whatever they had to end. Honestly, he wanted more but he didn't know how to make that work.

A good start, Matt decided, would be to apologize and tell DJ that Emily was the reason he'd come back to Boston.

Matt, feeling battered, released a long internal sigh. He hadn't felt so off-kilter since he was a child and a teenager, unsure of his place in either his parents' or grandparents' worlds. And that he hated feeling insecure was exactly why he never risked everything in a relationship. Since Gemma, the closest he'd come to love was liking Dylan-Jane.

But here he was on the knife edge of love. And it was a damn terrifying place to be. Because love hurt, dammit. It always had. It hurt when his parents chose their pursuit of pleasure—booze, drugs, partying—over his need for stability or a new winter coat or food. It hurt when he saw the frustration and resentment in his grandparents' eyes when their quiet, academic house was invaded by a sports-playing, smart-mouthed teenage boy, who ate more in a meal than they did in a week.

It hurt when he'd wanted so badly to be loved and had been forced to the periphery of their lives. That was why he'd fallen so hard for Gemma, Emily's birth mom. At seventeen, he'd dreamed of them marrying, creating a family, loving and being loved in return.

Her note telling him that she'd miscarried, that she was breaking up with him and moving away, had rocked him. From that day on, his relationships were only about the sex. He was comfortable with that, he knew how to handle it. He didn't know, as evidenced by today's screwup, how to deal with this churning cocktail of emotion that DJ whipped up.

She was—in the best, most exciting way possible— his biggest nightmare. She'd made him—as a grown, educated man—want to revisit those naive, foolish boy's dreams.

He could sit here and analyze this to death or he could do something, choose a course of action and stick to it. He'd start by telling DJ how he felt, see if she was, maybe, on the same page. He wanted to share his bubbling, nervous joy about Emily. But first he had to get through this damned dinner.

Fenella offered both him and Jim another serving of beef Wellington, but not DJ. Matt frowned. With her bland blond hair and faded blue eyes, Fenella—in her midfifties—was competing with her dark-haired beauty of a daughter. She knew she was fighting a losing battle, and that made her a little more pointed, a shade meaner. Every sentence she directed at DJ was condescending, every time DJ spoke Fenella interrupted. He'd been tempted to call her out, but he knew DJ wouldn't appreciate his interference so he'd kept his tongue between his teeth. He was convinced it was covered in bite marks.

But there was a point to this dinner and he wondered when they would get to it. After giving his stock answers to oft-asked questions regarding his more well-known trials, he felt a measure of relief when Fenella stood up and asked Jim to help her fetch the dessert, gaily waiving off their offer to help.

As soon as they left the room, DJ lifted her eyes to meet his. "Having fun?" she asked, her gaze frosty.

"No. It's as sucky as you suggested," Matt succinctly replied. "We need to talk."

DJ played with her heavy dessert spoon, tapping it against the edge of a side plate. "Yes, all right. I think it's time we cleared the air."

Good, great… *Calm the hell down, heart.* He could do this. Firstly, he'd apologize and explain about Emily, about why he'd been so off his game earlier. After he got that done—hopefully without making a totally mess of it—he'd tell her that he had feelings for her. Feelings that were new to him, feelings she'd hopefully reciprocate. They would agree to spend Christmas together, take some time to work out how they could see each other more often, how they could talk every day. They'd make it work.

Every problem had a solution.

He wasn't convinced. Matt felt like his internal organs were caught in a vise. What he wouldn't give to be staring down a war-crimes defendant or a three-panel lineup of the world's most educated judges. *That* he could handle.

Matt looked into Dylan-Jane's eyes and felt his panic fade. Anchoring himself, he fell into the depth of emotion he saw there. She looked scared yet defiant, emotional but holding it together. He was about to tell her that everything would be okay—he would make damn sure of it—when the door opened and Fenella and Jim returned, each carrying two tiny ramekins. Her eyes darted from DJ's face to his, but beneath her smile lay the heart of a barracuda.

Fenella placed a small dish in front of DJ, then walked around the table and reached over Matt's shoulder to place his dessert on the table in front of him. There was no need for her to push her breast into his shoulder, for her mouth to pass so close to his ear. Matt ignored her and kept his eyes on DJ, hoping she wouldn't notice her mother's inappropriateness. DJ, thank God, had her head down as she tapped the bowl of her spoon against the hard topping of her dessert. She didn't notice Fenella's fingers dancing across the back of his neck.

Matt gave Fenella a cut-it-out look and she responded with a sexy smile. Fenella slipped back into her chair and, judging by the speculative look she and Jim exchanged, Matt knew she was about to drop the conversational equivalent of a hand grenade.

"I'm sure you've forgotten, Dylan-Jane, because you seldom remember what is important to me, that I am the chairperson of Boston Women." DJ looked up, her eyes wary. She swallowed her mouthful of dessert and carefully replaced her spoon on the side plate next to her.

Fenella looked at Matt. He knew she was waiting for him to look impressed, but he'd never heard of the group before. He lifted his hands. "Sorry, should that mean something to me?"

"We are an exceptionally influential group of like-minded women—intellectuals, professionals, business people who gather to discuss topics of mutual interest."

Sounded like hell, Matt thought.

"We are a think tank, a discussion group, but we do one charity event a year and that's our Christmas ball. It's an extremely elite gathering of the movers and shakers of Boston and I intend to, formally, announce my senate run at this year's ball."

"Congratulations," Matt murmured. What else was there to say? And why did he feel like she'd yet to pull the pin on that grenade?

"We only issue two hundred invitations and guests are carefully debated. Invitations are coveted. Very influential people will be present."

She'd said that already. God, he needed this to be done so he could talk to DJ. She was important, this crap about a ball wasn't.

"Every year we have a keynote speaker and this year we've nominated you."

What? Matt jerked up, his eyes flying to Fenella's face. "Me? Why?"

"You're smart, successful and interesting. You're young and good-looking and have had interesting experiences, and successes, in international law and human rights. People remember your grandfather and he is a legal legend. People would be interested in what you have to say and the contacts you'll make will be out of this world."

Except that he didn't work in Boston, he worked in The Hague. Boston contacts wouldn't do squat for him there. He looked at DJ and lifted his eyebrows. "You going?"

"No." DJ's eyes turned flat and cold. "I'm not nearly important enough to warrant an invitation."

"Darling, I just don't want you feeling like a fish out

of water." Fenella's patronizing smile made Matt slam his teeth together.

"She has an MBA, Fenella, I think she can hold her own." Matt pushed the words out between his teeth.

Jim jumped into the conversation. "For you, there is no downside, Matt. It would raise your profile and, let's be honest, there will be a host of legal talent in the room. Your surname is gold and there's nothing wrong with being associated with one of the brightest legal minds of this generation," Jim said, his tone jovial. "Having successful, influential people around Fenella makes an impression. Knowing that you endorse her might sway some of the on-the-fence donors, people who are worried about the conservative slant she's taking."

Oh, hell no. "But I'm not endorsing her."

Jim ignored Matt's statement. "We certainly don't expect you to shout it from the rooftops. In fact, any overt political support at this event is frowned upon. People prefer more upbeat, motivational speeches, but the members of the committee were persuaded that you were the best choice. People will know Fenella has a personal connection to you. She will take the credit for you speaking."

They made it sound like he was just going to hop on through the hoops they were holding up. Like crap. He decided to test them. "I presume that my invitation will include Dylan-Jane as my plus one?"

Fenella's mouth tightened. "I'm afraid not. There simply isn't space at the main table and the tickets were snapped up months ago."

Yep, an F minus for lack of effort. Matt picked up his napkin and tossed it on the table. "Not interested." He looked at DJ and sighed at her colorless face. This was the crap she'd dealt with all her life? He'd endured two hours and he was at his limit. "Wrong answer, Fenella."

Fenella smiled. "Matthew, Dylan-Jane knows where she is most comfortable and it's not in a ballroom with two hundred people far more successful than she will ever be."

Matt shook his head, stunned at Fenella's lack of maternal instinct or common decency. Matt was on the edge of losing his temper. He rarely let loose, but when he did, international judges, opposing counsel, clerks and his staff knew it was best to run for cover. Taking a deep breath, he counted to ten, then to twenty, but the words still bubbled like acid on his tongue.

He wasn't going to be able to hold back—the urge to defend his woman was too strong, too primal. But before he could speak, DJ pushed her chair away from the table and flung down her linen napkin, her eyes angry and defiant.

She placed her hands flat on the table and glared at Fenella. "Take your ticket and shove it, Fenella. I would rather go to hell on a melting ice cube than endure hours in a stuffy ballroom listening to you put me down. In fact, I'm never putting myself through that again."

Fenella laid her hand on her heart and sighed. "Stop being dramatic, darling. I've had a nice night and you're spoiling it."

"You've spoiled many years of my life so I'm pretty sure you'll cope. The only reason you bothered to invite me to dinner tonight was to get Matt here. Putting up with me was the price you had to pay because my lover is a successful, well-respected human-rights lawyer."

God, she was magnificent—dark eyes flashing, cheeks flushed, breasts heaving.

Fenella and Jim exchanged a long look and Matt

thought, just for a minute, that Fenella might lie and reassure DJ that Fenella had wanted to see her daughter, that she enjoyed DJ's company.

Then Fenella shrugged and leaned back in her chair. "My highest priority is my career and my political ambitions."

And there it was, in black and white. What a princess.

"No, Fenella, your highest priority is yourself. It always has been, everything has always been about you."

"Do stop with the dramatics, Dylan-Jane."

Matt saw DJ's jaw tense and knew she was grinding her teeth together. "You refuse to see me, Fenella, for the person I am. I am a partner in one of the fastest growing design businesses in the city. I'm financially fluid and respected by the people I work with."

"The Brogan twins?" Fenella scoffed. "Please! Callie Brogan used to have some influence but since Ray passed away, she's not as socially active as she used to be. She's less than useless. Noah Lockwood has the cachet of the family name, but he keeps a low profile, so what good is he to me?"

"It's not all about you!" DJ shouted.

Fenella smiled, her eyes as cold as an Arctic wind. "Of course it is, because it sure as hell isn't about you."

Right, this had gone on long enough. He had to leave now because soon there wouldn't be enough bail money in the world.

But Dylan-Jane wasn't done. He saw the smallest of smiles cross her face, then her shoulders dropped and she looked at her mother with contempt. "Thank you, Fenella."

Fenella frowned at her odd response. "For what?"

"For saying that. Now I can walk away, completely guilt-free."

"This really is getting tedious."

DJ nodded. "I absolutely agree. And after I walk out that door, I'm done. I'm done with you and your narcissistic personality and your weird desire to put me down. I have no value to you and you sure as hell have no value to me. So let's break up, huh, Mom? What do you say?"

Fenella's mouth dropped open and Matt was completely sure this had to be the first time Fenella was ever caught by surprise.

"Now, let's not be too hasty..." Jim said.

DJ's cold glare stopped Jim in his tracks. "This is long overdue, Jim. I should've had the guts to do this years ago. Goodbye, Fenella. I'd say I'd vote for you, but that's a lie."

Then his woman—this amazing, brave, confident woman—picked up a full, open bottle of red wine. Walking away, DJ defiantly tipped the bottle upside down and a stream of red hit the carpet. He followed the river to the hallway, amazed and thrilled, by how quickly the stain spread. It was petty, admittedly, but fun.

After all, even he could tell the place definitely needed a splash of color.

Eleven

As DJ walked out of Fenella's house, she knew she would never be back. Never again would she worry about saying the wrong thing, waiting for the caustic bite of a sharp tongue, the stinging slap of a derogatory comment. She would never again wish that she was a better daughter, someone her mother could love. Her mom couldn't or wouldn't love her and DJ was done waiting for Fenella's approval.

DJ was done. Period.

As she hurried back to her apartment above Levi's house, she heard Matt's footsteps behind her. When they reached the Brogan house, his hand on her elbow stopped her in her tracks. DJ turned to face him, conscious of the icy air on her cheeks, the heat of their breaths creating a cloud between them.

Matt…

In the twinkling lights from the surrounding houses, she realized that she was done wishing with him, too.

She needed to face reality and, for the first time, DJ felt strong enough to do that. Her father had replaced her, her mom didn't even like her and, to Matt, she was a way to pass time. She couldn't blame him for that. They'd both used each other. It had been done with respect and gentleness; they'd both taken what they needed before going back to their respective lives.

The problem was that she now wanted more.

Deep inside, she'd always wanted to feel like she was the center of someone's world, to be someone's first choice. Matt couldn't give her that, but DJ knew she couldn't settle for less. It was time to be her own champion.

DJ looked around, shook her head at the pretty houses, the decorated lawns. It was Christmas, the time of the year when everything momentous happened. Her father leaving her, getting pregnant with Matt's baby, walking away from Fenella…saying goodbye to Matt. For good.

DJ scowled at the elaborate, oversize wreath Darby had hung on the front door.

"Matt." DJ jammed her hands into the pockets of her coat. Standing in the freezing cold was not the best place to have a breakup chat, but, on the plus side, the frigid temperature would keep their conversation short. "Look, I—"

Matt held up his hand and DJ stopped speaking. She had no idea how to verbalize what she was thinking anyway. She'd never excelled at talking…

"I need to explain about Emily."

"Matt, it's not important."

"It *is* important. I owe you an apology, but before I get to that, I need to explain that Emily is my biological daughter."

What?

DJ just stared at him, her mouth slack with surprise.

"I was seventeen when I had a relationship with her mom. Gemma told me she miscarried, then she moved away and I didn't know she carried the baby to term and gave it up for adoption. Emily contacted me earlier this year and we started corresponding. Part of the reason I came to Boston was to meet her, but she got cold feet and asked for some time. Today she called me and invited me to lunch right then. I *had* to go."

DJ took a moment to process his words, to make sense of what he was saying. Then anger, regret and resentment churned inside her. "You've known about your daughter all this time and you couldn't tell me? Instead you insinuated that I might be jealous?"

Matt pushed an agitated hand through his hair. And looked embarrassed. "Look, you've got every right to be mad, but before you blow me off, which I'm pretty sure you're about to do, I need to tell you that I'm—"

DJ held up a hand. She couldn't move off this topic, not just yet. "Hold on a sec, Matt."

DJ stamped her feet and hunched her shoulders. It was cold, sure, but this frigid iciness invading her body was a pain she'd never experienced before. It had nothing to do with the falling temperatures. "I need to get this straight. You come back to Boston and insist that I tell you what's worrying me. I tell you that I miscarried your baby. I tell you about my father leaving me and adopting his mistress's child. But I don't stop there, I also tell you about my narcissistic mother, who doesn't like me at all. I bared my soul to you, something I never, ever do and *you couldn't even tell me you have a daughter*?"

Oh, God, he really didn't see her as anything more than a bed buddy. She wasn't even his friend.

DJ shook her head. She hadn't felt this miserable since she'd watched her dad walk away that night two decades ago. What was it about Christmas and its need to kick her emotional ass?

"Dylan-Jane—"

"Don't you dare!" DJ said, nearly yelling. "Don't you dare utter some inane platitude, telling me you care about me, that you're sorry!"

"I am sorry. Very sorry," Matt murmured. "Let's go inside. We'll make coffee, have a rational conversation. DJ, we can fix this—*I* can fix it—if you'll just hear me out."

Matt reached for her hand, but DJ stepped back. She didn't need his comfort and she sure as hell didn't need his pity.

Sucking in her last reserves of energy, she took a step back, then another. Tossing her hair, she forced away her tears, needing to get this over with. "I'm calling it, Matt. We're done. We were wrong to try and mix what we had with our real lives. It got complicated, so let's… uncomplicate this."

Shock skittered across his face. *"What?"*

"Maybe it's time we both tried someone different, something different. I'm your go-to girl and I want to be someone's *everything*. You're the guy who can't give that to me."

Matt frowned at her, looking annoyed. "You're now making my decisions for me?"

DJ lifted her chin. "Matt, you couldn't even tell me about your past, that you once got a girl pregnant. My miscarriage was the perfect segue into that conversation, something like…'I can't believe this is happening to me again.' If you couldn't tell me that, after what I went through, how can I assume you will tell me anything personal, let alone how you feel about me?"

DJ threw up her hands in exasperation. "I love it how everybody thinks I have the problem communicating when you're a hundred times worse. At least I tried, Matt."

DJ saw a million emotions in his eyes, but because he didn't try to explain what was running through his mind, she had no idea what he was thinking. Yeah, it was way past time to stop flogging this almost-dead horse. It was far kinder just to put it down.

Despite not being able to imagine a world without Matt in it, DJ summoned her courage. "'Bye, Matt. I hope you'll be gracious enough to give me some space while you remain in Boston. And, merry Christmas."

"You don't believe in Christmas."

"Funny, I was beginning to."

DJ hurried into the yard and ran up the steps to her apartment before her tears started.

"DJ—" Matt called.

She'd never heard her name spoken with such regret and she wanted to go back to him, to soothe his pain away, but then the knot at the end of DJ's frayed rope snapped. One sob escaped, then another, and before she could release a third, she slipped into her apartment, closed the door behind her and sank to the floor.

Curled up into a ball, she finally let herself cry.

Mason heard the strident ring of his doorbell, wondering who was leaning on it at 10:20 p.m. on an icy winter's night. Walking from his study into the hall, he glanced up the stairs, thinking one of his boys would bound down to open the door. Only a teenager would be stupid enough to be out when the windchill took the temperature below zero.

No one charged down the stairs and the doorbell chimed again.

Annoyed, he yanked open the door and the small bundle on his doorstep whipped around. "Callie?"

He checked again... Yep, it was definitely Callie, red-nosed and looking nervous. "What are you doing here?"

"Are your boys here?"

"Upstairs," Mason replied, thoroughly disconcerted. "Is everything okay? Come inside."

Callie tipped back her head and shook her head. "I can't, not if your boys are here."

Damn, he was freezing and really, his boys wouldn't care if he had a guest. Seeing the obstinate tilt to Callie's chin, he sighed. "I can sneak you into my study, they'd never know."

"If and when I agree to date you, Mason James, it will be openly and honestly. I'm far too old to be sneaking around."

Okay, that sounded promising, but it still didn't explain why she was on his doorstep. "Can you put on a coat and shoes and come out here for a bit?" Callie asked.

It was ridiculously cold, but Mason was starting to realize there wasn't much he wouldn't do for her. Mason shoved his feet into the pair of boots he left by the door and grabbed his coat and scarf. Pulling on both, he closed the door behind him.

He stamped his feet and sent her a quizzical look. "What's this about, Cal?"

In the dim light of his porch, he saw determination sweep aside nervousness and then she pushed her hands into his coat and put them on his chest. Standing on her tiptoes, her mouth brushed his with the sweetest, hottest kiss he could remember.

She pulled back to whisper against his lips. "I thought about phoning you but I didn't want that, I wanted to be in your arms, I wanted to kiss you. Is that okay?" Callie asked, holding on to his coat to keep her balance.

Let me give that some thought... Yes.

Oh, hell, *yes.*

"Kiss away," he muttered, aiming for insouciant but hitting breathless. Now, there was a feeling he'd never, ever cop to. He allowed her to control the kiss, closed his eyes when her lips moved over his, kept his hands lightly on her hips as she gently sucked on his lower lip. He wanted to pull her in, take her, possess her, but this was a major move on her part and he didn't want to scare her off.

After minutes of sweet torture, he couldn't take any more. "Open your mouth to me, Cal, I want to taste you."

Her lips opened, her tongue darted out to meet his and he was lost. Groaning, he swept his hand under her coat to grab her butt, yanking her into him so she could feel how aroused he was, how much he wanted her. Forgetting his vow to take this slowly, to let her set the pace, he devoured her mouth, his tongue sliding against hers, dueling with her for control of their kiss.

Callie wanted this—*him*—as much as he did.

The thought slammed into him and he reacted, taking the kiss from lusty to fierce. God, he needed her, naked in his bed. Now, tonight, up against the wall, immediately.

He wrenched his mouth off hers, his lips exploring

her fine jaw, sucking on the skin below her ear. "Let me come home with you, Cal. This is killing me."

"Mason."

Hearing the need in her voice, he yanked his head back to look at her. She was so close to saying yes, he could see it in her eyes, in the way she said his name.

"Say yes, Cal. Please. I'm begging here."

Callie opened her mouth to speak, only to be interrupted by the annoying ring of her phone.

Mason let rip with a long stream of curse words as Callie fumbled for her phone. She stabbed the screen with a shaking finger and he heard sex in her voice when she offered a breathy hello.

Mason, not giving up, ran his thumb over her lower lip and back again. He wanted those lips on various parts of his body and he'd been so close to getting it.

"Yeah, yeah, I'm there. Give me ten minutes."

Dammit. Whatever was said had killed the passion and he knew the moment had passed. Seriously, was the universe conspiring to keep him from having her, knowing every inch of her?

"I'm so sorry, I've got to go."

Mason watched her walk down his path to her low-slung sports car, his heart thundering and his dick straining against the buttons of his jeans. "Callie?"

"Yes?" She turned and Mason saw that her nervousness was back. She expected him to castigate her, to complain about her being a tease. She rubbed her forehead and he noticed her trembling bottom lip. She looked from him to her car and back again. "I have to go, DJ needs me."

She'd drop everything for one of her kids. As frustrated as he was, he had to respect that. But she could spare him a minute to hear what he had to say.

"We can't go on like this much longer. It's time to fish or cut bait. In or out."

"Mason…"

He ordered his heart to ignore the pleading look in her big eyes. "We *have* to move forward, Cal. I'm not asking for anything more than a night, two, as many as works for us. I need you, naked, in my bed and in my arms."

"You're pushing me, Mason."

Yeah, well, someone had to.

But he wanted her fully on board with where they were going and what they were doing, so he forced a cheeky smile onto his face. "I sent Santa my letter. You are all I want for Christmas. So when he calls you to make arrangements, don't be uncooperative."

A quick, appreciative smile took his breath away. "I'll see you tomorrow at your place."

For a moment he thought she was agreeing to sex, then he remembered that her clan was coming over to the café to make a million cookies. Super.

Callie lifted her hand and slid into her car. After a small wave, she pulled away, but it was a long, long time before he went back inside to his warm house.

DJ was lying against Darby's chest, her legs across Jules's lap. Callie sat on the coffee table facing them, shoving tissues into DJ's shaking hand. She couldn't remember when last she'd cried this much.

"I think I'm dehydrated," she whimpered, her voice rough from sobbing.

"You can't be dehydrated, DJ, you've had three glasses of wine." Darby lifted her hand to pat the side of DJ's head.

"Then I'm drunk," DJ decided.

"Much more likely," Callie briskly replied.

Leaning forward, she wiped a tear from DJ's cheek and sent her a sympathetic smile. Callie had been DJ's second call when she'd picked herself up off the floor. The first had been to Darby, and within ten minutes all three women were in DJ's sitting room, doling out sympathy and wine in equal measure.

When you sent out an SOS this was what friends—no, *family*—did. No questions or qualifications; they just dropped what they were doing and ran. DJ looked at Jules, who'd obviously tumbled out of Noah's bed. She wore one of his sweatshirts and ratty yoga pants, and had shoved her feet into a pair of UGG boots. Darby wore men's pajamas, oversize. Callie? Callie looked as beautiful as ever, but why did she have what looked to be razor burn on her chin?

And God, that reminded DJ of how Matt would rub his stubble over her cheekbone, down her neck. She'd never feel that again. She'd never be held in his strong embrace, or curl her arms around his hard waist, or slide her hands down his thighs.

Oh, God, what had she done?

"You do realize you are not only mourning Matt, you are also grieving the death of your relationship with Fenella and your dad leaving you," Callie calmly stated. "As well as the loss of your baby."

"My dad left a long time ago, my mom is as mean as a rabid snake and I wasn't ready for a baby, so I'm pretty sure I'm only crying about Matt," DJ said, feeling exhausted.

"Now you're just being stubborn, Dylan-Jane," Callie said. "You've had a constant hope that things would get better between you and Fenella. You've always dreamed your dad would come waltzing in to claim you, to apologize for leaving all those years ago. Of course you're mourning your baby because, deep down in that place you won't look at, you've always wanted a baby. That's why you are also crying over Matt. He's the one person you could see yourself making a family with. They are all connected, darling."

"Matt was only ever just a bit of fun," DJ protested.

If she told herself that often enough maybe she'd start believing her lie.

"You conned yourself into thinking that was all he was," Callie told her, her voice insistent. "DJ, do you really think you would've kept seeing him for all these years if you weren't crazy about the man? If it was just about the sex, you would've stopped seeing him years ago."

"I don't know, Mom, he is pretty hot," Darby commented. "I might've stayed around just for the sex."

Callie ignored her. "You will be okay, Dylan-Jane, with or without Matt in your life."

DJ looked at the only real mom she'd ever known, desperately wanting to believe her. "How do you know?"

"Because when Ray died, I thought I did, too. For years and years, I wondered why I was here, what the point was." She heard her daughters gasp and held up her hand to keep them from interrupting. "I wasn't myself for a long time. I just…functioned."

"I know I can't compare my pain to yours, Cal. You were married to Ray for more than thirty years…but losing Matt still hurts."

"Yeah, love does hurt. But just remember, if you can feel pain so deeply, you can love just as deeply. That's the yin and yang, my darling."

"I want Matt to love me," DJ finally admitted. "But he doesn't."

Callie took DJ's hands, snotty tissues and all, in hers. "But, honey, that doesn't mean he's the only man you can love. While it's romantic to think there is one man out there to share your life with, it's practical to remember that relationships sometimes don't work out, people die, hearts break. It's a part of life, part of being human. But I'm begging you, DJ, don't retreat. Don't let this pain stop you from being open to finding and receiving love again."

DJ couldn't imagine being held, kissed and touched by anyone other than Matt. On an intellectual level, Callie's words made sense, but everything in DJ rebelled at the thought.

Yet she knew Callie meant well so DJ tried to smile. "Maybe by next Christmas I might be ready to throw myself back into the dating game."

"Oh, it'll be long before that. Maybe by then, Jules will have provided me with a grandbaby I can spoil."

"Can I get married first?" Jules demanded, shaking her head in exasperation. "And why don't you harangue our brother like this?"

"Oh, I hassle him about his love life and I also spend many minutes on my knees praying that God will send him a girl who will lead him in a merry dance. Since Tanna broke off the engagement—"

"She all but left him at the altar, Mom!" Jules interjected, frowning.

Callie waved away her correction. "Anyway, your brother is far too used to getting his own way with women."

The twins bumped fists. "Amen, sister."

"As for you, Darby Brogan, I have a wonderful feeling you are going to get exactly what you want…and more importantly, what you need."

DJ could feel Darby's smile. "I hope that means a baby, Mom."

"You'll get what you most need, Darby Brynn Brogan," Callie reiterated, before slapping her thighs and standing up. She bent over and clasped DJ's face in her hands before placing her lips against DJ's forehead in a long kiss. "I love you, baby girl. I could rip Fenella's throat out for hurting you, and if I could, I would kick your father's butt to hell and back. But you will be okay, DJ."

"You didn't threaten Matt, Mom," Darby pointed out.

Callie held DJ's eyes. "No, I didn't. I think that boy will surprise us yet." She gestured to the pile of tissues and the empty bottle of wine. "I'm going back to bed."

DJ thanked Callie and they watched her walk out, gently closing the door behind her.

Jules tipped her head to the side. "Was that stubble burn on her jaw? Do you think Hot Coffee Guy put it there?"

Darby scowled. "That's not the point, Jules. What I want to know is why I am the only one in this room not seeing any action."

Twelve

They'd both caught feelings. Like damn amateurs.

DJ was right. And it pissed him off to admit that.

He'd waltzed into her life expecting her to tell him everything. He'd demanded it because he was the guy who asked the questions, who got answers, who made assumptions and created strategy around what people said. He never allowed his perceptions to cloud a situation; he stayed emotionally uninvolved.

He hadn't realized that he'd been treating DJ like a client. Even though he knew he was falling for her, knew he was feeling more for her than he should, he'd still kept his distance, choosing to listen rather than engage. He'd treated her like…

God, he'd treated her like his parents and grandparents had treated him.

Looking from the outside in, he'd done just enough to remain in control but not enough to be a full—or even half—partner in the situation. DJ did what she did and he just reacted.

Matt felt rocked by the realization. He'd genuinely thought he was better than that.

Now Matt looked at the small wooden table and watched Emily's mouth moving, automatically tucking her words into the boxes where they belonged. Her plans for the New Year, her college roommate, her best friend. Listening to her, but still reeling from the night before, Matt desperately hoped his pounding head, tight throat and fuzzy thinking were a result of a sleepless night and not because his heart was curled up in a corner whimpering.

He'd thought he was tougher than that.

"So I'm thinking of dropping out of college to go smoke pot in a commune in Peru."

Matt heard Emily's words and knew they were a test, to see if he was listening. She'd have to do better than that; he could listen to three conversations and read a book at the same time.

"Over my dead body," Matt muttered, ordering another cup of coffee.

"So you were listening but you definitely weren't paying attention," Emily said. "I have to say, I'm a bit annoyed that I'm not the entire focus of your universe right now since I've only recently dropped into your life."

Matt wanted to feel bad about not giving her the attention she deserved, but he was feeling so crappy already that he didn't have the energy. "Sorry, I have a lot on my mind."

"Like?" Emily demanded.

Matt started to change the subject and realized that was something he always did when he didn't want to answer a personal question. But Emily, like DJ, wasn't a random person. Emily was his daughter. And if he wanted her in his life, he needed to let her in.

"I've been seeing someone on a casual basis for many years and she just called it quits."

"Ah. Couldn't have been that casual, then."

Matt frowned at her. "What do you mean?"

"If you are upset and stressed, which you so are, you obviously have deeper feelings for her than you realized. Does she have feelings for you?"

"I think she does."

"And the problem is?"

The problem is that I'm scared. Soul-deep terrified.

He knew what it was like to live with someone and not be loved, to be a part of someone's life and not be valued. Love, as he knew it, wasn't a guarantee for a happy-ever-after. But relationships didn't come with guarantees.

Maybe it was better that he hadn't laid his heart on the line, hadn't expressed all his hopes for what he and DJ could be. At least, this way, he still had his pride.

But his pride wouldn't keep him warm at night, make him laugh or feed his soul.

Dammit.

"It doesn't matter, I'm going to let her go and you and I can be a family," Matt said, leaning back so the waitress could put a cup of coffee in front of him.

"A part-time daughter you'd see once or twice a year? That's your definition of a family? No wonder your girlfriend dumped you." Emily rested her forearms on the table. She wrinkled her nose before nailing him with a look. "Do you want a family, Matt?"

"I have you," Matt carefully replied.

"That wasn't what I asked."

Sure, he wanted a family. He wanted someone to come home to, kids who ran into his arms, a wife who kissed him awake and blew his mind, and other body parts, at night. But that was a fantasy... He'd had two families and both had been terrible. With his work schedule, he was pretty sure he would be terrible at it, too.

"I work a lot, Emily. My life is crazy."

"So, uncrazy it. You choose how much you work. Last time I heard, there wasn't a law that said you needed to put in such long hours."

Ah, the folly of youth, so black-and-white. "It's not that simple, Emily."

"No, you're just making it complicated. Do you know why you want to call me your family, Matt?"

"Because you, actually, are?"

"Okay, biologically, yes, but I'm not, not really. This may hurt and I'm sorry if it does, but I already have a dad. He's the one I ride motorbikes with, who sends me stupid dad jokes, who once drove eight hours to take me to a dance competition. He's the one I would turn to if my life fell apart, he's the one who's going to walk me down the aisle. You will be my friend, I hope, but he's my *dad*."

Matt felt like a red-hot blade was being shoved into his heart. For the second time in twenty-four hours.

"But you want all that, I can see it in your eyes. You want a daughter you can take to dance class, a son you can take to soccer. A wife who loves you. You want a family."

Matt couldn't speak. If he did, he might finally lose it.

"There's this woman out there who might want that, too, with you. Don't you think you owe it to her, and yourself, to see if a family is something you can make together?"

"We both have issues…" It was pathetic but it was all he had.

"God, you old people are so lame. Everybody has issues, Matt. Deal with it."

He was getting schooled by an eighteen-year-old. That being said, he was still proud of the strong, sassy, in-your-face woman she was. "Your parents did a wonderful job with you, Emily."

She grinned. "I know."

Matt looked at his watch. "Do you want to meet her?"

"The person you nearly let slip through your fingers? Sure."

"It might mean making Christmas cookies."

"My mom is the Christmas-cookie queen. I smoke at making cookies. And, this way, I can make sure you don't chicken out at the last minute."

Yeah, she was smart. And too damn cocky.

Exactly like he'd been at her age.

DJ was trying her level best to get into the spirit of Christmas, she really was.

Mason had rearranged the café's tables so they were all in a long row and they had a sort of cookie production line going. Levi, Eli and Ben, under Callie's supervision, mixed ingredients. Mason and Noah rolled out the dough. Jules pressed out shapes and Darby put them onto cookie sheets, which Callie put in the industrial oven. Because DJ had arrived late, she was tasked with making various colors of frosting and putting them into bags so they could decorate the cookies when they cooled.

The twins, with their keen eyes for color, felt the need to supervise DJ's every step, and the making of the red icing had taken ten minutes longer than it should have before they were both happy with the color. Instead of resisting, DJ quietly followed their orders, thinking that it didn't matter whether they ended up with a fire-engine red or something darker. Red was red and her heart was still broken...

DJ looked down the table and caught Noah looking at Jules. DJ watched passion cloud her friend's eyes as Jules stared back at her man. Unable to watch, DJ moved on to Callie only to see her watching Mason, confusion and desire and fear on her face.

DJ's heart, that stupid, hopeful organ, still wanted what Jules had, what Callie and Ray had enjoyed for thirty and more years—a partner, somebody who made her life complete. A family.

Callie was right when she'd said that DJ needed more than what she'd been prepared to settle for. After being alone for a very long time, she'd thought being alone was safe, that she could be content with having a shallow relationship. But when Matt came into her Boston-based life everything changed. It suddenly made sense. He filled her world with laughter and fun and heat and really exceptional sex.

But Matt didn't see her as someone he could trust, someone he could lean on. She needed him to view her as an equal partner, as a friend and confidant as well as a lover. His silence told her, in actions louder than words, that she was, and always would be, just his bed buddy...

DJ picked up a bottle of green food coloring and tipped the bottle slowly so that a drop, then another, hit the white frosting. The first drop looked black and then, as it spread, it lightened into the brilliant green of Matt's eyes. In seeming slow motion, DJ saw her arm sweep the bowl off the table, watched as it hit the slate floor and shattered, green-tinged frosting exploding like a sugar bomb.

DJ looked down at the mess she'd made and burst into tears. It was all too much. Christmas and her dad and her mom and Matt and the emerald green frosting and the broken bowl and the ruined cookies and...

God, she *hated* Christmas.

DJ felt warm arms around her, a hand pulling her head to a chest and someone tugging a spatula from her fist. Sobbing harder, she pressed her wet face into a warm, masculine neck.

"Shh, DJ, don't cry," Matt murmured.

He was here? Even so, she honestly didn't think she'd ever be able to stop.

"I need to clean up. I made a mess."

"Mason's handling that."

Standing on her tiptoes, DJ looped her arms around Matt's neck and told herself she should let go. Walking away from him again was going to be harder than before. Hanging onto him like a wet limpet wasn't something she should be doing. She hung anyway.

DJ thought she felt Matt's lips in her hair, but then he was talking to Callie and Mason and his words didn't make sense. Then she heard a voice behind her, one she didn't recognize, but she couldn't find the energy to care. She was so tired...

"C'mon, DJ."

Holding her tight against him, Matt walked her across the room. At the front door, he lifted her coat from the hook. He carefully dressed her, pushing one arm into a sleeve, then the other, then buttoned her up before tightening the belt. Through her tears, DJ noticed Matt's brow was furrowed, his deep eyes worried. As Matt pulled open the door, DJ swiped the balls of her hands across her eyes, hoping to wipe away some of her tears.

Another batch just took their place.

On the sidewalk, Matt took her hand and walked her across the road to his car, yanking open the passenger door and guiding her inside. Matt slammed his door shut, started the car and fiddled with the heater before leaning back in his seat, his eyes finally connecting with hers.

When he made no effort to drive away or to speak, DJ gestured to the wheel. "Where are we going?"

"Nowhere. We have cookies to make and I want you to meet someone."

She was over anything to do with Christmas and she really wasn't up to meeting anyone new. This wasn't her finest moment.

"In case you didn't notice, this isn't a good time for me," she said, trying for sarcastic but hitting miserable instead.

Matt gripped the steering wheel with one hand and DJ noticed that his hand had lost all color. When she turned her eyes to him she noticed that his face was ashen, too. "And that's on me. I'm sorry, DJ."

"I'd like to tell you it's okay that you can't give me what I want—what I *need*—but I'm not there yet. That's why you have to keep your distance."

"Except that I don't want to."

DJ frowned. "I don't understand."

"I don't want to keep my distance. I don't want to be without you."

Oh, God, if this was a joke or a prank, she'd kill him,

she really would. And if he made some stupid suggestion that fell short of what she needed, she'd maim him.
And she'd make sure it hurt.

Before she could formulate a sentence, Matt picked
up her icing-splattered hand and kissed her fingertips.
The corners of his mouth kicked up. "Sweet. Literally."

"Matthew." His name on her lips was a plea for an
explanation. Or to let her go.

Matt lifted her hands to his lips, held her knuckles
against his mouth and closed his eyes. When he opened
them again, DJ—for the first time—saw all the way
down to his soul.

"I want more, Dylan-Jane. I want *everything*."

DJ stared at him, terrified that he was telling her
what she most wanted to hear. And she was equally
scared this entire encounter was a figment of her imagi-
nation. DJ pulled back, still half expecting him to open
the door and walk away into the snow.

"Please don't say that if you don't mean it," DJ whispered. "Please don't tell me that if you intend to walk
out of my life again."

Fury flashed in his eyes. "Why do you think I would
do that, DJ?"

DJ turned her head to look out the windshield. "Just
before my dad walked out of my life, he told me he
loved me, that he'd always love me, but I never saw him
again," she whispered.

"I swear to God…" Matt said, anger coating every
word. DJ saw him push his frustration and fury away,
and when his fingers slid around her neck and his thumb
stroked her jaw, his expression was tender. "There's
only you, DJ, there's only been you for the past seven
years. I'm not walking away, Dylan-Jane, and every

time I leave you, I *will* come back. That is my solemn promise."

She wanted to believe him, she did, but she felt like she was standing on a bridge with only a thin rope to stop her from slamming onto the sharp rocks below. If that rope broke...

"I want to be with you, Dylan-Jane, because you are the only person that makes sense. It's Christmas and, while you don't believe it, it is the season of miracles. You are *my* miracle, you've got to know that. I want to marry you and have babies with you and sleep with you and fight with you and, God, I want to love your delicious body for the rest of my life. I want you in my life, only you."

Matt waited a beat before speaking again. "Forever you. Be my Christmas miracle, DJ."

Then Matt spoke the words she most needed to hear. "I love you, Dylan-Jane. To me you are, and always will be, irreplaceable."

More tears slid down her face, but DJ didn't care. She let her body expel the last of her fear, her distrust. Holding Matt's face in her hands, she wept. Matt, because he knew her so well, just waited until her tears slowed.

"Are you sure?" DJ asked, her words rasping from the tears still clogging her throat.

Matt half smiled. "About loving you? Yes. About never leaving you? Yes. About being irreplaceable? Damn straight."

DJ felt a smile start to bloom on her lips. She shook her head, trying to think clearly. Matt loved her! They had a future! She was emotionally safe!

"I don't know what to say," she admitted, turning her mouth to place a kiss on his palm.

The pad of Matt's thumb rolled over her bottom lip.

"Then let me talk. We're going to get married, DJ, at some point, preferably as soon as possible. I haven't yet worked out how we'll manage two careers on separate continents, but I will—*we will*. And we will spend the bulk of our time together, that's not up for negotiation. This not seeing each other for weeks and months is BS and it's over…we *will* find another solution that works for both of us. It might mean splitting our time between two homes, but I don't care where we live as long as we are together."

A sunburst of happiness dried the rest of her tears and DJ opened her mouth to agree, but Matt shook his head and spoke over her. "I don't know how good I am going to be at being a husband or a dad, I didn't have great role models when it comes to either, but I swear I'll learn, DJ. I'll never cheat on you and you'll be my first priority, I promise."

She couldn't demand that of him; he had a daughter and she should come first. Putting their kids first was what good parents did. "You have Emily, Matt. I understand that she needs to come first."

"Emily has her dad, DJ, and a family she adores. I'm okay with that. But I want my own family, with you. I want to do better, be better at love and responsibility and raising kids than our parents were. You want to come along on that ride with me?"

There was so much hope and vulnerability in his voice. DJ slowly nodded as she held his intense gaze. "In time, I want another baby with you, Matt, maybe two. But before then, I want us to learn to lean on each other. I want to be your light when your work is dark, your rock when your ground feels shaky. It's going to be hard sometimes because life is hard, but if we put each other, and our kids, first we'll be okay. If we hold on tight to each other, we can love our way through anything."

Matt rested his forehead on hers, his breath sweet on her lips. "I love you, Dylan-Jane."

The sweetest words ever said. "I love you back, Matt."

"Want to marry me?"

God, *yes*. "More than anything," DJ whispered.

Matt's lips finally met hers and DJ's mouth curved under his. "Brace yourself, Matt, but I think I'm changing my mind about Christmas being the worst time of year."

Matt's low laugh drifted over her. She was the luckiest woman in the world because she was going to hear that laugh for the rest of her life. Not only that, but she also got to kiss this man, love this man, until she died.

DJ pulled back and looked at Matt. She really wanted to tell him how she was feeling, how happy he'd made her, how fulfilled she suddenly felt, but those damn words wouldn't come.

Matt nodded and smiled. "I know, baby. It's almost overwhelming, isn't it?"

DJ nodded. "I feel bigger, greater, like I'm about to burst out of my skin, like I am three sizes too big for this car. Like nothing is ever going to be the same ever again."

Then Matt kissed her and he felt both new and familiar, exciting and reassuring. He kissed her slowly, gently, his mouth telling her that she was loved, that she would never be alone again. That she would always, always have him standing next to her.

He was absolutely her Christmas miracle.

Then his tongue slipped between her open lips and passion rolled in, hot and demanding. Matt groaned into her mouth and his kiss turned possessive as he branded her as his. DJ didn't mind—it was, after all, the truth.

She was his and forever would be.

DJ wasn't sure how long they kissed, but when they heard the sharp rap on the window, her coat was off, Matt's hand was inside her bra and his erection was rock-hard under her hand. Thank God, the windows were solidly misted over. Matt cursed as he pulled away and when DJ thought they looked marginally present-able, she cracked the window an inch.

The three witches stood outside, smirks on their faces. "Well?"

DJ darted a look at Matt, who was leaning back in his seat, looking amused. He arched an eyebrow, silently telling her to answer Darby's demand.

"Well what?" DJ asked, trying to look innocent.

"I swear I'm going to kill you," Darby muttered. "Are you back together?"

DJ nodded. "Yes. In a way."

Darby made the sound of a momma wolf protecting her cub. Pushing a finger through the crack in the win-dow, one gray eye glared at Matt. "I swear, Edwards, if you think you are going to get away with not mak-ing some commitment to her, I will chop you up with a chain saw."

Matt raised an eyebrow and smiled at DJ. "She's warming up to me, I'm sure of it."

DJ chuckled. "Want to be a bridesmaid, Darby?"

"If you think I am going to let you go back to that half-assed relationship you had, well, you can just forg—" Darby faltered. She frowned. "What did you just ask me? Are you getting married? When? Seri-ously? Mom, Jules, they are getting hitched! Will you please get out of this damn car?"

DJ laughed, glanced down at Matt's pants, saw he was on his way to being decent and grinned at him. "We need to go back inside. Sorry, but they'll hound us until we tell them everything."

Matt's finger ran down her jawline. "I know they are part of the package, sweetheart, and I wouldn't have it any other way. And yes, we do need to go inside. I'd like you to meet Emily."

DJ jerked back in shock. "Your daughter is in there and you left her alone with strangers?"

Matt shrugged. "She's a big girl and you needed me." Matt opened his door and a snowflake drifted into the car. But before leaving the car, he sent her a look that melted her. "I love you so goddamn much, Dylan-Jane. Never doubt that, okay?"

Now, there was a statement she could wrap her head around.

Epilogue

Mason stepped into the entryway of Callie's home and picked up a glass of champagne from the tray on the hall table. He was late because he'd spent Christmas Eve with Emmet and Teag and, thanks to the snow, his ex had been a half hour late to pick up their boys. It was now close to midnight, but the party was in full swing and there were a lot more people here than he'd expected.

In fact, the house was heaving with couples in ball gowns and tuxedos. Mason ran a hand down the lapel of his own tux, briefly wondering when last he'd worn it. Three years ago? Five?

Did that matter? All that mattered was that he was here, at the first Christmas Eve party Callie had thrown since before her husband's death. Mason sipped his champagne, wished it was whiskey and tried to spot his quarry, which was impossible given the fact that he couldn't look past the broad backs of Levi Brogan and the three Lockwood men.

God, he was frustrated. He hadn't been alone with Callie since that hot kiss on his porch ten days ago. Time was up. He wanted her. They would be damn good together. But she had to decide to fight for him, too.

Mason looked around and his attention was caught by the opposite wall, which was filled with family photographs. Wanting to ignore them, but knowing he couldn't, he sauntered over. His eye was immediately drawn to a photograph of a dark-haired man sitting on a wall, his head thrown back with laughter. Callie's Ray, Mason surmised. Levi looked like him, Darby had his nose and chin, Jules his eyes.

Intelligence and good humor radiated from him and Mason, whose ego was fairly healthy, felt intimidated. How the hell was he supposed to compete with Ray Brogan? While Mason was rich enough, he wasn't the billionaire Brogan had been. Neither was he as sociable—tattooed math geeks didn't tend to be—nor was he, his mouth twisted, as good-looking.

Jesus, what the hell was he doing here?

Mason was about to step back when a feminine hand slid into the crook of his arm and a subtle perfume hit his nose. He knew it wasn't Callie because his heart rate didn't accelerate. He slowly turned to see Darby standing next to him, her gaze on her father's face.

"You would've liked him, you know."

The hell of it was that he probably would have.

"And he would've liked you," Darby added. "He would've liked the fact that you don't take any nonsense from my mom. He didn't, either."

Mason didn't know whether to defend Callie or not, so he changed the subject. "Quite a crowd."

Darby grinned. "Yeah, Mom was wild about how Fenella treated DJ and decided to teach her a lesson. She knew a lot of people who'd bought tickets to Fenella's function tonight would rather attend one of the Brogans' Christmas Eve parties so she called them all up and invited them over to help her celebrate both Jules's and DJ's engagements. Fenella is going to have at least a third fewer people than she expected."

Mason had to smile. His woman wasn't someone to be messed with. He looked over to where DJ and Matt stood on the edge of the dance floor, supposedly dancing but really just swaying to the beat. Their gazes were locked on each other and anybody looking at them could see their love…and their desire to get naked as soon as possible.

Darby nudged Mason and he turned back to look down into her lovely face, a face that would look a lot like Callie's in twenty years. "You look at Mom like that."

Ah, God, what was he supposed to say to that?

The switch to another subject had worked for him before, so he tried it again. "Have DJ and Matt worked out their living arrangements?"

Darby smiled, amused. "They are still working it out but they will. They love each other too much to live apart. Are you in love with my mother?"

Mason almost dropped his glass in surprise. "Uh…"

"You are, aren't you?" Darby persisted.

Of course he wasn't! He wanted to sleep with her, that was all. He opened his mouth to explain, but how could he tell the grown-up daughter of the woman he lusted over that this was all about sex?

Can't do it…

"Whether I am or not has very little to do with you." Mason managed to push the words between his teeth.

"Fair point," Darby conceded. She looked at the photo of her dad and when her eyes met Mason's, hers reflected sadness in their silvery depths. "I love—loved—him. He was the best person in my life and he adored my mom. And she adored him."

Yeah, he'd worked that out. It was time to go.

Darby held his arm in a death grip. "This hurts like hell to admit, but I never saw her look at him the way she looks at you."

Whoa! Every muscle in Mason's body tensed as he waited for her next words, but pride wouldn't let him ask her to elaborate. After a minute—a millennium—Darby spoke again. "Maybe she and my dad sparked off each other when they were young, but the two of you? God, one look and boom! It's disconcerting, I have to tell you."

She should see it from his point of view.

"You do something for her, Mason, and whatever you are doing scares her. She's resisting. Keep doing it, though, because you've made my mom enjoy life again. For that I will always be grateful."

He felt he should explain. "Darby, listen, it's not like that. I'm not going to be your mom's happy-ever-after. That's not what's happening here. I get that you are concerned about her, but please don't start thinking that I'm her knight in shining armor. Because that would be crap."

Darby laughed. "Mason, my mom is a strong woman, we *all* are. We come from a long line of strong women and the last thing we need is a knight, in armor or otherwise. Brogan women slay our own dragons."

With that parting shot Darby drifted back to the

crowd. Mason stepped away from the bank of photographs and glanced around, determined to find his quarry.

As if on command, the crowd parted and there she stood, looking glorious in a green fitted dress and sky-high heels, her blond hair tousled and her blue eyes dominating her face. She was talking to a man in his sixties who, judging by the look on his face, was working out the best way to get her into bed.

Hell, no. The only person she was going to bed with was Mason and it was time she got used to the idea.

He walked across the room, his eyes on her face, waiting for her to notice him. Her shoulders tensed, her back arched and her head spun around, blue eyes connecting with his. He debated whether he should go to her, whether she wanted to advertise their connection. Callie surprised him when she beckoned him over. When he reached her side, she lifted her fingers to touch his jaw. Her heels allowed her to brush her lips across his, giving him a longer than polite kiss.

Finally, his brain kicked into gear and he gripped the slim hand lying against his heart.

"What the hell are you doing?" he whispered, noticing that her eyes were dancing with amusement.

Under the amusement was flat-out lust. For him. He went rock-hard instantly so he turned his back to the room.

"A little show-and-tell," Callie said, taking another taste of his mouth.

Both hands were on his chest now and Mason knew the room was watching—the band had stopped playing.

Mason frowned. Who was this woman and what had she done with uptight Callie Brogan?

Callie looped her arms around his neck and ran her

fingers through his hair. "I'm kissing you to show everyone here that you are here with me and I'm about to tell you exactly what I want for Christmas."

He couldn't pull his gaze away from her face. "What do you want for Christmas, Cal?"

"There were two things on my bucket list you said you could help me with…" Callie said, her cheeks now tinged with pink.

He forced himself to remember her list. One was phone sex and the other… Holy, holy crap. "You want a one-night stand? With me?"

Callie's nod nearly stopped his heart.

"Just one night of pleasure with no expectations, no strings. No demands. Can you give me that, Mason?"

It was the only thing he'd asked from Santa, the only item left on his Christmas list. This was what he wanted…*all* he wanted.

So this was turning out to be the best Christmas ever in the history of Christmases.

Then, as he fell into Callie's startlingly blue gaze, the thought occurred to him that, maybe, one night might not be enough.

* * * * *

COMING SOON!

We really hope you enjoyed reading this book. If you're looking for more romance, be sure to head to the shops when new books are available on

Thursday
18th October

To see which titles are coming soon, please visit
millsandboon.co.uk

LET'S TALK
Romance

For exclusive extracts, competitions
and special offers, find us online:

f facebook.com/millsandboon

⊙ @millsandboonuk

🐦 @millsandboon

Or get in touch on 0844 844 1351*

For all the latest titles coming soon, visit
millsandboon.co.uk/nextmonth